I0699430

LESTER

BY KIMBERLY WHEELOCK

Copyright © 2024 Kimberly Wheelock

All rights reserved. No part of this book may be reproduced or transmitted in any form or by any means, electronic or mechanical, including photocopying, recording, or by any information storage and retrieval system, without written permission from the publisher.

This is a work of fiction. Names, characters, places, and incidents either are the products of the author's imagination or are used fictitiously. Any resemblance to actual persons, living or dead, events, or locales is entirely coincidental.

ISBN: 979-8-9882838-6-7

eBook ISBN: 979-8-9882838-4-3

Book design by Ash Wheelock Copyright © 2024 Ash Wheelock

Contact at ashwheelock.com

For my grandmother.

You are the heart and center of our family.

For my grandfather.

I wish there had been time to talk about the trains.

LESTER

"But the wilderness had found him out early… It had whispered to him things about himself which he did not know… And the whisper had proved irresistibly fascinating. It echoed loudly within him because he was hollow at the core."

-Joseph Conrad, Heart of Darkness

PART ONE

The locked pantry.

When the sun peered into the kitchen window at the exact right angle, the rays reflected off the shining metal, sending orbs shimmering and dancing across the cupboards and ceiling above her head. Everything on Grandfather's homestead was old and worn except for that padlock and the shining hasp it hung from. Every day, she ate her eggs alone and in silence, watching the tiny spots of light as they traveled along the ancient wallpaper, and every day, Talia wished she had the key to the lock.

"Too many god damned mouths to feed. Can't afford to take care of all your brats!" Grandfather spat the last out as he drilled the hasp into the door frame. Flakes of paint fluttered down to the scratched linoleum floor below. Her mother had been fixing dinner as he installed the lock. Grandfather would have a fried cubed steak and homemade mashed potatoes, while Talia and her siblings were served something scant, like a couple of cans of chicken noodle soup. Her mother prepared the meal in silence, accepting his anger. He had started on her the moment she arrived home from the bakery. Any response would only make his anger worse and preparing something more involved for the children would trigger a full-scale blowout.

The key never left its place from around her grandfather's neck.

All of their food was locked away. The refrigerator had an alarm affixed to it too. The device blared louder and louder if it remained ajar too long. Both were purchased within the first week of their arrival. After Grandfather caught one of the twins, Matthew, standing with the door ajar looking for a snack, her brother had been swatted, and the lock appeared. They had always been allowed to eat when they were hungry in their old house. He purchased it "special" for them because Grandfather was right about one thing: there were a lot of mouths to feed.

They came to live with him after her father was struck by a drunk driver while on his way to work. The driver survived, her father did not.

"God favors drunks, small children, and fools." She had overheard one of her mother's friends lamenting after the funeral service. It had been a terrible day. Her mother had sat in the corner of the room, flanked by her two closest friends, unspeaking and twisting a tissue in her hands. Sarah, her mother, unable to pay the mortgage alone, had no other option but to return to her familial home with her four children in tow.

The house lived at the furthest edge of a fading logging town named Palmer. The homestead was miles from its nearest neighbor, even further from the town proper, on the border of the Mount Baker-Snoqualmie Forest. Palmer was the entry point to a string of long abandoned railroad towns along the Green River. The tiny community was only a collection of homes, mostly trailers in various states of decay, and a store that was one part grocer and one part saloon called The Last Resort. Palmer didn't even have a post office, the closest was in the neighboring burg of Black Diamond where all the children went to school.

The homestead sat in a clearing at the end of a long dirt road lined with overgrown weeping willows. When they had visited Grandfather, before her father's passing, Talia had loved how the willow branches formed a tunnel of swaying curtains as they drove the lane. The expansive plot of land with all of its buildings and places to play made the property one of mystery, like the secret garden from one of her bedtime stories. The house itself was large with six bedrooms and several bathrooms. It needed a surfeit of repairs that had been neglected over the decades, including a new roof and a fresh coat of exterior paint. There was an old grey barn, which they were forbidden to go inside of. Grandfather said it was dangerous, but Talia saw him disappearing into the dilapidated structure several times a day and knew that wasn't the truth. Surrounding the house were an assortment of outbuildings: the pumphouse for the well, an old outhouse no one had used in so long it hardly stank, a chicken coop, a massive garage with no doors, and a collection of sheds in various states of disrepair. Beyond was the forest.

The homestead was in a beautiful location, but one marred by living with a man who hated her and her brothers' very existence. For that reason, Talia made herself scarce, and while she spent her time exploring all the corners of the property, she was often stuck monitoring her siblings when her mother went to work.

"I need you to make sure they don't get into trouble," Sarah had said, peering into her eyes, and pushing a lock of her umber hair behind her ear. "I love you, Tally." She did not say sorry with her mouth and instead said it with her gaze. Grandfather was best avoided. The eggs had been her first lesson.

During their first weeks in the house, Sarah would send the twins or Talia out to gather eggs from the free roaming chickens on the property. Eggs were free, so they were eaten for breakfast every day. Cole had gone out that morning. He returned holding a clutch of eggs, bundled in the front of his shirt. As he handed one to Grandfather, the shirt slipped, and a single egg rolled out, smashing to the floor. Cole stood paralyzed over the damage, the orange yolk bleeding out around its pale green shell. Without warning, a hand flew. Cole was backhanded, and the rest of the eggs fell, splattering in small crunches as they landed on the faded linoleum floor. Cole was slapped again for dropping the eggs, and there had been no breakfast for anyone that day or the next.

Her mother had been bitter about the incident, although Talia understood it was because of how Grandfather had yelled at her afterwards. He cornered her on the front porch when she arrived home, spitting out the phrase, "Should have used a rusty coat hanger for all the brains this bunch has!" which she hadn't understood. He topped that with something she did understand to be an insult, "Dumb, dumb, dumb, just like their daddy." and that's when she knew she hated him. A couple of mornings later, her mother pressed a basket into her hands. An old dish towel was laid into the bottom to keep the eggs from rolling around. She begged her with hollow eyes to be careful.

After that it was up to Talia, and she resented the task. The henhouse smelled of sour hay and bird scat. The ammonia odor made her eyes water. Sometimes, she would find a desiccated chicken corpse, half-pecked to death, with its rancid, rotting scent. No, there was nothing pleasant about Grandfather's now. If she never had to eat another egg in her life it would be too soon.

Then one day, it all changed.

As Talia daydreamed about what it would be like to have the key to the pantry door's shining lock, Grandfather appeared on unstable legs, grabbing hard onto the table. She startled but did not tear her eyes away from the lock. Talia was afraid to meet his gaze. He smelled strange and too sweet, like sugar was oozing out of his pores. He snapped two thick fingers in front of her face, and when she glanced up at him, saw he was oily with sweat. Something was wrong with Grandfather.

"Earth to Talia!" Craig said, snapping his fingers in front of her eyes. Talia came out of her memory. Her fingers rested lifeless on the laptop's keyboard, the cursor flashing waiting for the next prompt. She had traveled off in her mind and returned to the present to find her boss and a roomful of people staring at her. It was a bad habit.

"Did you get that?" he asked, his tone level. She hadn't. Craig knew it, and there was that look in his eyes. The same one her grandfather wore when he was ready to bring the hammer down. She was in trouble the first chance he got.

"I'm sorry. Could you repeat that last part?" she responded, using an ingratiating voice. The one coated in sugar. The one with no "tone." Craig blinked, gave an imperceptible shake of his head, then continued. He glanced over a time or two to verify she was documenting the conversation and went back to his obsequious self with the clients.

The meeting continued. Craig was playing the part of dutiful negotiator. His objective was to nail down the finer points of Pleasant Valley Farms' merger with The Eggery. His fee was being paid by the latter, along with a considerable off-record payment for settling certain aspects of the agreement. Those details made this less a merger and more of a hostile takeover, and Pleasant Valley Farms was the only one in the room unaware.

The Eggery Incorporated was a large-scale producer and distributor of eggs, owning several dozen facilities across the state. They touted themselves as an organic, wholesome option, an alternative to the mainstream producers and dairies. The Eggery sold under three different brands to gourmet boutiques and whole food markets. The people who bought their eggs were people who had the ability to vote with their wallet and could afford to buy based on their conscience. Talia had sat at this table with The Eggery merger team enough times to know they were actually in the business of removing the competition. They scouted out small, successful organic egg operations and separated them from their business for pennies on the dollar. This was the fourth merger that Talia had been a part of, and every time it was the same orchestration.

The mom-and-pop operations, in this case Pleasant Valley Farms, would arrive at the time they were told. Led to believe they were attending an unofficial meeting, the owners donned casual attire. Talia herself had laid it out this way each time. "Just an informal lunch," she'd say. They showed up too comfortable, at times underdressed, expecting an honest exchange of information. If an attorney came in on behalf of the smaller business, which was only half of the time, they were never prepared. Talia would lead them into the massive boardroom, seat them alone at the far end of the long mahogany conference table and make them wait. After enough time had passed, long enough to be uncomfortable, but not so long it was disrespectful, The Eggery team and Craig would enter.

The Eggery hid behind a holistic grass roots veneer. They preached simplicity and earth awareness in both their presence and marketing. All of their clothing was designed to look casual, but a trained eye knew it was anything but. One woman wore her hair parted down the middle in long, loose waves, smiling from underneath makeup meant to appear like she was wearing none at all. She wore flowing silks, loose linens, and cashmere. Her outfits cost as much as Talia's rent. Her male counterpart was decked out in Patagonia and Arc'teryx as if a spontaneous hike might occur at any moment. A luxury watch adorned his wrist that looked like an antique but cost a fortune. The same one had been delivered to Craig a few months ago, and Talia had Googled it out of curiosity. The price tag made her jaw hit the floor.

Once everyone was seated, and all pleasantries had been exchanged, the breakdown began. Everyone was friendly to the point of nausea, even when problems arose. Craig would prattle through the bulk of the contract as if it was all run of the mill standard terms and conditions. Questions were quickly subdued, but eventually, there would be a point of contention. It usually took the form of a percentage less here or fewer shares there. A point that was such a menial takeaway in the grand scheme of things, it represented a tiny hurdle in the overall course of progress. The change never failed to elicit a flicker of surprise between the small business owners. They knew it was incorrect, but somehow, every time, they were reluctant to put up a fight. Maybe because it seemed trivial, or maybe because there was still so much to be done. As a rule, no one ever wanted to make too much of a fuss.

Right before the break for lunch, when everyone was tired and hungry, Craig would work in a clause that would ultimately give The Eggery a full buyout option. A statement about production falling under a certain threshold resulting in The Eggery being awarded the option to buy out the original owner's shares at less than market value. It was psychological warfare. Craig had a magical way of handling this, rattling off the sentences as if they were commonplace and common sense. The reality was buried in language and legalese. It was human nature, no one wanted to look stupid. It was an even split how often they agreed or objected. When they agreed, they pretended to understand, and the buyout clause was forgotten halfway through lunch.

The objectors, on the other hand, would ask for clarification. Craig would distract them by feigning the sudden realization that he had made an error. He would roll the discussion back to earlier in the meeting, address the prior takeaway they had failed to object to, and restore it to the original offer. Although it was a nominal change, the clients would be relieved to win back the percentage or shares they'd agreed to, and they would forget the buyout option. If they accepted this, then the entire purpose of the meeting was fulfilled. Then, they would break for lunch.

When they returned to the too warm conference room full from the catered meal, their focus would be on staying awake rather than maintaining control of their shares. Everyone agreed at this point in the day, and the bulk of the merger contract would be completed by the close of the meeting.

Craig had caught Talia drifting at a critical juncture. Her attention had been locked in the past when the owners of Pleasant Valley Farms had raised their objection to the clause, their brows furrowed and confusion evident. Everyone was restless and anticipating lunch. She could see it in the absent-minded way one of the women picked at her nails or how Pleasant Valley's owner kept shifting position in his seat. The firm had promised an expensive catered meal from a nearby Italian restaurant. The group was ready for the break, but Craig was driving home his main objective, throwing around his ten-dollar words.

"As long as we have agreement on Clause 5.13, The Eggery can continue to offer the percentages we had previously discussed." He smiled, flipping through a yellow legal pad, and glancing over at the husband-and-wife team who owned Pleasant Valley. They were both nodding in agreement but avoiding eye contact. Talia's face heated, the full weight of her realization that she could have fumbled this at the most important moment. Craig paused, having gotten what he wanted, then tossed the legal pad. It landed flat on the tabletop, slapping against the mahogany-colored wood. All heads lifted at the sound.

"Why don't we break for lunch?" Craig offered. "As you all know, Luigi's catered today as a special favor. I couldn't decide on a dish, so there is a selection of gnocchi with a truffle butter sauce, spaghetti Bolognese, and veal saltimbocca. Hopefully, no one is offended by the veal. It's the best dish on the menu. Impossible not to order. There's a caprese salad, some antipasti, and someone is waiting to prepare the Caesar salad when everyone is ready." He stood, straightened his tie, and buttoned his jacket. The rest of the attendees followed suit, smoothing the fabric of their clothes, careful not to show how eager they were to step away from the table. Craig extended his arm to lead them out.

"Talia, will you hang back a moment? The rest of you, the room next door, on the left. Please don't wait to get started, and you must try the veal."

He opened the conference room door and indicated to the adjacent conference room where the warm aroma of oregano and Bolognese sauce emanated. His white teeth flashed. A murmur rippled through as the attendees exited, and only she and Craig remained. When he turned around, the grin was wiped from his face. He walked toward her with eyes downcast. Stopping in front of his place at the table, he straightened the pad of paper and each pen with a single extended finger. She was in trouble.

"Do we have a problem?" Craig said after a moment of empty air. He still did not look at her.

"I'm so sorry, Craig. I only lost focus for a second. Everyone does before the break. Everyone," she said, the last coming out thin. Craig moved like a bolt, shoving his chair aside so hard it slammed against the wall, and he came within an inch of her face.

"Do you fucking understand how important this is?" he hissed, stabbing a finger at her. She nodded, unflinching. It never helped to waver or shrink when he did this. It had never helped with her grandfather either. The best outcome was to agree.

"They might be tired, but we cannot afford to be. You need to be performing at your peak. Do you understand?" The vein in the center of his forehead bulged, the blood filling his face and turning it beet red. This close she noted the concealer under his eyes, hiding the bags that lived there. She nodded again, the absurdity of his makeup causing the corner of her mouth to twitch.

"What the fuck is so funny?" Craig demanded. She winced.

"Nothing. I'm sorry," she replied. He shook his head and took a step back, delivering a withering look.

"It's this, Talia. This kind of thing. This is why I couldn't advance you. You just don't have what it takes," he muttered. "You can skip lunch."

Craig was doling out a punishment: she was not welcome at lunch. It was a tactic he liked to employ, excluding her from a perk. Like last Christmas, when everyone in the office was handed an envelope containing their annual bonus, Talia received a gift card to Starbucks. He'd been angry she'd gotten his coffee order wrong, when in fact, the shop had simply given her the wrong drink. She accepted the punishment, although it had not been her mistake, just like all the others he had handed down over the last few years. There was no other choice.

"Alright," she replied, trying to maintain a flat expression. She saved the document with a quick tap, closed the laptop, then scooped up her legal pad and hugged it all to her chest like a shield. She was disappointed. She had been anticipating the catered meal and neglected to bring lunch from home.

"Good," Craig said, his eyes locked on her, then turned to leave the room. When he was gone, Talia exhaled a sigh of relief, but a small flare of anger lit deep inside of her. She went to her desk to set everything down, then fished through her purse for a protein bar she remembered having at the bottom of the bag. She ate it in three large bites with water to wash it down. After, she retreated to the ladies' room to sit alone.

Tears threatened to come the second she locked the bathroom stall, but she held them back. Craig would see her red-rimmed eyes, and the thought of giving him the pleasure was revolting. No amount of crying would fix the bind she was in. Talia Michaels was stuck.

She took a seat on the toilet and pulled out her Blackberry to check her email. She scrolled through, hoping someone had made a reservation with her guided hiking service. A fraction of her frustration lifted when an inquiry email appeared at the bottom of the list, and then she saw the name of the sender. It was from a former classmate: Chase Winters. Without even reading it, she slid her thumb over the button to delete it, then hesitated.

This must be a joke, she thought with a sinking feeling. She hated herself for her curiosity but in the end, it won out, and she opened the email.

Hey Talia,

I hope you remember me from school. I'm currently producing an online paranormal show. We've gained a lot of followers, and some of our vlogs have been a hit on social media. Maybe you've heard of us? Dark Dimensions. I have an opportunity for you, but we would require a hike outside of what you normally offer. We need help reaching Lester, and the Tacoma Watershed won't grant us access. We need an expert to help us navigate the forest because we want to do an investigation there. Would love to meet in person to discuss.

Best, Chase

It was a joke. It had to be. His choice of words about "needing an expert" in reference to Lester was all she needed to confirm it. Just like back in elementary school when they had followed her around calling her "ghost." Everyone knew her story. The poor girl who grew up on the edge of Palmer. Talia closed the email and turned off her phone. She deflated, dreading the remainder of the afternoon.

She returned to her desk where a courier waited.

"Been here five minutes," he said impatiently. He handed her the package and was gone before she could explain. Laughter bubbled up through the conference room's closed door. The package was addressed to Craig, but Talia tore open the mailer anyway. From the envelope slid a black laminate box with fine gold writing on the top. *Renaissance Chocolatier.* Clients often sent thank you gifts to Craig and this appeared to be exactly that. She rested the box on her desktop. The lid resisted, sliding free, and gave a small sound as it released. She moved the thin layer of golden paper and found herself looking over two dozen flawless chocolates that had the quality of tiny glass ornaments. Each treat was perfect in shape: one a sparkling red rose with tiny green leaves, another a pink heart with silver striping. They were exquisite. She guessed this box cost the sender a fortune. Talia considered the gift for a moment, replaced the lid, returned the box to the mailer, and then slid it into her purse.

CHAPTER THREE: TALIA - 1991

Grandfather smelled overripe, like a piece of fruit left out in the sun too long. It was a strange odor, unfamiliar and wrong. His pallid face hung over her and with a quick glance, she saw perspiration dotted his temples. Talia shrank in his presence. He leaned heavily on the wooden surface of the kitchen table, the way he canted suggested he might keel over without it holding him up. He snapped his fingers in her face to get her attention but said nothing. She stared down at what remained of her scrambled eggs, focusing on the tiny flecks of pepper dotting the yellow globs. The table shifted, its legs protesting with a loud scraping sound, and her plate moved along with it. She avoided looking Grandfather in the eye, she hated the way his gaze felt on her, but she gave in. His mouth hung open, gaping like a fish out of water, gasping at nothing.

Talia regarded him with deep interest. Grandfather was unwell. He made a sound, deep and guttural, which came not from his throat, but down within his chest. He strained and choked to form words; his mouth unable to solidify around the sounds. His eyes bulged as he looked down at her, then, oddly, the right side of his face fell as if it had been pulled by a string. The corner of his mouth collapsed into an exaggerated frown, the furrow of his brow went flat, and the skin of his cheek sagged. Yes, something was very wrong with Grandfather. He took a stumbling step, and the table slid further across the floor. Her plate teetered on the edge of the tabletop, and a bit of egg flew. He tripped over his own feet and went sprawling hard to the kitchen floor. He landed with a resounding thud that rattled the plates in the cupboards, jangled the cutlery in its drawer, and sent dust motes swirling in the sunbeam pouring through the kitchen window.

The girl stood in a moment of shock. Not knowing what to do next, she plucked her plate off the table and carried it with her unfinished breakfast to the sink, careful to set the stoneware down against the stainless steel without making a sound. It was a habit: silence guarded her from observation. She made it a game that only she was playing, competing to move through her day on soundless feet and with soft hands. She lost when she was noticed. She lost when she got hit.

Talia turned away from the sink and stood over her grandfather as he lay on the floor. Face down, he looked up at her but did not move. A low grinding sound emanated from his throat, and it made her think of stones rubbing together. She was smart enough to know how his face had fallen slack was an indication of something bad, and the sickly-sweet odor radiating off of him was part of the problem. He often smelled odd after a night of drinking, but today there was something fetid and rotten beneath it.

The house was empty this morning. It was just the two of them. Her mother had gone to the post office twenty minutes ago, taking her youngest brother, Jamie, along. Jamie could be a handful, and it was prudent for Sarah to take him rather than expect the other children to mind him. The twins, Cole and Matthew, were playing in the woods. They were not actual twins, but Irish ones, with only a meager eleven months separating their births. They were nearly identical. The only way to definitively tell them apart was the mole on Matthew's chin. Talia had already served them each a small plate of scrambled eggs, which they scarfed down like two hungry puppies, and vanished out the front door. Talia did not mind. In fact, she had fixed her own meal after because she liked to eat alone. That left just Grandfather and Talia. No one would come for a while.

Grandfather's hands shook as he tried to gain purchase on the scarred linoleum floor. He did not seem to notice his right one wasn't moving. Thick gurgles sprang from his mouth and a thin string of drool dribbled into a puddle under his cheek. Talia said nothing in response. He indicated weakly with a single pointed finger to the telephone hanging next to the pantry door. He wanted her to call for help. *But I'm not supposed to use the phone*, Talia thought. She was conflicted.

This man called her mother names. He complained and bitched about the four children he found living in his home, referring to them as "bad seed" and "crotchlings." This man never hesitated to slap them any time they did something he deemed unfit. He would often deliver a fist without any forewarning. The rules changed from day to day. What was acceptable on Monday would earn them a strike on Thursday. It never made sense.

Then there was the lock on the pantry door. When they lived in the old house in town with her father, there had always been food. In the morning there was cereal with milk, sometimes with tiny marshmallows in it. There were canned peaches, the syrup sweet and thick, with cottage cheese. For lunch, they had macaroni, green grapes, and goldfish crackers, and Talia remembered how her daddy had let her stand on a chair to stir the contents of the pot while he held her with one strong arm. When they wanted a snack, they were handed cheese sticks, buttery crisp crackers, and circles of pepperoni.

In this house, there was hunger. Lunch was a slice of bologna between two pieces of soggy white bread, and that was if they received lunch at all. If their mother was at work, they were better off not to ask for anything. The children would wait for dinner rather than make the request of their Grandfather. At least at school they received lunch every day. Breakfast was always eggs. On a rare occasion, they were allowed a piece of toast or a few slices of apple to go along with their morning meal. Some days there were hardly enough eggs for all of them.

The best meal of the day, by far, was dinner. Mother prepared and served a full meal because that was the expectation Grandfather set. He would sit at the head of the table, her mother sat at the opposite end, and between them, she would place a main dish, often a casserole or meatloaf, sometimes a roast, then next to it a vegetable and a side. Often, there were dinner rolls because her mother brought leftovers from the bakery. The owners let the employees take them home at the end of the day. They were allowed a knife tip of butter with their rolls, which her mother carefully doled out.

Grandfather would heap his plate full, taking several thick slabs of meat and piling a mountain of mashed potatoes onto his plate. The children were never allowed gravy if there was any to have, and they were not allowed seconds. Whatever was left over was to be packed away in the burnt orange Tupperware and stored in the fridge.

Grandfather would eat from the containers for his lunch the next day, and Talia was required to wash them.

Now, they were alone. He watched her with his one rolling eye, and Talia reached down slowly like he was a rabid animal caught in a trap. He made a feeble attempt to grab her hand. For a split second, she froze with his greasy fingers around her wrist, but there was no strength in his grip and his fingers slipped off. She lifted his head carefully, surprised by its heaviness, then grasped the key on its long chain, and slow, slow, slow she pulled it from around his neck. She took a step back, admiring the silvery metal flashing in her hand, then walked over to the pantry, fingered the shining new lock, and fit the key inside.

With a turn of her wrist, the lock snapped open. She lifted it from the hasp, then swung the pantry door wide. Talia had never been in the pantry before. The children were strictly forbidden from entering, so she was not prepared for what she found inside. The shelves were laden with food. It was piled on the floor, cans stacked two high, and boxes and bags were crammed without a single bare surface. There were boxes of cereal, dried pasta, and cans four deep on the shelves containing soups, beans, and an assortment of vegetables. There was a selection of canned fruits packed in syrup, and a stack of tuna fish in its thin cans. Hidden away were packages of cookies: molasses, chocolate chip, and fudge coated. Big bags of potato chips and pretzels tipped over, threatening to fall to the floor. There were bags of flour, rice, and white sugar. Everything she had been denied, everything he had kept hidden.

On impulse, the girl grabbed an open package of chocolate chip cookies and without any ceremony, tore back the cellophane and stuffed one in her mouth. The cookie was soft and dense, giving way under her teeth and filling her mouth with brown sugar and sweet chocolate. Without any restraint, she ate another, feeling the same sensations against her tongue a second time. Talia would receive a sound beating for this ordinarily but suspected there would not be much Grandfather could do about it after today. She sometimes had a sense about these things without knowing where the thoughts came from. It was like the idea would float into her brain and become reality. A part of her knew this would be the end of the lock. This would be the end of the fridge alarm too. It would be the end of the beatings and the foul words and the smell of the brown stuff he drank every night. No more nights when she would come into the living room to say goodnight and feel his eyes slide over her beneath her nightgown, like he was a wolf, and she was a rabbit. She had wondered how long it would be before he came for her, knowing it would happen. Eventually.

Her stomach twisted at the thought, not fully understanding what it meant. To suppress the sensation she ate another cookie, then another. Chocolate stuck to the roof of her mouth, and the dough mashed down between her teeth. She ate another, her hunger becoming a frenzy, cookie after cookie, until they were gone. Shame overcame her. Not knowing what to do with the empty package, and not wanting to get caught, she hid it behind a row of jars holding red sauce and exited the pantry.

Talia turned, meaning to close the door and lock it, then decided otherwise. Instead, she went into the living room and located her backpack. She flipped it upside down and dumped out its contents, sweeping the binder and papers under the skirt of the sofa with a kick of her foot. She returned to the pantry, giddy and excited. All the things she wanted were contained within, and she selected items with abandon. After the sack was filled to the point she could barely get the zipper closed, she pocketed the key, deciding she would hide it. She already knew her mother wouldn't take the time to look if it was gone. Out of sight, out of mind worked well with adults. She left the lock hanging on the hasp, hoping it would give the appearance that Grandfather had opened it. She took two steps away, thought again, and took the lock too.

Grandfather watched her from the floor. His hands trembled and shook. To her, this massive man looked suddenly feeble and weak. *Who's the rabbit now?* she thought. The corners of Talia's mouth turned up and her lips formed into a small smile. She would have a feast, and this man, this horror of a man, could no longer stop her. As a child, Talia could not conceive the sweetness of her revenge.

She exited the house, crossed the dooryard, and entered the forest.

Talia returned to herself drenched in sweat, brought back to awareness by her racing heart and the film of anxiety clinging to her mind. She sat up, scrambling to gather her thoughts. The eradicated box of chocolates lay on the bed next to her. There was nothing left except for the crinkled gold wrappers, each hollowed out of their treats. There was an aching pressure in her belly.

She only remembered eating the first candy, how delicious it had tasted, then everything after was a scorch mark across her memory. Glancing at the clock, she found she had been gone less than fifteen minutes. There was time. Talia heaved herself off the bed and into the connected bathroom. Returning to the apartment at the end of her workday, Talia found it empty despite the late hour. It was not unusual for her to work late. If Craig was at his desk, she was expected to be at hers. It hadn't seemed like a sacrifice when she started. She'd been too grateful for the opportunity to consider how that requirement would feel after years of servitude.

It was Friday night. Her roommate, Serena, was out with friends, enjoying her twenties. Not that Talia would know what that was like, she spent her Friday nights decompressing in front of the television set until she was too exhausted to keep her eyes open. She had a few friends but those few had long given up inviting her out. There was no boyfriend or partner, which was a fact she had mixed feelings about. She had tried dating, but it was always the same. They would have fun together, but over the weeks and months, he would grow tired of pursuing her when she constantly changed or cancelled plans and remained uninterested in moving the relationship into more serious territory. It wasn't really a surprise when they stopped calling.

Leaving the office, the outline and weight of the box in her bag made her giddy with excitement. As she drove home, she imagined what the chocolates would taste like and how they would feel in her mouth, and the anticipation carried her up the stairs to her third-floor apartment. Talia placed the box on her bed, reverential as she lifted the lid off, unveiling the arrangement inside. The metallic packaging in its interior held intricate and charming truffles in all shapes. Here was one like a blue teardrop with yellow and green speckles and another cut like an emerald and reflecting the light like an actual gem. The candies were in an array of colors with perfect details inlaid on each.

The first she selected was a white moon with a glittering pearl mica powder coating, making the piece shimmer under the light. Talia guessed each flavor, taking a bite from the moon and finding a soft nutty cream in its interior. The cream was cold on her tongue, flavor exploding in her mouth and making her head tingle. She was ecstatic to give into this small pleasure. She intended to return the lid and set it aside, hiding the rest for another day, but the binge came without warning. Talia faded out into bliss, like the high of a junkie, devouring each delicate chocolate with abandon. When she finished, she laid down to embrace the pleasurable sensations that coursed through her and lapsed into something of a dreamlike state. One that took her to the place hidden in the forest.

Talia dropped to her knees in front of the toilet, held back her dark brown hair and without hesitation, crammed two fingers down her throat. Nothing happened. She did it again harder and gagged, her mouth filling with saliva. She tried again. More gagging and nothing else. She'd hardly eaten today, and her body refused to give up the sustenance. Talia turned on the sink and stuck her head under the faucet, gulping the water down. Growing impatient, she grabbed the cup from the side of the sink, filled it to the brim, and chugged. When she finished, the fullness in her stomach made her feel like she would burst. She filled the cup again, forcing herself to drink, and holding her breath as she gulped the water down. Once the cup was empty a second time, she turned back to the toilet, her discomfort painful, and shoved her fingers down her esophagus. This time she belched, and her stomach twisted. Talia, growing impatient, gave it another forceful try, and this time, it came up. The first rush was full and forceful, the bulk of it water and some of the masticated chocolates. More followed, the rest of the chocolate and water, and she checked for the marker: the pearl mica moon. The flecks of white in her vomit indicated she was empty.

Talia relied on a marker. She usually chose one of the varieties of cheesy snacks covered in vibrant orange dust to signal completion. Salad was a reliable marker as well and served as an excellent pillow if she knew she would not be able to evacuate soon after the binge. It was easy to carry a snack-size bag of crackers with her in case the urge arose. Talia had grown up with the habit and could manage it with careful planning. But recently, the binges were catching her off guard. In the last year, there had been a few occasions where she woke up unaware she'd lost control. Like the night of the lasagna incident. She was lucky Serena hadn't caught her. Coming to awareness on the kitchen floor at three o'clock in the morning surrounded by a pan of lasagna, a half-eaten loaf of garlic bread, and a variety of sweet and salty snacks, Talia had little to no recollection of how the binge had begun. She rushed to pack away the mess before she could purge. The fugue state was alarming. If Serena had walked into the kitchen in the midst of it, Talia's secret would have been exposed.

Talia could usually control the urges and exhibit restraint when she needed to. There would be a trigger and a plan, the crucial piece centering on guaranteed solitude, then once the first morsel touched her lips, she could let go without worry. There was little memory of the episodes once she gave in, and when she returned to her senses, there was only a fleeting memory of a sunny afternoon and a dark forest. Tonight's binge had caught her by surprise and while it had been small, she had laid waste to a couple hundred dollars' worth of chocolate. She should have seen it coming; her binges often centered around expensive, hard to acquire foods. One episode she'd gorged on rambutan, which she had somehow managed to procure several flats of. Another time it was a saffron-laden shrimp paella dish. Sometimes it was all junk food, which was her go-to. Hundreds of dollars' worth of food gone in an instant.

Still kneeling, Talia splashed cool water on her face from the running sink and flushed the toilet, watching as the fine hand-crafted chocolates circled the bowl. She was empty, which was a relief after the pleasure of the food became painful. Looking in the mirror above the sink, only the top of her face visible, she could see the dark circles under her light green eyes. A good night's sleep had eluded her for the last couple of weeks.

Talia was grateful the weekend had arrived, and since it was Labor Day, she would be out of the office for three days. The extra day was critically needed after the debacle with The Eggery, and she had a hike scheduled with her guide business.

Out of high school, and on her own, Talia got a job at a local coffee shop. The pay was average, but the tips were outstanding. It was nice to have money, but there was never enough. She applied for a credit card and was rewarded with a shiny black Visa. It took her no time at all to rack up the balance, often buying Chinese food and shopping at gourmet markets to sate her binges. She financed a car a little out of her price range and got a second credit card to offset the extra expense.

The reality of growing up without any money meant she had no idea how to manage her finances. Driving home on a winter night, unable to see through the driving rain, she plowed her pricy new car into a stopped pickup. Talia's car was totaled. She walked away with a broken ankle and a severe case of whiplash, then discovered her insurance had lapsed. The credit card she'd used to pay it was overdrawn, and the charge was denied. She offered her paltry savings to the man to fix his dented bumper, which he accepted.

Saddled with a car payment, credit card bills, no car, and a broken ankle, Talia buckled down. Over the course of a few months, she scraped together enough cash to get a junker. The engine light was always on, but it ran. Her insurance payment was astronomical. Her ankle healed, but her medical bills went to collections. Her situation wasn't pretty, but she was managing. When her roommate moved back home, Talia offered the room to a former coworker because she couldn't afford the rent. The woman stayed three months, only paid for the first, and stole half of Talia's belongings when she left. To add insult to injury, Talia discovered she'd been hiding the eviction notices that the landlord had left. She was drowning in debt, and with nowhere to go, Talia started living out of her car.

It was then that Craig appeared, like a proverbial knight in shining armor. He came in for a latte, looking beleaguered, and lamenting about how his legal receptionist had quit. Talia, overwhelmed with debt and considering bankruptcy, told him she needed a second job, and he offered her the position on the spot.

The money was fantastic, so good, in fact, she didn't need the second job and quit the coffee shop. She found a place that would accept her eviction, bought a more reliable car, and worked to pay down her debt. After her first month, Craig offered to cover college courses so she could become a paralegal, and she jumped at the chance. She enrolled at the local community college to work on her associate's degree.

During her second quarter, things shifted. Craig demanded she stay later through an important merger, and she missed her final. She begged the professor to retake it and passed. Making it through by the skin of her teeth and convincing herself she would simply have to work harder, Talia enrolled the following quarter. Work demands prevented her from attending, and she failed her courses. Craig was unhappy, but he and

Talia agreed they would revisit the issue after the next term. He started treating her differently.

Working late one Friday night, Craig ordered dinner: a cheeseburger and fries for himself, and a boxed salad for her.

"I noticed your pants are getting a little snug," he remarked. "You should get to the gym." The following Monday, a bottle of weight loss supplements sat on her desk. She was embarrassed but chose to ignore him.

One cold December day, Craig tossed her the keys to his Lexus.

"She needs a wash," he said.

"Do you need me to run it to the carwash?" she asked.

"No." He leveled a cool gaze at her. "The mitts, soap and buckets are in the back storage closet. Pull it around back and use the hose there." She sat at her desk too astonished to speak.

"Is that a problem?" he asked, cocking his head. She recognized the look in his eyes and stifled her objection. Talia donned her winter jacket, but it did little to keep her dry, as she wiped down his sleek black car. He came out to inspect when she finished and handed her a towel.

"Make sure there are no water spots."

The message was clear. He had pulled her from the gutter, and he would continue to treat her like she belonged there. Talia reminded herself at least he wasn't trying to sleep with her and kept her nose to the grindstone. She looked for other jobs, but nothing paid as well as what she was earning. She couldn't afford to quit, trapped at a dead end.

Twenty-three-year-old Talia looked for an outlet, and the idea came like a lightning bolt. People loved Mount Rainier. There were endless trails within the national park and surrounding forests that offered stunning views of the mountain. Growing up on the edge of civilization, the last house at the end of a gravel road to nowhere, she knew those places like the back of her hand. She set up a website and offered guided hikes around the area.

The business flourished. Talia found her niche. The other guide companies either ran sightseeing tours with minimal hiking or were assisting people in climbing the 14,000-foot volcano. There was less in between, and although her competitors had the more popular areas locked up, she offered what no one else did: solitude and a rugged backwoods experience. The work was seasonal, operating primarily from mid-May to late October, and she was booked most weekends. There was some pushback from Craig about taking additional time off, but she worked hard during the week to keep things on an even keel. She had planned to expand into snowshoeing, considering leaving the firm altogether, when the recession hit. Business dried up. The thing she relied on to keep her sane, vanished.

After that, Talia lost her conviction. She broached the subject of school with Craig once more. He told her that ship had sailed. She was desperate with no sense of what direction to take. Craig's mistreatment escalated. Along with the punishments and remarks, he micromanaged the work she did, required longer and longer hours, and denied her time off. She needed to get out before she snapped. Everyone around her had a life to envy. They were getting married, starting families, buying homes, launching careers, and traveling, while Talia was stuck with no future. All she had wanted was to avoid ending up like her mother, broke, desperate, and under the thumb of an abusive man. Despite her own best efforts, here she was, and she hated herself for it.

Kneeling there on the bathroom floor, lost in rumination, the sudden pain in her knees brought her back to reality. She wanted to crawl into bed but went to her closet instead, selecting the hiking boots and clothes she would need for the following day. Next, she pulled out her large daypack and verified all the safety and first-aid gear was where it should be. Tomorrow, she would lead a short family hike to Silver Falls. This hike was more of a guided tour, her least difficult selection, that attracted an older client base. She prepared as if her clients would arrive empty-handed, filling her pack with a variety of snacks and several bottles of water.

With the chore complete, she pulled off her day clothes and slipped on a t-shirt and sweatpants. For a long moment, she sat on the edge of her bed, the weight of the day and the years pressing down on her. She was exhausted but knew sleep would not find her. Instead, she headed into the bathroom to wash her face. She flipped on the overhead fan to clear the sour smell hanging in the air. She brushed her teeth first, then running tepid water, she scrubbed, rinsed, and applied moisturizer.

Calmed by the ritual, she opened her laptop to confirm payment and review the information about the family she was guiding. At the top of her inbox, the message from Chase Winters sat, goading her. Reading his name made her stomach drop, and the school yard memories slipped in.

"Are you messing with me?" she asked the screen, scanning the short message a second time, and growing angry. Not even in adulthood could she escape the torment of her peers.

Talia never forgot receiving that new sweater in first grade. It was fuchsia with a fluffy white kitten wearing a tiny blue bow on the front. Bright colors were all the rage. The only thing she could have wanted more was a Hypercolor t-shirt or a box of neon-colored crayons, but both were out of the budget and therefore, out of the question. She wore the sweater to school the next day, taking care in dressing and choosing barrettes to match. Arriving to class, proudly donning her new garment, Talia was met with snickers from the popular girls. Unbeknownst to her, the sweater had belonged to Eve Lawrence before it ended up in a bag of clothes donated to Talia's mother by one of the local churches.

The other kids had kept their distance before, making sideways comments about her clothes or hair. The most common remark was "Ew," but no one had gone out of their way to make her miserable until now. When Eve saw the sweater, she stalked up to Talia.

"This was mine you know," she said. Talia, surprised and embarrassed, shook her head. Eve grabbed the garment, fingering its hem until she found the hole, and shoved her finger through it.

"We got rid of it because of this," she said, wiggling her finger and laughing. "But I guess you probably like wearing someone else's throw aways." She walked off, laughing, her perfect blond hair bouncing with each step. A squad of girls trailed after her, each rolling their eyes and giggling. Every bit of Talia's earlier happiness evaporated. The first chance she got she went into the bathroom and stuffed the sweater into the trash. Her mother didn't notice when she arrived home without it, but her mother didn't notice a lot of things those days.

While very few of the families in Black Diamond were affluent, they were all doing better than hers. The sweater was only the beginning. Her classmates ridiculed her endlessly, her poverty in evidence by the oversized hand-me-downs she wore. Chase Winters was not the main culprit. That role was left up to the queen bitch: Eve Lawrence. After that confrontation over the sweater, Eve's focus was set to the task of making every one of Talia's days more miserable than the last. Chase had been on the periphery, watching as they tormented her and never interfering on her behalf. He was guilty of the occasional wolf whistle as she walked by or a pinched nose as he passed by her desk.

Talia considered texting the number to tell him where he could shove his request and then decided against it. Bullies had to be ignored.

Just leave it alone. He probably wants a reaction, she thought. *Cause why would anyone want to go to Lester?* She switched gears, finished checking all the information for the following day, then closed her laptop and laid down on her bed.

Lester.

Talia tried to suppress the memory of the place that terrified her as a girl. She shut her eyes against it, but sleep refused to come.

Talia was in search of the perfect picnic spot. Her brothers played out of sight along the banks of the Green River. The sound of their sticks cracking against each other echoed off of the trees behind her. She followed the footpath to the old pump house, stopping before entering the forest. A momentary tug of hesitation held her back. She was leaving them to fend for themselves. Tall trees loomed ahead of her, the sunlight leaking through in places. The forest called to her, beckoned her forth with a warm caress of a breeze, and she continued on. The twins had each other.

She headed away from where her brothers played, keeping the river to her left. She had been in the woods before but always stayed within sight of the house. Talia wanted to go somewhere new, somewhere hidden, to enjoy her stolen treasures. A place that would be her own. She was in no hurry, her appetite sated by the chocolate chip cookies.

The land beyond Palmer was full of rich green life. The forest was a mix of deciduous and perennial trees: Douglas fir, red Cedars, Oregon ash, black cottonwood, and big leaf maple. Where the river flowed, the trees grew tall as they strained for the sun high above the valley floor. Evergreen trees dominated the surrounding hills.

Here on the forest floor, where the young girl walked, a riot of plant life grew, feasting upon the dark fertile soil. Perfect white trillium bloomed amongst the gigantic ferns, creating a field of dazzling flowers as far as her eye could see. Ahead, she spotted an old willow tree, its branches swaying lazily in the wind. All the willows had been planted here and on an ordinary day, it would be the spot she retreated to. Her mother told her the story once how when the house had been built, the wife had grown up on a piece of land with weeping willows and loved them so dearly, she begged her husband to ship three dozen here to the distant reaches of the Pacific Northwest. It was why the massive trees lined the lane to Grandfather's house, and why there were a few here scattered amongst the forest.

Thimbleberry dominated the understory, the broadleaf of the plant dotted with vibrant red berries like jewels set in their mounting. The tiny soft berries were similar to a raspberry, but not as sweet or tangy. She absent-mindedly pulled one from a plant, felt it squish between her fingers, and tossed it away. There were not her favorite berries. She preferred the blackberries that grew along the road, especially closest to the river. Those came later in the season. Already the small white flowers on the vine were beginning to fade to reveal the soft green of the new berries. Another month, and they would be swollen, black, and ready for consumption. Once they were plump and fat, they would pick them by the bucket full for jam. Her mother would sell the preserves to the bakery where she worked to make their famous, seasonal blackberry jam tarts. It was a lot of work, but it brought in extra spending money. This year the money was earmarked to help pay for Talia's school supplies, and she hoped desperately her mother would buy her the pair of patent leather shoes she had been begging for.

Talia traced the rim of the river gorge along a faint game trail, the vegetation thick around her. She followed the path, looking around for a spot that called to her. Talia would know when she saw the perfect place for her feast. The day passed, and the distance from the homestead grew. She walked in a daydream, thinking of shopping with her mother and what she might be allowed to buy. It was a rare treat; one she was looking forward to. Heading into third grade, she was hoping for a new start. That last two years the only clothes for her had been second-hand or thrifted, and the other kids made fun of her for it.

Talia had been walking a long while lost in her reverie when she spotted the outcropping of stone overlooking the river. It was in the sunlight, and she could set the forest at her back to look down upon the shifting blue green of the water. It was the spot. Her spot. Carefully plucking her way to the tree line, Talia stepped out into the light, the midday sun hot on her face. The river was a constant song through the canyon, its rushing waters carrying up the valley walls. She sat on the rock and looked around to admire this place high above the river gorge. She had traveled uphill quite a distance and wondered vaguely how far she had gone, until she opened the backpack.

Talia removed a bag of potato chips swollen with air, a package of frosted cookies, a half-eaten bag of pretzels, two cans of peaches with pull tops, a full box of cereal, two cans of soda, a couple snack size boxes of raisins, a box of cheese flavored crackers, and a brand-new bag of beef jerky.

First, Talia opened the crackers. She selected one, plucking a single cracker out between her pointer finger and thumb, pretending to be a dainty lady at tea and nibbled carefully on its edges. The salt delighted her tongue, the cheesy flavor intense. She cracked open a can of soda, something she was only allowed when they had fast food, and the carbonation fizzed in her face, the bubbles sizzling up from the can. She took a long sip. It hurt her mouth in a way she enjoyed. A small burp escaped her lips when she finished, and it made her giggle. She scooped out a couple more crackers, enjoying the flavor each time it filled her mouth. After hearing over and over how they couldn't afford food, she was astonished by the wealth of snacks in her home. The remedy for her hunger had been behind the pantry door all along. It was a betrayal, implemented by her grandfather but enforced by her mother. The person she trusted the most in this world had lied to her, and that realization came like a gut punch.

Talia disappeared into where the hunger lived. The single crackers turned into handfuls. She ripped open the closed bags and boxes, restraining herself as she tasted the first bits of food, then shoving whole fistfuls into her mouth, mashing it between her teeth, and swallowing it down with a swig of cola. Frenzied, she grabbed pieces from this package and a few fragments from another, then trying them all at once to reveal a new flavor, like the saltiness of a chip combined with the sweetness of a cookie. Or how a handful of cereal tasted with a mouthful of cola. The girl ate and consumed, unaware of what she was forcing down her throat or how much, disconnected from the swelling in her stomach and how she was beginning to grow full. The salt and the sugar danced across her tongue in various textures and tastes, calories filling her body and brain with the pleasant rush of endorphins. Cracking open a can of peaches and slurping down the syrup, greedily pulling out the fleshy fruit with her fingers and hardly chewing them before swallowing, another already in her mouth. The beef jerky took too long to chew, so she set it aside. The rest went down easy and was gone, leaving only the second can of peaches and the jerky.

With the food devoured, Talia let the warmth from the sun sink into her bones and fill her with the languid perfect sleep of a full stomach. At complete peace, existing in a bubble of total satiation and relaxation, it was a high like nothing she had experienced before. Everything was right with the world for this singular moment. She forgot about her daddy and how much she missed him. Gone was the face of her mother, the flat line of her mouth and the dark circles under her eyes. Not a single thought for her younger brothers and needing to protect them from the old man. And finally, Grandfather. Not a memory of his episode in the kitchen, or the trouble she might be in for abandoning him. She drowsed in the sun's embrace fulfilled and feeling like nothing else in the world mattered except this moment.

After a while, she did not know how long, a cloud passed over the face of the sun. Cold awareness returned. She woke to wrappers strewn about, the soda cans lay empty, drunk to the last drop, and all that remained were crumbs at the bottom of each package. Not that she was hungry, in fact, she was quite sick. Her stomach bulged, overfilled, and protesting. A flare of panic lit in her chest. The sun was sinking in the sky, and she did not know where she was or how far she had walked. And yet the thought of turning toward home was too overwhelming to consider.

Nausea crept in, the pressure in her belly intensified. The thought of everything she had eaten mashed together made her gag, and it sat there at the back of her throat. She burped the cola, a thick choking heave, and vomit rose to the surface. Talia leaned forward onto her knees and crawled to the side of the outcropping. Her eyes watered, her nose ran, and her mouth filled with saliva. She was going to throw up. All of the comfort she felt had turned to pain. She wanted it gone. Talia vomited a hot stream down the side of the cliff. Although grotesque to her at first, she realized it was a perfect end. Every heave disappeared below her, far and away. Some ended up on the steep slope underneath her. With the pressure relieved, she continued to eject the meal until the bright orange crackers came up signaling she was empty. She sat back panting from the effort. Wiping her mouth with the back of her hand, there was a modicum of disgust but also of something prideful. A special secret. Just for her and her alone, and it made her feel powerful.

The girl gathered up the packages, stuffing the garbage into her backpack and making a mental note to abandon it along the way. She would not leave the mess in her special place. She kept the beef jerky and the last can of peaches, saving them in case she grew hungry later. After ensuring she had collected all the evidence, the girl returned to the forest dazed and out of focus from her episode. Talia considered what to do next. She had no desire to return home. She was second guessing her earlier premonitions about

Grandfather's extended illness. Her disappearance, theft, and refusal to call for help would be met with retribution. She would undoubtedly receive a thorough beating if Grandfather recovered. She hiked further upriver and ignored the progress of the sun.

Birds called to one another from their perches. Talia walked idle and careless through dense greenery, worry nibbling at the edge of her thoughts. She picked her way through the forest, undecided and conflicted, knowing she should go home and not wanting to with a ferocity she'd never experienced before. Unaware she followed no trail, her wanderings took her deeper into the forest. She wondered in her child's mind, if she continued to walk, if she could reach a different place, one where she would find a new family, one with a mother and father who desperately wanted a child. She imagined how they would adopt her and change her name. They would spoil her with beautiful dresses, shiny shoes, new toys, and all the food her heart desired. It was a pleasant idea. Talia would miss her mother and those softer moments when they were alone, and she was happy, which was rare these days.

It was not until the forest grew dim, and the sound of the river vanished amongst the trees, that she realized she was lost. Without the water by her side, she was disconnected from all sense of direction. Talia hadn't thought to pack a jacket or a flashlight. She searched for the sun overhead, trying to orient herself, but under the cover of trees she could not remember what direction it had traveled from and was unable to determine where the sun was now. She decided to get to a high place, hoping to find it or the river so she could make her way home.

When a mountain appeared in front of her, Talia walked up its steep slope. The tree line disappeared as she scrambled up the dusty, loose soil and jagged rocks. There were precarious spots where she clung to the rocky face, nimbly planting her footfalls, and finding how efficient and unafraid she was. She was agile and traversed the mountainside easily. Once she reached the top, she was surprised to see how high she had climbed. There was a rush of relief when she spotted a fire lookout on stilts sitting only a short distance away.

Looking out, the impenetrable forest surrounded the peak in all directions. The sky had grown dusky, and defeat overwhelmed her. The wilderness went on for miles, a patchwork quilt of dark green swaths of old growth, and light green squares where the trees had been cleared. There was nothing in those spaces that spoke of civilization. She was lost.

She crossed the peak and went to the building, grateful to find it unlocked. It would be the safest place for the night. She found a bare cot, and after digging around in an army locker, sourced an old wool blanket smelling metallic and dusty. After shaking out any spiders, she crawled underneath the blanket and regretted her secret hope to find a new family. Her only wish on that cold night was to be back in her mother's arms. Too tired to be afraid as night drew in, she pulled the blanket over her head and fell into an exhausted sleep.

Talia dreamt about the forest again: an ocean of waving branches threatening to swallow her as she traversed the heart of darkness. The dreams left her uneasy and disoriented. She had risen with her alarm, alert and awake despite their dark memory. She quickly dressed, grabbed her pack, and headed out the door.

She would meet her group at the Ohanapecosh Visitors Center for their hike to Silver Falls. This was the only hike she did within Mount Rainier National Park. The other local guides had the best features of the park locked down, so the majority of her selections were in the backcountry guiding lesser-known trails. The basic package Talia offered for this section was for Silver Falls and the Grove of the Patriarchs. There were options to extend the hike or backpack further to Deer Creek or Tamanos Creek. It was an accessible hike for people who lacked experience. As a bonus, it was less populated than the high-profile sections like Paradise and Sunrise, allowing for solitude in the lush forest.

Upon reaching the Visitor's Center, Talia recognized her group immediately. The family of four consisted of a middle-aged man, his two sons, and elderly mother. She was struck by the two boys, near carbon copies of each other, except one had big ears and the other wore glasses. She suspected they were Irish twins like her own brothers. These two were pale, soft children, and when Talia approached them, they were huddled together in a corner over a Nintendo DS. While one moved his deft thumbs over the controls, the other watched and made quiet comments in his brother's ear.

My work is going to be cut out for me, she thought, amused. Both their father and grandmother were standing over the three-dimensional scale map of Mount Rainier that sat in the center of the room, pointing at different locations.

"Good Morning! I'm Talia," she greeted them, extending a hand. "I am guessing you are Dave and fam?" Dave took her hand to shake it. His hands were big and soft much like Dave himself: a large man with a heavy middle and thinning light brown hair atop his head. He had a gentle smile that made his eyes twinkle. Talia liked him immediately.

"I'm Evelyn, but you can call me Lyn," the older woman spoke from behind Dave. He moved aside, and his mother came forward to shake Talia's hand as well. Evelyn was fit for her seventy-five years. The only indicator her body was giving in to old age was a slight hunch to her shoulders.

"Good Morning, Lyn! Are you guys ready to head out? The Grove of the Patriarchs is only a short distance beyond the falls, so we can always change our minds if you want to extend the hike," Talia suggested. Dave called the two boys in a hushed tone. Neither responded. Dave walked over without a word and held his hand out requesting the console. The boy with the glasses offered up the toy, and Dave made it vanish with a practiced maneuver. Talia appreciated the shared familial connection, the unspoken language between them. It made her nostalgic for what had been stolen from her. This man knew his children, and he was gentle. She liked Dave even more, which made her miss her father.

"We're ready," Dave grinned.

"Alright, let's go," she said leading them out of the building. "I invited you to start at the Center so you could get a taste of the park's history. The map gives a great perspective of Rainier's scale. I'll take us past the hot springs on our way to Silver Falls. The pools aren't much to look at anymore, but I am sure it's as close as any of us want to get to Rainier's volcanic activity." Talia's guide persona led the way. The role allowed her to shed the myriad thoughts that grabbed for her attention and provided her with natural confidence and knowledgeability. She liked how people trusted her and treated her with respect on the trail, it gave her a sense of worth that was so lacking in her day-to-day life.

"First, and most important, I brought water and snacks for everyone. Granola bars and some dried fruit, something light with a bit of sugar is good to have for a hike. I might even have some chocolate," Talia said, winking at one of the boys, who met her with a blank stare. She quickly suppressed the memory of the night before and the box of chocolates.

"We do have water. It never hurts to have more just in case. Right, boys?" Dave replied, playing in to her enthusiasm.

"Perfect!" she said. "So, I've met Lyn and Dave. Who else is joining us today?" They were following the walkway behind the center and stopped in front of a massive section of tree on display. The cut circle was from an old Douglas Fir and had markers on its rings to designate notable events that had occurred during the tree's life. Talia turned and looked at the two boys. They glanced at each other, another unspoken conversation. It was something she recognized from her own brothers' behavior.

"Noah," the boy with the glasses spoke first.

"Lucas," the one with the big ears said in a voice barely above a whisper. He looked away, not meeting her eye.

"Hi Noah. Hi Lucas. I am going to get right to it. One thing about Mount Rainier is that it has really big trees." She indicated the weathered brown section behind her and held her arms against it to demonstrate its size. Talia pointed to a small black placard in the center of its rings.

"This tree was born in 1293 and lived to be almost seven hundred years old." She indicated the marker on the outer rings. Talia tracked her fingers along the ridges next to the placard denoting when the tree was cut. "Can either of you two tell me anything that might have happened while this tree stood?"

The boys looked uncomfortable at being asked a direct question and shifted their weight from foot to foot. Dave gazed down at them, waiting for a reply. Lucas caught his father's glance and looked away, as if eye contact would require his response.

"I doubt you will get much from these two," he said, his tone light but admonishing. "Today was a hard sell. If they could spend all day holed up with their video games, they wouldn't even get up to use the bathroom."

"Dad," Noah whispered his plea, embarrassment all over his face. Dave continued anyway.

"We came all this way to visit Nana." Dave turned to face the boys to remind them. "I told you when we came out to the woods, you were going to be here with us."

The rebuke was a soft warning, but also one that suggested if they persisted in being reticent, he would not be as calm in the future. Talia had a hard time imagining Dave being anything but gentle with his sons. The thought of him as her father warmed and saddened her. Dave turned back to face Talia's presentation and gave her a subtle nod to continue.

"The Declaration of Independence was signed when this tree was 483 years old. Nearly one hundred years later we have the first documented climb of Mount Rainier and the American Civil War beginning. You can see the markings of Mount Saint Helens previous eruptions and when there was a mini-Ice Age recorded. It is incredible to think how long this tree survived, and there are many more along the trail, particularly in the Grove of the Patriarchs. Let's continue." Talia beamed, wholly in her element.

"Mount Rainier boasts several mineral springs which were harnessed to bring tourism long before the park was established. While they are no longer in use, they were important to the history of both Longmire and Ohanapecosh. You can see over here where there were plans to install a pool," Talia said when they arrived at the hot springs. She indicated where there was a deep depression filled with murky water and pond scum.

"For a time, these mineral springs were part of a health resort, and visitors claimed the hot springs cured all kinds of ailments like arthritis and psoriasis. You might've seen photographs of the resort and the bath houses inside the center. Rumor has it the springs were regarded as holy by the local tribes, so when the land was taken and commercialized, a lot of people thought it was cursed. The resort was plagued with issues and changed hands several times before closing permanently when the park purchased the land. The park decided to let the area revert back to its natural state, but the evidence of the resort's plans remains. It's critical we understand our impact on the environment and how long the land can take to recover from human use. That's why it's so important to remember we stay on the trail," Talia spoke as they walked the muddy path. Evelyn stayed beside her while Dave prodded his sons along.

The hot springs produced a mild boggy odor, only faintly sulfuric, that gave way to the crisp smell of Douglas fir and damp rainforest. The faint rush of the Ohanapecosh River carried up to them on the trail from the valley below. Filaments of its glacial blue color were visible between the trees. The quintet travelled through the forest, the air cool despite the warming day, and admired the landscape, from the tiny orange-yellow mushrooms growing on dead cedar trees to the piles of moss-covered stones.

"It's something to think that a glacier just said *here* and left this. It's been here for centuries," Talia said over her shoulder as they passed a massive boulder the size of an SUV. Its surface housed a host of bright green moss, a couple small ferns, and a tiny vine maple spreading its branches for the sun.

As they neared the final half mile, Evelyn faltered in her stride, and Talia fell behind to keep pace with her.

"How are we doing?" Talia asked. Lyn glanced up at her, smiling with thin lips. Her age showed in the fine lines around her mouth and the wrinkles near her sharp blue eyes. She was a beautiful woman. Talia hoped she would age so gracefully.

"Oh, I'm fine. You don't have to hang back here on account of me," the older woman said, waving her off.

"Don't be silly," Talia replied. "There's a bench up here before the last bridge. We can take a break there." Lyn nodded, accepting Talia's invitation.

"Getting old is for the birds," Lyn laughed. "I wish you could have seen me in my prime. My father was an alpinist. He worked on search and rescue teams and operated a mountaineering company. I could do everything. Climb a sheer rock face with a thirty-pound pack. Hike fifteen miles in a day. Pull a full-grown man out of a ravine."

"It sounds like you were a regular badass," Talia replied. Evelyn laughed hard enough she stopped and grabbed her side.

"You're right. I was a total badass," she said. Talia grinned.

"Were you in the same line of work as your father?" Talia asked when they started to walk again.

"No." Lyn shook her head, focusing on her feet. "I was home with the kids. That was at a time when a family could survive on one income. I have two sons and a daughter. We stopped at three. That was a small family in our neighborhood. Catholics. You should have seen the pack of them running around like it was Lord of the Flies. I was home, but it didn't suit me. I was raised to be a woman, not a wife."

Lyn passed a knowing glance off to Talia as she spoke.

"My husband knew exactly what he was getting into when he married me. He took no issue when I volunteered for the Forest Service. I loved it. There was always a mother who would take the kids. They were all too happy to help, said it kept their own kids preoccupied. I would head out from time to time to assist on a rescue or on weekends, take a trip up to the mountains. When the kids got old enough, I would pack sandwiches and bring them. Dave was a lot like those two, except he always had his nose in a book. If we had those Gameboy things back then, he would be just like those two," Lyn rambled, and Talia listened, welcoming the older woman's musings. Evelyn was funny, fierce, and independent. Everything Talia wanted to be.

The bench was next to a large rushing creek with a wide bridge spanning over it. The boys and their father wandered out into the center, while the two women sat together on the bench like old friends. Talia took out a bottle of water, unscrewed the cap, and without asking, handed it to Lyn. The older woman accepted it without question and drank.

Talia used an innate sixth sense to anticipate other people's needs. She had relied upon it since she was young. It was how she survived so long with Craig whose every little tic and mood she could read and, at times, manage. Her uncanny ability to predict what people wanted and needed had aided her throughout her life, and with Evelyn, it was no different. Talia followed the water bottle with a half-unwrapped granola bar.

"I could have done this trail blindfolded with my hands tied behind my back," Lyn said, taking a small bite from the bar. She chewed and looked at it thoughtfully, as if a little surprised to find it in her hand.

"You are doing amazing, most seventy-five-year-olds I know would have turned back after the hot springs," Talia said. Lyn snorted.

"I know you're right, but when you've been betrayed by old age, you'll understand," Lyn replied. She drank her water and ate her granola bar. When she was finished with both, Talia packed away the garbage.

With their break done, she led them the final tenth of a mile to Silver Falls. The family was captivated by the onslaught of water pouring into the chasm below. Talia looked on at Lyn's mesmerized expression, enjoying the woman's pleasure in reaching their destination, then assisted her down to the best viewpoint. Dave hung back and pulled out his camera to take pictures, staging the two boys next to his mother with the powerful waterfall in the background. Talia stood aside watching the scene unfold. Dave gave instructions to the two boys who had straight faces. Lyn, on the other hand, looked radiant surrounded by her grandsons. She gave them a heartfelt squeeze and the smiles came.

Talia's phone vibrated in her pocket. It caught her off guard, cell service within the park was non-existent and, somehow, she had a signal. Turning away from her party, she pulled her phone out and felt immediate regret. Craig's name was flashing on the screen. A sharp pang of anxiety ran through her, followed by a wave of nausea as the phone buzzed urgently in her hand. She almost answered out of habit. She used to feel pride in his reliance upon her, but she had come to see the device as a short leash. When Craig called, she was expected to answer, and she dreaded it ringing during her off time.

It was tempting to believe it would be a simple thing, but it was never a quick question or reminder. He would demand she come into the office. Craig had killed enough of her weekend plans as of late, she knew how this would actually go. On the other hand, if she did not answer, there would be hell to pay. Anger flooded her. Was she not entitled to a weekend? He had not asked her to work. What was left to punish her with? The promotion to paralegal was gone, the raises were infrequent, and the promise of higher education had proved to be a pipe dream. What was left to take away? The rationalization emboldened her.

When the call stopped, Talia powered down her phone and returned it to her pocket. She would not be answering his calls today or for the rest of the long weekend.

There would be fallout and for the first time, she didn't care. She turned around to find Dave waiting for her. He held his camera out.

"Would you mind taking our picture?" he asked, eyes shining. He was having the time of his life. She let her anxiety get carried off by their enthusiasm, even the boys were grinning at something whispered by their father. Talia was exactly where she wanted to be.

"Say: Silver Falls!" she cried above the roar of the water and snapped the picture.

Morning broke. Talia, having spent a restless night in the lookout, sat up from the musty old mattress and sneezed. A dead moth lay beside her. She flicked the corpse to the floor, and it left a bit of white powder on her fingernail. Upon discovering the chill in the air, she wrapped the blanket around her shoulders, then reached into her backpack for the can of peaches. Once she popped open the top, she slurped the juice, then plucked a piece of the soft fruit from the tin. She ate in contemplation. She was not sure where she was or how to get home.

After polishing off what amounted to her breakfast, the girl stepped out into the cool morning, hugging the scratchy wool blanket around her. The air smelled fresh and faintly of dew. Vast mountain ranges capped in snow lined the northeastern horizon. Beyond, a few stark white peaks appeared as ghosts in the far-flung distance. She spotted a remote lake reflecting the early light. Dominating the southern viewpoint was Mount Rainier. Miles of untainted forest spanned in all directions. Talia squinted, looking for the break in the trees where the river would be and was dismayed to find she could not be sure. As she tried to quell the panic that was slowly rising into her throat, a glinting flash caught her eye.

Talia leaned forward against the wooden railing, squinting to sharpen her vision, and remembered how she had uncovered a set of binoculars inside the lookout while she searched for a blanket. She went back into the building and dug around in the locker at the foot of the bed until she found the heavy black lenses. Dashing back out to her prior position, she focused on the place where she had last seen the spot of light against the endless green. It took a moment, but she found a clearing. In the midst of it was a building with a metal chimney positioned at the exact right angle to reflect the early morning sun. A burst of hope ran through her. A building could mean people, and people meant rescue. Relief flooded through her.

Taking the wool blanket and binoculars with her, Talia proceeded down the mountainside. The dew dampened the soil, firming it, but making it no less precarious. She moved fast, preoccupied with reaching the structure she had spotted, but her feet kept sliding out from underneath her. The third time it happened, she grabbed a scraggly subalpine tree to prevent her from winding up on her backside or, worse, falling down the mountain. Talia restrained her movements, her thighs aching to hold her weight on the downward grade. Slower than she liked, she dropped below the tree line and back into the forest, losing sight of her intended destination. She prayed she was heading in the right direction.

It was another slog through the forest, one that she was more cognizant of the second time around. Gone was the dreamy quality of the prior day when she had maintained a certain level of denial about her situation. With the acceptance that she was really and truly lost, here at the fore was the prickling nervousness that she would never be found.

She walked for what felt like hours in places where the trees grew together so dense no light reached the forest floor. She imagined she was trapped in a cage, and it made her feel claustrophobic. Everywhere she turned the monoliths soared above her. The undergrowth was equally thick, and she struggled to find an adequate game trail to cut through it. Her arms itched with a dozen tiny scratches as she squeezed between trees and shrubbery. She eventually found a well-used path she could pass through unscathed. The only sound was the wind through the treetops, which seemed to grow louder with every step.

Light appeared ahead. Realizing it was not the wind she had heard, but the rushing of the Green River. Her pace quickened to reach the break in the trees. There she hoped she would see the house, and if not, she could follow the river instead. She was back to a landmark familiar to her. There was solace in this, she was safe. The trees came up to an eroded bluff along the water's edge. She was careful to stay back from it, seeing the river frothing and gnawing at the loose dirt underneath her feet.

On the opposite side of the river was the white house with the metal chimney. She was saved. It was the one she'd seen from the tower, but it was standing on the edge of a town. Talia took a step back, shocked by her discovery.

Prominent in the foreground was a large dark building next to a set of railroad tracks. A collection of homes and old structures in varying states of collapse formed the backdrop. The white house was apart from the others. She followed the tracks with her eyes and saw a long, low metal bridge spanning the river.

She ducked back amongst the trees, hugging the embankment for fear she would stray too far and lose sight of the river again. When she reached the trestle, she stood out in the open looking across. The tracks followed the river away from the town and disappeared into the mountains. She wondered vaguely where they went, noting two poles where a sign had once been.

Talia crossed the bridge, the sky overhead a brilliant blue. Sweat sprang up where the pack rested on the small of her back. She stepped one plank at a time, the water moving below her caused a strange sense of vertigo. She focused on a grassy patch of earth on the opposite end of the trestle and took steady breaths. Reaching the other side, she stopped again in wonder. A town in the middle of the forest. Like a fairy tale. Many of the dwellings were dilapidated with sunken in roofs. Ivy threatened to overtake the last standing walls of what used to be homes. There were piles of bricks and rubble where she suspected old storefronts had once sat. There was an assortment of buildings, and what was left told the story of a different time when this place was a hub of activity. Now, it appeared no one was here.

Talia followed the railway to the large dark structure with a set of stone stairs leading to its entrance; a platform extended out along the tracks. She read the tarnished bronze placard beside the large double door.

Lester Station

She took a step back, stunned. She knew the rumors, the legends about this abandoned place, it was common knowledge in her small corner of the world. And she was here. She wheeled around, a new sense of fascination overtaking her.

What remained of the streets were overgrown with weeds. Talia walked down the center of the tracks glancing around at each of the empty buildings. She looked back at the white house with the metal chimney, larger than the others, its flaking paint reminding her of the pantry door back home.

Before her was a house, faded burgundy from years of neglect. It was a narrow building and appeared to only hold a single room despite its high roof. Another, in a similar style, was a sunny yellow with tiny green lichen growing on its surface. Many of the houses were small. She regarded the layout of the town. Set back from the residences, were a collection of squat utilitarian cabins. Behind them, was another large building peeking out from amongst a stand of tall trees. It looked new compared to the other structures, and she wondered what it could be. Everywhere she looked there was more to see and marvel at. Although several buildings were still standing, there were many that had collapsed and given in to rot. All once homes of people who had long ago abandoned them.

She heard a creak behind her, and when she half-turned, she saw an old man standing on the porch of the large white house. He was thin and well-dressed, his clothing tailored to fit his frail frame perfectly, the pants the exact length over his shoe. They were clean, and the material of good quality. In contrast, his hair was long, shoulder length, greasy, and he had a scraggly, unkempt salt and pepper beard to match. As she rolled her eyes over him, they landed on his shocking blue eyes, and she found herself mesmerized.

"Hello," he said simply. She watched him, frozen. "Where did you come from?" Those eyes were like blue fire. She had come here to find someone and found someone she had.

"Where did you come from?" he asked again. She did not answer and took a couple steps back, tripping over one of the rails and sprawling hard onto her bottom. The man watched, but did not draw closer. She scrambled up, brushing her hands off on her pants.

"Where did you come from?" he asked a third time. His cold eyes penetrated her. She couldn't look away. She was terrified.

"Palmer," she replied. He cocked his head to one side and took a single step down from the porch.

"Do you know why you are here?" he asked. Alarm spread throughout her body. She did not belong here. There was something wrong with this place. There was something wrong with this man.

"You are a special one. Very special." he nodded and took another step down. Talia's feet were stuck in place as she watched him take another step, and another, until his final footfall reached the grassy earth. "Yes, there's something very special about you. Let me count your ribs." He started toward her, and all at once, she came unglued.

With a clumsy turn, she ran, and the old man gave chase. At first, she paralleled the rail line for fear she would lose her bearings. The backpack bounced against her backside, heavy with the binoculars. She hazarded a glance back to see how close he was and nearly tripped over her own feet. He was falling behind, his age too much to overcome.

Talia was exhausted from the prior day's hike and knew she could not maintain her speed for long. She cut right into the heart of the abandoned town. The man followed. She whipped to the left, which she discovered was a mistake. The structures in this section had collapsed into piles of rubble on top of old foundations. There was nowhere to hide. She cut right, going deeper into the town, and further away from the river.

"Girl!" the man cried, managing to produce a lungful of air. He was leaning forward, hands on his knees, trying to catch his wind. "Goddamn this body." She used it. She put distance between them, turned right again and was now heading toward the cluster of cabins in the back of the village.

"Girl, come on out! I want to show you something!" the man called.

When she reached the cabins, she set her back against one of the buildings, and held her breath, hoping the man with the terrifying eyes would give up. The structure shook with the vibration of footsteps within. He was not alone. Someone was inside the cabin.

Talia ran toward the railroad tracks, hoping to get over the bridge and away from this town. But ahead of her, a small group of people were waiting on the station platform. Talia balked. They were watching her with interest, but no one moved to intervene. She knew they would not help her. They were strange like the man. She diverted again and followed the tracks to the other edge of town beyond the station. Having come full circle, she was aware that a few of them were following her, but not with much urgency.

Talia ran with everything, the air burning hot and fiery in her chest. Adrenaline coursed through her veins. The backpack slammed wildly, and she ran as far as her little legs would take her. The rails bent around an outcropping, and once she was behind it, out of the sight of her followers, she hid. She climbed back into the forest, found a rotted log next to a large tree and crouched within the depression of earth. They searched for her, passing through in a carefree fashion. One man said to another, "She didn't go far." She waited, then waited some more.

When she could restrain herself no longer, she crept out from her hiding place. She headed away from the town of Lester, along a gravel road caught between the forest and the rails. Ahead, a short distance away, she spotted another bridge crossing over the Green River. She picked up her pace and when she reached it, started across, wanting to put as much distance as she could from the town. She took one look back when she had reached the halfway point and saw the buildings from a distance. The man stood there at the edge of the abandoned city, watching her cross the trestle. The others were gone, only the old man remained. He spotted her, then threw his hand up, and waved. Her heart skipped, terrified he would pursue her despite the mile between them. Instead, she watched him walk away.

Talia hurried to the other side of the bridge, slowing only to cast glances behind her to ensure she was not being followed. After crossing, she kept the river on her right and didn't stop walking. Her lungs ached, and her legs throbbed, but she was too afraid they would find her to stop. Gone were the thoughts about finding a rich mother and father and having parents all to herself. Forgotten were the decadent dinners, the beautiful dresses, and a big house with a manicured garden. Talia would return to the homestead, although a part of her wished she could disappear rather than face what was waiting there. She wondered if she truly belonged anywhere and was starting to suspect there was nowhere in the world safe for her.

Talia followed the river until it grew dark. Her legs throbbed, she grew thirsty, and her stomach whined for food. She remembered the jerky and ate bits of it as she went. Just as she decided to pull out the wool blanket and find a log to curl up next to, she heard voices calling from deep within the forest. She froze. Had she heard what she thought she heard? For one terrifying moment, she thought she had doubled back, and these were the people of Lester. She listened. Someone was yelling her name. Suddenly, there were many voices and tiny pinpricks of light flitting amongst the trees like errant fireflies. Her name echoed like birdsong.

"I'm here!" she called. "I'm here! I'm here!" A light swung in her direction. She wanted to run and found she had no strength to move faster.

"I think I heard something!" a male voice yelled. Other beams moved toward her, and their voices grew louder, calling her name. Relief washed over Talia as she picked her way through dense understory of thick fern and shrub.

"I'm here! I'm here!" she screamed. The lights converged, and she was swept up by big arms that held her tight. She was home.

Talia ignored her phone until late Sunday morning, then gave in to the impulse to power it on and assess the damage. She was rewarded with over thirty notifications: fourteen missed calls, twenty text messages and several emails. All but one was from Craig. He was asking where the file had been saved with the notes and contract from the merger meeting. The request itself was confusing. Files were stored in the shared drive with a designated folder for The Eggery. The last three texts gave her pause, each simply read: *Call me.*

All of the calls and messages stopped Saturday evening, so Talia hoped he had located the file. On Tuesday morning, she would feign stupidity and tell him she had gone camping and had no service. She was willing to face his anger with her newfound resolve.

There was a single text from a number she did not recognize, and she immediately regretted opening it. Chase Winters had not given up. It read: *Hi, Chase again. Hoping you saw my email. I would love a chance to meet up with you. Give me a call.* Talia frowned at the message and his persistence. She ruminated about ignoring the request as she languished in bed and dozed. Lester infiltrated her sleep. She dreamt of walking on an endless track of railroad, stretching to the horizon as far as the eye could see. The forest grew darker around her, knowing as you know in dreams, she was approaching the town, and the man waiting there. When she woke, she determined to call Chase to tell him she wasn't interested. She needed to put an end to the whole business. She was done with the dreams, done with the memories.

While researching to start her guide business, she had discovered there were a couple of websites dedicated to providing trail information to hikers. People could leave reviews or reports on conditions, along with directions and photos. On a whim she searched the trails near where she had grown up and was surprised to find reports on Lester.

There was no reaching the ghost town anymore. The main road was gated and guarded. It was widely known there was a northern access point that required a long drive and a hike in, but a quick review of the ghost town forums assured the visitor that the Green River Headworks, the entity that managed the Tacoma Watershed, was monitoring the area and trespassers would be prosecuted.

There were some interesting stories in the forums. One person reported having a gun pulled on them by one of the Headworks guards, while another was simply escorted off the property. A particularly amusing post detailed the adventure of a kayaker who had ferried himself up the waterway against the current. The guards spotted him and tried to flag him down. When he ignored them, the guards continued their pursuit, eventually attempting to follow him in their own raft. The kayaker thought he'd lost them, until he came up to a net strung across the waterway. Unable to continue upstream, he drifted back down river, while the guards followed in their truck. Weeks later, netting blocked access to the waterway where the watershed began.

Growing up in Palmer, it was odd the level of manpower utilized to keep people out of the watershed. It was done under the pretense of protecting the water quality, but the locals agreed it was overkill. The entrance to the watershed road had NO PARKING signs every fifty feet and cameras pointing in all directions. There was a guard house at the entry with a massive chain link gate, and a giant sign declaring: VIOLATORS WILL BE PROSECUTED. It was not an idle threat. Every local knew someone who had hunted in the watershed or wandered in by mistake, depending on the version you got, and had been fined an absurd amount of money for trespassing. It was hardly worth the effort to navigate to Lester, and for what reason? Even if it was a prank, she would put an end to it.

Hi Chase. Sorry, I've been busy since you reached out. I don't offer hikes to Lester. No one does. It's illegal to trespass into the watershed. I won't be able to help but take care.

She scanned the text a couple times to ensure she sounded casual without any hint of the annoyance she felt and sent it. Seconds later the phone came alive in her hands. Chase was calling. Talia tried to dismiss it and accidentally answered. Flustered, she sputtered out a, "Hello?"

"Talia Michaels! How are you? Thanks for getting back to me. I understand your reservations when it comes to Lester, but that's why we need your help. I really think this is an opportunity you wouldn't want to miss," Chase said barely pausing before getting right to the point. Caught off guard, Talia stammered a response.

"There's no way in," she said. Her words sounded unconvincing even to herself.

"But *you* know a way in," he replied. Her surprise was replaced by irritation.

"Look, Chase, this isn't what I do. I'm not interested," she stated, making her tone as firm as she could muster.

"I would love the chance to explain in person. What are you doing tonight? Can you meet with me?" he asked. Sensing her reluctance by the silence on the other end of the phone, he continued. "We won't be alone. The whole *Dark Dimensions* team will be here along with the homeowners. We are conducting an investigation for the vlog. You should come down and see for yourself." She started to decline a final time, unwilling to entertain this line of discussion further, when Chase interrupted her protests, his tone soft.

"I'm serious, Talia. Our show is on the cusp of taking off. We have a chance to get picked up by a network. We just need something to push it over the edge, something that will go viral, and Lester is it. Can we talk face to face? It's been a long time since we've seen each other, and a lot has changed. I didn't just reach out to talk about Lester. Please come. At least see what we're all about," he begged, a hint of desperation creeping into his voice. "You can still say no after you hear me out." Her reservations were breaking down. She had to admit she was a little curious. The big night she had planned consisted of rotting in bed and watching bad reality TV. Getting out of the house sounded more appealing.

"What's the address?" she asked.

"Perfect!" Chase cheered and rattled it off. "One hour. Show up any time after, but it would be best if you came before nightfall. You are welcome to stay as long as you like. All of our filming takes place after dark, and we won't have time to talk when the cameras are rolling."

It made sense to her why Chase had been so popular in school; he was unabashed and charming. Despite their shared history, and her resistance, he won her over.

"Alright. See you in an hour," she said.

"See you soon," he replied, and the call disconnected. Apprehension filled her. She wasn't sure what she had agreed to but figured she could back out if things became uncomfortable.

"Well, I guess if I get murdered at least I won't have to go back to work," she said to herself.

***

Kent's East Hill neighborhood was a rabbit warren of winding roads, each circling back on the other. Talia was confident she was lost. The afternoon sky was grey, overcast, and threatening rain. By chance, she found the street she was looking for and spotted the brickwork on the front of the raised ranch house. Several vehicles and a large white van were parked outside. She slid her car in behind the others, then gathered her emotions before getting out. It had been over a decade since she had seen Chase in person. She'd come across his picture on other people's social media profiles, but they were not mutuals. This was the first time she'd heard about his vlog or the paranormal research team he was working with.

Before Talia could exit her car, Chase stepped out onto the covered porch and down the steps toward her. She was struck by the sight of the cute kid who had matured into a good-looking man. It reminded her again how unsurprising it was that he navigated the social circles he did. His sandy blond hair, buzzed at the temples but with some length on top, was styled to fall to the side. He was a pretty boy, thanks to the dark eyelashes accenting his blue eyes. His clothing, a dark band t-shirt over blue jeans, looked effortless and casual. His smile was a brilliant white with a row of perfect, straight teeth. He looked like he stepped out of a catalog.

That's what they mean when they say Prince Charming, she thought, opening her car door.

"You made it!" he said, his pleasure at seeing her evident on his face. Talia flushed pink at his elation, her younger self responding to the attentions of the best-looking guy in school. He held out his hand, and when Talia went to shake it, he instead helped her step out of the vehicle. It was unexpected, and a little flattering, until she remembered he wanted something from her. As they stood eye to eye, she realized she was still clasping his hand and dropped it. He was the same classmate that had teased her in school simply because she had the misfortune of growing up poor. She was here to see what was so important that he had begged her to come.

"It's good to see you," she lied.

"It's been a long time," he replied. Enthusiasm radiated off of him like a contagion. It was tempting to allow herself to be swept up by it. Her desire to be accepted and fit in was undeniable, but she let her reservations remain.

"It's bizarre, isn't it?" Chase said, a little unsure.

"Yes," she replied. "It certainly is."

"I wasn't exactly nice to you in school, Talia. I am glad you came. I owe you an apology and it's long overdue. I am sorry for how we tormented you. Us kids were horrible. I was horrible. You didn't deserve to be treated that way. I know I played a role. In hindsight, I wish I hadn't. I wish I could say I stood up for you. There were times I wanted to and knew it was the right thing, but…" He trailed off. Talia cut in.

"I understand. It's hard to go against the group. It's long forgotten, but thank you," she lied again, surprised by the ease with which she was able to do so. Perhaps she wasn't ready to accept it. She would have preferred to demand answers to explain why he had stood by and watched it happen. Why did he participate if he knew it was wrong? Why didn't he help her? But the worst part was how the pain overwhelmed her when it should be a distant memory. On a subconscious level, she believed she deserved what was done to her, and it filled her with shame.

"I started to write the message more times than I can count, but it felt wrong to apologize that way. I wanted you to see that I'm not the same person I was back then. I wanted you to know that what I did was wrong, and I am sorry." He frowned. Chase was uncomfortable humbling himself and admitting his failings. Talia didn't mind how awkward he felt making amends. He should have been an ally when she had truly needed one, but she recognized it was hard to ask for forgiveness. The apology was clumsy but seemed genuine.

"Thank you for allowing me the chance to say it." He gave her a pained look.

"I am a little caught off guard," she replied.

"I am sorry, I didn't want to do that over the phone. You deserved the respect of it being delivered in person. If you want to turn around and leave now, you can," Chase said. Her resistance softened, and she rewarded him with a laugh.

"Since you aren't hopping back in your car, I assume that means you are willing to stay?" He delivered an incandescent smile. "Before we head in, I want to give you the lay of the land. First, we are here at the request of the homeowners. Did you, by any chance, get to check out the vlog? We aren't anything as well produced as *Ghost Adventures*, but we are starting to get a following."

Talia shook her head, feeling a little foolish she hadn't taken the opportunity to look it up when she had the chance.

"I didn't. I didn't even know you had a vlog until you emailed. Does anyone else I know work on it?" she asked. He shook his head.

"Nope, just me. I'm like a producer. Actually, I'm a lot of things, but that's irrelevant. You didn't come here to listen to the history of how I got into this. We are here because the family requested our presence. They believe their daughter is trying to communicate with them."

Talia's expression must have broadcasted her confusion because Chase immediately explained.

"Their daughter passed away, but they think she is reaching out to them. They asked us to come investigate. I know it goes without saying, but please be respectful to them and their home. Be mindful that they are still in mourning. Avoid crass jokes about what we are doing. Trust me, it can be hard not to. We all know it can seem a little silly to outsiders."

"Am I allowed to ask what happened?" Talia asked.

"She drowned in the pool," Chase said, matter of fact, his face looking grim. "I know what you are thinking, but they asked us to be here. One of their friends follows the vlog and suggested they contact us. They asked us to investigate."

"I invited you so you could see what we do and understand what I am asking for. I don't want to waste any more of your time, so I'll get straight to the point. Our team wants to head in a different direction. We are all fine investigating households with an active haunting, but we want to get away from families with lost loved ones. It seems we've developed a niche in this area, and it's proven to be too complicated. The shoots are emotionally heavy, so we don't get to really show our personalities and what makes us unique. Editing ends up taking twice as long because we have to consider the family. And these episodes open us up to liability. If anyone is unhappy about the content, or the comments on the vlogs get out of hand, there's always a potential for dispute. Our time is getting eaten up monitoring the chat threads on those videos. On top of that, the feedback from our viewers is that they want to see us investigate places with a history, like what other paranormal research teams do. They want to hear the stories behind the haunting. You are here because there's one story that's never been done and that's Lester."

The word itself made Talia shudder.

"Why?" she asked. "You know as well as I do nothing good ever happened in Lester."

He laughed.

"That's exactly why. It has such a rich history, so much great back story. And it could put us on the map. No one is doing this kind of thing right now. We wanted to start with Lester as a launching point and continue to explore sites in the outdoor arenas and national parks. We already have a list of episodes we want to do in and around Mount Rainier and the Olympics. I think it will get us picked up by a network. We want to be the next *Ghost Hunters*."

"There's no other ghost town like Lester. People have been out there, and everything is exactly as they left it. Structures are still standing: the depot, people's houses, even the schoolhouse. It's not very well known, except to locals, because no one can get to it. Now, imagine if we did and filmed it."

"What about Franklin or Melmont?" Talia asked. "Those are accessible." What was left of the old coal mining town of Franklin was almost forty miles downriver from Lester. Franklin boasted a small cemetery with several ancient headstones, an old mine covered by a grate, and a collection of rusting mining equipment too big to remove from the site. Melmont couldn't even be considered a town anymore. What remained were a few old building foundations buried in the forest near Mount Rainier.

Chase nodded, tossing a look back at the house.

"We did Franklin. The headstones were cool, but we didn't get much content. It had a staged vibe, like the headstones were dumped out there. Summer said she heard a voice calling from the mine, but the audio didn't come through." He grew silent and gave her an earnest look. Her heart skipped. She had no idea why he was looking at her that way.

"I want you to reconsider. Take us to Lester. It will be worth your time."

Talia shook her head, "I don't know…"

"Hey, let's go inside. We can finish this conversation later. I want you to meet everyone," Chase interrupted. She wanted to refuse him and decline to participate, realizing she never should have come if she really meant to say no. But when he led her toward the house, she put up no objection and followed him inside.

Chase started with introductions, first to Angel and Danielle Rodriguez, the couple whose home they were filming in. When they entered the main living area, Angel was helping the crew arrange furniture to accommodate the shoot. Danielle stood beside the fireplace where a row of saints' candles burned on the mantle. She fidgeted with a gold beaded rosary and swayed from one foot to another. Her eyes looked watery. Chase shifted his tone and stride when he approached her.

"How are you holding up, Danielle?" Chase asked, placing a casual hand on the woman's arm. She startled, pulled from her reverie. Talia, aware that her presence here in this woman's home was out of place, stiffened. Danielle appeared not to notice and offered a limp handshake during their introduction, her eyes on Chase. She did not ask who Talia was or why she was there.

"I'm okay." Her expression was flat. He tilted his head a bit, and her lower lip quivered. "No, really, I am. I'm ready. I'm so grateful your team is here. We can finally get some answers." Chase rubbed her arm, nodding, then gave it a quick pat and severed himself from the exchange. Danielle hardly noticed when he and Talia walked away.

"Alright," he whispered. "These two guys working with Angel. The one on the left is Alabama. Just call him Bam. It's not his real name, but when he starts talking, you'll get it. He's our camera guy."

Alabama was barrel-chested and a full head taller than Talia. He might have been intimidating had he not caught her eye and flashed a big grin at her. He kept an impressive red beard, but his hair was concealed by a frayed baseball cap with a fishing lure hooked onto the bill. He reached out to shake with his enormous hands. She liked him immediately.

"The other guy is our newest intern. Lane. We brought him on to help with general stuff, add some fresh blood, and try out some different things. He's actually part of the brainchild behind Lester. I can't believe I didn't think of it first, but the minute he suggested it, I knew."

Lane gave a stiff nod to Talia. He was stocky, with short dark curls and serious blue eyes. They were framed by long beautiful lashes that made him inherently attractive, but his stony demeanor put her off. They moved on.

The house was larger on the inside than it looked from the street. Off the entry was a massive formal dining room and beside it, a long hallway with doors to unseen rooms. Everything was dated, the original construction evident by the overhead light fixtures, out of style laminate trim, and the old brickwork fireplace. As if on cue with her thoughts, Chase spoke up.

"They had plans to renovate. Their daughter died not long after they moved in," he said as he led her to the back corner of the house. "Recently, they started in the bedroom downstairs since it was out of the way. Something to stay busy as they tried to heal. That's how Angel described it. You'll see. That's when they started having experiences." They entered the kitchen and attached breakfast nook to find two more men and a woman. One of the guys was accepting a careful application of makeup from the woman. Her hair was a jet black with streaks of astonishing violet color.

"Guys, this is Talia. She's the one I told you about."

"Lester?" The other guy asked, swallowing whatever he was eating, then offered his hand. "I'm Glenn." He looked like he was hardly a day over eighteen with a flop of wavy black hair covering his dark almond-shaped eyes. A whisp of a moustache graced his upper lip, and he gave her an easy smile. He had crumbs of orange cheese dust at the corners of his mouth. "Sorry, quick snack break." She laughed and took his hand.

"Glenn is camera two and our general assistant," Chase interjected.

"That's code for bitch," Glenn chuckled.

"I know all too well," Talia replied.

"I'm also the one you come to for anything technical. The resident geek." Glenn ran a hand through his hair, and it flopped back in front of his face.

"He is also the youngest," Chase said, giving Glenn a knowing look. Turning to the woman. "This is Summer, make-up artist and resident medium. And the guy she's trying valiantly to make attractive is Dean, the front man and mastermind behind this little endeavor of ours."

Summer glanced over her shoulder but was too preoccupied dabbing powder onto Dean's forehead to do more than say a quick, "Hello!" Dean's eyes were shut, accepting the foundation, and offering no acknowledgment. They were both dressed in dark clothing, bordering on the edge of goth, and their likeness in appearance made Talia wonder about their relationship status.

"A medium?" Talia's eyebrows arched, impressed. Summer put a finishing touch on Dean's nose and turned around.

"It's really not that exciting, hi!" She reached to shake Talia's hand and gave her a full appraisal with a warm look on her face. Her frame was tiny, but her makeup was as vibrant as her hair, lips bright, and eyes smudged with heavy shadow. Her nose, lip, and eyebrow were pierced with shining silver hoops. She looked like a dark pixie.

Dean stood up, checking his forehead, hair line, and sideburns in a handheld mirror. His eyebrows were a shade lighter than his hair, so Talia guessed black was not his natural color. He was tall and thin, with a vague similarity to James Dean, given the pompadour and chiseled jawline. Between his dark eyes and classic look, she understood why he was their lead man. He paid her no mind.

"Dean, this is Talia. The guide I want to hire to take us to Lester," Chase repeated himself a bit forcefully. Dean didn't look over at her, instead he fixed a rogue hair that was hanging in front of his eyes. Talia offered her hand. When his eyes finally slid over to meet hers, he didn't take it. Instead, he gave a barely perceptible nod, then turned his hard gaze onto Chase. Talia was taken aback by his coldness, withdrawing her hand, and flushing with embarrassment.

"Are we set up to get started?" Dean asked him.

"They are arranging the living room so Bam can get the shot," Chase replied. He leaned in and whispered to Dean. Something flickered across Dean's face, and he glanced at Talia for a split second.

"So, Chase has told us a lot about you," Summer said, stealing her attention.

"I had no idea I was being discussed," Talia replied, a bit apprehensive.

"He said you knew how to get to Lester. That you got lost out there when you were a kid. And it was a big deal. That the whole town was out in the woods looking for you, and you reappeared like out of thin air. That must have been a scary experience," Summer said.

An ache crept into Talia's skull. She was both surprised and angry at how casually the details of her childhood trauma had been passed along to this perfect stranger.

"And this guy is really trying to drag you back out there?" Summer placed a hand on Talia's arm. Talia calmed, comforted by Summer's warm nature and reassuring smile. "Dean and I aren't totally on board. To be honest, I'm on the fence. It could be good for the show, but it sounds like it's remote, like maybe it's not safe for us to go out there?"

"We could hike there in a day, but it would be a full day. It's not anywhere near civilization. I've been there a few times. I run a guided hiking company, but I don't take people to Lester. It's really not that exciting." The lie was out before Talia realized what she was saying. She had never been back to Lester in person, although it was a place she frequented in her dreams. That was how she knew exactly how to get there. Chase, somehow, had that part right. She didn't understand why she was saying any of it, except that there was a part of her that wanted to impress them with her expertise. Summer squeezed her arm, and as if she had read something on her face, changed the subject.

"Are you staying for the whole shoot? Let me give you a quick tour of the main action," Summer said. Talia followed her to a stairwell just off the kitchen. It led down into a finished basement smelling of cut wood and dust. They clomped noisily down the stairs as Summer talked. The first door they came to was closed.

"The last owner had a workshop in there and left everything behind when he sold the house. He was elderly, and his kids were moving him in. They didn't have room for the equipment. There's an office here." Summer pointed to the next door which led into a small room with a computer and paperwork spread about haphazardly. "Down here a little further, there is this random room. Whoever built it used these strange concrete bricks for the walls. The floor is concrete too. It's always been super cold when I go in and honestly, it gives me the creeps." She opened the door, and the freezing air spilled out. The space held a couple of stacked cardboard boxes and an old rocking chair. There was a small toy train set on the floor. Summer swung the door shut. They moved further down the echoing hallway into a second living room with a sliding glass door looking out onto a patio and an empty inground pool.

"That's where it happened." Summer indicated the pool. "The girl drowned. Just an accident. Nothing sinister. But things have happened since she died." Summer ducked through another door set off the main living area and flipped the light switch. The room beyond was painted a navy shade too dark for the gloomy subterranean space. The only natural light came from a sliver of a window high on one wall. Scattered across the floor were drop cloths, paint buckets, and a ladder from when someone had attempted to brighten the space and paint over it in eggshell. The reason why they stopped was clear: there was a host of tiny handprints splattered in paint at waist height.

"This is why they called us," Summer said, locking eyes with Talia. "Chase told you I'm a medium, and I feel like that sounds way more impressive than it actually is. I get glimpses, impressions of things, like people's thoughts or emotions. It's pretty rare, but sometimes I can see more. I exaggerate my abilities for the show. I utilize some cold reading with live people, which sounds… not nice. I like to think we bring families together. We give them closure and understanding at times of devastation and loss.

Everyone else on the team dislikes doing these, except for Dean and me. We wanted to keep to our roots. Old school. Stick to how we started. It's hard being here though. You've met the mother? Danielle? Such a sweet woman, and she blames herself completely. She was working in the garden when it happened, right beside the pool. The girl struggled, went under for a minute before Danielle realized something was wrong. She pulled her out and after she spit up the water, she was breathing normally. They took her to the hospital to check her out. Doctors released her in good health, but, later that night, she died in her sleep. Dry drowning. Ever heard of that?"

Talia shook her head.

"Neither had I. It's all so sad. We want to do interesting investigations though, and our fans respond better to the vlogs with more exciting content. Chase has been moving us away from family gigs, but that means we are having to find other places to investigate. It's a double-edged sword. There is a reason why we agreed to do this one. I'll show you." Summer led Talia back down the narrow wood-paneled hallway to revisit the shop beyond the stairwell. She swung the door open and stood back, allowing Talia to look inside. It was another cement block room. Planks of wood were propped against the back wall, and the floor was covered in a layer of sawdust. Pegboard hung from one wall with various handheld tools dangling from carefully placed hooks. A drill press and table saw stood in the center of the room. Talia glanced over at Summer, unclear what she had come to see, and Summer pointed at the ceiling. Over the table saw, a twelve-inch circular blade was lodged into the beam.

"They haven't come down to the basement since that happened," Summer said. "I don't think this was the little girl."

Things were different after Talia came home. First, and most noticeably, Grandfather was absent. It was as if the house had been lifted from under a dark cowl and been brought into the light. When Sarah returned from her errand on the day Talia disappeared, she found the two boys sitting on the porch with hang dog expressions on their faces, their Grandfather lying face down on the kitchen floor unable to move, and Talia missing. Grandfather was transported to a hospital in Enumclaw where it was later learned he had suffered an embolic stroke. He survived, but the prognosis was not good. His ability to speak coherent sentences would be permanently impacted due to significant damage to the area of his brain responsible for speech. Movement on the right side of his body would be limited at best. When they discharged him from the hospital, he was admitted to a rehab center to determine if he could recover any movement. The doctors were hopeful with physical therapy he could restore some mobility and maintain a bit of independence, but Sarah had her doubts.

Questions were never asked about Talia's disappearance. The assumption was made that her grandfather's stroke scared her so badly, she went into the woods and got turned around. No one wanted to know where she went or why. She became the girl who survived a night in the forest, a forest known to be a hot spot for missing people. Her return was cause for celebration.

In the days following Talia's return, the townspeople filled their home full of food, the community responding with speed and generosity. Not that it stopped idle speculation. For years, Talia heard casual mentions from the locals about how lucky she was given their proximity to the cursed town of Lester. A lot of people from Palmer were afraid to even say the ghost town's name out loud for fear it would bring the curse to their doorstep.

The pantry door remained open. No one questioned her about the missing key from Grandfather's neck or the absent lock. It never came up.

For several weeks after the incident, Talia had the pleasure of being by her mother's side as if they were stuck like Velcro. She received extra-long hugs, was allowed to sleep in her mother's bed, and got to ride in the cart when they went to the store. To have her mother's undivided attention was a secret wish fulfilled. Their home, in the absence of her grandfather's intimidating presence, became a place of happy mornings, play, and affectionate touch. The only way Talia could have been happier was if her father was alive. There was a surreal quality about it, like entering a parallel reality, and this was the version of her life if things had worked out right. She never wanted it to end.

After those few glorious weeks at home, basking in all the attention Talia's heart desired, the new school year arrived. She was reluctant to go, but her mother rewarded her with a pair of those patent leather shoes she had been hoping for.

Talia found her experience on her first day back to school to be very different from those in years past. She had become something of an overnight celebrity. Snide remarks were replaced by curiosity and awe. The other children wanted to say they knew the girl who survived overnight in the haunted forest, like she had some kind of superpower. No one made fun of her clothes or teased her about being poor. The other kids allowed her to cut to the front of the lunch line, they even wanted to trade their best snacks with her for the ordinary things on her tray. Everyone was nice. There were compliments about her hair, brushed and put up by her mother that morning, or her outfits. She found herself with no absence of kids to play with at recess, and the children would argue about who got to pair up with her. Talia even made friends; other children wanted to be her friend.

Talia was riding a high. For the first time in her life, she was receiving her mother's undivided attention. She bossed her brothers as she pleased. And the best part of all? There was no foul-smelling fat man saying mean things or stomping around the house. No one yelled at her mother. Grandfather was gone. She no longer lived in fear of his evil appetites. Talia was free to be a girl again.

It would prove to be a short-lived reprieve, and it was Eve Lawrence who was responsible for spoiling everything.

"Look, it's the dead girl," Eve said to her small posse, all dressed alike with colorful barrettes in their hair, pleated skirts over primary-colored tights, and patent-leather Mary Janes. They were walking into the school up the front walkway. The buses were unloading students, which incidentally coincided with the moment that Talia's mother had dropped her and her brothers off. Talia caught them out of the corner of her eye as she slammed the car door and shrugged on her backpack. It was a new insult, and she was not sure what it meant or what Eve was up to. A pit of dread formed in her stomach at the prospect of this new game.

In response to Eve's insult, the other girls giggled, covering their mouths to conceal their glee. They all looked over at Talia, and Eve stood tall and proud, a smirk stretching across her face, each of her perfect white teeth on display. Talia wished each of them would fall out.

"The dead girl! Are you a ghost, Talia? Are you haunting us?" chirped Eve's first lieutenant, Hilary, as they followed her up the walk to the brick school building. The girls laughed again. Talia picked up her pace and headed inside. After entering her classroom, Talia made herself small while she hung her jacket and bag in her cubby, then sat at her desk to wait for the lesson to begin.

Within an hour, the first note landed on her desk. She'd been writing out the words from the chalkboard on her paper for the next spelling test, filling the worksheet out dutifully like the rest of the class, when an expertly folded piece of paper slid across the wooden laminate. It startled her, and she glanced around to determine the culprit. Everyone's heads were down on their own papers. The teacher sat at her desk bent over the gradebook.

Talia took the note, slid it into her lap, and unfolded the paper. In the center of the blue lined page was a crudely drawn skull and crossbones. *RIP* was emblazoned across the top. Talia bit her lip, angry, and her cheeks flushed with blood. She didn't understand what this was. Usually, she knew what the girls were up to, but this game she was out of the loop. So ready to leave the old version of her life behind, Talia had warmed to the experience of making new friends immediately and grown unaccustomed to keeping up her hardened shell. It left her vulnerable. She had not realized how hard it would be to remove the target from her back.

Another note came a few minutes later despite Talia trying to keep an eye peeled for the perpetrator. This one read: *Are you dead? Check yes or check no.* Both options had tiny boxes next to them, and she found the *YES* box had already been checked on her behalf. This time she stood up and walked to the front of the class to throw the note into the trash. Upon returning to her desk, she caught the furtive glances between Eve and Hilary, and their barely contained laughter. As Talia passed between them, Eve stuck her leg out and tripped her. Talia's hands and knees took the brunt of the fall, skinning one knee and bruising the pad of her hand. The whole class erupted in laughter.

Mrs. Stevens stood and demanded the class settle. When the laughter subsided, she asked Talia if she was alright. Talia nodded, miserable, and slunk back to her desk. She had been cast down by Eve's group of mean girls, and today would mark the end of any status she had gained. The notes continued. One was a drawing of a ghost. Another included a lengthy set of questions asking what her favorite thing was about being dead and if she could still eat food or disappear whenever she wanted. Instead of getting up again and risking more embarrassment, Talia hid them all in her desk.

When lunch arrived, Talia approached the table where she usually sat with her newfound friends and spotted them sitting across the cafeteria. She picked up her tray to join them, then realized they were refusing to look in her direction. The girls she had befriended in the last couple weeks were avoiding her like the plague. It was like she had contracted a contagious virus, one that made her invisible. Somehow, the other children could sense her status change as if it were a neon sign flashing above her head and chose to steer clear rather than be likewise tormented. Eve's clique would make sure to loop in anyone foolish enough to be Talia's friend. After finishing her food, Talia slid out of the cafeteria and made her way down a long corridor to the library. Mr. Wilson looked up from his desk. He smiled when he saw her, but she could tell he was going to turn her away.

"It's too nice to be inside today," Mr. Wilson explained. He normally allowed her to remain through lunch, but today he was forcing her out. White hot hatred filled Talia. She would never forgive him for refusing her sanctuary behind the stacks of books. She glanced over at the old clawfoot bathtub full of pillows, her favorite spot to read, wanting nothing more than to disappear inside of it until she had to return to class. Talia had a growing confidence that something was in store for her. The game was afoot. She could sense it. The same way she could read the people around her. Like she knew the real reason Mr. Wilson didn't want her there was because he was waiting for a call from his partner, who was another man and that was a secret, and they were in the middle of an argument. After lunch he had an empty period which would allow him to see the conversation through. Instead of trying to plead her case, Talia resigned herself and headed to the playground.

Stepping outside where the blazing sun was baking the asphalt, Talia was despondent. She watched the children swinging and climbing the metal bars of the playsets, the colorful plastic slides faded from long exposure to the elements. The field beyond the playground was empty, and she decided to walk to the furthest reaches of the yard, past the monkey bars and swing set. There, she could sit on the cool grass until the bell rang calling them inside. She hoped the distance would deter anyone from bothering her. She slid past the playground, staying close to the red brick building, and out into the open grass, turning her back to the school yard. No one noticed the loose group of third graders gravitating toward Talia as she went.

The gathering had been rallied by Eve "Evil" Lawrence and her horrible, no-good second in charge, Hilary Smith. On this hot day, the playground teachers were distracted, busy monitoring the basketball games being played under the cool covered area at the opposite side of the yard. Talia unknowingly led them out into the field, which could not have played into Eve's hand any better. The kids caught up with her where no adult would see. Talia was unaware she had company until it was too late.

"My dad said you went to Lester," Eve announced. She projected her voice to be heard by the group. Talia stood in the middle, horrified to find herself being surrounded and in the center of Eve's trap. She looked for a friendly face and found none. Here was Chase Winters with his posse of boys: Gabe Swanson, Toby Hoyt, Marcus Turcott, and a couple others whose names she could not remember. The bulk of the group consisted of girls. They all belonged to Eve's clique or were "cling-ons," vying for Eve's attention in the hopes of being incorporated into her club. Some she suspected were only curious.

When the word Lester was spoken, Talia understood. The ghost town, the scary place all the children whispered about. People told stories about what existed there, the horrors that had been perpetrated in the town of Lester, the haunted place at the end of the rail line. Talia had disappeared and gone to Lester, now she was a ghost.

"How do you like being dead?" Eve asked, a sneer on her lips. The other children laughed like it was the funniest thing they had ever heard. Talia frowned, careful not to show her fear and remained silent.

"If she's dead, how come she's not all rotted?" one of the boys asked. Eve shrugged, but Hilary piped up.

"Cause she's a ghost, remember? And no one can see her," she said. "What did you see out in the woods, Talia? Did the ghosts eat you up?"

Talia recalled the man with the icy blue eyes, old, but much older underneath. She shuddered despite the warm day. She had an urgent need to be out of the circle. Talia made a feeble attempt to break through, but the children pushed her effortlessly back to the center. That was when the game began. She tried again to exit the ring, and the person she touched would gasp and laugh.

"Oh! Did you feel that? I swear something touched me!" the first exclaimed. The other children looked around as if she was invisible. She shoved at what she thought was a thin place and another girl shrieked, "Fingers like ice. Brrrrrrr!" The group dissolved into laughter. Talia withheld her tears as this continued. Every time she touched someone, they would act like nothing was there. They saw through her like she no longer existed, and for one "Did you hear that?" Eve asked the air above her head, then she looked over at Hilary. "It was like the wind was speaking, but no one is there!" Hilary burst into a fit of giggles, and the other girls tittered alongside her. Talia tried to crawl through Chase's legs, but he blocked her retreat.

"Let me go." She used her voice, trying to push through another imagined crack in their forces. Not wanting to give up their game, one of the boys shoved her back, harder this time, and she fell.

"You're dead," Eve said. "I think we need to bury you." Talia, horrified, aware all eyes had shifted to her. Hands grabbed her and forced her down onto her back. Others ripped at the grass, tearing at the fresh green blades, throwing it on top of her. All of them began chanting, scattered at first, then in unison: "You're dead! You're dead! You're dead!" Talia tried futilely to sit up and was pinned by unseen hands. They would not release her. She screamed, lost in terror and blind with fear, and the children grew louder.

"You're dead! You're dead! You're dead!"

Talia fought, hot tears coursed down her face and screams escaped her lips. She swung at the blank faces of her tormentors, each just out of reach. The kids laughed and chanted. The piles of grass continued to come, and some went down her throat causing her to cough and gag. Snot ran down her nose, and the grass stuck to her cheeks, clinging to her wet tears and slimy upper lip. The children surrounding her laughed and chanted.

She felt it before she knew what was happening. The coughs racking her body, uncontrolled, and her lap was hot, burning hot. All at once, she was soaked and laying in a cooling puddle. She had peed her pants. And when the grass fell away, everyone would see. She lay still, hoping with every bit of her being that she could actually be invisible so no one would see. Someone screamed.

"Ew, the ghost pissed itself!" the voice cried, delighting in using the swear and emphasizing the hard consonant. The other children all squealed, equal cries of disgust, and the taunts shifted into something new.

"Peed your pants!" They chanted. "Peed your pants!" Peed your pants!"

When the bell rang, calling them back to their classrooms, many of the outliers scattered, tearing back across the field to get into their seats in time. Eve and Hilary remained behind while Talia lay on the ground, trying to conceal the crotch of her pants, the saturation evident, and wiping the blades from her face and hair. She looked at her lap to find a tiny perfect buttercup lay there, and the sight of it made her wish she really was dead. At last, she was allowed to stand. Tears poured from her eyes as she brushed her clothes off. She wiped her face with her sleeve.

Eve stepped up to Talia, face to face, with her horrible mean girl sneer.

"You're dead now. No one will ever see you again! Pee Pants!" she laughed as if she had made the funniest joke of all time. Hilary joined her, and they ran off to class.

Talia dragged her feet as she returned to the school building, dreading facing all of her classmates. When she arrived, she was late, and the lesson was in full swing. The teacher stopped and turned toward her as she entered the classroom.

"The door opened by itself!" Chase Winters called from the back of the classroom. Everyone laughed. The teacher whipped around, shooshing the class. She turned back to Talia to say something, then noticed the fragments of grass clinging to her hair and shirt, her ruined ponytail sagging against the elastic, and her face puffy from crying.

"Talia, are you alright?" Mrs. Stevens asked. Talia nodded and headed toward her desk, but Mrs. Stevens stopped her. She crouched down and looked Talia in the eye.

"Who did this to you?" Mrs. Stevens asked. Talia's eyes stayed down on her scuffed patent leather shoes. Every eye was on her.

"I don't know," Talia replied as quiet as a mouse. Mrs. Stevens stood up and went to the classroom phone, dialing, and pulling the long cord so she could step out into the hallway to make a call. Talia drifted back to her desk and sat down behind it. She placed her head down on the laminate, wishing she could disappear. The note hit her in the face.

She did not want to see what it said but was compelled. She unfolded the loose-leaf paper to: *You're a ghost. You're dead.* Here was a headstone drawn in fat pencil with the epitaph reading *RIP TALIA* in block letters. Below it, in tiny script, she saw the acronym meant: *REST IN PEE.* She put the note in her desk along with the others and let loose a painful wail.

Mrs. Stevens hurried back into the classroom, hung up the phone, and gathered Talia up to escort her to the principal's office. Before her mother arrived, they asked her many times what had happened, but Talia held her tongue. It would not benefit her to reveal her bullies. Eve would retaliate because that was who Eve Lawrence was.

Her mother picked her up. She said a few sharp words to the principal about the lack of monitoring on the playground, which the principal accepted without argument. Once in the car on their way home, Sarah asked her one time what had happened, reassuring her if she told, Sarah would make sure it never happened again. Talia, thinking how Grandfather had been allowed to treat her without her mother's intervention, said nothing because she knew it was lie. In response, when they got home, her mother gave her a bath and changed her into jammies, cuddled her up on the couch, and made popcorn covered in butter. When everyone ate dinner, she was allowed to eat on the couch in front of the TV, and after her brothers were put to bed, she was served a bowl of vanilla ice cream with a ribbon of fudge and peanut butter running through it.

Talia never identified the culprits. The school was all too happy to sweep their lapse in attention under the rug. Sarah suspected Talia had thrown some kind of hysterical tantrum and was too embarrassed to admit it. Since it appeared to be due to residual trauma from getting lost in the woods, she didn't want to force the issue.

The children at Black Diamond Elementary rotated between teasing her mercilessly about peeing her pants or pretending she was a ghost and therefore, did not exist. The torment was relentless. Eve Lawrence had fixated on her and to Talia, it seemed like the nightmare would never end.

The next school year, everyone collectively lost interest. It was like she had actually become invisible. The other kids still called her "ghost" from time to time, but for the most part, she passed through her school days as a nonentity. She had no friends to speak of, the teachers never called on her, and she could barely pass through the halls without someone bumping into her. Truly, like she did not exist at all. Except for Eve. Eve never quite let it go, but by the time they reached high school, Talia had learned how to steer clear of her. Eve had grown preoccupied with how she looked and would spend most of her time preening in front of a bathroom mirror or hanging onto her boyfriend. If Talia saw her coming down the hall, she headed in the opposite direction.

The bullying taking place in her third-grade year was not the biggest problem Talia faced. The real issue began when Grandfather returned home after his stroke.

It was a room Talia longed for as a girl. Everything was pink, from the curtains to the paint on the wall to the bedspread covering the tiny twin mattress. Over the bed hung wood cut letters spelling out her name: *Maya*. A tiny desk sat with a Lisa Frank diary on its top, a pencil with a unicorn topper placed next to it. A glittery pink castle stood in the corner, the dolls abandoned and the courtyards gathering dust. Maya had been a well-loved child.

Talia crammed herself next to Chase in the doorway, careful not to rub shoulders with him. The room glowed with the soft light of a single candle. Alabama's face was bathed in the cool blue aura of his camera screen. He leaned against the opposite wall filming Summer and Dean, who were seated side by side on the twin size bed.

Prior to filming, Chase explained how they avoided using night vision during home investigations. Relying on natural color and light seemed to help the viewers connect to the emotional nature of the content. Night vision created the opposite effect: distancing the viewer and resulting in an uptick in callous and inappropriate comments posted to the website.

"We were almost shut down right when we started gaining traction because we didn't take those things into consideration. We made a lot of stupid mistakes, but we learned," Chase told her. "Stuff like that could have ruined us."

"Ready?" Dean asked, holding up a small tape recorder. Summer had her eyes closed, communing with herself. She took a deep breath and released it long and slow, blowing out through pursed lips.

"Maya?" Dean asked aloud. "Are you here with us?" The little red light on the recorder was lit. There was a long moment of silence, then Summer jumped, shaking the whole bed. Her eyes flashed open, and her brows knitted together.

"Did you feel that?" she asked, touching the side of her face. "Someone blew into my ear. Oh, I have goosebumps," she whispered. Dean broke character.

"We need to do that again," he interrupted, looking from Chase to Bam, a flicker of irritation crossing his face. Summer muttered an apology.

"You need to be authentic. Do you want people to think this is staged?" Dean's tone was saturated with frustration. Summer's lips flattened.

"It is staged, Dean," she said, then scoffed. "Fine, let's do it again." She twirled a finger in the air, rolled her shoulders, and closed her eyes once more. They launched into a question-and-answer session with the answers unheard. Bam yawned from behind the lens. When Dean did not like how his question came out, he would ask again with more gravitas or a different inflection. Just when Dean's arrogant behavior was almost too much for Talia, Chase pulled at her elbow, and they moved away from the door frame.

"They always have to work out some kinks and find their flow in the beginning," he told her.

"So, the show is fake?" Talia asked. Chase hesitated, considering her question before he answered.

"How do you say… Well, it's exaggerated," he paused, searching her face to gauge her reaction. "We always get footage of a voice on a recorder, or someone getting touched to keep our viewers engaged. It's common practice in the industry. Everyone does it. But we see real phenomena. A few weeks ago, we caught incredible footage of an orb floating around Lane. We've all heard voices, actually felt a random touch, or seen objects move. The problem is we don't always catch it on camera, so we've learned to set up a few things and work them in. If nothing else happens during this investigation, at least we have that. I know it sounds heartless, but if we don't catch anything, it does amount to a waste of time. Then we have nothing to show our audience. It's all covered in the waivers."

In the living room, along with Danielle's collection of candles, a couple of strategically placed lamps were emanating soft light. Danielle and Angel were seated together on the sofa clasping hands and looking tired. Each had a cup of coffee within arm's reach. Glenn acknowledged their arrival.

"We are all good in here." He shot them a thumbs up and returned his attention back to the Rodriguez's. Chase did not linger and turned away to check out the other areas of the house. Before the cameras went on, there had been a brief meeting where Chase and Dean had assigned everyone's locations. Glenn, Danielle, and Angel would remain in the living room with a tripod and a recorder for the majority of the night. Lane was set up with another tripod next to the pool. As the newbie, he was the low man on the totem pole and would have to sit outside alone for the duration. Summer, Dean and Alabama, behind the camera, would move through the known hot spots: Maya's bedroom, the half-painted room downstairs, and the woodshop. Chase and Talia would be moving between each group and checking in with a camcorder.

The final scene would bring the whole *Dimensions* team together beside the empty pool to offer a ceremonial healing and cleansing ritual to allow the Rodriguez's to say goodbye and hopefully find closure. They had signed the waivers, understood the events of the evening would be filmed and possibly broadcast, and that the crew was not affiliated with any religious sect that purported themselves to be capable of exorcism. They could not guarantee any outcome from the investigation or cleansing. Chase had explained it all to Talia when she signed one for herself. It also functioned as a non-disclosure agreement.

"Do you need a cup of coffee?" he asked. Talia shook her head, unexpectedly awake and riding a strange buzz.

"Why don't we go and check in with Lane?" They started down the stairs, their footsteps echoing as they went. Chase did not bother turning on the light but instead pulled a palm-sized flashlight from his pants pocket and popped it on.

"You get used to operating in the dark. I should have snagged a flashlight for you from the van. Can you see alright?" Chase asked.

"I'm fine, just don't abandon me," she replied. He agreed and took her hand. A rush of trepidation passed through her. *Careful,* she told herself. But hadn't she secretly hoped for a chance to be accepted? Especially by someone who had rejected her. That by being worthy of acceptance it would prove there was nothing wrong with *her.* That was the real hidden wish: not an apology, not an acknowledgement of the pain, but for someone to actually *see* her. To *belong* somewhere.

Labelled the "Palmer Girl" well into high school, the other students had still called her "living dead girl," or, worst of all "ghost," behind her back. There had been no escaping that moniker. And she was a ghost. No one invited her to football games, school dances, or dates, and her pariah status persisted into adulthood. Coworkers didn't invite her out. People's eyes passed over her on the street, and servers never heard her requests. Even the couriers in the office barely acknowledged her. This small connection was evidence she existed.

His hand was warm. She intentionally kept her grip loose out of fear he would realize whose hand he was holding and flinch away. To her surprise, he did not drop her hand until they reached the exit to the pool. He let go to slide back the glass door, and they stepped out onto the patio. When the contact ended, she flexed her hand, struggling to decipher how she felt.

Lane slouched in a lawn chair, looking bored. Solar lights disbursed along the fence illuminated the yard, and frogs croaked nearby. The night was mild despite the grey clouds from earlier in the day.

"How you doing, brother?" Chase asked.

"Feels weird sitting out here talking to myself," Lane replied, he shifted in his seat.

"You'll get used to it. After a while, it starts to come naturally."

Lane yawned, stood up and stretched his lower back. "If you say so."

"Don't worry," Chase offered. "You'll get better spots in the future." He turned to Talia, and said, "If you are up for it, you and I are going to do a little work in the bedroom down here before the others join us. Who knows? Maybe we'll capture something." Chase raised his eyebrows, waved her through the door, then followed.

"You don't think the parents staged the handprints?" she asked in a hushed voice. Chase considered the question as they went through to the painted room.

"People have done stranger things to get us to investigate their homes, so I guess I wouldn't put it past someone. But the team talked about it beforehand and agreed the explanations were too far-fetched. The first theory was the most obvious: they brought a child over and had them make the prints. It's possible, and the most likely explanation, but then you have to accept that the child might tell their own parents or friends and expose the whole scheme. That's pretty macabre. Would you take that risk? Or… or they fashioned some kind of hand using a mold or a 3D printer. Glenn educated us on how difficult it would be, so we considered maybe one of those silicon molds. In the end, to accept any of those theories, we have to set aside everything we know about Danielle and Angel. They aren't the type. But, if they made the handprint, it's pretty convincing. Take a look."

He flicked on the light. Talia examined the prints, leaning down to get close to the wall. She saw what he meant.

"Do you see the palm lines? The fingerprints?" He leaned in next to her, their faces inches apart. She saw the detail, the whorls at the tips of each finger and the broken palm lines with tiny fractures splitting off.

"It would take a very dedicated person to fake fingerprints like that. Why go to all that trouble? What's the payoff?" he asked.

"People do peculiar things when they are suffering," she replied.

When she stood up again, they were uncomfortably close. She blushed and averted her gaze. Chase grinned.

"You know, you aren't what I thought you would be," he mused.

"What did you think I would be?" Talia replied, feeling her walls come up.

"I'm not trying to be rude," Chase said. "I guess I half-expected that reserved girl I knew in school. You seem so different now, so composed. It's kind of intimidating." Talia was caught off guard, unsure if he meant it to be a compliment or an insult.

"Thank you?" she said after some hesitation. They stood in silence looking at each other, too close and too intimate. Bam and Summer's voices carried ahead of them as footsteps approached down the hallway. The crew entered: Dean in the lead with Bam and Summer right behind him. Summer was chuckling at something indecent Bam had said. Dean gave the pair a cool look when he entered. Talia stepped back, embarrassed, and not sure why.

Chase joined Dean by the doorway, and they consulted over how they wanted to film the room. Summer came over to check in with Talia.

"How's it going?" she asked.

"Whadaya mean 'how's it goin'?' It's her first spook show. Somethin' always happen to the newbie," Bam interrupted. His southern accent laid heavy over his words like syrup.

"Care to explain?" Talia asked, taken aback. Summer shot a look at Bam, then returned her focus to Talia.

"He didn't tell you? Why am I not surprised," Summer sighed. "When we are investigating a house, if the house is actually haunted, it's usually the new person who has the encounter." Talia's eyes shot wide.

"Chase might have conveniently left that part out," Talia said. "So, it's real?" She was skeptical about the omission and wondered if she was being set up. Summer touched her arm.

"Don't worry, we've all been there," she said. Talia relaxed, grateful for Summer's presence.

"We all get haunted on occasion. I reckon, it's some kind of spirit joke they always takin' it out on the virgin," Bam admitted, fiddling with the camera. Summer threw an elbow into Bam's side, and he doubled over.

"Ignore him," she said. Talia almost laughed aloud despite her alarm at what they were suggesting. She liked them both and was grateful they had made it a point to involve her. Dean, on the other hand, seemed reticent. It was evident he was unhappy about Chase inviting her to participate in the investigation, and he was demonstrating his displeasure by avoiding her and keeping his distance. Talia thought he was rude, even if she understood his frustration.

"Alright, you guys ready?" Chase announced. Bam nodded, lifting the camera. Summer withdrew her hand from Talia's arm, closed her eyes, cleared her throat, and shook out her body. At the end, she took a long cleansing breath in. On the exhalation, her eyes reopened. Bam fiddled with a few settings on the camera, peering through the viewfinder, then positioning himself in the room to capture the best angle of both Summer and the handprints on the wall. Dean moved into the shot beside her. Talia stood back, watching the well-oiled machine of their process operate.

"No, I want you here." Summer reached for her. Talia glanced between Chase and Dean. Chase nodded, "Go with it." She shifted her weight from foot to foot, uncertain and unsure where to stand. Suddenly self-conscious, she smoothed the front of her shirt and removed her hair from behind her ears.

"Just be natural, you're beautiful," Summer said, pulling her in next to her. Talia noticed the admonishing glance she shot at Dean, which he ignored. Instead, Summer nodded at her, "Don't worry, there's nothing to it."

"Ready?" Bam asked.

"Okay, three, two..." Chase dropped the final number, and the camera's red light came on. Dean's face shifted, filling with childlike wonder. His whole persona changed. She was surprised how convincing he was when only moments before he was surly and irritated. He gestured to the handprints behind him.

"The evidence doesn't get any more real than this," he said, waving Bam closer to capture the wall. "You won't be able to see the detail, but we will include some high-res images on our website for you skeptics. We've verified these are not faked or fabricated. Look at the lines here. It would have required a lot of energy for a spirit to manifest this amount of detail. That's why Summer and I are going to spend the majority of our night in this particular space to see if Maya will communicate with us. Also, we have a special guest tonight. Talia is here with us, and you guys know how it is with first timers!"

Chase had told her it was fake, and she had seen them "playact" first-hand, but worry gnawed at the back of Talia's mind. She continued to grin stupidly for the camera not knowing what else to do.

"Maya's not wasting any time," Summer announced, her eyes closed and tone sharp. She gripped Talia's hand hard, and her eyes opened wide. "She's attaching her energy to you. It feels..." she hesitated, "protective."

"I don't feel anything," Talia replied, her smile faltering. Summer sucked in a gasp; her eyes closed again. Talia couldn't discern if it was an act and if she should be playing along. Dean locked eyes with her. It was the first time he had met her eye all night.

"I can sense the presence here in the room, it's electric," Dean held up his arm and rubbed at it absently. Talia, confused, looked to Chase for direction. He gave her a little nod and continued to watch.

"It's so hot in here," Summer whispered, fanning herself with her empty hand. "She's here with us, and she's asking for help. Wow, Maya. Oh, Maya, honey. She's telling me she's protecting them, that's why she's still here."

Dean was moving out of the shot but still committed to the role of bewildered investigator as he walked around the room. Summer was frozen in place, her breathing heavy. Talia tried to relax and open herself up to the experience, wishing they would cut the scene and try again without her.

"Maya says she had to stay to protect them..." Summer paused. "Wait, something else is here."

An icy finger ran down Talia's spine at Summer's statement. Goosebumps rose on her skin despite the growing heat of the room. This was no act. Something unseen was here.

"There's another presence in this house," Summer reported. Something stroked Talia's arm, burning her, and she jerked in a half-turn to find no one there. She was peripherally aware of Bam shifting the camera's focus to her, but she was too alarmed for it to fully register.

"What was that?" Talia whispered, startled. Summer squeezed her hand.

"Maya, are you here with us?" Dean asked, the recorder manifesting into his hand as if out of nowhere. "If so, show us. I'm going to set this paintbrush right here. I want you to move it if you can." He placed one of the paint brushes on the top rung of the ladder, balancing it so the barest glance would make it fall.

"Dean, I can assure you, she's already here," Summer responded with a wince. "She is coming through so loud."

"Maya, can you move this paintbrush? Show us you are here with us." Dean employed a subtle hand motion to direct Bam to film the brush, but Chase shook his head and indicated for Bam to keep the camera on Summer and Talia. Something was happening. Summer gasped.

"She wants to show me something. She keeps insisting, something about the stairs…"

"Maya, is there someone else here with you?" Dean asked.

"Not someone. Something," Summer corrected. A thick electric energy was filling the room. It surrounded Talia and caressed her skin once more. She jumped. Chase was careful to stay behind Bam and out of the shot. When she glanced over to him, she was unsure if his expression had changed. Did he look concerned?

"It's been feeding," Summer said, her voice a monotone. Talia glanced over to see her eyes had rolled back into her head. Her grip on Talia's arm was hard and painful.

"Come."

Summer pulled Talia across the room, through the doorway, and down the hall toward the woodshop. She wanted to resist, but Summer compelled her to follow. She glanced back, frightened to see Chase behind them in the narrow passage, urging them forward. Bam squeezed past, the camera trained on them, and Chase pointed the flashlight to illuminate the way. Summer swept the door open, stopping short as she crossed the threshold. She took a shaky breath, and uttered a quiet, "Oh."

Talia noted the saw blade stuck in the rafter over their head, assuring herself this was staged, an act. Nothing here was real. Chase had explained how it was amplified and exaggerated for the audience. The look of Summer's eyes. The handprints. The breath against the ear. The sawblade. She told herself it was all fake. An orchestration. Exaggerated.

The painted room had grown intensely warm to the point she was suffocating, but here, freezing air poured from the shadows. She looked to Summer and saw her breath coming out in faint puffs.

"It's here," Summer said in a voice distant and removed. "Maya says it's here." Talia could not see deeper into the room. The blackness pervaded every corner. Summer brought her a step further inside, her face a mask of horror, but Talia couldn't pull away. She had an urgent desire to leave, even with the three men standing behind her, she did not feel safe. A predatory gaze was upon her.

A shadow in the furthest corner drew her attention. Her heart galloped and yet, she took two cautious steps forward, leaving footprints in the sawdust. A shocking wave of heat flooded over her.

"Careful," Summer hissed. "She says it's hungry."

Talia could not see into the darkest recess of the room with her naked eye. She perceived an infinite space, empty and vast, but something was concealing itself in the corner. She disregarded Summer's warning and stepped into its aura. Her awareness shifted, and she understood it was not the absence of light, but that something was cloaking itself in darkness and drawing all the energy to itself out of the room. From the void, the thing generating the black hole unpeeled itself from the corner where it had been hiding.

Each long spidery limb unfurled and elongated, sinewy and stretched, too strange to be human. The entity's malformed appendages braced itself against the rafters above. With each of its many legs unfolded, it hoisted itself from its nest and brought itself to its full height, impossibly tall and encased in a black exoskeleton. Her throat locked. Each of its hundreds of eyes were upon her, each a pool of liquid obsidian regarding her.

Yooouuu, it formed the word with great difficulty. Talia's eyes watered, unable to avert her gaze. Unbelievable pain gathered in her, filling the base of her throat. She choked, desperate to heave it up.

I caaan taaaste yooouuur paaain, it murmured, blissful and intoxicated. It was reaching for her. Talia was paralyzed. She flashed back to the house in Palmer. Back to her grandfather eyeing her like she was an animal caught in a trap. Back to the terror in her mother's eyes.

"We can never tell, Talia."

The endless forest.

The man with the blue fire in his eyes.

"Let me count your ribs."

The creature was inches from her face, and when its long limb wrapped around her, like a python pulling her to its mouth, she whimpered.

Ghooost. Ghooost. Ghooost.

It quivered with anticipated ecstasy, its desire for her an eager throb pulsing through her body. Its gaping maw opened, unhinging and widening, stretching larger and larger, monstrous and immense. It surrounded her as she choked on a scream, and everything went black.

Grandfather returned home after Thanksgiving, and he brought the hospital with him. Rehab turned out to be a failed endeavor. Grandfather made no lasting or meaningful progress in restoring mobility, but he had adapted to being waited on hand and foot quite well. Talia overheard this said to her mother during a phone call with the hospital staff. Talia had sat stock-still and perfectly quiet listening to the tinny voice coming through the receiver.

"How can he refuse to do any more therapy? Is there really nothing else that can be done?" Sarah asked, a thread of desperation woven into her voice. She was yanking on the fine hairs at her temple, and there was a lost, frantic look in her eye. A pit formed in the center of Talia's stomach, understanding something bad was happening. It wasn't just the tone of her mother's voice, but the exhaustion coming through the phone. "There are no other options if he refuses to do the work," it said.

A week later, two men delivered a hospital bed and an array of equipment required to care for Grandfather at home. They were efficient, sparing no movements as they built the bed and connected all the equipment. The couch where Talia and her mother snuggled together, eating popcorn, and watching old movies, was moved aside. One of the men showed her mother the different settings to adjust the bed and how to bring the sides both up and down. While that was happening, the other man was checking the functioning of the heart monitor on Jamie, who was giggling mercilessly. Red numbers lit the screen.

"He's refused a catheter, so we included a few boxes of diapers. His insurance won't cover those," the man advised. "You'll be billed." Sarah sighed, pulling at the same clump of hair. Agitation and frustration pulsed off of her mother, and it made Talia want to hide.

"But it covers all of this, right?" Sarah asked, indicating the bed and monitoring equipment. The man nodded. The bed sat empty that night, an ominous reminder of the person who would return and dominate the space. The following day, Grandfather came home. A silent ambulance with its red light turning crunched into the gravel dooryard. The EMTs pulled him out of the back of the van as the four children watched from the porch. Dismay washed over Talia. Her mother was going to learn about the pantry and how she had stolen the key. She would be in real trouble for not getting help and running away.

The paramedics moved Grandfather into the house, hoisting him from the stretcher to the brand-new bed. They hooked up all the wires, made a few adjustments, and were gone as fast as they had arrived.

"How are you feeling?" Mother asked him. The stroke had taken a dramatic toll on the once sturdy man. Grandfather had lost a considerable amount of weight, and it aged him. The fat that once smoothed over his wrinkles was gone. His skin looked as if it had been draped over a bag of bones. Liver spots dotted his face and the back of his hands. The month indoors had faded his sun-kissed skin to pale and translucent, and Talia could see the blue veins in his arms and legs. He couldn't lift his head for more than a second, let alone leave his bed. Once overpowering in his presence, the massive man was diminished both in size and will.

The right side of his face sagged, and he waved feebly with his left hand. There was a whiteboard on his lap with a magnetic marker stuck to its surface. He was familiar with the object. With a shaky hand, he scrawled, "FINE," the letters almost illegible. When Talia drew closer, Grandfather glared at her. He made no sound or movement to write. She half-wondered and half-hoped he had forgotten about that day. If he did remember, he gave no indication. The waves of animosity he directed at her were the same for all of the children.

Sarah hired a nurse to come during the day. Grandfather's insurance covered the expense. The nurse was a heavy woman with box dyed burgundy hair and painted on eyebrows. Her double chin had a mole with a single dark hair protruding from it. It was a curious thing for Talia to see a woman who spent so much time attending to her appearance to ignore such a flagrant grotesque detail. Her name was Sandi with an "I." Sandi came when mother was at work, and while she was nice to the children, Talia noticed right away when no other adult was around, Sandi with an "I" didn't do a whole lot of anything. The children became her little go-getters. If she needed a glass of water or to have the channel on the television changed, whichever child was within earshot would be responsible for fetching or doing for her. Unless it was Jamie. Sandi caught on quick that Jamie was unreliable. He would either demonstrate his latest karate move or get silly and become intractable.

Most of the time, she planted herself in Grandfather's old armchair with her fat white legs kicked up on the ottoman watching daytime television. Everything from *The Price is Right* to afternoon talk shows where the guests screamed and threw chairs. Sometimes she would put on a cooking show which inspired her to fix a snack. Sandi did care for Grandfather. She fed him, changed his diapers, checked his blood pressure, doled out medication, and held one-sided conversations with him. Talia could see it annoyed Grandfather, how Sandi talked at him more than she talked to him, but it wasn't like he could put up much objection. She didn't avoid pulling her weight when it came to nursing Grandfather, but if she forgot to grab a diaper before she had him partly undressed, she never failed to ask one of the kids to hop over and get one for her.

One thing they learned early on was that Sandi's nursing ended at five o'clock sharp each day. Once the clock rolled over, little hand on the five and the big hand on the twelve, she was out the door, come hell or high water. One evening, the phone rang just after four, and Talia heard her mother begging on the other end of the line for Sandi to stay late. The oven had flipped a breaker at the bakery, and they were behind with several ordered cakes, so she would need to stay.

"State don't pay me overtime, Suge. Are you going to pay me out of your own pocket?" Sandi rasped into the phone. She left at five, and their mother arrived ten minutes later looking harassed and exhausted.

The truth was her mother was drained dry and being pulled in every direction at once. The dynamic between Talia's mother and her grandfather was no different than before his stroke. It was clear Grandfather was punishing her mother for his present state of being.

First, Grandfather began demanding dinner the minute she walked through the door. It was a scribbled message before she even took off her coat, and he would tap, tap, tap the marker on the whiteboard until she came to see.

"Hang on, Dad, let me put my stuff down," Sarah would say. If she didn't come fast enough, he would start slamming his whole fist on the whiteboard or the tray table if it was in front of him.

"What good is a nurse if she never does anything? Why doesn't she feed you before she leaves?" her mother would mutter, half-hearted and beaten down. Sarah asked Sandi about it, and Sandi shrugged.

"He's never hungry when I try to give him dinner at four. He refuses to eat. I'll try again this week," the nurse told her. Sandi did try, and Talia watched her grandfather slap the spoon away night after night. The last time he hit the dish and flung the mush he was conscripted to eat all over the wall and curtains. And when Talia's mother came through the front door, he was slapping at that whiteboard like a hungry seal doing tricks for his trainer. Sandi gave up and apologized to Sarah.

"I think he really wants you to do it," Sandi said.

Talia learned it was better to make dinner for herself and her brothers. Whatever amount of time it took Sarah to make their Grandfather's dinner and spoon-feed it to him, was the amount of time their meal would be postponed. If he was being stubborn that day, he would demand to hold the spoon himself, and she would hold the bowl within his reach. That took even longer. While her mother fed Grandfather whatever prepared meal was at hand, Talia would go into the kitchen to get the water boiling for butter noodles and open a can of vegetables. She made a lot of meals that winter, choosing uncomplicated cans of soup or noodles covered in sauce or cheese. Her mother would bring home day-old bread from the bakery, which Talia slathered butter onto and served to each of her brothers. No one complained, the three boys were happy to be fed.

As soon as the household got into this routine, Grandfather developed a new trick. Talia watched Nurse Sandi change diaper after diaper, announcing to no one in particular the quality of his excrement. She'd do a quick wipe down and fan him off to dry, before placing on a new diaper. When over the course of a few days, Sandi had only uncovered diapers full of urine, Talia could see the surprise on her face, but she carried on with her business, making passing mention of this to her mother.

That night, after she had painstakingly fed him dinner, Talia's mother finally had a moment to eat, hours after arriving home. As she brought the first bite to her lips, the undeniable sound of her father filling his shorts came. Talia had retreated to her room hours prior, but she heard her mother gasping and retching as she cleaned him up.

"Jesus, Dad! I'm going to have to bathe you. Have you been holding this for three days?" Sarah howled. The smell crept into Talia's bedroom, and she forced her window open to let the freezing night air pour in and wash away the overpowering aroma of feces that had filled the house.

And so, it went. Before Sarah could even get in the door and take off her jacket, Grandfather was loading his shorts to the brim. Only after she gave him a thorough cleaning could she prepare his dinner and spend the next hour feeding him. If that wasn't enough, he started with another tactic to get underneath Sarah's skin.

After his dinner, when she would try to fix something for herself to eat, he would holler unintelligible gibberish at her, dictating something on his whiteboard and slamming his palm against it until she would come over and answer his question.

"Christ, Dad, this is the first chance I have had to sit all day. Just watch TV for a minute," she would yell from the kitchen where she hurried to fix herself a simple sandwich or scrape up her children's cold leftovers. His demands were trivial at times: a change of socks, the light too bright in the living room, wanting to sit up and then dropping the remote he used to adjust the bed out of his reach. At other times, his requests were vague and required a certain amount of guesswork to meet. She would work at the solution, trying to sound out the word on the whiteboard as Grandfather would grumble and bark in his foreign tongue. Her failure thrilled him, and Talia could smell his elation as it radiated off of him. It pleased him because it was a game. This was evidenced further when Sandi was there alone, Grandfather wanted next to nothing. He was content to watch whatever programs Sandi had on and let her feed him his breakfast and lunch with ease.

Sandi grew bored with so little actual work to do. She refused to assist with housework and had agreed to only the smallest amount of child-minding, so she wandered the house as Grandfather slept. Talia harnessed her superpower of being invisible and stalked Sandi on silent socked feet. Talia had memorized which stairs and spots in the floor would creak and knew how to close a door by holding the knob turned and shutting it, letting the latch slide into place noiselessly. She mastered all the ways of avoiding detection both at school and at home.

Things disappeared, and Talia watched Sandi disappear them. Grandfather's baseball cards, the old ones in the special plastic cases, were slipped casually into her pocket. A coin collection was unceremoniously dumped into Sandi's purse. A small China cow that had lived on a dusty shelf went missing, and no one noticed except Talia. The theft became more brazen over time. One day Sandi loaded several black garbage bags full of clothing from Grandfather's closet into the trunk of her car. One of Grandfather's special medals, the gold one with the eagle and the shadow box it was mounted in, disappeared.

Sandi helped herself to other things. Sandi would pretend to place Grandfather's pain pill into his little cup along with the others, and with a barely perceptible sleight of hand, palmed it and turned away to slip the capsule into her own mouth. Sometimes, she would just double up the dose for Grandfather, so he would sleep the afternoon away.

Other times, they both got one. Sandi helped herself to everything in the cupboards and pantry without restraint.

Talia's mother did not notice. She had no capacity to monitor what the nurse was getting up to in her idle time. She woke, dropped Talia and her two brothers at school, Jamie with the sitter, and went to work. Afterwards, she came home to care for Grandfather, which took hours, and then, with what was left of her day, would put together a quick meal for herself, check on her children to tuck them in for the night, rush through a shower, and head to bed.

Then came the late-night demands. Having slept all day, which was happening with more and more frequency, Grandfather would be awake long into the night. He would moan and hit his fist on the tray table until her mother would wake and make her way down the stairs to check on him. After a week or two of this occurring almost nightly, Sarah made a bed on the couch. She tried calling the hospital social worker after losing sleep for three weeks, begging the person on the other end for a night nurse. The social worker said only the day nurse was covered, and anything additional would have to be paid for out of pocket. There was no money for that, so the problem persisted.

Grandfather kept her mother busy at all hours of the night, and Talia saw her wilt and fade into a husk of her former self, living only to face each new day and the challenges it would bring.

One winter morning, Talia woke in the predawn hours. Needing the restroom, she walked out onto the landing quiet as a mouse and looked down onto the living room and kitchen below. Her mother sat at the kitchen table smoking a cigarette, something she rarely did. Sarah kept a stale pack in the back of the junk drawer with a book of matches stuffed into the cellophane. Another was buried under the booklets in the glove box of her car. On occasion, she would sneak off into the forest to sit on a stump and take long slow drags off the butt, blowing the smoke out in careful rings. Talia had come upon her once, and she sometimes found the stubbed-out butts in an ashtray hidden in a nearby tree hollow.

Her mother's eyes were on Grandfather as she ashed into an empty coffee cup. She blew tight perfect circles of smoke, never averting her gaze. He was awake, and they were staring at each other in tense silence. There was a storm gathering between them. The whiteboard rested on the tray table, which had been removed from his bedside and sat several feet away. Sarah flicked the ash off the end of her cigarette, and Grandfather made a low howling noise. Talia's mother stood up and pointed her two fingers holding the smoking stick at him.

"You make another sound, and I will stuff your fucking mouth full of socks," she told him. Rage seethed off of her. What had long simmered below the surface was ready to overflow. There was a dark presence in the family home, and it was no ghost. It was demanding, endless with its need, and intent on destroying her mother.

A week later, Talia returned home after school to find Sandi gone, and her mother there. She had been fired. Between the frequent absenteeism and simple exhaustion, the mistakes were piling up. After another sleepless night, Sarah had dozed off, and the bread in the oven had burned. It was caught before it started a fire, but it had become a regular occurrence for Sarah to fall asleep on the job. Combined with a number of small incidents like dropping a candy thermometer into mixing dough and spilling an entire twenty-pound bag of flour on the dirty kitchen floor, it was the last straw. The bakery was done. Luckily, the State would pay her mother to care for Grandfather around the clock.

It wasn't enough to cover all the household expenses. Talia remembered driving to the social services office to collect welfare and how her mother had wept in the car afterward. It was a small saving grace that there was no mortgage to pay.

For a time, the pressure came off. Talia's mother, no longer pressed to maintain a job and arrange for a sitter for Jamie, relaxed and fell into round-the-clock care of her father. While this was an improvement for Sarah, things grew worse for Talia. As her mother slipped into a strange cycle, mimicking her grandfather's pattern of sleeping late into the morning and long afternoon naps, Talia found herself back to preparing breakfast and walking the mile long driveway to the bus stop with her two brothers. More than once, they were too late to catch the bus, and they would have to turn back and shake their mother awake. Sarah would keep them home rather than make the effort of driving them to school.

Grandfather remained unpredictable and kept up his unending demands, making them harder and harder to decipher. He refused to use the whiteboard. When he was brought food, he would reject it and knock the spoon out of her mother's hand. If he could reach it, he would slap the bowl, sending the contents flying everywhere. He laughed every time her mother had to change his diaper and if he could, he would let out a resounding fart the moment she pulled it off. He slept less and refused his medications.

Her mother no longer resembled the bright-eyed, pink-cheeked young woman she had once been. Her skin had grown sallow, and her formerly shining hair hung lank and frayed. Her color had drained away, her essence dissipated with every demand Grandfather made. It was like a hunger, and he was intent on sucking every last drop of her dry.

As the weeks became months, the pressure, released by her mother's full-time presence, was boiling over once more. The storm was about to break.

Shortly after midnight, Chase walked her out to her car. The cloud cover had cleared, and every star was shining in the sky. Talia was happy to be out of the house and breathing fresh air.

"Are you sure you're alright?" he asked, concerned. Talia was annoyed with the continued inquiries into her well-being. She wanted to go home and climb into bed.

"I'm honestly fine," Talia replied. "I must have forgotten to eat today."

"Really, though, did you see something in that room?" he asked. Production stalled when she collapsed in the wood shop. She had woken up on the downstairs couch with the team standing over her. She was confused at first, disoriented from waking up somewhere else, then the memories flooded in. The experience left her embarrassed and ready to leave. She claimed low blood sugar and a bit of stage fright must have done it. Summer did not believe her, but no one forced the issue.

"Not a thing."

He levelled a gaze at her, waiting for her to reveal the truth, then acquiesced.

"Alright," he replied coolly. Talia grabbed onto the handle of her car door, waiting to be released from the conversation.

"Look, I'm sorry for inviting you here. I was hoping if you saw what we are doing, you would feel comfortable taking us to Lester."

Talia's surprise and irritation must have registered on her face because Chase stopped speaking.

"As much as I would like to help, I have a full-time job and a part time business. I can't afford to step away for that amount of time. This has been fun."

"What if it was a permanent gig?" Chase blurted out. "We've discussed making you a regular. Dean and I agreed adding another female would mix up the dynamic. You and Summer have amazing chemistry. You could be our fearless outdoorswoman, and we'd give you a bio all about how knowledgeable you are with folklore and the history of the areas we explore. Even if you didn't want to sign on forever, we could affiliate. It would be good exposure for your guide company."

"Dean agreed to keeping me?" Talia replied, incredulous. "No offense, but I don't think this is for me, Chase." He reached out and placed a hand on her shoulder before she could turn away and looked firmly into her eyes.

"Talia, if this show goes the way we anticipate, you'll be watching us on TV years from now wishing you'd said yes. I have a blank check with your name on it if you take us to Lester. No joke. I guarantee we will hit the numbers we are anticipating. That episode is going to put us on the map. No one has anything on Lester, and its history is full of ghost stories. Even if you don't want to stay on, take us to Lester, take the money, and you will never have to see me again."

The offer struck her dumb. "That's not fair," she scoffed, wanting desperately for it to be true.

"Name your price."

She stood there for a moment, considering.

"How about ten thousand dollars?" she replied, triumphant, waiting for him to decline. He appraised her.

"If that's the price, we want to hire you. We'll call it hazard pay. There's a risk you, we, could be arrested for trespassing if we are caught, so it's warranted. Does that mean you'll take us?" he asked. He'd called her bluff. As tempting as it was, the thought of returning to Lester gave her pause.

"I need to think about it."

"Okay, then think about it. We'll talk soon. Drive safe." He delivered a winning smile, gave a quick nod, and returned to the house with a wave goodbye.

Talia sat down in her car before her knees gave out on her. After starting the engine, she took a moment to process the overwhelming proposal that had been laid before her. A blank check? A job on the show? Was this real? Chase had hardly blinked when she gave him the number, a number she thought was outrageous enough to decline.

Finding herself wide awake in the predawn hours of the day, Talia stopped at a twenty-four-hour grocery to buy a gallon of milk and three boxes of Fruit Loops. Returning home, she detoured into the kitchen to grab one large spoon and a giant mixing bowl, then retreated all the way into her private bathroom with her purchases. She emptied one entire box into the bowl and dumped a third of the milk on top of it. She took spoonful after heaping spoonful, mindless and numb, shoveling the cereal down her throat without registering the taste.

Her mouth was raw after the first box, but she poured in the second with more milk. Her closet was visible through the bathroom door, and it stood open to the darkness inside. The creature from the Rodriguez's basement peered out from within.

Although she had experienced sheer terror as the entity had gripped her, there was a recognition, a sense of familiarity. It's hunger was hers. She poured in the last box of cereal, still ravenous, and swallowed each bite despite the fullness in her belly. The taste of oversweet sugar, and the fake fruity flavoring was intoxicating. The creature watched her, shivering with excitement and delighting in her pain. The last bowl went down in a trance, and she disappeared into herself. She disappeared into the forest.

***

The creature was gone when she woke. Sometime after her binge, in the midst of her trance, it had vanished. There was a lump in her esophagus like she'd swallowed a baseball, her mouth and throat sore. She spent most of Monday sleeping, soaking in her extended absence from work.

Tuesday morning, Talia woke full of dread. All of her prior resolve was gone. Her planned excuse sounded hollow on her tongue. She turned it over and over in her mind as she dressed. For the entirety of her drive, her stomach churned with rancid anxiety.

When she arrived, she found the lights on, and Craig already sitting behind his desk. Before she could set her purse down, he called to her from behind his cracked door. Her breath caught. She hoped to settle in before he started in on her, but she would be glad to have it over. Talia passed through the door to Craig's office and hovered there. He was freshly showered, hair damp, and the scent of his aftershave hung in the room.

"I wasn't expecting you. I don't have your coffee, but I can get it," she said.

"Where's the Eggery file? The one from Friday?" he asked.

"It's in the shared folder where we put all open contracts," Talia replied.

"Show me," he rolled back from the desk and gestured at his computer for her to take control. Talia hesitated. Craig was calmer than she'd ever seen him. He waved impatiently at the computer, so she hustled over, manipulating the mouse to the shared folder and clicking it. A window popped open with a collection of files.

"It's right here," she glanced at him from over her shoulder. "See?" He nodded.

"Open it," he advised. His eyes had taken on a flat quality and her senses prickled with foreboding. She returned her attention to the computer once more and clicked open the file. The document loaded and words came onto the screen.

"Tell me, Talia. Can you read that?" he asked. She skimmed through the paragraphs. The words were nonsense. The structure was there, the punctuation appropriate, but the words were not real words. It was almost sensical, but gibberish, reminding her of a poem she had read in high school. *Twas brillig and the slithy toves.*

"Did the file get corrupted?" Talia asked, scrolling through the pages. She checked the file history, and the last person to make any changes had been her.

"I already spoke to IT. It's not corrupted, it originated like this." She turned to face him full on, and he sat with his fingers steepled together, each elbow resting on the arms of his chair.

"No, I wrote up the notes," Talia argued.

"Get away from the computer!" Craig shrieked, shooting out of his chair. Talia shrank away, positioning the desk between them.

"You're fired."

"What? Craig, I didn't do this! There has to be something wrong with the file!" Talia objected.

"There's nothing wrong with the file, there's something wrong with you! Not only did I discover this fuckery when I was trying to file these documents, but I called and texted over a dozen times with no response. We discussed this. You were advised you would be on call until this latest contract was fully negotiated. You agreed to working nights and weekends upon request. You were not available."

"I was camping. I had no service," she offered weakly, desperate, and knowing her prepared excuse would hold no water.

"This bullshit with you has been going on for too long. You aren't reliable. I hired you to become a paralegal and you proved you could barely handle the most basic classes. Such a waste of energy, you are hardly qualified to be a legal secretary. Now, out of nowhere, during one of the most important mergers of my career, you forget how to type? This takes the cake, Talia. I have to call another meeting and redo everything. Do you understand what that means? They'll be sure to bring their attorney and argue every point that isn't in their favor. This is going to take months to resolve. We fucked our client. You fucked our client. You're done. Clear your personal items from your desk. Get out. And don't expect a reference," Craig yelled. "In this economy, you'll be lucky to find anything. A million people would die to have this job."

She had underestimated the depth of her error. If she had answered the call, come in on a Saturday, even if the file looked like that, at least there would have been some chance of recovery. Instead, Craig had three entire days to sit in his frustration and fume about the implications of her mistake. He handed her an envelope.

"What's this?" she asked.

"Notice. Since you didn't finish a degree or program, your debt to the firm for all the tuition we ponied up is due in thirty days, in full, or it will be sent to collections."

"But," she stammered. "I don't have it."

"That's your problem," he replied, pointing her out of his office. She stepped out, turning to beg him to give her another chance and he shut the door in her face.

Shaking and holding back the flood of tears Talia hastily grabbed an empty box from storage and gathered the few personal items at her desk. She fled the building.

Returning to her apartment, she considered the file, unbelieving she would produce something that errored. She remembered clearly typing up the meeting notes. It was masterful how perfect it all seemed. She wanted to believe in his drive to punish her for not answering his calls, he had altered the document himself to create an excuse to fire her. She could not prove it, but he took an obvious enjoyment in making her suffer. The only part Talia could not reconcile was Craig's willingness to sabotage a crucial merger. The simple fact was, he wouldn't. Which left only one possibility: Talia had written the document. And if that were true, she had bigger problems than losing her job.

***

Two days passed, and Talia hardly left her bed. She struggled to process the events of the prior week. A grey sky cast a gloomy light through her window blinds. Talia stared at the ceiling, willing herself to disappear. A knock came at the door, and Talia pulled the covers over her head.

"I'm fine," Talia called, irritated by the intrusion into her depressive solitude. Serena had been hovering, concerned by Talia's unusual behavior.

"Someone's here," Serena spoke through the shut door. "Purple hair. Piercings." Talia sat up. *Summer?* Talia was not presentable; still in two-day old pajamas, hair bedraggled and a questionable body odor. She threw back the bedcovers, immediately exhausted by the effort, and shoved her feet into a pair of flip-flops. She pulled on a sweatshirt and fixed her hair into a ponytail. When Talia entered the living room, Summer stood by the door.

"Chase said you weren't answering his calls. And you also didn't respond to any of my texts. I was worried," Summer said, then seeing Talia's flat expression, continued. "Sorry to surprise you. I decided to come by because I wanted to show you this." Summer removed a laptop from the bag at her side. "Is there somewhere we can talk?" Summer asked, casting a sideways glance at Serena who was monitoring their conversation over the breakfast bar.

"Oh! I'm sorry!" Serena exclaimed, realizing she was eavesdropping. She pointed a finger at her bedroom and then disappeared through the door, shooting a curious glance at Talia. Summer stepped into the living room, her black boots and leggings contrasting with the cream-colored carpet and light green sofa. Summer sank into the too soft couch, then strained to set the laptop on the coffee table. Summer's awkwardness made Talia feel a little better. Summer opened the computer and looked up at Talia expectantly.

"Well, it doesn't take a psychic to see you are not happy." Summer observed. "Is it because I'm here or because of what happened at the Rodriguez's?"

Talia considered.

"A little of both. I told him I would think about it, and I've been a little preoccupied. And as for the second part…" she considered what to say next and decided on honesty. "Nothing like that has ever happened to me before."

Summer snorted.

"Okay, good, it sounds like we can put aside the pretense you fainted. Maybe the boys bought it, but I certainly didn't. You saw something down there," Summer said.

Talia bristled.

"It wasn't a trick? One of your little 'exaggerations' for the audience?" Talia asked, a bit sharper than she intended. Summer rolled her eyes and smoothed her leggings.

"Wow. Alright, we can exaggerate a caress on the skin, air blown against the face, and sometimes we will go so far as to stage something moving off camera. All of it is subjective experience, questionable on any level as reliable data. So, what if we use it to garner a little more interest? There was no faking what happened in that basement, Talia. We were all stunned. What's real comes through and in this case, it absolutely did." Summer turned the laptop toward Talia and pressed play.

The screen lit with a setting Talia was familiar with. There was the door to the Rodriguez's basement, and Summer pulling Talia down the hallway toward the woodshop. It was dark, and the women were only visible in the circle of Chase's flashlight. It was difficult to see. She watched as they disappeared into the darkness of the room below the stairs, until the beam caught up to them a few steps later. Their hands clasped, Summer at the door and Talia peering into the depths of the room. She watched the moment unfold from the perspective of an outsider.

"It's here," Summer said and pointed at the darkened screen. She paused the clip and increased the brightness. When she hit play again, the Talia in the video stepped forward, and there was a flicker of movement in the darkness. Talia's stomach lurched at the sight of the entity on the screen, a shadow across the blackness, then the image grew too fuzzy to see anything. She swallowed hard. It was nothing like being there, but this was evidence, real evidence, of what she had seen.

"I didn't notice it the first few times we watched through all the footage. Lane pointed it out. The guys are going absolutely bananas to release this. I insisted we talk to you first," Summer said, leaning forward and pausing the video. Then added, "We need you."

"I told you I get impressions. That's true. It's a form of empathy. As cliché as it sounds, I only get a glance at what's behind the curtain. With people, it depends on how open they are. Some are easy to read because they lay themselves bare and leave it all on the table. Not too hard to know what is going on with them. Other people are closed off or able to compartmentalize so well that they conceal aspects of themselves. I can get behind those blocks if I work at it, but only if I have the right energy myself. It takes a lot of effort. And just like I can read energies on our plane of existence, I can pick up on the ones from beyond. They are like us. Some are up front, obvious, and others are too far behind the wall. I get flashes or ideas, like I said. I have been known to cold read or exaggerate a narrative off of those glimpses. It's not hard to do. But with you around, it's like training a spotlight onto every energy in my proximity."

Talia was taken aback, but stood there, silent, and listened.

"It was a half-truth to say I couldn't see the thing in that woodshop. I didn't see it with my eyes, I experienced it in my mind. It was the most intense contact I have ever had. It was like it was rifling through my brain, pulling out the pieces it wanted, and I couldn't stop it or throw up my defenses fast enough. I have never experienced anything like that before."

"Okay. What you are trying to tell me?" Talia asked, folding her arms.

"Do you even know what you are?" Summer asked, eyes narrowing. "You are a mythical creature, Talia. You're a medium. A sigma empath, like me. Do you have vivid dreams? See auras? Know things or how people are feeling without even having to ask? Psychic abilities are very common with a sigma empath, they are typically lone wolves and have a strong connection to nature. Talia, you have a gift."

"But you aren't just any medium. I've never seen what you can do. You magnify abilities in others. When I'm beside you, it's like my power gets cranked up to ten. As soon as you walked into the room, I read you like a book. You got fired. I could have dug deeper, but I stopped. As for your roomie, she has it bad for that guy. Does she know he's never going to give her the time of day?"

There was a second where Talia was too stunned to speak.

"I'm right, aren't I?"

Talia nodded. The guy in question was a serial breadcrumber, and Serena couldn't seem to help herself no matter how many times he blew her off or brought another girl around.

"Is that how you got my address?" Talia asked.

Summer snorted. "No, dummy. White Pages. One quick Google search later." Talia hung her head and laughed despite herself.

"All jokes aside, I am here to sell you on Chase's crazy idea, and I absolutely have underlying motivations. I know you told Chase you'd think about it, but he admitted to me you'd already said no. If you aren't willing to do it because of him, I get it, but you *should* do it because of me. Chase wasn't lying when he told you we were on the cusp of making it big. We are about to breakthrough into the mainstream. Lester could put us on the map. We have a producer from a major network who has been sniffing around, but he doesn't like the personal stuff. That's why a few of us want to move away from the episodes like what we did at the Rodriguez's. We went through and tracked our viewership on those episodes, and there was a pattern. The saddest episodes lose a significant audience about twenty-five percent of the way through the video. The vlogs with less emotional content and interesting back stories are the ones getting all the traffic and ad revenue. But I'm not here to sell you on joining *Dark Dimensions*."

"What are you talking about then?" Talia asked, sitting down next to Summer on the couch and eyeing the laptop like it was a bomb.

"The same producer considering taking on *Dark Dimensions* wants me for an offshoot: an entirely female led ghost hunting team. It hasn't been done before on any platform. At first, I shot it down. I didn't want to be a Powerpuff Girl or Buffy, and I figured I would be better off sticking it out with the boys. But the producer is firm. They've seen what the guys are offering before, the network wants a whole new dynamic. They said I could keep doing guest appearances on *Dimensions*, but we would have our own thing," Summer explained.

"We?" Talia laughed.

"Yes!" Summer scooted closer so that their knees were touching. "I want you to come with me. After what we did together, we could be unstoppable. *Dimensions* has never had an experience like that. The footage is amazing! You and I together could access real paranormal activity. No faking. I heard Maya like she was right beside me, physical and real. It's never been like that with the other side before. They always sound far off in the distance or like they are talking underwater. Usually only a word or two comes through. I knew what she wanted, and she led me. She led me into that room."

Summer's eyes had grown wide, her excitement palpable and contagious. It overwhelmed Talia, but she enjoyed it. The earlier tension was forgotten, and she remembered why she had felt so drawn to Summer to begin with.

"And I would get paid? Cause I need a job."

Summer nodded.

"Yes, you would get paid. Just say yes, Talia. I promise you won't regret it," Summer said.

"I don't know. This is a lot. I get this email from Chase about going to Lester, which I tried to ignore. Now, here you are telling me I have latent psychic abilities, and you want me to join a paranormal research team. Actually, scratch that, you want me to help you launch your own paranormal team. I barely know you. I barely know if I am willing to work with Chase. I don't know if I even buy into this 'psychic empath' thing you are selling." Talia shifted, pulling her knees up to her chin. Summer looked dismayed.

"He really undersold what he did to you in grade school, didn't he?" she said, more to herself than Talia. She took Talia's hand and looked into her eyes. "All the more reason to come with me, we'll do Lester because it will help everyone, then you and I can start our own show. We don't need to bring them. Well, except Bam. I entirely plan on poaching Bam."

"What about Dean?" Talia asked, surprised.

"What about him? He isn't my boyfriend if that's what you were thinking. Dean isn't even his real name. I love him, and he's one of my closest friends, but the longer we do the show, the more pompous he becomes. *Dimensions* is a knockoff of all the ghost hunter shows that came before it, and he is so resistant to trying anything new," Summer scoffed. "Honestly, you wouldn't know it based on how those guys play it, but *Dimensions* was my idea. They won't tell you that. Not Chase, and definitely not Dean. But it was my idea, and that's why I am confident you and I can do this together."

"You don't even know me," Talia replied, feeling herself warming to the idea. The ten grand would put her square with Craig, which was her most pressing concern, and leave her with a little extra.

On top of that, there was an opportunity for something greater. And while there was no way to be sure the offer was real, Talia wanted it. Summer directed a cold stare at her, the jet-black eyeliner she wore framed her sharp blue eyes, making them sparkle like jewels.

"I know you grew up poor. Not like Hamburger Helper poor, like one step away from a cardboard box poor. I know you have been tormented by more people than have loved you and that has made you fiercely guarded. I am completely serious about everything I have put on the table. I know you have an immense amount of untapped potential. That is not hyperbole or any of that 'you go-girl, rah-rah' bullshit. You are full of power, and we have only scratched the surface. Talia, I need you to help me build an empire. Say you will."

Despite her fears and many reservations, Talia found herself uttering the words, "I will."

PART TWO

William Madigan, known as Mads to his friends, woke to a chorus of birdsong, a symphony on the air itself. He poked his head through the flaps of his damp canvas tent to find the two pack mules were the only other members of the party awake. Bored and tethered, one of the animals was shifting its weight from foot to foot, while the other was straining for an out of reach, but desirable, bit of vegetation. The fire was cold, but predawn light illuminated the sky. The last stars, the ones he could see above their small clearing, faded as the night receded. His thoughts went to Abigail, and the memory of her warm body against his. Mads closed the flaps to his tent and pulled the blankets over his head. He faded into a suspended state warm in his bed with the avian song surrounding him.

Mads woke fully a short time later to Indian John's soft footsteps while he went about the business of rousing the camp and preparing the morning meal. As he stirred the campfire, the embers crackled like glass. Tents rustled as the camp came awake.

The sun's rays peeked through the top of the tree canopy. The forest was so dense, Mads was surprised any light made it to the earth below. He laid his head outside the tent doors. Golden sunbeams ignited the fog clinging to the treetops. It set the forest on fire. The branches, warmed by the sun, released their dew. The effect was magical as ethereal mist swirled amongst the fiery rays. He committed the enchanting vision to memory.

"Fairy light," Jack muttered. Mads glanced over to find the old man's head outside of his tent, admiring the tree canopy for himself.

"None of that nonsense before breakfast," Ray called, the rasp of sleep in his voice. Old Man Jack ignored their boss and rolled his head to look at Mads square on. He gave the boy a wink.

"Aye, the Fae are nothing to be trifled with, and we are in their realm now," Jack grinned, his Irish accent thick. Mads couldn't help but smile back. The old man was full of nonsense, every old logger was, but Ray was in a mood and having none of it. He climbed out from his tent, stood tall, and lobbed a pinecone at Jack's balding head.

"You'll curse us with that gobshite. Enough!" Ray said, then turned to Indian John. "Coffee. Please."

"Waiting on water," John replied without taking his eyes off the growing flames. Ray sat on the earth next to him and held his hands out for the warmth. Kindness, another Skopamish Indian, returned with a sack of water. He offered it silently to Indian John, who poured it into a pot for coffee. Mads did not know John's real name, only the Christian name given to him. He did not seem to mind the title, while Kindness barely tolerated the anglicized version of his true name.

Their group was the advance crew, setting up the early camps for the logging team that was working its way up the river valley behind them. The Indians had been hired as their scouts to take the group into the forest and navigate the terrain where the surveyors had laid out the railroad's trajectory. The superintendent trusted Ray to do the job but trusted the tribesmen's wealth of knowledge more. They prepared the meals, tended the fires, and, so far, had never been wrong about the landscape they were traversing. They assisted from time to time with the actual work.

William Madigan was the youngest of the posse at seventeen. He had lucked into working on Ray's team because he was strong, and skilled with the ropes. The foreman needed a workhorse to offset Jack's waning strength. Because Jack could still climb a tree faster than anyone else in the entire logging outfit, he was necessary. The other two workers, Wyatt and Carson, had an exceptional skill set, but tended toward laziness. Mads suspected they were sent because they created too much of a distraction for the other workers, and the foreman needed to get rid of them. Raymond was enough of an asshole to keep them in line.

Mads hardly remembered anything before the forest. They had moved to the Washington territory from South Dakota. It was a journey he had no memory of, and his mother was loathe to discuss. They had set up near Commencement Bay as part of a settlement that was later named Tacoma and established a farm where the soil was rich and dark. He had always been big for his age and while he liked the physical work of the farm, he had no head for books. He had tried to stick it out in school because his mother was adamant about him attending, often citing what a privilege it was for it to be available at all. He made it to the age of thirteen, then quit to join his uncle who was logging in the mountains to the east. While most people would not dream of leaving a civilized life for the untamed wilderness, he had, and Mads loved every second of it. He had been born again, embracing the spirit of adventure. He had been William when he left home but he was Mads here in the mountains. He was a different person in the woods: the risk taker, the wild man. He had ruffled the feathers of a few experienced loggers with his arrogance and made no secret how little he cared. He knew he was a natural to the work. He had proved himself time and again, doing what others would not and willing to take risks to get the job done. It had earned him respect and the nickname.

After spending a few years working in a settlement named Perkins Prairie, a mucky muck from the Northern Pacific came through recruiting and offered him a substantial pay increase to work clearing the future rail line east of Palmer. The tradeoff was that there would be little down time, and they expected it to take a couple of years. The railroad had a deadline, Lincoln had seen to that, according to the rumors, but it meant they would be doing double duty to clear the forest in order to lay tracks. Mads signed on. He was recognized by the foreman for his talent and work ethic so when the advance team needed to clear camps, he was offered the job.

He rolled over in his tent, watching Indian John make his black tar coffee.

"Moving day. We need to lay out a site near Friday Creek. I want you all packed up in an hour. We need to make about seven miles before the day is out," Ray announced.

Kindness clucked and shook his head, while Mads and Jack groaned. Downriver it was easier to stay close to the riverbed because it was flat and forgiving. The further into the watershed they went, the more difficult the terrain became. Each day they were traversing multiple ridgelines through a forest so dense it sometimes stood against them like a wall.

"We aren't going to make it seven miles. Do you see what's ahead of us?" Mads asked. They had all seen the mountain, whose shadow they were sleeping under, and the one behind it was even taller. Raymond shot him a look. Despite the boy's mouth, he liked him, so he tolerated his attitude.

"Sounds like you need a hanky." Ray pulled a kerchief from his chest pocket and waved it at the boy. Mads gave him the finger.

"Keep it down, would ya? Some of us are trying to sleep," Wyatt grumbled from behind the walls of his tent.

"Something about this part of the forest," Jack said to no one in particular, staring overhead at the beams of light cutting through the boughs above. "It feels alive, like we are inside a giant beast, like the belly of a whale. You can feel its heart beating in the earth." He had a strange look as he spoke, both lost and fearful. Silence fell over them.

"Are you getting senile? Knock it off with that fairy shite," Ray blurted, then stomped off to piss. Mads looked over at Jack, a man who had felled more trees than the other four loggers combined. It was nothing short of a miracle, given how long he'd been working the forest, that his only missing appendage was the little finger on his right hand. He still had both eyes and all four of his limbs. For his time and experience, they called him 'The Bull of the Woods,' and that meant you heeded his warnings.

"You mind my words. There's something here." Jack looked over at him.

"Stop, you're giving me the willies," Mads said, rubbing the gooseflesh off his arms. He gave the older man an awkward smile, hoping for reassurance, but Jack's serious expression remained.

Jack rustled out of his bedroll and stood. His clothes hung off his lanky frame, suspenders keeping his pants from sliding down his narrow waist. He stepped close to the fire and nodded at Kindness, who handed him the first steaming cup of coffee. Mads followed in turn, and when Raymond came back from the tree line, after kicking first Wyatt's and then Carson's tents, he accepted a cup as well.

The two men appeared out the front flap of their dew-covered tents a moment later, both with blood shot eyes and swollen faces. Last night, with their work done for the day and without a word to the others, the pair had wandered off to sit by the river and pass a bottle of spirits between them. It was another night of debauchery, as much trouble as one can get up to in the middle of nowhere, sharing stories about the trees they had brought down, the women they had bedded, and recollections of drunken nights that had come before. With nothing better to do, and each with a belly full of liquor, they had started a boulder throwing contest by the light of the moon. Their cackles, and the sound of rocks crashing against each other, woke the sleeping camp. Raymond, not one to do well with nighttime disturbances, had enough of it as soon as it had begun, and started hollering at them to turn in or he would dock them both a week's worth of pay. The pair rolled back into camp, sodden with alcohol and stifling laughter like a pair of schoolgirls, dissolving into giggles when Carson was overcome with an interminable case of the hiccups.

"How ya feelin'?" Mads said, bending down and speaking loudly. Wyatt groaned in response.

"Knock it off. I need some coffee," he muttered.

"Get out of bed, and get some then," Raymond spat, then took a sip from his own cup.

Breakfast was berry-laden mush slopped into each of their cups once they'd polished off the last dregs of their coffee. Kindness had collected the huckleberries the day before, wandering higher up into the hills to find them. They made the meal more palatable, although a few were too early and made Mads jaw ache with their sharp tang. The group gathered their bedrolls and tents, strapped them up into their packs, and hefted it all onto their backs. Their equipment, the ropes and wedges, were carried by the mules, along with their camp supplies. The Indians collected water for the group, strapping it to their chests for easy access during the hike. Both Kindness and Indian John carried rifles, ostensibly for hunting, but also for protection. The tools of their trade, the axes and crosscut saws, were carried by the five loggers as they went. Mads, Wyatt, and Carson carried an ax in each hand, while Raymond and Jack were tethered together by two ends of the pair of long saws they carried, a man on each set of handles. They left behind their riverside camp and moved into the trees as the sun rose over the surrounding peaks.

They were lucky to be set on this task in midsummer, the nights were mild and damp, and between the elevation and the cover of the forest, the men stayed relatively cool despite the blazing sun. The Pacific Northwest was known for being under rainy conditions in all seasons and the woodlands reflected it. Many of the trees were evergreen, Douglas Fir and Western Red Cedar, along with pockets of vine maple and cottonwood, particularly by the riverbanks. At higher elevations, you could find the blue green of the Noble Fir and higher still, the twisted subalpine fir and Mountain Hemlock. The understory was a riot of life. The smallest tiny grey mushrooms grew on rotting stumps surrounded by shaggy moss and feathery lichens. Giant prehistoric ferns dominated the forest floor along with red huckleberry shrubs dotted with fruit; all verdant and thriving amongst their taller brethren.

There was the smell of fish in the river, and Mads thought a couple of salmon would make a fine dinner. The river cut a natural valley through the western foothills that the rail line would follow. The Green River was collected from dozens of natural spring water creeks. It was not prone to the volatility of a glacial river, but it swelled with snowmelt and excessive rainfall in the cold months. Forested peaks surrounded them on all sides and as they moved deeper into the river gorge, an unending sea of trees confronted them. It would be a feat to get a steam engine through the range ahead, but the surveyors had found the pass and scouted the line. It was progress, and it was coming at full speed. As they established the camps, loggers would move in and bend the landscape to their will.

As a small group of men heading into the wilderness, it felt less like progress and more like they were pioneers in untamed lands, seeking their corner of the earth. Mads had built the cabin inside his mind a hundred times or more. He would hew the logs by hand and build a small but cozy homestead near a creek. After, he would ask for Abigail's hand, steal her away from her parents' household and show her the place where his heart could be found.

They'd met in Perkins Prairie shortly after he arrived. Mads was immediately smitten. She had put him off, the oldest daughter dutiful to her parents and her younger siblings, but she allowed herself to be pursued. Before the railroad job had come along, he had planned to ask her and had nearly forgone the railroad's offer. When Abby caught wind of it, she pushed him to go with the promise she would be waiting for him when he came back. He loved her mightily. She was the most beautiful woman he had ever laid eyes on, and the way she looked at him with those grey-blue eyes made his heart stop. She would love living in the woods. She admired all the different wildflowers he brought and knew every one of their names. She loved when the sun shined or when the rain poured. Her shoes were always dirty, and her cheeks were always pink. They would live together in the wilderness, away from everyone. He held this image in his mind as they made their way over the miles.

Kindness and Indian John led, navigating through the understory as if they walked on air. In contrast, Jack and Raymond blundered through as best they could, tripping over their own feet and yanking each other along by the crosscut saws they carried. Wyatt and Carson trudged at the rear of their little procession, while Mads walked alone ahead of them. Aside from the occasional argument between Jack and Ray about the speed with which the other was moving, the men were silent as they cut through the wilderness.

They were moving up a steep incline, the crest of which Mads was able to see through the thinning trees. It was midafternoon based on the position of the sun. Kindness had held up and turned to look at John, his brow knitted together with concern. They had climbed above the river canyon, but the faint rush of water echoed up the rock walls from below.

As they reach the precipice of the peak, a fetid smell wafted through on the breeze. It was Wyatt who noticed first.

"Who had the beans last night?" he remarked.

"We all did," Carson muttered back to him.

"Smell that?"

"Smell what? You shit your pants again?" Mads called over to him. Wyatt scowled at the reminder, it was a story he would rather everyone forgot, and when Mads turned away, he felt Wyatt's glare sting the back of his neck.

"That's hot spring. Stinks like the devil's asshole. We might have ourselves a party tonight, boys!" Wyatt crowed. Raymond's ears perked up.

"If you want to party again tonight, you can head back down to the main camp," Ray told him.

Mads had heard about hot springs in the foothills. Loggers talked about finding them from time to time, but he had never encountered one himself. He reached the top of the mountain where they stood on a rocky ridge overlooking the river and a flat valley below. The Indians had stopped with the mules, having a discussion in Lushootseed of which Mads only knew a few words. John had taught him all the dirty ones.

"What's the problem?" Raymond demanded, sweat beading across his forehead.

"Something different in the air," Indian John replied, delivering a placid look punctuated by a shrug.

"Fairies," Old Man Jack muttered under his breath. Ray jerked the saw. "None of that!"

Raymond used the opportunity to pull the spyglasses from his satchel and scanned the terrain. Jack wiped the sweat from his brow, relieved for the break.

"There," he pointed. The Green River snaked through the valley below. "Do you see that draw right there." Mads looked, noting where Raymond indicated a strip of land bent inwards, and the trees a richer shade of green.

"That's Friday Creek," Raymond said. He returned to the other end of the crosscut saw, and they began their descent. It was difficult to pick their way down the mountain, but the sunlight on Mads face was a pleasant change. They would reenter the tree line shortly. When they reached the base of the peak, Kindness continued forward.

"We still have daylight to make the confluence. We should keep moving," he called back. That was when Carson piped up.

"I'm not going any further," Carson announced. Ray turned to look at him.

"We haven't reached our target," he replied.

"Well, I don't much care." Carson threw down his axes and sat on a fallen log. "We've been over three peaks since we left this morning, bushwacking the whole way. My feet hurt, I need water, and I want something to eat." Wyatt took a seat next to him and slung his pack off to the ground.

Indian John backtracked to where they stood, moving with the stealth of a cat, his movements fluid and soundless. Kindness continued on with the mules. John's dark eyes met Ray's.

"We need to continue," he told the boss. It was known that Ray trusted both Kindness and Indian John implicitly. They were honorable men, and Raymond was reading something off of John that wasn't being spoken out loud. He nodded a response.

"Get up," he barked at Carson, throwing a water sack at him. "Take your water. We are moving on." There was a story Raymond told once around the campfire about how they had been scouting for the company to find premium forest to log, when Ray had come down with influenza. His fever spiked, and his lymph nodes swelled. He could barely move, let alone continue the trek through the forest. They posted up to camp for a few days. Late on the second night, a mountain cat appeared by the fireside as it burnt low. Its yellow eyes glittering as it regarded the sick man lying beside it. The cat must have been half-starved to approach.

How Raymond told it, he was too delirious to warn John and Kindness out loud, so he spoke to them in a dream. They woke and fought an epic battle with the creature. Kindness admitted Ray was almost certainly hallucinating. They ran the cat off without any bloodshed and spent three days nursing Ray back to health.

"I would have died that night had they not been there," Raymond said, looking down at his hands. "I owe them my life." Raymond ensured the two Natives were well compensated and treated with respect.

They made it another half mile when they reached a clearing, and Carson threw another fit. Raymond consulted Kindness and Indian John. They conceded the location would be sufficient, although the expressions on their faces said otherwise. Each man claimed a level spot for their tent. Kindness cleared the forest duff for a cook fire and laid out the mess. Indian John grabbed his fishing pole to head toward the river. The afternoon was humid and close, with time before dinner, Mads decided to join him.

"Hold up, I'm coming," Mads called. The river was a short walk away and when they reached the bank, Mads found an eddy of water where he pulled off his boots and socks and dipped his feet in. John walked into the river up to his knees and cast his line. They languished the afternoon away, Mads meditating in the sun while John brought in three large salmon, cleaning them on a smooth flat stone. They returned to a crackling fire in twilight, with a full moon slowly rising into the sky. The men ate heartily that night, each taking down several portions of freshly grilled salmon and stewed wild carrot. When his belly was full, Mads laid down on top of his bedroll, his head outside his tent to watch the stars appear and drifted off to sleep.

He was shaken awake by Indian John, his face inches from Mads's own. His fingers were pressed to his lips. The moon was high in the sky, illuminating the clearing with its cold light. Mads stayed silent, watching the man crouched next to his tent. The fire had burnt down, and a small lantern glowed upon his face. His eyes were wide and watchful.

"What is it?" Mads whispered.

"Something's happened," John replied. Mads sat up, the last traces of sleep fading with the realization that they were alone and someone deep in the woods was moaning in agony. A knot from the fire popped, and Mads flinched.

"Come on," he said standing and pulling an ax from a nearby tree.

"Where is everyone?' Mads asked, as he rolled up and onto his feet.

"Wyatt went to find the hot springs. He should have left it alone."

"He was never going to leave it," Mads snorted. Wyatt couldn't leave off anything. The more you told him not to, the more he couldn't resist.

"Where is everyone else?"

Indian John gave no answer.

Mads grabbed a lantern and another long-handled ax. The small light he carried as they entered the total darkness of the forest brought him little comfort. The lantern's flame flickered, only able to reveal two steps in front of his face. He was holding back the night, as if the trees and darkness would overtake him completely if not for the tiny flame he carried. The two men walked so close together their arms touched. Wet sobs echoed off the trees. The sound surrounded them, seeming to come from everywhere. Mads followed John's lead, stepping soft and gliding silently through the black forest. The lantern guttered and smoked. He prayed it wouldn't go out.

As he began to question their errand, a moan erupted directly to their right, and John disappeared into the dark after it. For one frightening second, Mads was alone. He pressed forward in terror until he found John kneeling over a body. Raymond's crumpled figure lay in a pool of blood.

Mads dangled the lantern over him and assessed the damage. Ray held his stomach, hands sticky and matted with dirt and fir needles. His bicep was slashed, the fabric of his stained shirt torn. Tattered skin was exposed underneath. There was a shallow cut across his cheek. Around him, the forest floor was disturbed where he had dragged himself to the base of a massive cedar tree. Raymond was in serious trouble.

"He went in, and something pulled him under. He got pulled under. Thought he was screwing around, but he came back up. Came back different. Different eyes. Different smile…" Raymond trailed off, shuddering, and looked up at them with wet eyes. A tear slipped down his cheek.

"Ray?" John asked. "Who? Who went in the water?" Ray gave no answer but stared hard into the darkness. Mads turned and held up the light. The oppression of the trees closed in around them, like a thousand eyes watching, and the sensation of *presence* prickled his scalp. The lantern's light seemed to diminish, as if the illumination it provided was being sucked away.

"John, I don't like this," Mads whispered, unnerved.

"Who did this?" John demanded. Raymond looked up at him, frightened.

"Don't trust him, whatever he says, don't listen. Something's wrong with the water." he whispered, urgency in his voice. "There's something wrong with the water!" He labored to breathe, then his eyes went distant and glassy. John stood abruptly and moved into the darkness.

"Hey!" Mads yelled. He gave chase, fearful he would lose him in the forest, and Mads did not want to be out here alone. John moved fast, in and out of the lantern's glow. Mads crashed after him, his heart pounding.

"Where are you going?" Mads asked. John gave no response. They were climbing uphill. Soft laughter tinkled in the distance, and all of Mads's senses went on high alert. Another round of chuckles bubbled up, turning into cackles of laughter, growing louder with each step they took.

They erupted out of the tree line to find the moon high overhead, showing them the way. Mads held the lantern low to the ground as they navigated the rocky incline. John stopped and indicated for Mads to do the same. The moonlight revealed a grotto carved into the cliff. Amongst the rocks was a collection of obsidian pools surrounded by twisted whitebark pine. It was a beautiful place, but there was something unsteady about it and how the pools seemed to alter reality. They were oppressive black holes in the earth, like negative space. John was staring at their smoky surface, entranced. Mads sensed their pull and, with much effort, averted his gaze.

"There is no reflection," John remarked. Mads saw it too. The moonlight did not reflect in the water. Mads hesitated to draw closer with the lantern, knowing it was the pools themselves drawing the light in, as if consuming it directly out of the air itself. Unconsciously, Mads sight returned to where they lay, impassive and insane.

Something wrong with the water.

Wyatt emerged out of the darkness, stepping into the close circle of light thrown by the lantern. He flashed a wide grin.

"Oh, hey, so good of you to join us!" Wyatt laughed. "The water's fine!" A dark substance smeared his forehead, and as Mads drew closer, he saw the substance splattered his arms and stained his clothing. It was blood, and it was drying in a handprint where someone had gripped his collar.

"What did you do?" Indian John muttered. Wyatt's grin stretched impossibly wide. Mads was chilled when Wyatt's gaze shifted to him. His eyes were black as midnight, and deep within them, Mads saw the pools reflecting back.

"Do you want to see Abigail?" Wyatt asked. Her name flared a warning in Mads's mind. He had never spoken about her before with any of them. How could Wyatt have known?

"Mads, she's right over there. In the water. You can go see her right now." Wyatt gestured toward the hot spring at his back, the steam coming off its surface in whisps and swirls. For a second, Mads imagined he heard her sigh. Soft light emanated from deep within the interior of the water and color shimmered across its surface. It was her sigh, the same exhalation that escaped her lips when he took her hand or placed a kiss on her temple. A shadow passed over the pool, and Mads glanced over, expecting to find her there. The water called to him like a siren song.

"William," she whispered. "Come with me. Come build me a cabin, William." It reached for him. She reached for him, and his mind gave in. John grabbed his arm.

"Don't listen," he said, he fixed his eyes on Mads's face. The tendrils of her voice withdrew from the center of his mind. Something else was here, something in the pools.

Wyatt's eyes flitted between the pair and cocked his head.

"You see it, don't you?" he said, sliding a hand behind his back and withdrawing a long blade. "It was hungry." Wyatt launched at John. The Indian, unprepared, barely deflected the blade with the handle of the ax. He kicked Wyatt in the stomach, and the possessed man fell back a step. He laughed, turned his head up to the night sky and howled, hovering at the edge of the shadows.

"Better watch out Injun, I'm coming for you!" Wyatt held the blade up at eye level, pointing the tip at Indian John, then turned and vanished into the depths beyond the grotto. John watched him go, guarding himself with the ax.

"We need to go," John said, breathless. "We need to get back to Raymond." They made their way down the hillside. John followed a nearly invisible trail, and Mads stayed close behind out of fear a false step would send him over the cliff's edge. They reached a landing below the hot springs and heard someone panting. The gasps grew louder as they approached and for a cold moment, Mads believed whatever was inside of the pool had escaped.

"Carson?" Mads asked, bringing the lantern forward and cautiously approached. Carson cowered behind a boulder. He lifted his head in response to Mads voice. Two black holes punctured his face where his eyes should have been, and streams of black ichor flowed down from them.

"Jesus Christ," Mads whispered, his stomach turning violently.

"Mads? Is that you?" Carson rasped in a thin frightened voice. Blood pooled around him. He was covered in it, having sustained an uncountable number of injuries. He coughed and sputtered up a clot. "Do you have any water?" John stood at Mads's back watching the woods. They heard another peal of laughter echo from somewhere above them.

"Yeah, it's me. I don't have any water, but let's see if we can get you back to camp," Mads said. Carson's face fell, and he laid his head against the boulder.

"Yeah, okay. Why is it so dark?"

Mads exchanged a glance with Indian John.

"It would be nice to have something to drink," Carson cleared his throat. "They went in the hot springs, and something happened. They both changed. Wyatt's eyes went black. Stay out of the water. Old Jack and Ray were with us. I don't know where they went. Wyatt went after Ray with that blade. I stopped him, but that's when he got me." He swallowed thickly. His brow continued to move, his eyelids fluttered, but no eyes looked out of those bleeding holes. He coughed a few more times, and another thick clot came up. He strangled on it. Indian John stepped past Mads, propped Carson up and angled his throat open. He grasped Indian John as if he were drowning and the other man was keeping him afloat.

"It's not Wyatt anymore," he spat out, a mist spraying across John's face. He did not flinch away. Carson struggled, sucking in a great gasping lungful of air. As John repositioned him, Mads could see the several chunks had been taken out of his shoulder and collarbone where he was steadily gushing blood.

"Aw, man." Mads head swam, and he had to avert his gaze. John glanced over at him.

"Sit down so you don't fall," he said, then to Carson. "It's okay, brother. You've warned us. You don't need to hang on anymore." Mads knelt in the dirt, setting down the lantern, and focused on his breathing. He had seen many traumatic injuries in the forest, but none as horrifying as this. Carson struggled for air.

"You are safe to leave this plane. Step into the next. We will protect you as you go," John spoke quiet words, whispering something else only the dying man could hear. Carson sucked his final breath and exhaled a sigh so deep and so long, Mads felt his spirit slip out on its current. Then he was gone. John took a moment, then laid the body down beside the boulder.

"We will have to track him," John said after a moment of silence.

"Are you kidding?" Mads replied. "Wyatt's out of his goddamn mind if he did this."

"Whose voice did you hear?" John demanded, bringing himself to his full height. He continued without missing a beat. "I heard my father speak. He told me to climb in, and I would be redeemed for giving up my true name. I can still hear him speaking to me, saying I am a disappointment for standing with the white man."

Mads caught a glimpse of the wounded expression on his face.

"This place is poison. We need to find the others and go. Kindness did not want to stop here. He sensed the dark spirits."

Without a sound, Wyatt emerged as if he had been slipping between the space amongst the shadows. The wicked grin splayed across his face.

"Too bad about Carson, but he interfered," Wyatt said, shooting a passing glance at Carson's body. He then turned his gaze onto John, ignoring Mads.

"You are a disappointment, redskin. How would you like to be scalped? A little retribution for what your kin did to mine. We just wanted a little land, there's so much of it here!" His tone was rising.

"You redskins don't deserve to live amongst us. Better yet, you deserve to live in a hole!" Wyatt laughed, his eyes, pits of obsidian, regarding them with cold indifference. Wyatt shot out lightning quick, his knife raised. John ducked. A shot rang out so loud Mads threw his hands up over his ears. Wyatt collapsed, dropping the blade, which John snatched up. Wyatt rolled onto his back in the dirt, bringing his hand up to the place where the bullet had exited the center of his chest. Kindness appeared and stood over the top of him, holding the rifle to his face. Wyatt grinned.

"Chicken shit. Yellow bellied coward," Wyatt chuckled, looking to Kindness. He turned and met Mads's eye. Those dark eyes. "You can swing an ax, but you really are a limp dick. Scared little boy running through the forest. Don't leave me, John!" He imitated the timid voice of a child.

"Tuck your tail and run, you sissy. She wants a real man. Your Abby, she don't want a wittle scawedy cat like you. A pale boy, soft in the middle. Soft all around I bet. She wants to get fucked by a real man, why do you think her daddy won't let her go?"

John's ax was within arm's reach. Mads grabbed the still warm wood of its handle and used the tool to stand.

"Don't listen to him," Kindness said, remaining in his place.

"She doesn't love you. She loves her Daddy. Daddy! Daddy!" Wyatt screamed in a high voice. Mads swung the ax and buried it into Wyatt's skull. He hadn't realized how hard he was breathing. When he looked up, he found Kindness aiming the rifle at him. Mads lifted his arms up in surrender, and Kindness lowered the weapon.

"Ray will survive," John said to Kindness. "We might be able to rig a litter and carry him out. We need to turn back. Abandon this place. Have you seen Jack?"

"No, but he was here. We should go," Kindness replied, pulling the ax free of Wyatt's skull, then handed it to Mads. Mads accepted it reluctantly, then puked up his dinner.

They left Carson and Wyatt's bodies behind. Ray still had a chance. They retraced their steps and found him unconscious. As Kindness and John worked Ray up to standing, gathering him up to be carried back to the campsite, Mads heard the voice of his love calling to him, coaxing him back to the pools. Abby begged, offering up everything a man could want. Mads found himself both disgusted and aroused, she was dirtied in his mind by the things the darkness said. They limped along with John and Kindness dragging Raymond between them. Mads trailed behind with the lantern and ax, trying to deny the voice worming through his brain. There was a chuckle, and Mads wheeled the light around. The Natives stopped ahead of him. At the base of a massive old growth cedar sat a young man.

He didn't look up when the light fell upon him, he was preoccupied by his hands and chortling. Mads drew closer.

"Jack?"

Only an hour ago, Jack was his senior by decades, and when Mads discovered him sitting childlike giggling in the middle of the forest, the two were the same age. There was muscle and sinew in his body, instead of the thin bones of an older man. His skin was firm and without wrinkles, he had a head full of hair, and his beard was a rich dark brown without a grey hair in sight. Jack chuckled. His eyes were different, not black like Wyatt's but an icy blue. He was restored to his younger self. Jack held up his hands in front of him, wiggled all ten fingers, including his once missing pinky finger, and laughed.

"It's the damndest thing!"

The gravel crunched beneath Talia's feet as she stepped from the van. She scanned the wall of trees before them. The breeze caressed the long grass along the lane and kicked up tiny cyclones of dust. The *Dimensions* team removed their gear from the vehicle. She grabbed her own backpack from where it had been stashed and slung the weight of it over her shoulders. They were departing for Lester.

"Back on Friday at five p.m. You do not leave until you see us," Dean provided instructions to the driver, his tone adamant. "You wait until midnight. If we don't come out, you drive until you have service, and call the authorities to get search and rescue out here. Because we will be here. Someone will be here." He repeated the instructions a second and then third time.

Talia pulled out the map and compass, orienting her direction, as the others strapped into their packs. She had gone over their route a dozen times since Summer convinced her to sign on. There were no direct routes to Lester that were accessible to the public. The main road and railroad were inside the watershed and surveilled by the Green River Headworks. There was a massive gate just outside of Palmer, and the Headworks utilized notoriously aggressive guards to keep would-be visitors out. The ghost town forums reported that the northern entry point was also under surveillance by the Headworks.

After scouring a collection of topographic and road maps, she found a forest service road that entered Lester to the east, but it presented a logistical nightmare. It was an unreasonable distance to travel on foot. With four-wheel drive vehicles it was doable, albeit cost prohibitive, and created other potential problems like road washouts, fallen trees, and impassable gates.

They were left with an entry point through the forest from the south, the same route Talia followed as a girl. She sourced a collection of Green Trail maps and cobbled together a network of old trails and forgotten roads that would detour around the watershed. The condition of their route was questionable, and Talia anticipated some bushwhacking would be required, but the entire team had agreed to the trip. They would camp at the lookout their first night, or what remained of it, and arrive in Lester the following day. Her navigational skills were about to be put to the test.

It was an inconvenient trek given the amount of equipment they needed for the vlog, and Talia had spent the better part of the week working closely with Chase to ensure everyone on the team would be carrying a manageable weight. It had been an absolute feat to parse their gear down to the essentials between food for a five-day trip, tents and sleeping bags, along with an extensive array of cameras and ghost detection devices.

Bam was the only one who made anything close to an argument.

"We gonna Blair Witch it, eh?" Bam asked. He lifted his cap off by the brim and scratched his head thoughtfully, then sighed with feigned gravitas. He was lamenting leaving behind his favored Blackmagic shoulder camera. "Won't be good quality."

"What's wrong with this one?" Talia asked, indicating one of the smaller handheld cameras.

Bam clucked and shook his head.

"You would have to carry it along with your other gear. It's going to add a lot of weight," Talia conceded with a shrug. "And you will have to figure out how to deal with the battery."

"That'll do," he saluted. The matter was closed, and Alabama brought his camera.

To reduce their overall load, everyone would share tents except Bam, who was too big to share, so his tent would store all the cameras and equipment in case it rained. Chase and Talia had sourced ultralight two person tents and a solar charging system to offset carrying a week's worth of batteries.

Bam, Glenn, and Lane were tasked with carrying the camera equipment, while the rest of the group brought the accommodations and food supply. Everyone was required to have one day's worth of food, a water filter, and an emergency blanket to survive alone in case they were separated. Talia assisted everyone in packing their wardrobe. They would each be heavy, but it was unavoidable. With their weight in mind, Talia split the hike into Lester over two days.

She surveyed the group, adjusting and fitting their packs like she had shown them, and her confidence grew. They were ready to embark.

"Are we good to go?" Chase clapped his hands. "Alright, then after you, m'lady."

"Okay, follow me!"

Talia entered the forest, and the *Dark Dimensions* team followed behind her. The first mile was quiet as everyone adjusted to carrying their pack and managing the terrain. Talia had warned them how difficult it would be to backpack for the first time, but they had all ignored her, eager to come.

Talia's feelings were still mixed about taking the team to Lester, and she had wondered many times over the last week how it would affect her. Her memories of the town were so co-mingled with the events around her grandfather's collapse, and the hardships that followed, the time period had become fragmented in her mind. She had long tried to cut off those recollections because they were disturbing and lacked clarity. In the daylight, it was easy to chalk it up to the imagination of a young girl lost in the forest. Late at night, when darkness fell, and the quiet earth settled in, she knew she had not imagined a single second of it.

The prospect of the hike and being surrounded by new people filled Talia with nervous energy. She had established herself amongst the members of the group. Summer and Talia were fast friends. Already they were texting throughout the day, finishing each other's sentences, and had met up a couple of times for drinks. Talia was drawn to her, and it was a whole new experience to pick up on someone's ideas the very moment they produced them. Talia imagined this is what having a sister was like.

After spending every day of the last week with Chase planning the logistics of the trip, her cool sentiments about him had warmed considerably. She enjoyed working with him. It was strange how well they related to each other. He was not the same person she knew in high school, and Talia was forced to accept his apology had been sincere. More and more, she caught him looking at her when he thought she wouldn't notice, and it secretly thrilled her. She didn't want to like him because she didn't trust him, and yet, she found herself considering the prospect. Everyone else, excluding Dean, had accepted her immediately.

Lane kept up the first few miles without breaking a sweat. She wondered about his background, trying to remember if she'd gotten around to asking him what kind of hiking experience he had. Her interactions with Lane over the last week had been limited. She knew almost nothing about him beyond his newness to the team. She could tell he fancied Summer, but Talia was confident every guy had a crush on Summer.

"How much do you know about Lester's history?" Lane asked.

"I know quite a bit. I grew up here. These woods are notorious for missing people. So many, I can barely remember them all," Talia replied. They followed what remained of the trail as it wound through the forest. The foliage had closed in and concealed the path. Sunlight poked through in small bright pockets, the earth giving the sweet smell of evaporating dew mingled with late season flowering plants and ripe berries. The wind tangled the branches overhead, and Talia took in a long lungful of air.

"We've gone through the records, historical and modern. It's hard to keep track," Lane said, waving a fly from his face. Talia glanced back and noticed the others had fallen behind.

"We should let them catch up," she said. He came to a halt, pulling his water bottle out and taking a sip.

"From the beginning, it seems like Lester's had a dark history. People say it's cursed," she continued. "Like the massacre."

"Everyone only knows the outcome. To this day, no one knows why Donovan did what he did. What do you know about the Stampede Pass Tunnel?" Lane asked.

"Almost nothing." Talia shrugged.

"On record, only twenty-eight men died during construction. Given the size of the project, that's unheard of. But there's almost no mention of the Chinese who worked on the tunnel, and they far outnumbered the other men. Their deaths weren't documented anywhere. The company just shipped their bodies back home to China in boxes. If they were concealing the number of the dead, how accurate do you think their other accounts are?"

"So, you're saying a bunch of people died, and then a company lied about it?" Talia joked. "Of course, they would sterilize the actual history to make it more palatable. Do you think they are hiding something?"

"Yes. I think a lot of men died there, and I don't think it's being made public for the same reason there are guards and fences around the watershed. Another example. The tunnel was dug out from both sides of the mountain, and the owner of the company offered a reward to the first man to connect the tunnels and pass through. The thing missing from every account of that day is who won the prize. The records include all kinds of trivial details, like the type of food served at the celebration, and how many cases of whiskey they ordered, but not a word about the winner. One of the books I read about Stampede Pass even referenced an overseer's journal where the pages from that day were removed," Lane explained.

"The journal is strange, I'll give you that," Talia acknowledged.

"A lot of workers for the tunnel came from the camps near Lester," Lane said. "When you start looking closer, there are too many coincidences."

Glenn and Bam came through the brush.

"This must be where the party's at." Bam grinned, lugging his camera over his shoulder, his cheeks flush with exertion. He had exchanged his favorite baseball cap for a black bandana. "I am sweatin' like a whore in church."

"Where are the others?" Talia asked.

"Those three are dragging, they say go ahead," Bam replied. Talia didn't like his answer.

"Let's slow down until they catch up," she replied.

"The fire at the sanitarium is another example, but there was more before that," Lane continued. "The doctor who bought the property and built the hotel was killed in a hunting accident after he married Dr. Lana Handel."

"I know, it was all very convenient," Talia offered. "Handel wasn't a real doctor. She got her medical license through a loophole in the legal system. Once her husband died, she started marketing the sanitarium as a health and weight loss clinic to sell her starvation cure. She would get her patients to sign over their estates and then starve them to death."

"She was real piece of work," Lane said.

"No kidding?" Glenn said.

"Totally swindled them," Talia explained. "She was nicknamed 'The Starvation Doctor.' She didn't just starve them though. She tortured them. She made people take long soaks in scalding hot water to sweat out all the toxins. Clients were forced to have daily enemas, for hours on end. She would clean them out, along with their wallets."

"Solid dad joke," Bam chuckled, offering up his fist to bump.

"Thanks." She returned the gesture.

"Her lawyer was in on it too, although he disappeared before the trial. The whole bit was working for her until she killed one of the Williams twins," Lane said. "The sisters were super rich: old British money. The surviving sister managed to get help, and the authorities shut Handel down."

"She was tried for murder," Talia said. She knew this tale. A local author had written a book about it, and all the locals had read it, including her.

"After they found bodies buried on the property and determined each of them had transferred their estate over to Dr. Handel, they had a good case against her. She was vocal in the beginning about her innocence and how people sometimes died because they were too sick from the start. One day, she stopped talking and never said another word. Didn't testify on her own behalf and went to prison without a peep," Lane went on.

"You're right! There was a ton of speculation she was covering something else up," Talia said. "It all ties in with the rumors about the missing people. Everyone always connects back to the cult."

"Was there a cult?" Bam asked.

"I think it's mostly a way to make sense of all the weird stuff that's happened out there," Talia replied with a shrug. "The town's been plagued with problems that a cult would have no control over. There was a train accident in 1911. Spanish Flu and Smallpox hit the town pretty hard too. The massacre was just the icing on the cake."

"But why'd they think there was a cult?" Bam pressed.

"It's a way to explain it, I suppose. I think there's something ancient there, something that existed long before any man came across it," Lane replied. Talia remained silent, considering her reservations about Lester. Her prior unease returned. What had she stumbled upon in Lester all those years ago? Had she imagined it all, or had she uncovered something darker?

They moved into a denser part of the forest where the trees were so tall they blotted out the sun, and the gloomy understory grew cold. A flicker of movement crossed the narrow trail in front of them. She stopped.

"Hold on," she said. The guys stopped behind her. The overgrown salmonberry shrub rustled. Something was in the thicket. Talia's heart pounded. She had the horrifying idea that the shadow creature, the one from the Rodriguez's basement, was there waiting for her. She took a step back.

Summer's laughter erupted behind them, and the thing hiding in the salmonberries crashed out onto the trail. A piebald deer, with splendid splashes of white across her tawny brown body, stood startled in the trail, her ears twisting with confusion.

"Whoa!" Glenn exclaimed. The doe turned and trotted off. Talia clutched her chest.

"Heavens to Betsy, I need a change of drawers," Bam announced. Talia, then Lane, burst out laughing.

"What are you guys doing?" Dean asked. Summer and Chase were with him, and Talia was glad to see they had caught up.

"You didn't see the monster that jumped out at us?" Bam laughed.

"They've been eating the mushrooms," Summer sighed, play acting as if she had been long suffering their antics, which sent them all into fresh peals of laughter.

"We should really keep moving," Talia interrupted, catching her breath.

"Fun sucker," Bam teased, then moved his hulking mass up the trail, swapping his camera from one shoulder to the other.

"How much further?" Glenn asked, falling in line.

"A ways," Talia replied. Summer groaned but saddled up behind Talia.

"Chase, you should tell Talia everything you found out about Lester," Lane said.

"Which part?" Chase asked.

"Your favorite bit. The boring part," Lane replied. This earned a few chuckles from the group.

"Oh, that part," Chase said, nodding. "What's boring about the most insane landgrab in history?"

"Oh my god, yawn," Summer said, sarcastically rolling her eyes.

"Okay, so maybe not the most insane, but once you hear it, you have to admit the details are downright strange. When I started researching Lester, this was actually what I came across first. The Green River was declared a watershed way back in the early 1900's, which you know of course, you lived on the edge of it."

Talia nodded.

"The railroad was already there, and a collection of towns had sprouted up along the line. The surrounding area is all national forest land. It was protected, but public. The City of Tacoma started buying land bordering the river under the pretense of building a dam. A lot of it was owned by private logging companies, who would be allowed to continue to operate. Later, they moved on to homeowners citing water quality and filtration. The city was snatching up every bit of land anyone wanted to sell, but they hit a snag with Lester. People didn't want to move, so politically, the Headworks, backed by Tacoma, started doing everything they could to shut down the town." Chase paused.

"Around the time of the massacre, BNSF was closing operations in Lester. They had diesel locomotives and didn't need the helper stations to get the engines over Stampede anymore. After the massacre, trains hardly stopped in Lester at all. When the jobs went, so did the local businesses. By the time the grocery store closed, there were only about one hundred or so residents left."

"You were right. This is the boring part," Glenn said to Lane. Chase ignored this, keeping his eyes downcast to watch his step, he continued to explain.

"Another thing worth noting was the dispute over the shared land use agreement with the National Forest Service. Historically, it allowed public access to all national forest land. The Forest Service and the City agreed to hammer out a resolution. They worked on it for over a year, only for the Tacoma officials to pull some underhanded maneuver and present an agreement in line with the city's objectives. They completely disregarded the terms both sides had agreed to. Did you ever hear about the Battle of Lester Gate?"

"What's that?" Talia asked, surprised she hadn't heard this story before.

"The Headworks installed and locked a gate on the main road in and out of Lester. A crew from King County came and tore it down. Really? You've never heard this before?" he asked.

"No. I only knew the stuff about the hotel and the massacre and the missing people. It's why everyone says Lester is haunted," she replied.

"The legal issues are even worse. Lester is in King County, and the city of Tacoma is in Pierce. King County sued the City for putting up the gate, and the City won. How did the City of Tacoma overcome King County, the wealthiest and most populated county in Washington State? They did the same thing to the National Forest Service and successfully negotiated a land agreement with the railroad, which is unheard of. Politically speaking, that's a lot of power."

"They always said it was water quality," Talia said. "Seems strange to let them kill the trees and run machinery in a protected area."

"Right, but if it's to protect the water, why let the railroad run at all? Why let logging continue? But a hundred people can't stay in their homes? The city bought the townsite for a song and a dance and then made the killing blow by backing legislation to close down the school district. Lester was done when the Legislature passed a bill that closed its school district for good. It was one of only two districts in the state to close. After that, there were no jobs left in the town. The Headworks conceded to allow a few of the last residents to stay, but their landholding was non-transferable: once they died, the property was condemned. The last living resident there had some notoriety."

"Are you talking about Greta?" Talia asked.

"Yes! Greta! I think the watershed is a cover, a perfect one. But you can't convince me that's the only reason. That's why I believe there's something more there. I think they are hiding something," Chase mused.

"Like what?"

"UFO's," Bam chirped.

"Sasquatch," Summer said.

"The lizard people," Lane laughed. A collective chuckle rippled through the group.

"Whatever it is, I don't know, but they have been trying to control it for the last century and used every tool at their disposal. Tacoma won fights they had no business winning. They forced everyone, and everything, out to let it sit empty. Explain that," Chase said, his tone forceful.

"Do you think its supernatural?" she asked after a long silence.

"Yes," Chase replied, vindicated. "It's kind of wild no one else has connected all of this together. For some reason, it seems to slide right off the history books. I think whatever 'it' is brings out the worst of humanity. I'll bet it's unlike anything we've seen before. Lester is a hotspot for violent and strange activity. Considering the number of residents in Lester's history, it has to have one of the highest violent death rates per capita in the United States."

"It's like that one town in Texas. La Plata, but the opposite. In La Plata, they had a violent crime rate of zero. It turned out to be something in the water," Glenn said.

"Whatever it is, we are going to find out," Chase replied.

May Third would go down in infamy as the day Norman Dyer was the first man to cross through the Stampede Pass Tunnel.

Norman first heard about the contest two years prior while sitting in a tavern in Pasco. The two men next to him were passing through on their way to drill a tunnel through the Cascades for the railroad. Norman was looking for a change of pace. He'd grown up in the desert, surrounded by a flat expanse of parched land and low dry mountains covered in scrub, and spent most of his life working as a farmhand. The job sounded exactly like what he needed. He offered to buy the two men a beer and asked them about the job.

The transcontinental line through the Cascades had been completed utilizing a system of switchbacks. The grade over Stampede Pass required multiple Decapod steam engines to get cars over it. The method was both slow and dangerous. The tunnel was an ambitious project, commissioned to expedite traffic, and the Northern Pacific wanted it finished as soon as possible.

Two crews worked on either side of the mountain to cut the passage through. It was hard work: in the beginning, the job was getting done in feet per day using hand drills. To encourage the crews, a contest was set. Whichever man passed through the bore tunnel first would be awarded $1,000, along with a steak dinner and whiskey for his entire team. It was the contest that sold him. It was not borne from a want of money; it was a want of glory. Norman wanted to go down in history as the person who completed the Stampede Pass Tunnel.

After he joined the east-side construction team, he learned he was not the only man in pursuit of this goal. For one, there was Silas Boyd who bragged to high heaven he was responsible for four of every six linear feet they excavated out of the tunnel. He was young, obnoxious, and full of ego. The labor of the Chinamen that worked invisibly alongside him accounted for nothing. There were five of them to every white man in Tunnel City and for good reason: they labored harder and longer, performing more difficult and dangerous work at every turn. They were paid far less than their white counterparts and were not entitled to the rights of the American and European workers, so the company filed them in. It was common practice. No railroad in the American West existed that Chinese hands did not build.

Silas did not care for the Chinamen. Many of the workers shared the same opinion, but few broadcast it like Silas did. At the end of one day, Silas balanced a gold panning plate on his head, yanked back his eyelids, and started shouting "ching chong bing bong" to get a rise out of the other men. It didn't go unnoticed. For weeks, every drill he used broke, the rock in the header wouldn't get cleared, and no one came when Silas hollered for assistance. Work eventually returned to normal. Silas never connected his behavior to the backlash, and what good is a lesson if the student doesn't learn?

Then there was Otto. Otto was friendly, affable, and a drunkard. When he was on a sober streak, Otto moved fast and clean. When he was hungover, it was a wonder he was even upright. He was regularly caught napping in the darker recesses of the tunnel. Occasionally, Otto showed up still drunk from the night before, and when he did, he spent more time sloppily telling everyone they were his best friend than he did working a drill.

Last was Benny Robbins. Norm knew Benny was the east-side's best chance of winning. Not only was he built like a horse jockey, short and thin, but he was fast. It was Benny's freak strength that sealed it though. Everyone talked about it. No one could beat Benny at arm wrestling. He could lift rocks over his shoulders that others could hardly move. He scared people, and the other workers kept their distance, although no man on the crew would admit it. Norm was fast and wiry too, but coming up against Benny, he would lose every single time.

Norm decided to create a little insurance. The person he turned to was Li Wei. Li was one of the Chinese supervisors: he oversaw the work being completed by the Chinese workers and connected with the white bosses on their behalf. He spoke English, well enough to translate, and all of the men respected him, except Silas, who respected no one. Li was regarded as the person to go to for anything you might need, and Norm had it on good authority several men had gone to him to procure a remedy or panacea.

The tunnel was nearly complete. When they were deep in the darkness, with only the faint light from the string of filament bulbs overhead, in the brief seconds when all work would stop, there was the sound of scraping and hammering in the walls. Recently, the sound of men's voices could be heard.

Confident the following day would find him entering the west end of the tunnel, Norm prepared a cold box, buying ice and several bottles of root beer. He worked the cap off of one of the bottles, careful to remove it without warping the metal. When the bubbles settled inside the bottle, he sipped a little off the top, then poured in a bit of the bone-colored powder from the envelope Li had slipped to him three days prior. He went through this process for three of the bottles, marking the caps of the "infused" root beers. After pressing the bottle caps back on, he heated them to help with the seal. He admired his handiwork; they were indistinguishable from the others unless you knew what to look for.

Norm arrived at the work site before any of the other workers. He brought the cooler to the mess area and hid it behind a scrub pine.

"What's that?" Silas had snuck up behind him. He poured himself a cup of coffee from the one of the pots. They were alone for the moment.

"Want one?" Norm leaned down, snagged a bottle from the icy cooler, and tossed it to Silas.

"Dandy." He slid the root beer under his armpit and picked up his cup of joe. "Good thing it's cool in the cave, supposed to be a scorcher today." He squinted up at the sun.

"That's why I thought these would be a good idea," Norm said. Silas rewarded him with his idiot grin.

A few of the "firecracker" men, the group of Chinese explosives handlers, passed by with tea in their hands. The Chinese had a separate mess, separate camp, and separate food. Everything was separate. It was simple racism, although some argued the Chinese had questionable cooking methods. Norm thought the food smelled wonderful. Silas took that as his cue to go.

Norm waited around, taking a cup of coffee for himself, and biding his time. When Otto appeared, it was plain he was hungover. A cloud of whiskey surrounded him. His eyes were red-rimmed and watery, skin ashen, and a full day of stubble covered his face. From the look in his eyes, Otto was somewhere between falling asleep and fighting back the urge to vomit.

"Otto." Norm nodded toward the cooler. The man looked at him, the offer not registering. Norm reached into the cooler, found one of the marked bottles, and held it out to him. Excited by the brown bottle, Otto reached for it immediately.

"Root beer," Norm said. Otto barely masked the look of disappointment but accepted it anyway. He popped the cap off with a bottle opener slid from his pocket and took a tentative sip. When he found it agreed with him, he took a couple of long swallows and belched appreciatively.

"Ooooh, I needed that," he said. His smile revealed the gap of a missing tooth. "Thanks Norm, you're a pal." He took another drink, collected his helmet, and moved toward the tunnel opening. Norm had a pang of guilt; Otto hardly needed the help this morning. *Insurance,* he reminded himself.

As the morning sun warmed the hillside, he continued to loaf around by the cooler, watching the incoming men come to grab coffee, slide on their helmets, and sling their pickaxes and drills over their shoulder, then meander toward the tunnel. Li Wei passed by him.

"Li!" Norm waved and tossed him a bottle of root beer. Li was caught off guard, but his face lit up when he saw the drink. He came over to Norm.

"You set me up?" Li asked, chuckling a bit. Norm shook his head.

"Wouldn't dream of it," Norm replied. Li used a tooth to open the bottle and took a sip. His face puckered from the bite of carbonation. When the taste set in, he beamed and nodded at Norm.

"Good luck today. Hopefully, magic powder help," Li laughed, tipping his helmet to him.

"I expect it will," Norm replied. Li nodded at him again, then moved on to the tunnel.

Norman's dawdling was drawing attention from the mess cook. He had no explanation for why he was still standing around with his thumb up his ass, especially if the foreman swept through. As he was grabbing a couple of bottles to carry into the tunnel, hoping to find Benny inside, the small man came jogging up. He looked harried and was clearly rushing, which made it all the more awkward to stop him.

"Hey, Benny!" Norm called. Benny shot him a look as he ran past. When Norm tossed him the bottle, Benny snatched it effortlessly out of the air. He looked down at the brown glass and back at Norm with confusion.

"What's this?" Benny asked.

"Root beer. Grabbed a few last night," Norm replied. A flash of distrust crossed Benny's face. He reversed his step, walking backwards into the tunnel as he faced Norm. Benny was not buying what he was selling.

"You just wanted to share?" Benny chuckled. He glanced down at the bottle again, skeptical, but with a trace of humor on his face. Norm panicked. He held up his own bottle, worked the cap off with his belt buckle, and took a deep drink, gasping a little when he finished. Benny eased a bit.

"You asking me out on a date?" Benny asked.

"Yeah, I'm a nice guy," Norm quipped back, then walked past Benny without meeting his eye. The tactic worked, Benny shrugged and slid the bottle into his back pocket. Norm was dismayed. Dealing with the others was a moot point if Benny didn't drink his root beer. Silas and Otto might present an inconvenience, but Benny was the real competition. He fought back a sinking feeling.

They stepped into the darkness of the tunnel, their eyes adjusting to a string of filament bulbs that glowed overhead. It was then he heard a clink and *tsssssss* as the cap popped off the bottle. Relief washed over him.

"This is pretty good," Benny said as they continued forward. Relieved, Norman smiled to himself. Groups of Chinese were widening the tunnel, removing the bench layers to bring the passage to its full width and height. They did not look up at the two men as they passed and continued to load rocks into the bins of the narrow steam engine used to move the cleared debris.

Norm pulled a lump of wax from his pockets, rolling it between his fingers to warm it, then placed a ball in his ears. The clanging of metal on rock quieted. The cavern continued to narrow as they went, closing in the longer they walked, and it was a long walk, at least three quarters of a mile. They would walk fifteen to twenty minutes to the bore.

At the end of the heading, they found Silas and Otto working side by side, chatting amiably. Norm caught the last fragment of their conversation.

"He changed sides last week. Said there was something off with some new guys from Dean's Mill. They work fast, but you didn't want to get in their way. Nasty business," Silas explained to Otto, who was only half-listening.

Norm tuned the rest out, stepping in beside them. He picked up his hand drill and set it to the stone. Benny followed suit. The work was hard. Structure and support were under constant evaluation. The engineers would check if the rock would hold before ordering blasting through the walls or allowing the use of the air drills. It made progress slow to switch back to hand drills for the time being, but as the headings drew close to meeting, caution was warranted. His thoughts drifted, his hearing dulled by the wax, and he fell into a rhythm.

The foursome had worked up a good sweat when it started happening. Silas stopped working. He crouched down, seeming in a state of deep focus. Silas stood up again, picked up his tools, then stopped. His confusion and frustration evident. Silas glanced back down the tunnel and grimaced. Norm chuckled a little to himself. The kid glanced around, checked on the other guys, and then adjusted the front of his pants.

"I need to take a shit!" Silas announced loudly and dropped his tools. Norm did his best to suppress a smirk as Silas duck-walked to the front of the tunnel with his hard hat carried in front of him. Norm returned to his drill work, hoping and praying any second he would break through to a hollow space on the other side. Moments later, Otto cursed and swore.

"What the hell?" he spat. Without ceremony, he reached into his pants and rearranged what he found there. Norm nearly choked on his own laughter.

"I need a break," Otto said as low as he could above the din of echoes bouncing around the cavern.

"What's the problem?" Norm asked, removing a ball of wax from his ear, and feigning as much innocence as he could muster.

"I haven't had a boner like this in over ten years, and today I could punch through the rock with this hard on. It actually hurts. I need to go. I can barely see straight. All I can think about is my goddamn dick," Otto was laughing as he spoke, but he was distressed. Guilt leaked back into Norm's thoughts, but there was also a glimmer of pride. He might be able to pull this off.

"I'll be back if I can get rid of this thing," Otto said, his eyes watering. Norm could not tell if they were tears of pain or amusement. The old man abandoned the site. Norm had hardly picked up his drill again when he caught Benny watching him from the corner of his eye. He pretended to be unaware, instead shaking his head at Otto's departure as if to say "that guy," and continued to work on the rock in front of him.

For a while it was only the two of them working side by side, not speaking and breaking the stone layer loose from the back of the tunnel. Benny slowed, hesitating. He surreptitiously fussed with his pants. He shot a glance over at Norm, who did his best to appear not to notice. Benny knew. He dropped his drill, walked over to Norm, and shoved him hard.

"What was in those sodas, friend?" he asked, inches from Norman's face. Norm took a couple steps back and held up his hands. Benny grabbed the front of his shirt.

"What the fuck was in the root beer?" Benny demanded. "You're a real son of a bitch. This is about the contest, isn't it?" Benny cocked back his fist. "Dick powder in the soda? Are you a pervert, Norman? Were you hoping for a little action? I'll tell everyone you are a fucking fa..."

Norm winced, shutting his eyes against Benny's incoming fist.

"No. No. Do not fight," Li urged, pushing himself between Norman and Benny. He worked on loosening Benny's grip. "Some time happen, special property of gun powder."

"What?" Benny asked.

"Gun powder give you big dick," Li lied smoothly. He made a fist to show Benny, then shrugged and laughed. Everyone, except Silas, had a soft spot for Li, and Benny was no different. He dropped Norm's shirt, but shoved him again, hard. Li grabbed him before he could go down. Benny brushed past Li and ambled his way up the tunnel. Norm's plan had worked. It was left to him and Li.

"It work," Li said, suppressing his laughter. "Will wear off in a couple hours, better get to work." Norm nodded. Li brought out a small stick of dynamite, and Norman's pulse juddered. Li affixed the stick into a crack, working it into the stone until only the long fuse stuck out. Li gave it an appraising look, nodded, then pulled out his matches.

"Are you sure it's safe?" Norm asked.

"I am engineer. Just small hole."

Norm was unsure, but he had already come this far. He said no more and gave Li a thumbs up.

"Stand back," Li said, lighting a match and bringing it up to the fuse. Norm dashed away, laying low behind a pile of stone. Li ran after him like a mad man and lay down beside him, plugging his ears. Li wore an ecstatic grin on his face. The blast came, and the ground shook. Debris blew past the pair, and the tunnel filled with dust. They remained there for several beats as the air cleared, then stood up to inspect their work. Squinting, Norm focused the headlamp on his helmet and scanned the wall.

"I go get hammer," Li said and hurried off.

Norman looked closer. There was an opening, a small hole had been punched through. He placed his eye against it, peering into the space on the other side. He heard workers in the cavern, saw their shadows further down the tunnel, but he saw no one. Norm was the only one aware it existed. He would have to be careful. If the west-siders saw him before he was through, they would be working double time to expand the opening and climb through themselves. Norman put the hand drill to work clearing the rock. Methodically, he widened the hole to make it big enough to slide through.

Norm moved fast. He would only have a moment before the west-side's team noticed him through the bore. They might try to stop him from getting through if it meant their side would lose. Working on the gap in the stone, quietly removing pieces of the wall, his heart pounded in his ears. After the last two years, here was the culmination of all his effort. While he had not done it alone, he had sweated and toiled to prove himself. When he was promoted to the front line, he fought hard to push their team forward foot by foot. He'd earned this. With a final hunk removed, the hole was wide enough to slide through. He got down on his knees and peered through. He was still alone, so he proceeded to birth himself onto the other side.

The ground was cold and hard, the stones scratching through his shirt as he carefully pulled himself through, minding to avoid dragging his softer bits across the sharp earth. Squeezing between the rock, his hips resisted. He wriggled and squirmed until they slid past. He pulled himself onto the floor of the west-side tunnel and stood. He'd done it, he was the first through the bore. The prize would be his. Norman Dyer would go down in history.

Two men trained their headlamps on him. They said nothing. Norm grinned at them, wanting to laugh out loud. Glory was his.

"You did it!" He heard Li's voice say from behind him. Norm turned to find his head stuck out of the hole, looking up at him and laughing. Before Norm could reply, the two men came forward, grabbed Li, and yanked him through. Li screamed, struggling in vain to fight them off.

Norm was a coward, and just like a coward he had no intention of intervening, so he turned to run away. He understood they would not allow a Chinaman to claim the prize, but expected since they had witnessed his achievement, they would let him exit the tunnel to validate his victory.

Norm fled, crashing into a wall, and wound up sprawled out with a rock in his ass. The wall was not a wall, but a man with the stature of a bear. He leaned down, seized Norm by his throat and brought their faces together. The man's eyes were bottomless black pools, opening to a world of darkness beyond this reality. A place of sheer terror, oppressive bleak existence, and evil. The man sealed off Norman's air with his grip, and his bladder let go.

"There was never a chance for you," he said. He threw him to the ground, brought out a cannister, and poured it over Norm's body. The pungent, toxic fumes gagged him and burned his eyes. Kerosene. Norm sputtered, unable to breathe with the gas filling his airway.

On his hands and knees, trying to find an escape through his blurred vision, he saw Li. One man held Li's arms behind his back, angling them upward so Li was forced to bend forward until his head was almost touching the ground. He begged in Chinese, speaking rapidly, but his supplications were going ignored. The other man came forward with no hesitation and sank a pickax into Li's skull. It made a sickening crunch. Norm screamed. Li's face went slack, and they dropped him carelessly onto the cavern floor. Norm tried to scramble away when he was kicked in the ribs. He dropped face down onto the earth.

"We are going to bury you in the walls," one of the men laughed. Norm dived for the hole and was kicked again. One of the men yanked the ax out of Li's head, and a chunk of skull came with it, exposing the meat underneath. Norm screamed again, choking on the gas. He coughed and flailed for the hole he'd entered through. Pain flared in his side, one of his ribs was surely broken, but if he could just get back to the eastern side.

One of the men approached, flicking a match alight with his thumb, and tossing it into the puddle surrounding Norm. The gas flared blue and consumed him. There was no air to scream again, only scalding white hot fire. Norm's skin burned, blistered, and began to melt. He watched one the men lean down to examine the hole. They were stealing his achievement. And that was Norman's last sight on earth. All went black as his eyeballs burst in their sockets, boiled from the inside. His skin melted, and his nerve endings burned away; the pain dissipated. As he lay dying, he thought of their eyes, eyes like coal. Eyes full of darkness, cold and unfeeling, like windows into the soul of the universe.

Talia scoured the mountainside to locate the route up to the fire lookout. The old trail they had followed hadn't seen a hiker in ages. The deeper into the wilderness they went, the more overgrown it had become. After a stretch of long abandoned service road, the path to this spot was no better than a game trail, but if her calculations were correct, the structure was at the top of the ridge.

They made a long pit stop next to a shallow creek to gather water, eat, and rest before the final climb. The late afternoon sun was beginning its slow descent into the western sky, but the air was thick. Everyone, except for Lane who appeared to take the trip as a personal challenge, was exhausted.

"Are we really going up there?" Summer asked. She had been careful not to whine throughout the hike, but her resolve was faltering.

"It's not as bad as it looks," Dean reassured her. Summer shot him a disbelieving glance.

"Why can't we just camp here for the night?" she asked.

"I thought about it," Talia replied, squeezing water through her filter into her water bottle. "Is that what everyone wants to do? I figured it would be easier to finish with this at the end of a long day rather than wake up and start with climbing a mountain." The plan was to start in the morning next to the lookout, traverse down the ridge, and follow Lester Creek until it met the Green River. From there, they would cross the river using the same train trestle that she had when she was eight.

"Today," Lane said.

"Today." Glenn seconded, soaking his feet in the cool water. Bam was beside him doing the same.

"Let's get it over with," Bam said.

"You guys were supposed to be on my side," Summer groused.

"Majority rules," Dean said.

"Come stick your feet in the water. They'll feel better," Bam said.

Talia extended their break another thirty minutes. They started up the thin mountain path at a snail's pace with Lane as the exception. He wore a focused, almost grim look, but seemed unphased by the challenge. The tree line gave way to exposed hillside and scraggly subalpine firs. A cluster of huckleberry shrubs full of dark indigo berries lined the trail. They both stopped to pluck a few while they waited for the remainder of the group to catch up.

"We're close, aren't we?" Lane asked, monitoring the slow pace of the team as they trudged up the path. Talia nodded, her mouth full of tart berry juice.

"This is exciting for you, isn't it? I can see it on your face. You love this," he observed.

"Am I that easy of a read?" she asked, a little embarrassed at her own transparency. "You know, I came out here when I was a girl."

"Chase said something about that," Lane said as he picked more berries.

"What exactly did Chase tell you?" she asked, plucking a few more for herself and popping them into her mouth. The breeze refreshed her, and the sweat on her temple dried. The rest of the group still had a few switchbacks to navigate through, so they had time to enjoy it. They were closing in on the final few hundred feet up the mountain, and the last section was precarious. Talia wanted to ensure everyone was together.

"He said you grew up in Palmer. That you lived on the edge of town in the woods, like nowhere close to civilization," he said. "He was murky on the details but said you wandered off and got lost in the forest. Your grandfather had a stroke, and police suspected you went to look for help because no one taught you how to use the phone. No one knew where you went. Did you come this far?" Lane asked.

To hear her history so casually retold with the narrative of her false heroism made her stomach sick. She tossed the last of the berries in her hand over the cliff and reached for her water. The fruit in her mouth had turned into glue.

"I knew how to use the phone," Talia replied sharply, catching herself off-guard. She softened. "I stayed in this lookout."

"Have you been to Lester?" Lane asked. His full interest was on her.

"Yes. I found it."

Lane's eyes widened, exaggerating their deep blue color.

"And?"

"And nothing." She closed the question with a long drink of her water and gazed out over the miles of forest below them. She could sense he wanted to ask more questions, thankfully the others had almost caught up.

"Couple of bloody mountain goats, you two!" Bam hollered, his face beet red. He looked half-crazy, the bandana forcing his wild hair to stand on end. He carried his camera under one arm. "We're moving like a herd of turtles!"

"Take a break, get some water," Talia ordered, all too happy to change the subject. "We are done after this climb. It's only a short distance along the ridgeline to the lookout." Summer nodded, unable to speak as she gasped for air, and bent forward bracing her hands on her knees. Every one of them was struggling, and it showed in their soaked shirts and heaving chests. Dean's hair had managed to remain perfect despite all the miles they had hiked. Chase squeezed past the others to where she stood next to the huckleberries.

"Are you good?" he asked her, out of breath. The deeper question was in his eyes. Lane, sensing this was a more personal inquiry, moved up the trail to give them space.

"I'm good," she replied.

"You sure?" he said.

Only she knew the real story about her experience in Lester. Everyone believed there was an underlying trauma associated with her grandfather's stroke, and she allowed them the assumption rather than provide the actual details. The only thing she felt for her grandfather when he collapsed was relief. It was laughable someone had made up a narrative where she didn't know how to use a phone. She knew it stemmed from their poverty; stupid and poor went hand in hand. And she was ashamed to admit she was grateful they had stereotyped her because otherwise she would have to explain why she abandoned him during his medical emergency.

Talia never told anyone about the locked pantry in her childhood home. Looking back, she suspected her mother had been secretly grateful she'd broken into it and hidden the lock and key. How would she have explained that to the authorities when they arrived? The alarm on the fridge had also disappeared by the time she returned home. The police drew their own conclusions about why an eight-year-old had walked into the forest and therefore, there had never been a reason to call in child protective services.

If anyone knew the real food situation in Grandfather's house, her disappearance would have been reframed as a bold escape, and further investigation would have revealed the bruises on her little brothers' bodies.

Talia understood all of this at her young age. She knew there was something wrong at Grandfather's house the same way she knew telling a grown-up or teacher about the abuse, and the way Grandfather looked at her, would likely result in her losing the only parent she had. If she told someone, she would be left with no one. It was never even an option for her. Instead, she stored away those dark secrets behind the pantry door in her mind and secured it with a bright, shining lock.

In truth, time had made the lock grow rusty, and the hasp loosen from the frame. The years of facing insurmountable debt and the crushing failure of her business, along with Craig's ongoing cruelty, had tested the strength of her defenses and threatened to tear it all down. Her control over that secret pain was failing, and she knew it was only a matter of time before the lock no longer held.

"I'm doing great," Talia replied. She wasn't sure whether to be flattered or annoyed by the attention.

"You just seem a little tense," he replied, reaching out to touch her arm. His hand was warm on her skin. Talia laughed, and it was genuine.

"I'm definitely stressed, this is a tough climb, and I'm worried about all of you making it up. Everyone except for him." Talia indicated to Lane, who had ranged ahead in order to map out their trail. Given the team's overall lack of experience, she was relieved there was at least one knowledgeable person she could rely on.

"Yeah, you're right," Chase admitted a little sheepish.

"Are you guys ready? I want everyone together for this next part," Talia called down to them.

"Uncle!" Bam responded, there were a couple of chuckles from the gang.

"I'll take that as a yes," she said to Chase. "Are you ready?"

"I am," he said, his eyes locked on hers. There was something exchanged in that look. Her face heated, but she didn't avert her gaze.

"Then let's go," she called past him.

Talia picked her way up the mountain, following Lane's footprints in the dust. She took cautious steps to ensure the ground was firm and stable before allowing it to bear her full weight. She pointed to handholds for the others. The trail was wide enough for a single person, but the mountain face was sheer.

As they neared the top, the pitch grew steeper. Talia had been in difficult situations hiking before, but not with six people in tow. She found it a little unbelievable she had done this as a child. The danger hadn't even occurred to her. *It was still safer than what you were returning home to*, she thought. Above her, she watched Lane slide over a precipice with his body pressed against the rock.

"Looks like the trail washed out a bit here," he called down to her. "It's sketchy." A pit formed in Talia's stomach. Lane was right, there was a four-foot section of the trail that had slid down the slope, leaving only a lip of stone sticking out of the cliffside.

"What do you mean, 'it's sketchy?'" Summer demanded; anxiety evident in her tone. Talia hurried ahead to gauge the difficulty.

"Did you test that?" Talia asked, indicating the rock. Lane nodded.

"It's stable," he responded. She hugged the cliff face and stepped onto the lip, no wider than a handrail. She shuffled across on the front of her feet, the heels of her boots stepping on nothing but air. It was precarious, but entirely doable. The gap was minor, and the ground on either side of the split was firm. A fall would result in a short slide to the trail below.

"Talia, Summer is going to need help," Chase said across the gap. He put his hands onto the dusty earth above as Talia had done before him and slid across. She flattened herself so he could pass by her, their bodies pressing up against each other. The proximity gave her a rush.

"Hey," he said.

"Hi." She smiled brightly. She pointed up at Lane.

"Follow him, he's going to show you where to go. I'll get her," she replied. She removed her pack and set it in the widest spot she could find, then navigated back across the gap. Talia passed the others as they came up. Dean met her with a worried expression on his face.

"Can you help her?" he asked. Talia nodded and scooted around him. Summer crouched at the bottom of the switchback taking long deep breaths. Talia leaned down and grabbed her hand. Summer looked up, surprised.

"I'm okay," she said, trying to wave Talia off.

"You clearly aren't," Talia said. "Let me help you." Summer took in a shaky breath.

"So, funny story: I have a fear of heights," she said. "But in my defense, no one said we were climbing a mountain."

Talia laughed. "You're completely safe. I will walk you through it." Talia moved into a position below Summer. "Just focus on your footing and hand placement, and I will tell you where to step. Don't look down."

"Okay." Summer said in a thin voice. They had only gone a few steps when Summer stopped.

"I can't do this," she choked out, her body frozen in place. Talia remained behind her.

"Yes, yes, you can. I know you can," Talia replied.

The others had navigated across the gap without any issue, and Lane had led them up the short embankment to the top of the ridge. Spotting the trouble, he was already heading back down to their position, while the others waited and watched.

"I can't move," Summer replied, turning her head to lock eyes with Talia. They were wide and full of fear.

"I'm going to remove your pack." Talia reached around Summer and undid the clasps on her chest and hip belt. Summer whimpered as the full weight of the bag sank onto her shoulders. She rocked, off balance, and nearly toppled over. Talia caught the bag with one hand, and Summer with the other.

"Shit," Summer hissed through gritted teeth. Talia swung the pack to the ground.

"Okay, here we go," Talia's tone firm. She pressed her body against Summer's, wrapped an arm around her waist and walked step by step up the trail until they reached the gap.

"Oh my god," Summer choked out, she tried to turn away, but Talia held her.

"Take my hand," Talia said. Summer shook her head but put her hand in Talia's anyway. Easing past, Talia stepped out and balanced on the rock lip, one hand clasping Summer's and the other on the cliff wall.

"Eyes on me," Talia commanded. "I will bring you across, but you have to listen to me. I climbed this mountain when I was eight. Can you believe that?" Summer shook her head. "I'm going to hang onto you. Do you see this lip I am standing on? Face the mountain and step onto it with your toes, I've got you." Talia slid back until their arms were outstretched. Summer placed her left foot on the lip, her eyes flicking down to where the ground slid away.

"Okay, good. Now look at me, Summer. Look at me," Talia spoke calmly, her grip on Summer's hand had grown filmy with sweat. Summer slid her right foot next to her left, and Talia stepped back again across the gap. Summer's whole body was shaking.

"I can't," Summer whispered.

"You can. I am going to pull you over. I won't let you fall," Talia said.

"Why am I so afraid?" Summer said, her eyes filling with tears.

"Because you have nothing else to be afraid of," Talia replied. Summer was freezing up, Talia could see the terror on her face. She shored up her grasp on Summer's hand, gripped her arm with her other hand and planted her feet.

"Ready?"

"No."

"Count of three. One…"

"No."

"Two…" Talia yanked her forward, mid-word, before Summer could brace herself against it. Talia's footing slid out, but Summer was in her arms. She thought, for a brief second, she had made a serious error because they were falling. They were going down together. Then Lane caught them.

"Gotcha," he said. Relief washed over Talia.

"I thought for sure we were going down," Talia replied.

"Not even close. You would have landed on the trail," he replied. Summer's teeth were chattering.

"Lane, will you grab her bag? I'm going to help her the rest of the way. Summer, it just gets easier from here," Talia said, as they walked up the final rise.

Summer said nothing.

"You did amazing," Talia responded, rubbing her friend's shoulder. Summer nodded and wiped a rogue tear from her face.

When they reached the top, Dean was the first to Summer's side.

"Are you okay?" he asked. Summer nodded, and he put a protective arm around her. The others approached giving Summer high fives and proclaiming her achievement. Bam howled like a wolf. Dean looked back at Talia and mouthed a, 'thank you.' As a group they moved toward the fire lookout, visible ahead of them. Talia waited for Lane. She admired the landscape, familiarity sweeping over her with the breathtaking view. Lane popped up with Summer and Talia's packs over his shoulders. He passed Talia's off to her.

"Thank you for your help," Talia said, as Lane fitted back into his own backpack. "Do you want me to take Summer's pack?"

"Eh, I think I got it," he replied casually. "And you're welcome."

"What did you do before you started with the team?" she asked.

"Built and repaired cell phone towers in Alaska," he responded, snapping the buckles into place, and adjusting his straps. "I was a lineman before that, but they pay you more when you are hanging up there at four hundred feet in the air. I'm used to doing crazy shit." When he grabbed one of the straps on Summer's pack, Talia took the other to share the load.

"And you came to do this?" Talia asked, a little surprised. They walked together with the bag between them.

"I'm just taking some time off between projects," Lane replied.

"If I had known you could do this, they certainly wouldn't have needed me," Talia replied.

"Not true. We absolutely need you," Lane said. The group ahead was approaching the fire tower. They celebrated Summer's success, and the completion of the day's hike.

"Hey ladies!" Bam hollered across the bluff. "We made it!" Talia waved back. Their voices echoed as they hooted and yelled.

"This is pretty cool," Lane said as they walked.

"Agreed," she replied. It looked exactly the same as it had twenty years prior, and after this night, she would never return again.

Wrapped in her thick winter coat, Rose Travers watched rain splatter and run in thick rivulets down the windowpane of the train car. The other passengers murmured optimistically about the warming weather. Rose did not hold the same elation. Her restlessness was like a dull, painful itch under the surface of her skin. March First would be the sixth day the passengers on the Northern Pacific Stampede line would be trapped on an unmoving train just outside of the town of Lester.

The snow accumulation was so dense through the mountains, the train could not continue to its final destination, the terminus of the rail line, in Tacoma. They were waiting for the snow to clear. The decision was made that the passengers would remain on the train. She had gathered this information by employing her usual habit of eavesdropping on adults in conversation. It was how she learned the hotel was unreachable for the same reason the train could not move. The shops and stores were closed. The tavern was an option because an enterprising fellow had dug out a path to the front door. The passengers could only reach it if they were willing to wade through the uncleared streets to get there. The passengers utilized the sleeper cars, and while the food supply was dwindling, everyone was eating. In the end, even if they could have debarked, there was nothing to do and nowhere to go.

In the prior days, Rose had cozied up in her seat, reading and watching the snow fall through the condensation coated glass. It had been a romantic notion at first, whiling the hours away, safe and warm, sinking deep into another world as puffy flakes drifted outside. Later, it became something to occupy her when the other children were too much to tolerate. They were often annoying, and she'd finished all of her books.

She'd played dolls with Natalie, but the younger girl kept insisting on story lines that centered around homemaking and taking care of babies. Rose found this endlessly dull. When she would try to break out of the narrative, and pretend like her doll was a trapeze artist, similar to the one she had seen in the circus back home, Natalie became petulant. Rose tried to cajole her into playing something else altogether, proposed the two dolls were a pair of lady robbers in the Old West, and Natalie slid into a full-on fit at the suggestion. She had thought since Natalie was six and Rose eight, and therefore more worldly and mature, she could convince her to go along. Instead, she withstood the tantrum with patience, played along with Natalie's storyline a little longer, then feigned exhaustion, claiming she was in dire need of a nap.

Another day, Rose played marbles with a cluster of three boys around her age. Rose had never played marbles before, and being new to it, she found she had no talent whatsoever for the game. The boys had lent her a few pieces to start, each taking a couple from their own purse, to make it an even four to play. At first, she had greedy thoughts of winning all the colorful glass orbs for herself, until she discovered the oldest boy was something of a shark. Round after round, he amassed a fine collection, and being the sore loser she was, her interest waned. With her last marble gone, she excused herself. The boys, entrenched in their own battle of the wills, did not notice or care.

One of the Northern Pacific's staff gave her a deck of cards, and Rose valiantly rallied the other children into playing Old Maid. Her father had taught her the game back home and while she knew how to play, teaching the others was another matter. She stumbled over the instructions and half-forgot rules, only to remember them again mid-play. She grew frustrated that they didn't *know* what to do. When the other children grew bored, they fidgeted and wiggled, and eventually stopped paying attention. The more Rose tried to maintain a sense of order, the more of a free-for-all it became. She withdrew from the group having lost all control and retreated to a table in one of the dining cars where she played a game of solitaire.

As the number of days piled up, all Rose could think about was getting off the train. The novelty of travelling across the country had lost its appeal somewhere around the border of Idaho and Montana. They had been trapped for six whole days mere hours from their destination. The anticipation and stagnation made Rose want to scream with boredom. The other passengers were in a similar mindset.

Shortly after exiting the Stampede Pass Tunnel, there was an announcement that a weather event would force them to stop. This caused a significant amount of frustration from the passengers of the Northern Pacific. To remedy their troubles, many of the adults collectively decided to join together in the saloon car for the length of the day. The drinking began in earnest, and the revelry filtered through the surrounding cars. What started out as good fun soon turned sour, and by day three the bar car had grown so raucous, a fight broke out and a few glasses ended up smashed. The conductor admonished the passengers as if they were schoolchildren and enforced a strict two drink limit per day. Later, he amended it to three, and then four, drinks because he was beholden to the same set of rules, and it was spoiling his good time.

As the days stretched on, the air inside the cars had grown close and fragrant with the odor of sour armpits and unwashed bodies. There was an uptick in hushed arguments amongst the other passengers. While these quarrels served to entertain Rose in the short term, it heightened the lingering tension.

On the morning of the sixth day, when people woke to find the storm had transitioned from snow to rainfall, there was a general increase in positive energy. They were nearing the end of their confinement. Rose glowered out the window at the landscape covered in heavy blankets of powder as dark clouds raced across the sky. On the opposite peak, the trees danced, their boughs bending under their freezing weight, shedding their heavy burden to the ground below. She watched in a trance, having lost interest in attempting to coordinate or associate with any of the other children. Her father sat next to her, taking tender sips of apple juice, and nibbling a dry, unbuttered piece of toast. He was hungover again.

"How are you doing, Rosie? Are you getting hungry?" he asked, patting her leg. She shook her head without looking at him. She loved her daddy, but she was angry with him for abandoning her day after day to go sit in the lounge car with the other adults. As much as she wanted to lash out at him, she restrained herself. Her present state was the best she could do. She wished she had stayed back east with her mother and three siblings if this was a sign of things to come.

The rest of the family would follow in the summer. Her older sister had stayed behind to help her mother with the younger two: her four-year-old brother, Johnny, and the baby, Sue Ellen. She suspected, though, her mother had foisted her upon her father, brought along because she was a, "handful." Her father had presented it to her like she was, "Daddy's Special Girl." In truth, Rose was Allen Travers' favorite. She was precocious, had no tolerance for bullshit, and was known to be quite bullheaded, much like Allen's father, whom he admired. Allen could swear sometimes the words Rose said were channeled from the old man himself.

Allen Travers was moving the family to Tacoma. He had been hired as an engineer to help design a water system to sustain the growing city and its surrounding farmland. They were, in fact, overlooking the source of Tacoma's water system from where they sat. The land sloped at a gentle grade to the basin where the Green River ran. It was a swollen flume of deep sapphiric blue in winter. When he had travelled here six months ago to interview for the job, the water had been a glassy green hue, hence the channel's namesake.

Lightning flashed, igniting the train car with light. After a few seconds, thunder followed echoing through the valley from miles away. A woman screamed, and one of the children cried. She suspected it was one of the young boys she had played marbles with and felt smug. Unafraid, and having grown up in the Midwest where thunderstorms and tornadoes were the norm, Rose searched the sky for the next bolt to cross it.

"You sure you don't want something?" Allen tried again, sensing Rose's contempt for him. He was also hoping a bit of whiskey would ease his discomfort. Allen Travers was not an alcoholic, but in the absence of anything else to do, the alcohol calmed his nerves and helped pass the time.

"No," Rose said trying to make her voice sound angry but not too much. It didn't have the effect she hoped it would. She wanted him to ask her what was wrong and talk to her. She wanted him to stay, but instead, he stood and adjusted his trousers.

"Alright, well I'll be back in a jiff," he replied. She glanced up at him, the shock of her father's abandonment apparent on her face. She realized he was going to get a drink and had tried to cover it up by pretending he was going to fetch something *she* wanted. She folded her arms and knitted her brows together, then turned away from him, and sat back to look up at the sky. Allen noted the look of disdain from his daughter. He had a momentary flash of guilt. *No matter how much she reminds me of my dad, she still looks like her mother when she's angry,* he thought. For a moment, he missed his wife desperately and wished she were due to join them with the other children before late June. With that thought, he took his sadness down to the lounge car to get a drink and chat with the other passengers.

Rose marked the darkening sky. The lightning accelerated in frequency, and the thunder grew louder and longer, as the storm passed overhead. The rain washed over the train in torrents, distorting her view of the forest on the far side of the river. As the water poured over them, she imagined they were in a submarine under the ocean. Her father had told her about the underwater boats, explaining to her in great detail how they were used to navigate the seven seas and could go for days without rising to the surface. She imagined she was the captain of a submarine, the other passengers were her crew, and they were embarking on a journey into the arctic where unknown forms of life awaited.

Thunder rocked the train. Rose adjusted her narrative. She remained the captain, but they were under attack. An enemy boat was bombing their submarine with torpedoes. They were dead in the water, their motors seized up, and her crew trying to restart them with little success. She was imagining this, lost in a daydream about the engines roaring back to life and growing louder as they warmed. Once they reached full power, they could shoot off beyond the reach of their adversary. Except, there was a vibration underneath her, and it was growing so evident it pulled her from her fantasy. She peered over the tops of the other seats, seeing the other passengers, too, were standing and attempting to discern the source of the growing squall around them. The earth was shaking, the whole train juddering on the track. Its parts clanged together wildly, and for a split second, Rose believed she had willed it into existence, she had willed the trains engine to start, and they were moving again. The rumbling was deafening. People were shouting, barely audible above the din. The train rocked hard enough, Rose wondered if it was going to tear itself apart. On instinct and fear, she dropped to the floor and crammed herself under the seat as far as she could manage.

The wall of snow hit and swept the train off the track. The force picked up the cars holding one hundred and nineteen souls and carried them into the river valley below as easily as if it were an angry child kicking a toy in a fit. Rose hooked her arms around the leg of the seat as the car tilted, hanging on for her life as the train rolled onto its side. The earth was grinding and scraping beneath them. She found herself on the ceiling, looking down onto the other row of benches, as she braced herself against the wall using the bolted leg of her seat. She watched as the other passengers, unprepared, fell and slammed underneath her with screams of shock. One man's neck made a horrible crunching sound when he landed, and she was sure he was dead by how his body lay after.

The side wall of the car sheared apart as fallen trees pierced through the metal and smashed into the train. The collapse of logs over her head shattered half the windows, and she ducked away from the spraying glass. The metal below her peeled back as she dangled, bracing herself as best she could in the tiny space. Watery snow poured forth through the torn openings and broken windows to fill the car. The train jarred, and she was nearly knocked loose from her position. Rose pistoned her legs to brace against the seat for fear of falling and being consumed by the flooding snow below her. Her little arms wanted to give up, but adrenaline ensured her strength did not fail.

The snow buried people alive. Screams for help erupted all around her as arms flailed and bags flew. The car slammed hard into the rock of the riverbed and ground to a halt. Her arms gave out, and she fell into a heap of frigid ice and debris, half filling what remained of the car.

A hot tickle rolled down her cheek. When she touched it, her hand came away with blood. Rose knelt in the freezing snow, dazed. The rumble grew quiet as the last of the avalanche and collapse of trees came to rest, leaving only the sound of water pouring steadily in from all the cracks and gaps surrounding her.

There were muffled cries below her. One arm of her coat was torn, but she still had the thick jacket around her. She shoved her hands in its pockets for her mittens, pulling them on to protect her fingers from the cold. There were shouts from the men above them, calling down to the people below. Rose wanted her daddy. She cast about for a way out of the mangled train car, to get away from the sound of the other passengers begging for their lives. She took a step forward, and her foot slid down, the snow precarious, and she struggled to get free.

The screams for help grew frantic, the sound of their terror filled what remained of the car. She was the only one left standing who had not been crushed under the blanket of watery suffocating snow. A blue hand clamored for her from below the ice and wrapped itself around her ankle, pulling her down. She would die down there if it succeeded. She tried to scream, but the air froze in her chest as she was slowly dragged below.

Rose was rescued from the train, the only survivor in her car. The screams of those buried by the avalanche would haunt her in the dead of winter. They would call for her: the voices of the people alive and trapped. In the dark of night, when the wind kicked up, and the thunder rolled, their icy grip would close upon her, and she knew, if she looked below the blankets, she would find their dead, pale eyes looking back.

Talia stood on the lookout's balcony, high above everything else in the surrounding landscape, watching as the sun made its final descent. Stars were beginning to light in the darkening sky, but the display of color held her captive. She could see the mountains to the north, Granite Peak and beyond the ghost of Mount Baker, illuminated by the setting sun. To the northeast, the collection of peaks that made up the Wenatchee Mountains were only a few valleys over as the crow flies. Their snowcaps were a distant memory in the lateness of the season. Mount Rainier, visible to the south of the lookout, was barren on its eastern flank, exposing the grey andesite below. The ridge where the lookout sat cast a shadow of a sleeping giant on the forest below, right down to the point of his nose and pucker of his lips. Talia admired the beauty around her and was overcome with a sense of calm.

The group set up camp in a flat area a short distance from the actual structure. The four tents were clustered together in a rough semi-circle with all the doors turned toward each other. The mountaintop they sat on was devoid of anything except scraggly subalpine trees, noble firs, and huckleberry shrubs that did little to create a windbreak. Luckily, the breeze was gentle.

In the dim light, Lane was demonstrating for Glenn and Chase how to use the backpacking stoves to boil water. Summer had already crawled into her sleeping bag and fallen asleep. A jubilant conversation sparked up full of laughter and a fair amount of teasing. Glenn's attempt at imitating Bam sent everyone, including Dean, into howls of laughter.

She embraced the revelry but was removed from it. A familiar chord struck: the pervasive sense of loneliness, both isolating and strangely comforting. Growing up not only as an outsider, but an outcast, it was a state she was accustomed to. The good humor of the group was not directed at her, and for that, she was grateful. She could accept being separate as long as she was not the butt of the joke. In meditation of her surroundings, she was at peace with herself.

The stairs behind Talia creaked and broke her from her reverie. Chase appeared at the top of the stairs.

"Am I interrupting?" he asked, crossing the platform to stand beside her. He leaned up against the railing close enough for their arms to touch.

"No," she replied.

"How are you doing?"

"Good. We made it this far. By tomorrow, we will be in Lester."

"No, Talia, how are you doing?" he asked. He was checking in, and she wasn't sure how to interpret it. Talia glanced at him. He stared into the distance, the warm orange light glowing on his face. She looked away.

"I'm great," she replied, confused.

"We've gotten to know each other pretty well this last week, and it's been awesome," Chase said. "But it looks like you are isolating yourself a bit. You know you don't have to do that."

Talia considered this. It was true; they'd spent a part of each day together over the last week going over all aspects of the trip, and during that time, a connection had formed.

"You know, I appreciate that you apologized. I do. It's more than anyone else has done over the years, but it doesn't change the past. I was not able to form meaningful relationships when it mattered, and I struggle to do it now. This is what it looks like. Even when I am accepted, there will always be some part of me that questions if it's real or if there's an ulterior motive. It wasn't just one incident or two, it was twelve years of my life," Talia sighed.

"Talia, I…" Chase tried to cut in, but Talia held up her hand and kept speaking.

"My dad died young and left us with nothing. Eve decided one day she wanted to pick on me, and she never let off. It got better in high school, but by then, I had been labelled a social pariah, so it wasn't like people were flocking to be my friend. No one wanted to come near me because it made them a target. With the few friends I made, all it took was a soda dumped in their lap or being called a name in the hallway, and I was back to being alone."

Chase hung his head.

"I got used to it. For a long time, all I wanted was to belong somewhere. To feel like I fit. After a while, all I wanted was to just be left alone. Some things you never fully recover from." When she finished, he was watching her with soft blue eyes.

"Talia, maybe I don't have any business saying this…" Chase began. Talia cut him off.

"If you are opening with that, careful with whatever you are about to say," she scoffed.

Chase hesitated, then angled his head as if inspecting her.

"It's been ten years," he said simply. "'We cannot simply sit and stare at our wounds forever.' When do you choose a different path?"

She found she had no response.

"When do you move forward and let go? If you build your walls so high no one can get over them, you are ensuring you will be alone. Is that really what you want?"

His words were a slap. Her heart beat a little faster, and her eyes stung, the anger welling up.

"That's not fair!" Her voice raised an octave. He had hit a nerve. Chase placed a hand on her shoulder.

"I'm not trying to hurt you, Talia. Everyone wants you here, especially Summer. And me. We want you to join us. Please, don't isolate yourself. Be a part of the team." He was holding her out at arm's length and staring at her with a hopeful look on his face. He brushed a rogue strand of hair that had come loose behind her ear. Chase drew closer, and for a split second, she anticipated a kiss. As the moment hung, she considered if she wanted it to happen. Deciding she was unsure, she retreated back a step. His arms dropped to his side.

"I know I was part of the problem, so let me be part of the solution. Come sit with us," Chase said, gesturing toward the team. Talia nodded. She followed him off the platform back to the camp.

"Our hero!" Bam yelled, leading them into a round of applause. Talia flushed. Summer, freshly awake from her nap, grabbed her hand and pulled her down beside her.

"Sit next to me," she said. Talia did as requested, and Summer leaned in, conspiratorial, like sisters.

"Thank you," Summer said.

"Forget about it," Talia replied.

"Stop being modest, I would have turned around and gone home if it wasn't for you," Summer said, her eyes sincere. She grabbed Talia's hand and squeezed.

"It's true," Dean offered. "She had that look in her eyes, she was getting ready to bail."

"Do you remember that time Summer dipped on us, and when you called her, she was at that diner down the street eating pancakes?" Bam laughed.

"What about when we caught her sleeping in the closet?" Glenn chimed in.

"I don't know is that as embarrassing as drinking too much coffee and needing to take a shit in the middle of an investigation," Summer laughed. "Remember that, Glenn?" Glenn hung his head, but only to conceal a gleeful face.

"I deny all accusations!" he replied. The others cackled.

"And he tried to blame the terrible smell in the hallway on a ghost!" Chase laughed.

"Remember the first house we did after we brought on Glenn? What we found?" Bam asked.

"Don't remind me. What a weird place," Chase replied.

"Well, don't leave us all in suspense, Chase. A couple of us don't seem to know that story," Summer smiled. Her eyes glittered in the firelight.

"Alright, alright. We got an email about poltergeist activity, and when I interviewed the guy, he had this massive house. One of those old Victorians in Seattle. All the standard stuff, right? Coming downstairs to all the cupboards and drawers open in the kitchen. Lights turning on and off in the bedroom. Doors slamming shut. Night of the investigation, Bam and I are in one of the second story bedrooms, and we hear footsteps overhead. The guy never said anything about a third story. So, we try to find a staircase, check all of the bedrooms, and nothing. On a whim, I look inside a closet and behind a rack of coats is a staircase. We go upstairs to check it out, and it's a room full of dolls. Each one had its own specially lit pedestal, like they were tiny Miss Americas. He had a Little Red Riding Hood, complete with a picnic basket under her arm. There was Bo-Peep, a Swedish girl with braids and an embroidered skirt. There was even a Shepard boy with that little hook stick."

"A crook," Dean cut in.

"Yeah, that," Chase continued. "He never uttered a word about the room. He didn't say the third floor was off limits. Not a mention about his doll collection. It was the strangest thing. We thought about asking him and decided it would be better to leave it."

"Never did figure out what was making those sounds. Gave me the willies. Footage is somewhere, but never added it to the show," Bam offered up. Summer's mouth was hanging wide open in mock surprise. A small smile played on Dean's lips.

"How did you not show us this room?" Summer demanded. Chase shook his head. "It was too creepy."

Bam nodded in agreement. "Something wrong up there." His eyes were wide with emphasis. He turned to Chase. "But he wanted us to ask about it, right? Like when the investigation was over, you could see it on his face he was waiting for us to bring it up."

"You knew about this and never told me?" Summer turned to Dean, incredulous. Dean shrugged.

"I only saw it later in the footage. I wanted to include it, but those two were adamant. They said no," Dean replied coolly.

"Strange you would cut the weirdest thing you found in someone's house, it's almost like we are working on a ghost show! Sounds like a literal gold mine!" Glenn said, glancing at the others. Chase continued his story.

"He kept asking us if we were sure we didn't find anything unusual. He offered to let us look around some more. I think it was a set up. He even called me a week later and asked us to come back because the activity had escalated in his bedroom. We declined, and he offered to pay us."

Summer threw her head back and cackled.

"You guys robbed us," Glenn muttered, shaking his head.

"Guy was weird." Bam shook his head in disbelief. "We had to edit the footage down cause he was worse than a jack-in-the-box, popping up all over the house."

"He was happy with it, though." Chase met Bam's gaze. "Did I ever tell you that? After we posted the final vlog, he called again to tell me how impressed he was with our work. He even said the house was cleansed. Acted like he hadn't called at all to get us to come back."

The stories continued, each of them sharing their own mishaps and misadventures. Talia embraced the present moment, despite the strangeness of it all, being here with this group and being accepted as one of them. Summer scooted over to lay her head on Talia's shoulder. Summer's skin was hot against hers, and it brought forth the unbidden memory of her mother and their nights cuddled up watching movies and eating popcorn. It'd been a long time since she'd been that close to someone. She embraced the comfort it brought her.

"You're with us now," Summer said.

***

After an early night, exhausted from a full day of backpacking, Talia woke the following morning, nestled in her sleeping bag. She was reluctant to climb out to meet the cold that awaited her. The others shifted in their tents as they slowly roused. Summer slept fully submerged in her down bag, only the streaks of her vibrant purple hair were visible out of its opening.

Talia rose, careful not to disturb Summer as she pulled on her boots, and exited the tent to make herself a cup of coffee. The instant packets were a life saver on space and easy prep. It was no mocha, but it served as a wake up. She was surprised to see Dean already awake and looking to the east from the fire lookout in anticipation of the sunrise. She gathered the necessary supplies, deciding to join him.

"Morning," she said making her way up the creaking steps to the platform. He acknowledged her with his eyes. "Want some coffee?"

"Yeah, that sounds great," Dean smiled.

"Are you always an early riser?" she asked. He nodded.

"I don't sleep much," he replied. They fell into an amicable silence. She set up the stove, poured in the water, and lit the burner. Within a minute, she was adding bubbling water to each of the mugs. She offered one to Dean, which he accepted and braved a tentative drink.

"Oh, that's hot," Dean whispered, blowing on the cup and taking another slurp.

"Amateur," Talia said back, taking a scalding sip off her own mug. He gave up a chuckle. A haze had settled over the valley below giving the illusion they were on an island above the clouds.

"What an incredible view," Dean said. Talia nodded, admiring the soft color over the mountains.

"Thank you for taking care of Summer yesterday. She means a lot to me. I don't know what I would do if something happened to her," Dean said.

"Anyone would have done that," Talia said, a small swell of pride filled her chest.

120

"No, no one would have done that. Thank you," he said, the sincerity evident in his tone and expression. He regarded her with more than the casual indifference he had previously shown her.

"I don't warm up to new people right away. Thank you for being patient with me. You are clearly a welcome addition and qualified for the job. A lot of people don't respond well when I don't immediately throw open the doors, but I don't really care how it makes people feel. It weeds out the ones who aren't worth the energy. It's the people who expect to be trusted without earning it, those are the ones I have to watch out for. People who have an expectation of how you should behave are entitled and with expectations, comes resentment. I hope you understand."

"I do," Talia replied. "You require people to earn your trust rather than automatically giving it. And some people feel like they are entitled to be trusted. Been there, and I'm the same. You have a leg up on me though. I don't know how to trust people. Not fully. I can't seem to shake the feeling that a bucket of pig's blood might drop on my head, you know?"

Dean nodded in acknowledgment.

"Oh, I know that feeling all too well," he replied, taking a long sip from his steaming cup.

A zipper ripped open from one of the tents, and Glenn emerged, face swollen with sleep and hair standing on end. He noticed them at the lookout and gave a quick wave before he wandered toward some shrubs to relieve himself.

"Don't give me too much credit. I don't really trust anyone. I trust you though. You helped Summer and risked serious injury to do it. What you did for her says a lot about who you are. Summer is my best friend. She's been here from the start and helped mold my original idea into what it is today. I couldn't have done any of this without her. I'm sorry I've been a dick, but you passed the test. That sounds lame now that I am saying. Doesn't it?" Dean said.

"Incredibly lame." Talia gave an exaggerated frown, and Dean burst out laughing. It was contagious, something genuine shared between them. The sun peered over the horizon and rose into what would be a clear, beautiful day. They continued making quiet conversation until the rest of the team emerged from their tents. After a quick breakfast of oatmeal, camp was packed away for their departure to Lester.

The trail down the other side of the mountain was poorly marked. Talia stayed a few steps ahead to redirect anyone before they went too far astray. The early departure had left everyone a little worse for wear. They were quiet, with sleepy minds and fatigued bodies. She navigated them around the rocks clinging to the cliffside and down a dusty set of switchbacks. It was a slow descent into the mist and gloom below.

Between the preternatural silence, and lack of sunlight, the forest was surreal. Not a single bird chirped, no breeze blew. It had a timeless quality, as if they were passing through a suspended state of animation, a liminal space. Talia kept catching glimpses of movement from the corner of her eye and could not shake the feeling of being watched.

The proximity to Lester was stirring suppressed memories within the recesses of her mind.

It was the image of the old man that came to the fore: his thinness and grizzled features, the pallid color of his skin, but more than anything, it was the energy in his eyes. The way he had looked at her like he had seen beyond time to the end of the epoch.

Let me count your ribs.

The words came on the air as soft as a whisper. Talia spun around.

"Did you say something?"

Summer drew back, startled.

"No," she replied, glancing around, then back to Talia. "Are you good?"

Talia nodded.

"You seem jumpy," Summer observed.

"I am. The last time I was here I was eight. There was a part of me that almost convinced myself I had made the whole thing up," Talia said. Summer linked arms with Talia, and they walked side by side.

"What did you see?" Summer asked.

"Back then, or now?" Talia responded, sliding her water bottle out with her free hand and taking a long pull off of it.

"Someone was out here?" Summer inquired, her tone low and conspiratorial. Talia nodded. A spark lit inside Summer's eyes.

"I've never told anyone before. There was a man out here when I got lost. He was old, but he seemed older. He was saying things that didn't make sense. He scared me, so I ran away and followed the river home. I still dream about him sometimes," Talia said.

Summer was quiet in response, considering Talia's revelation.

"Do you think he was homeless? Or lost? Was he living in Lester?" Summer finally asked.

"It was something different. It felt different," Talia said. It was strange to let out this information after keeping it a secret for so long. She had told herself so many times it was all in her head that she had almost convinced herself that was the case. But she remembered the people. She remembered the man. Rather than explain it, she chose to limit the truth, wishing she hadn't shared any of the details at all, and wondering why she had.

"Well, you were eight. Maybe he was concerned about a little girl wandering around the woods by herself?" Summer said. Talia shook her head.

"It was something different," she repeated, uncomfortable with her disclosure. "Maybe you are right. Maybe he was squatting in one of the houses out here."

"Have you told the others?" Summer asked.

"No. You're the first person I've told."

"We've established you are sensitive, which I'm assuming you didn't know at the time. Maybe it was a visitor from the other side?" Summer offered. Talia broke away from Summer.

"I don't know," Talia frowned. The prospect she had encountered a ghost, many ghosts, seemed like a reach, but it would explain the encounter. It would explain the strange things he said and the odd quality of his eyes. The sense that he was beyond time.

"Maybe? Please don't tell the others. I barely remember, and I don't want to be on the receiving end of a bunch of questions," Talia said. She shot Summer a pleading look, and Summer nodded, dropping the subject altogether. The rest of the *Dimensions* gang was catching up, so Talia forged ahead until she found Lester Creek. They followed the stream along its natural course to the river. Eventually, they emerged where the river split the forest. The marine layer of clouds had burned off, revealing a crystalline blue sky.

Near the confluence of Lester Creek and the Green River, a train trestle spanned the waterway and downriver was the town of Lester. The village looked almost the same as Talia remembered, and the full memory of that day flooded back to her. The log train depot and the schoolhouse set at the back of town remained intact.

"That's Lester?" Chase asked. The others piled up behind him, staring at the abandoned town across the river.

"Cool," Glenn said and high-fived Bam.

They stumped across the river on the railroad bridge, following the tracks. It was in good repair, sturdy as the day it was built.

"Do we have to worry about a train coming?" Glenn asked.

"Unlikely," Talia replied. "They mothballed the line back when I was a kid."

They followed the tracks into the town proper. The collapsed houses from her memory were gone, leaving only empty foundations, the enclaves in the earth like open graves. Once manicured lawns and gardens were overgrown with weeds and waist high grass. One house was a burned-out hulk with only the blackened framework and the last remnants of a sagging roof. Vines of bright green ivy wrapped around the charcoal columns, and snowy white bindweed flowers bloomed amidst the wreckage. The main street was reduced to rubble, the former structures had long since been torn down or collapsed, and left behind rotting posts grey with age. Piles of demolished brick lay scattered here and there, covered in long grass and dandelions. Glenn plucked a brick from one of the piles, hefting it with one hand.

"Do you think these are worth anything?" he asked. Dean and Chase exchanged glances. Bam laughed out loud.

"Sure, buddy. One problem: who is going to carry all those bricks out of here?" he asked. Glenn considered this and dropped his treasure.

"Some people pay good money for antiques. I bet someone would be interested in century old bricks from a ghost town," he replied, a little defensiveness creeping into his voice. Chase patted Glenn on the shoulder.

"I get it, but I'm not carrying those 'century old bricks' all the way back home. If we find some other artifacts, like something of actual value, I would be happy to…"

"What about a creepy ass doll? Does that qualify?" Summer interjected, nudging a dirty porcelain doll with a half-smashed face. The toy was propped up against a foundation where it stared at them with one glass eye.

Talia kept moving toward the center of town. Once there had been a road and a town center, but all that remained was bare dirt with scattered blades of grass and weeds.

"We should camp close to the river," she suggested when her unease became too great. The afternoon had grown warm, and she was aware of the slick of sweat on the skin under her backpack. Before receiving a response, she walked a short distance away to a flat spot near the river where a field of buttercups swayed gently in the breeze. On the edge of the meadow, the forest rose again and climbed up onto the face of Bald Mountain. It was on the edge of the town, the furthest point she could get away from Lester. She unclasped the buckles of her pack and dropped it to the ground.

"Here's good," she called.

"Where does that go?" Chase asked. Talia glanced at where he pointed. A road disappeared into the wood away from the town, barely noticeable with the overgrown tree boughs concealing it.

"I'm not certain," Talia replied.

"We'll have to check that out later," he said.

"Why don't we stay in one of the houses? Some seem to be in pretty good condition," Dean asked.

"If you want to see how well one hundred-year-old floorboards will hold up when all six of you are sleeping on them, be my guest. I have zero interest in sleeping in an old dusty building with spiders and mice. I'll be fine right here," Talia replied.

"Good point," Dean agreed, then meandered over to where Talia was unpacking her bag and dropped his stuff next to hers. The others followed suit. Talia eyed the white house where the man had appeared on the porch. It looked the same. It stood out from the others, somehow cleaner, as if it were encased in a bubble that had protected it from the abuses of time. Something about the house struck her as wrong, as if it were disconnected and separate from the other remaining buildings. She knew this was a strange thought, stranger still how her eyes continued to be drawn to it, as if she half expected him to step out at any moment. Chase clapped his hands startling her, then looked up to find the group standing around her in a loose semi-circle waiting instruction.

"Man, I'm so excited we made it! This has been the culmination of a lot of work, all thanks to you guys," Chase said. "Let's get base camp set up first, then coordinate what filming we want to get done tonight over lunch? Sound like a plan?"

"Sounds good, boss," Bam said, slapping Chase on the back. "My tent's in your bag." Tents went up, and air mattresses were laid out. Lane brought several large stones from the riverbed to form a fire ring. He dug a small pit in the center and cleared away the surrounding dry grass. Glenn and Dean sourced a worn log stripped of its bark and dragged it next to the ring for sitting. Bam unpacked all the camera equipment, checking to verify everything had survived the trip and was ready to go. Talia had disconnected from the chatter around her as she processed the surrealness of returning to a place that lived in her memory.

"I'm going to go take a look around," Talia said. Summer glanced up at her as she unrolled their air mattresses, a look of concern on her face. "Do you want company?" Talia shook her head.

"I'll be right back," she said over her shoulder. Their laughter echoed off of the buildings as she walked between them. She meandered to the other side, able to inspect the site from her adult perspective. It was more or less the same as when she was a child but without the fear. There was something eerie about the town, more than its continued existence as an abandoned place. It had a cursed history, but there was an unmistakable energy surrounding Lester. In all the years she had dreamt of the place, it had always been colored through the lens of her terror. Returning was strangely like coming home. Eventually, she turned back toward the river and walked along the tracks toward the old railroad depot.

The structure itself was made of cedar poles and planking stained a dark chocolate brown. The color had faded over the years with exposure, but the building itself was sturdy. The surrounding platform had given into weather and rot, and a collapsed section in one corner had fully returned to the earth.

Talia peeked into one dust covered window to see inside, etching out a small circle in one pane with her fingertip. The building had a main lobby with a vaulted ceiling. There appeared to be offices in the back with a second story above them.

The interior looked to be well intact with the exception of a considerable number of cobwebs in the rafters. The ceiling of the main lobby was vaulted giving it an open airy quality. There was no evidence of vandalism or graffiti, which she would have expected to find. The ticket counter remained, along with a couple of pew-style benches, where at one time people sat and waited for their departure. She turned to walk to the other side of the building, passing by another pane of glass as she went. Out of the corner of her eye, a shadow passed over the window. She peered inside and saw nothing.

Talia walked around the front of the building, the conversation from the campsite carrying downwind. Upon rounding the corner, one of the doors to the depot stood wide open as if to welcome her. She glanced around, unsure. *Had it been like this all along?* The stone steps up to the platform were clean of debris and without weeds growing through them. Talia considered this. She turned, looking into the depot where shadows loomed in the afternoon light. There was a presence in the darkness, its energy pulsing from the shadowy corners within. The blackness called to her, its whisper reaching its fingers into her brain.

Talia resisted, locking her mind against the assault. A single beam poured through one of the dusty windows, and radiated off of the wooden floor, illuminating the room. The light, unable to reach into the deepest recesses, left one corner cloaked in shadow. Talia's eyes focused there. It had followed them here.

This is where it all began, the shadow creature whispered to her. *The emptinesssss. The hole you will never fillll.*

She heard a footstep behind her and whirled around. Chase stood on the other end of the platform. He held up his hands in defense.

"It's just me," he chuckled. "Didn't mean to sneak up on you like that. I thought you heard me."

"Sorry, you scared me," she replied, grabbing her chest.

"I don't blame you. There's definitely a ghost living in there." He pointed inside. Talia glanced back to the corner where the creature had concealed itself. There was nothing there, the shadows had been chased away.

"I found it like this," Talia indicated to the open door. "Isn't that strange?"

"Probably an animal," he shrugged.

It was reasonable, but she didn't accept it. Something else about the space was rubbing her wrong, but she couldn't quite put her finger on it.

"Are you alright? You look worried," Chase said. She was comforted by his concern for her.

"Yeah, I think you spooked me is all." She smiled at him.

"Well, come on back. Lunch is ready."

It was an Act of Congress that led to the eventual establishment of the town of Lester. In 1862, the Pacific Railway Act was passed to establish a transcontinental rail line. When no direct route had been built, the possibility was raised that the Northern Pacific Railway might lose acreage awarded to them specifically for the purpose of developing a transcontinental line. With that incentive, the Northern Pacific employed Virgil Bogue to find a passage over the Cascade Mountains into Western Washington. This proved to be a challenge for many companies hoping to be the first to reach the West Coast, as several had surveyed the area previously and opted for a different route. Bogue discovered the thoroughfare that would bring people through the Green River Valley. What he wrote about it:

"A little after nine 'o'clock [March 19th, 1881], appeared a sharp bend in the ridge to the north, as anticipated, whence we descended, along a well-defined crest, so rapidly that in less than an hour the barometer marked only 3,495 feet [from a 5,500 foot summit], at a point where, for a little distance about us, there were no trees. To the east, a spur cut off much of our view, but facing west we looked down Sunday Creek. Beyond its confluence with Green River, were the mountain to the south, covered with dark fir forests, and back of them, the great snowy mass of Mt. Rainier sharply defined against the blue sky. It was a beautiful scene, and so impressive that for a moment all were silent. – Virgil Bogue, date unknown, Northern Pacific records.

What is recorded for the history books, and what actually occurred, are often two very different narratives, and when it came to this particular region of the world, that was often the case. The printed version conceals a darker history at work behind the scenes. With the pass scouted, work flooded the forest. The trees were logged, and the land cleared to make way for the railroad.

Bogue considered naming the landmark Garfield Pass out of regard for the current standing president, but the members of his company encouraged him to name it after himself, which was common practice among engineers. Bogue declined. It came to be called Stampede Pass, and a few different narratives about its naming can be found in the records. In one, the story told in a memoir written by one of his fellow engineers, and a member of the early clearing party, detailed a relatively tame story. While the men were debating whether to name the pass after Garfield or Bogue, the mosquitos came out. The swarm was so terrible and relentless, likely the result of a hatch, it forced the men to flee the area. He likened the event to a stampede, the way both horses and men reacted to the onslaught.

There is a conflicting, and more popular, narrative about the naming of the pass that comes from Bogue himself. Progress from the trail clearing team had slowed. To get the men back to work, a particular foreman was brought in, one known for being quite the hard ass. When the workers caught wind of this development, many quit. Later, when they were hanging around the camp's kitchen, with the expectation that they would be served lunch, they were reminded that meals were reserved for current railroad employees, and they were no longer entitled to a meal. With that, there was a "stampede" off the mountain.

The real version, while similar to the second, lacked a few key details. Bogue did bring in a new foreman, not because labor had slowed, but because the original foreman had been injured while clearing work camps ahead of the main trail. The man had returned to overseeing work on the main trail for a time, but it was not to last. Complaints were made that the foreman would wake screaming in the night; inconsolable, terrified, and, at times, violent. Growing more unstable by the day and crippling the team he oversaw by preventing much needed rest. He was released. Bogue hired Maxwell Bishop. Bishop was an outsider, but he earned the respect of the workers quickly. Trail clearing moved at a rapid pace until work reached the area between Champion and Friday Creek.

Overnight, Bishop underwent a personality change. Where he had been firm but reasonable, he became indifferent, delusional, and aggressive. The shift was so astonishing, some of the men joked he was possessed. After logging a particularly difficult piece of terrain, the men were exhausted and ready to call it a night, but Bishop told them all to get back to work. After another hour, they finished their work and headed to camp for dinner. When they arrived, Bishop turned them away. When they objected, Bishop told them they weren't going to eat until he told them they could. A couple of the men stood their ground, and Bishop brought out a whip, attacking several of the workers who had stood against him. All the men left the mountain that night, without dinner. Half went to track down Bogue to complain about the new foreman. The other half left and never came back.

Trains began running as early as 1886. While a tunnel was in development, the line utilized switchbacks up and over Stampede Pass. Growth continued throughout the Green River Valley. Several towns sprouted up along the river, fed by the rail line: Lemolo, Maywood, Nagrom, Kendon, and Dean's Mill. Helper stations were established for the steam locomotives to receive a final coal reload before traversing the grade up the mountain's steep switchbacks. Weston was the location of the helper station on the west-side, and Easton was the station on the east.

Work on the tunnel began in 1883 and concluded in 1888. Its construction was a feat of engineering. Over twenty-eight months, excavation was completed by teams working from both sides of the mountain toward the interior. Reports vary on the exact number of people who worked on the tunnel, but generally place the estimate around 300 workers. These often fail to mention the 1,500 Chinese workers that contributed their labor, and that number is considered to be underreported. Only the white deaths were recorded and totaled twenty-eight with another thirty-nine injured. The Chinese deaths went undocumented. The bodies were simply boxed up and shipped back to China.

A $1,000 reward was offered to whoever broke through the tunnel first and promised a steak and whiskey dinner to the winning man's side. When the headings met, there was a scramble to obtain the reward. The west-side man won, emerging bloody and a little worse for wear. Nothing further is said about what happened to the east-side man he encountered in the bore. History recorded the sanitized version. No one was counting if another box was sent to sea.

The tunnel, when completed, ran a total of 1.8 miles through the mountainside. It arched in the center to assist with drainage, but the length and design prevented exhaust fumes from escaping. The lack of ventilation and buildup of exhaust nearly led to the asphyxiation of passengers and workers alike. No deaths were reported.

The following year, the territory of Washington became a state on November 11, 1889.

As traffic over Stampede Pass increased, there was a need for bigger facilities at the helper stations. By nature of its location and the surrounding landscape, Weston was limited in its ability to grow. The Weston facilities were moved to Dean's Mill, which amassed a collection of facilities including a six-stall roundhouse and a two-story combination depot.

Lester was founded in 1892, named for Lester Hansaker, the station's telegraph operator. The town entered a period of growth. With regular trains moving through the valley, Lester established itself as a town, complete with a post office, general store, and schoolhouse. During this time, the infamous bath house and hotel was built, which would later become the Green River Hot Springs Hotel and Sanitarium.

The Green River Hot Springs Hotel and Sanitarium, also known as the Kloeber Sanitarium, was built on the edge of town by a wealthy man, Dr. J.S. Kloeber, in 1900. He had purchased the existing hotel and bathhouse, along with an extensive parcel of surrounding land. Everything to the east of the town, and a substantial portion of Bald Mountain, was owned by the doctor. He placed NO TRESPASSING signs along the edge of the forest. Some of the townspeople argued the woods belonged to the town, so Kloeber hired a local hunter to manage the area and escorted those out he found poaching there.

The hotel itself was top of the line for its time, complete with indoor plumbing, a bowling alley, billiards and game room, and shooting gallery. He spared no expense. One morning a pile of crates was unloaded at the depot holding fine china designed to Kloeber's specifications and special-ordered from Syracuse. An orchestra was hired to play during meals. Renowned for its luxury and craftsmanship, the core of the hotel was the twenty-seven mineral hot springs located on the property. The water was piped into the hotel's suites for a one-of-a-kind experience. Immersion in the mineral springs reportedly treated a variety of ailments and aid in relaxation. The Green River Hot Springs Hotel and Sanitarium was the pinnacle of extravagance, and a fantastic success amongst the wealthier crowds.

Lester became a working town of railroad workers, loggers, and merchants with a visiting population of upper-class patrons to the hotel. Dr. Kloeber remarried, not long after his first wife passed, to a one Lana Handel. Lana, also a practitioner of medicine, was a fasting specialist. The hotel focus shifted in earnest to attract visitors who sought health and vitality by advertising the healing waters, massage, and the new world-renowned fasting cure. The fasting cure rapidly grew in popularity. People travelled from around the world seeking solutions to their various issues. As the Green River Hot Springs Hotel and Sanitarium began offering weeklong retreats and extended stays, tragedy struck.

Dr. Kloeber went out to hunt elk in the forested acreage of his property and was discovered hours later shot, whimpering and delirious from blood loss. Ironically, he was the most qualified person to treat his gunshot wound. Kloeber muttered about a "fountain of youth" as they transported him back to the sanitarium and, in his final lucid moment, begged to be taken up the mountain. He died with his wife by his side. It was chalked up to an accident, but everyone knew no hunter worth their salt would have made such a grave error.

Mrs. Kloeber wasted no time returning to her maiden name and, granted a license to practice medicine in the state of Washington, was now known as Dr. Lana Handel. The ownership of the hotel and its surrounding properties transferred to her. She continued to promote her fasting cure.

Winter, the year 1910, was particularly severe. Before snow sheds had been erected along the rail line, a particularly foul snowstorm held a passenger train hostage for six days on the tracks just outside the town. When the weather warmed, there was hope that the train could move on to its final destination. Instead, it broke loose a massive avalanche that swept the engine and all of its cars off the rails into the river valley, killing ninety-six people. Only twenty-three people survived. It was thought the incident would be the end of Lester, and while travel to the town faltered, visitors were undeterred.

The same year, the City of Tacoma quietly filed for water rights over the Green River Watershed which encompassed all of the Green River Gorge from Palmer to Stampede Pass.

Dr. Handel's hotel single-handedly kept commerce in the town of Lester flowing. The opulence of the sanitarium attracted an affluent crowd that flooded money into the businesses and hands of the townspeople. On the heels of that money were rumors of a cult. The stories told in backrooms and secret whispers were of virgin sacrifices in the mountains, demons, and the occasional mention of a witch, to explain the number of disappearances that had occurred in those few years. Some people said the place was cursed. The connection was considered to be circumstantial. The increase in population to the remote and rugged town coincided with the increase in disappearances. It was easily explained away as happenstance.

Scandal ruined Lester's prosperity. In 1912, when Dr. Handel was tried for the murder of London Williams and the attempted murder of India Williams, the townspeople were shocked by the allegations against her. Before she could be charged, the Green River Hot Springs Hotel and Sanitarium burned to the ground. Records reported it as a wildfire, although the surrounding area was unharmed. During the cleanup, the bodies of several of Handel's missing patients were discovered buried on the property. The hotel was never rebuilt. Dr. Handel put the land up for sale as she attempted to appeal her case. It never made it to market, purchased by a private investor.

In the aftermath, the town entered a period of calm. The first dam was built near Palmer in 1913, and the following year, World War I began. The Spanish Flu pandemic swept through the Green River Valley, followed by Smallpox in the early 1920's, but Lester continued to grow. A road was cut in to connect all the towns along the river in the 1930's. Soundview Pulp opened a gravel pit in the area and employed many of Lester's citizens as the dieselization of the railroad-initiated layoffs. Soundview Pulp would later become Scott Paper. As part of a use agreement over the town's bunkhouses for Scott Paper, the company provided a considerable donation for the building of a new schoolhouse.

After the Northern Pacific announced the decommissioning of the majority of its steam locomotives, the workforce in Lester was reduced to a skeleton crew. After years of prosperity and growth, this transition signaled a town in decline. As if to punctuate that shift, Donovan's Massacre rocked the small town of Lester. Residents left the town in a flood. People would later speculate in the wake of all those deaths that it was the potential loss of his career that pushed George Donovan over the edge. The real story was that no one knew what happened. One day he woke up and snapped.

As the railroad transitioned to automation, the City of Tacoma sent in survey teams, buying up the vacated plots of land and looked for a location to build a new dam further upriver. This marked the point when the Headworks began its stranglehold on the town of Lester.

"Action," Chase said. Dean was in front of the camera with Talia and Summer beside him, standing silent. Dean's showmanship was on full display. The sun was descending in the sky and, for the time being, the fading day was creating the right effect. Soon, they would lose the light. Glenn and Lane were back in camp rigging a lighting arrangement together with whatever supplies they could find.

Talia was doing her best to act natural in front of the camera. She still felt like a bug under a microscope despite the coaching Summer had given her about where to look and how to behave.

She had checked her appearance beforehand, using Summer's tiny cosmetic mirror to ensure no food was stuck in her teeth and fixing her hair as best she could. Summer gave her eyelashes a quick coat of mascara and styled her hair. When the camera went on, she was brutally aware of her hands and spent an awkward minute unsure of what to do with them.

"The Green River Hot Springs Hotel and Sanitarium was a luxury mountain resort established in the late 1800's along the rail line over Stampede Pass. The twenty-seven on-site mineral springs were the main attraction, which drew in a wealthy clientele seeking a healing experience they could find nowhere else. The hotel burned down in 1912, reportedly due to a wildfire, and we are standing on what is left of its foundation today. Although only open for a couple of decades, it was owned by one of the most notorious serial killers of her time," Dean spoke excitedly to the camera. It was supernatural how different he seemed, like he was slipping on a new persona. Talia had nothing to do except stand idly by as Dean laid out the space they were in, and what they were hoping to uncover.

Dean moved on to Handel's victims. "While a few of Handel's patients had gone through the coroner's office, others were found buried on the property. There were a handful that were never found. What led to the unraveling of the doctor's scheme was the Williams sisters."

Chase cut the scene.

"Let's move into a closer shot while Dean talks about the Williams sisters. You two won't be in the frame," Chase indicated at Summer and Talia. Bam unshouldered the camera, and Talia relaxed.

The hotel grounds were nestled into the base of the mountain that served as Lester's backdrop. Glenn had done his own exploration and found what was left of the hotel's site a half a mile outside of the town. The former gardens were flourishing with overgrowth and surrounded on all sides by dense old growth forest. English ivy and field bindweed had overtaken the stone foundation and collapsing brickwork. The white flowers of the latter were closed against the night. The rhododendrons on the edge of the property were massive, thriving despite their neglect. Talia wandered through the lush green gardens and disappeared behind a blackened column with ivy clinging to it. She discovered the largest lilac shrub she had ever seen and idly wished she could see it bloom. Summer was not far behind her, sweeping her feet through the grass and scanning the ground hoping to discover something hidden.

"How long does it take to get used to being filmed?" Talia asked.

"There's really nothing to it," Summer said. "You'll get more comfortable over time."

"Was it that bad?" Talia frowned.

"You looked fine, but I could tell you were terrified," Summer reassured her.

"I just don't know what I am supposed to do when the camera is on me," Talia replied.

"You know what, forget about the camera. Unless they give you a specific direction, act like it isn't even there. It helps if you have a character to play, but until you figure out what you want 'her' to look like, two things: engage each of your senses, and be open. Paranormal investigations are about discovery, and if you close yourself off, then you will shut out all the experiences. If you start getting too caught up in your own head, start with your five senses. What do you taste? What do you smell?" Summer advised. "And talk to yourself out loud. No one knows what you are thinking. Ignore the camera, but talk like there's an audience."

Talia nodded, listening intently.

Glenn and Lane returned carrying cameras and strange devices along with a homemade lighting rig fashioned out of a white t-shirt and a tripod of branches lashed together with paracord. Lane shoved a small electronic box into Talia's hand.

"What's this?" she asked.

"Spirit Box," he replied, his expression stoic. "Let's you talk to the dead." Talia shot a nervous glance at Summer.

"It's a piece of cake," she said, then to Lane. "I'll show her what to do." Lane passed off another device to Summer, then returned to the main group.

"It's really simple, you ask questions for the spirit you are intending to contact, or any spirit for that matter, and see if it responds. Most times, it's a garbled mess, so even if there's a response, we won't be able to understand it. Other times, it's clear like a radio broadcast."

"So, it's a radio?" Talia asked.

"More than, but essentially, yes. It scans all radio frequencies non-stop. and the idea behind it is that a spirit can use those frequencies to speak to us by stopping on words or phrases from broadcasts. Some people say it actually picks up the radio waves the dead are using to communicate. It's an interesting tool," Summer explained, then held up the object in her hand. "I really like to use this thing. We call it a puck. It can be pretty wild."

"A puck?"

"It's similar to the Spirit Box, except that it uses a text interface rather than audio. I think it's the spookiest thing we use. The responses we get on the puck are precise and relevant like eighty-five percent of the time. We will use it if we start picking up an energy. It would help if we found an object, even if it was just a glass bottle. It helps with the link."

Talia looked around at the crumbling foundation, overgrown with weeds and flora, and wondered how far below the surface they would have to go to find artifacts from this place's former life.

"Ladies!"

Chase appeared and held a small camera out to Summer.

"You two can stay over here and look around. We are going to keep the focus on Dean for now and have him rejoin you later," Chase explained. Talia nodded. Summer gave him a thumbs up.

"He's such a control freak sometimes," she muttered under her breath as he walked away. Talia was taken aback by the vitriol in her tone. Summer noticed her surprised gaze.

"Sometimes he rubs me the wrong way." Summer shrugged, and Talia sensed she was being intentionally vague. Summer closed any further inquiry by opening the LCD screen on the side of the camera and readying it to film. Talia fumbled with the Spirit Box. After yanking up the antenna, she found the switch and turned it on. It erupted with a rapid pulsing sound in her hand, the static loud as it moved through channel after channel, endlessly scanning. She started at the sudden noise in the quiet place, watching the numbers on the spirit box change in time with the palpitations of the box. She listened for a voice or sound she could distinguish through the white noise. Talia looked up and found Summer was focusing the camera on her, obviously filming. Summer rewarded her with a grin.

"You ready to do a little investigating?" she asked.

"I guess?" Talia replied weakly.

"Is anyone here with us tonight?" Summer spoke aloud. They could no longer hear or see the guys, but their lights reflected off the tops of the trees, marking their distance from each other. A hollow wind wound between the walls and swept through the treetops, rattling the leaves of the bushes, and disturbing the warm night air. The rapid bursts of white noise from the spirit box set her nerves on edge.

No response came. Talia directed the device, feeling silly holding what amounted to a toy radio while pretending to listen for ghosts. Summer's face glowed in the reflected light of the camera. Talia remained where she stood as Summer turned and walked toward the forest. She wondered, not for the first time, what she was doing here.

The question itself, not asked aloud, received an answer.

RUN the box replied. Or had she imagined it said that? Summer was too far away for Talia to ask if she had heard it too.

"Is someone here with me?"

DONE

The word came in a short burst, like it had been clipped. A door opened up at the periphery of her gaze. It was clear only in her mind's eye and would vanish the moment it was looked at full on. Something, someone, had stepped through and joined her. She was no longer alone. Sweeping around, Talia half-expected to find a person standing beside her and found no one.

"Who's there?"

DONE

The box pulsed in her hand. Talia struggled to interpret the response, until it dawned on her.

"London?"

HUNGRY the box fired off. There was no mistaking the word. She scanned around her again, wishing Summer had stayed close.

The spirit box's rapid pulsing ebbed into a slow heartbeat, throbbing, and filling her ears with its sound. Talia's stomach rumbled, and she was hit with a pang of hunger so sharp she doubled over. Pain ripped through her, and all her limbs grew heavy with exhaustion. She was starving, desperate with hunger. She considered how far it would be to walk back to the camp alone and was too fatigued to even formulate the thought. Exhaustion seeped into her bones. Talia, weak and struggling to stay on her feet, was pushed without warning. As she fell, she could hardly catch her breath to scream. Everything around her went black.

If time passed, she was not aware of it. She found herself looking up at an orb of light in the darkness and wondered to herself when the moon had risen. Except, the light was not the moon, but a window to look out through her own eyes. She was in the background, shoved aside. A passenger in her own body.

"Hey!" Talia screamed. Her voice echoed around her in the cavernous black space.

"I'm so hungry," her own voice said with a British lilt, the response a quiet echo in the recesses of Talia's mind. Her hijacker's response. London Williams. Summer was returning, and London used Talia's body to approach her. Talia sensed her eagerness.

"Hello?" London called. Summer perked up, cocking her head to the side. Summer's face soon filled the lens Talia was looking through. Talia scanned around for an exit, but she was trapped at the bottom of a well.

"Can you please help?"

Summer's brow furrowed.

"Talia? Are you alright?"

"My name is not Talia, it's London. London Williams. I need assistance."

Summer's jaw popped open, realization sinking in. She brought her camera up to eye level.

"London. Did you stay here at the hotel?" Summer asked.

"Well, yes, we are here, aren't we?" The British accent growing stronger, the voice changing, and not sounding like Talia's own. "I came here for the cure. Ellen had returned after travelling the States, and she looked radiant. Lost what seemed like two stone and was quite the braggart about it; told everyone she'd come here. I wrote to Dr. Handel myself, and she sent back a pamphlet. It seemed wonderful! I had to come to the sanitarium. But she's not what she seems I'm afraid. This place is not what you think it is. Please, though, do you have anything to eat?"

"Talia, are you pulling my leg?" Summer said, her eyes narrowed.

"I'm here!" Talia cried out, casting about for a way to reach the hole and climb out. There was nothing in the space, only her and the orb of light. She was locked in the void.

"Have you seen my sister?" London's voice was fading in volume, and Talia realized with horror that her view of the outside world was shrinking. Summer was responding, her mouth moving, but she could no longer hear what was being said. She stared into the shrinking circle, willing it to grow and clumsily trying to force London aside, but London was resisting giving up control.

The light was reduced to nearly a pinhole, and terror welled in Talia's throat. A long-fingered hand closed on her shoulder. It was the creature from the basement.

Taaaliiiaaa, it hissed, its hot breath caressing her ear. She shuddered, paralyzed with fear.

Sufferrr

Its long spidery limb wrapped around her and pulled her to its gaping maw. She couldn't breathe.

Yesss, embraaace your paaain

She screamed, the call ripping through her like a lightning bolt. Without warning, she was forced to the front. In her body once more, the spirit box crackled in her hand.

RUN

The box fell silent. The white noise ceased, and nothing further came through. Summer was staring at her, eyes wide with shock. The hand holding the camera was shaking.

"Summer?" a voice yelled from what seemed like a mile away.

"We're here!" Summer replied without taking her eyes off of Talia. "Talia?"

Talia nodded, wobbling on her feet, then lowered herself to the ground. Summer crouched beside her.

"Are you alright?" she asked, finally, reluctantly, setting the camera aside.

"I don't know. What was that?" Talia asked. Her voice cracked. The relief of being alone in her body again, being in control again, overwhelmed her. The sky was the final shade of blue before full night, and a few stars pierced the curtain of darkness. Time had passed while she was inside.

"I think you channeled," Summer replied. The rest of the *Dimensions* team came crashing through the grass and rubble.

"What happened? Who screamed?" Dean asked, kneeling down, and placing a hand on Talia's shoulder. His face was full of concern. "Are you alright?"

"I'm not really sure," Talia replied.

"Oh my god! Talia! You channeled. She fucking channeled London Williams! I wouldn't believe it unless I had seen it with my own eyes. And I got it on camera. I heard her voice, Dean. It had a British accent and everything. She was telling me about coming to the hotel and Dr. Handel. She asked about her sister!"

Dean looked between Talia and Summer. Summer leaned forward, gripping Talia's other arm.

"What was it like?" Summer laughed, grinning from ear to ear.

"I don't know," Talia replied, her voice quiet. "I was here one minute, I sensed a presence, then it was like I was at the bottom of a well. I could see through this lens, like I was looking through a periscope. I tried to call out to you, but…" She trailed off, her brow furrowed, and she shivered at the memory of the creature wrapping itself around her in the void.

"I think we should call it a night. Let's go start a fire and go over the footage," Dean offered.

"I agree," Chase stepped in and offered a hand to Talia. Summer was already standing and fumbling the camera up to show an excited Glenn. The low light was fading to pure darkness. Turning on his headlamp, Chase placed an arm around her to walk back to their campsite. Talia leaned into Chase, comforted by his touch, as they picked their way through the rubble and onto the overgrown road that led back to their camp. The others remained, their excited chatter fading into the background as they walked.

"What time is it?"

"Close to eight," he replied. "Crazy how fast the sun went down." They left the gardens and entered the forest. The trees with their reaching branches had overtaken the road, leaving a narrow lane for the pair to pass. He kept his arm around her as they walked in step. His presence helped ground her into her own body while she sorted through her mingled thoughts. London's memories were fading but still present, and Talia kept slipping into the distant past. She felt unreal.

"How long were we out here?" she asked, shivering.

"A couple hours," he replied. Talia placed a hand to her head.

"Feels like we just started." She rubbed at her temple. He stopped her, turning his headlamp to keep it from shining in her face.

"You are really shaken up. Just take it easy. We'll get a fire started and whatever you saw, it will start looking better once we get you warmed up. I might have packed some hot chocolate. I think sugar would do you good," Chase said.

"Was that part of the sanctioned allotment?" she attempted a joke.

"It most certainly wasn't, but life isn't any fun if you don't break the rules," he replied, a smile tugged at the corner of his lips. They were close, and she liked their closeness because it reminded her that she was alive. She leaned into the heat coming off of his body. Gently, he lifted her face and kissed her with warm lips. She softened into it. With one hand around her shoulders, the other slipped onto her waist and pulled her into him. Pressed against each other, he pulled back for a split second, then kissed her again. Her body responded as if on instinct. A fire lit deep within her. He stopped, pulling back only inches.

"I'm sorry," he whispered, resting his forehead against her. He was a little out of breath. "I shouldn't have done that, but I've been wanting to since yesterday. I told myself I wasn't going to, but…"

"Do it again," she whispered. She wanted the contact, the physical touch and sensation, bringing her fully back into this world. She wanted his arms around her, holding her in the here and now. He didn't hesitate, as if reading her mind, he wrapped himself around her. A fire washed over her, and she matched his urgency. She gripped his shirt, digging her nails into the small of his back. He bit her lip, gently, the pain a welcome sensation, and kissed her deeply once more.

The voices of the others grew louder, and as much as she wanted to fight it, she broke apart from him. Her shivering had ceased, and when she looked up at him in the soft glow of his headlamp, his eyes were starry. They said nothing but continued walking on with their arms around each other, the terror of her possession forgotten with the sensation of her heart beating within her own body.

***

As Chase set about starting the fire, the others trickled into the campsite riding a high. Glenn carried the camera containing the video evidence of Talia's channeling like it was a holy artifact. The grin on Summer's face looked as if it might crack, she was grinning so wide.

"Only in Lester for a few hours and we already have killer footage!" Glenn said to Bam, high-fiving. Only Lane seemed subdued, while the others discussed how the rest of the investigation would take place over the next two days.

"I think Talia and I should be stationed in the schoolhouse tomorrow night," Summer suggested. "We might have an opportunity to make contact there." Dean nodded along with this.

Talia remained silent, her mind thrumming with conflicting emotions. She watched as Chase finished putting together a modest fire, large enough to produce heat but requiring everyone to huddle close to feel it. He brought out several packets of instant cocoa with the tiny marshmallows and boiled water to prepare a mug for Talia. Bam produced a bottle of Fireball.

"You carried that out here?" she asked, giving him an incredulous look.

"Can't keep a good time down!" Bam replied, the apples of his cheeks pink from the first sip of liquor. Talia rolled her eyes.

"What else did you guys smuggle in?" she asked.

Glenn pulled out a small cannister with green buds and rolling papers.

"Oh, you had better roll one of those!" Summer laughed and bit her lip. "I might have slipped in a little more make up than what I was originally going to bring."

"Totally brought the book you said not to," Dean replied.

"Deck of cards. Cause you always need a deck of cards," Lane said.

After a few passes of the bottle, a joint was lit and handed around. A light-hearted haze settled over them. Talia allowed herself a few sips of the liquor but passed on the joint. The liquor warmed her stomach and spread to the rest of her body. With her head fuzzy, she was able to finally relax.

"Alright, alright," Summer announced. "You as a horror trope and go." She pointed to Glenn.

"That's easy. 'Token Asian guy,'" Glenn said. "Which means I will probably die first."

"Why is that?" Talia asked.

"Cause minorities don't survive in horror movies. Plus, I'm a dude. It's one of the rules. You've heard of a 'final girl' right?" Glenn asked. When Talia shook her head, he continued. "It's Sidney Prescott of *Scream*. Ellen Ripley from *Alien*. Think Laurie Strode in *Halloween*. She's the OG. The women always make it to the last act, unless they have sex, of course."

"Cause slut shaming is a horror trope," Summer added, flipping her glossy black hair. "I don't know what's worse, that or getting 'fridged.'"

"Which brings us to 'the sacrifice' or sometimes we call them 'dead meat.' Their only purpose is to be killed," Glenn said. His eyes were already bloodshot and half-lidded.

"That would be me," said Lane, leaning back to rest his head against the log.

Glenn shook his head. "No. You're 'the tough guy.'"

"I resent that remark," Bam said in the most offended tone he could muster before breaking out into laughter. His drawl had grown syrupy with the liquor.

"As much as I love horror, some of the tropes are done. Running upstairs when they should run out the front door, the car that won't start or not making sure the villain is actually dead. Like stab him a couple more times for good measure!" Summer said. Dean passed Chase the bottle which he accepted.

"A howling cat jump scare," Chase interjected. "I hate that trope." He took a long pull from the liquor and gave a mirthful smirk, wiping his bottom lip. He handed it off to Talia. She held it but didn't drink.

"Some of those are mainstays. It's not horror without it. Like 'the old man with the warning.' Right?" Dean said. "Characters stop at an old country gas station before a camping trip, and an old guy tells them to stay away. They don't listen."

"My favorite movies are the ones where you can't tell if she's crazy or if it's a ghost," Chase said.

"Classy. More misogynism," Summer rolled her eyes. They started to argue.

"So, what would be my trope?" Talia asked.

"You're the 'final girl,'" Glenn said. "Especially after the footage we got tonight. You can channel. That definitely makes you the 'final girl.'"

"Oh my god, I know right? When I walked up on her, her eyes were glazed over, and I was talking to London Williams. It was crazy. She was telling me everything that Handel was putting her through," Summer said, ignoring what Chase was trying to say to her

"How do we verify that was information that came from London and not some book?" Lane asked, his tone annoyed. His eyes remained closed, and his arms were folded over his chest, but he was tapping his foot.

"Don't be such a spoil sport," Summer said. "This could be huge for us. Is there any other paranormal show right now that has someone who is an actual full-blooded medium?"

"I don't think so," Dean replied. "There's a few sensitives out there."

"Yeah, well, we all know what that means," Summer snorted.

"If there was a way to ensure the audience could see the reality of it and know it isn't just an act," Glenn considered, a little slurred. Lane slid the joint out from between Glenn's fingers, taking a last drag before tossing the roach into the fire.

"Let me see the camera." Summer held out her hand and urged Glenn to hand it to her. He gave it over. Summer fiddled with the controls, rewatching the clip.

"There!" she cheered, louder than usual, and handed the camera back to Glenn. "Do you see her eyes?"

"Sure, but…"

"Do you see what's different?"

"It's kind of hard to see," Glenn squinted, then his expression changed. "Whoa. Her eyes are a different color."

"Exactly!" Summer cried. Bam leaned over Glenn's shoulder to see and looked across at Talia.

"She ain't wrong," Bam said. They passed the camera around until it reached Talia, who looked at the paused image of herself. To see herself, not as herself but looking out of London William's eyes, she shuddered and handed the camera off. Lane's eyes were open, and he was observing her. Talia took a small sip off the bottle. Summer continued prattling on.

"We could do an episode where we test it," she said. "Show her talking to someone she's never met and channel someone they know."

"No way to prove to the audience they didn't just talk beforehand," Glenn said.

"You're right," Summer replied thoughtfully. Chase noticed Talia's discomfort.

"Are you alright?" he asked. She nodded. He frowned. The group grew quiet.

"That don't look okay," Bam piped up.

"Oh." Summer glanced around. "I'm sorry. I didn't think…"

"We've been doing this for so long and nothing like that has ever happened before," Dean said. "We didn't take into consideration it might be unpleasant for you." Summer looked ashamed.

"Oh, it's fine," Talia replied, blushing.

"No, it's actually not," Dean said, a little brusque. "We don't minimize each other's experiences. If that scared you, I would resoundingly speak for all of us when I say you are not required to do anything you are uncomfortable with. If you don't want to do something, you will only receive complete understanding." Talia hung her head, embarrassed further by Dean's earnest response, but when she looked up again, she saw every member of the group nodding in agreement with his words.

"It was pretty frightening," Talia admitted. "She shoved me out of control over my own body, and I couldn't get back in." The chills returned to her. Although Chase was next to her, it was Summer who scooted closer and put an arm around her, resting her head on Talia's shoulders and slipping a hand in hers.

"You are one of us now. We won't make you do anything like that again if you don't want to," Summer said.

"I don't think you should go back to the hotel grounds," Dean said.

"We still want to use the footage though, and we can make a statement about it. Something about how you were so sensitive to the energies around the hotel, we chose for you to avoid it," Chase cut in. He looked across the fire at Dean. "Everyone has had difficult experiences in the field."

"Or, if you want, we can cut it," Dean said. He said it to Talia, but his gaze was locked on Chase. There was a tension between the two men, a subtle and almost imperceptible way they were communicating without saying a word.

"Don't cut it. I think the footage will be good for the show, but I don't know if I am ready to do that on a regular basis," she acknowledged. "I'm not comfortable being ghost bait."

"That's fine," Dean said. "Let us know if you change your mind. I don't know about you guys, but I am exhausted." He stood and the others murmured their agreement.

"It will be hard for you," Summer whispered, so low no one else heard her. "You draw them in like lamplight in the darkness."

Summer stared into the fire.

"What did you say?" Talia asked.

"Hmmm?" Summer glanced over, half-lidded and sleepy. Everyone had grown quiet and contemplative, staring into the fire. No one had heard her but Talia.

"What is that?" Dean asked. The group turned toward the forest. Reflective orbs danced amongst the darkness. First only a few, then dozens and hundreds appeared, flitting between the trees. Talia's heart stopped. Summer gasped. They were eyes, a countless number, watching them from the void. Chase stood and flipped on his headlamp.

At the edge of the tree line was a massive herd of elk densely packed together. It was impossible to see where it ended. The animals stared with their many reflective eyes, then took cautious steps forward. They flooded past, unafraid of the people who looked on.

"Wow," Glenn said aloud. Every member of the team was on their feet as nearly a hundred cervids passed by them. Summer took Talia's hand. They watched in silence as the herd moved through their camp, past the town of Lester, to the river beyond.

The move to diesel engines is often cited as the cause of the exodus out of Lester and its neighboring towns, and while there was some truth to that narrative, the railroad was a false flag. What was rumor before was growing teeth. There were whispers after the massacre, questions about the cult's involvement. No one believed George Donovan would have done what he did on his own, and people continued to go missing without a trace. There were claims about the hotel grounds being haunted. Something had come unseated in the town of Lester.

As people moved away, the City of Tacoma, the entity behind the Green River Headworks, established their stronghold over the watershed. As soon as a resident spoke a word about selling, the Headworks was knocking on their door. All the properties flanking the Green River were purchased, condemned, and demolished with swift efficiency. One resident suffered a heart attack and had to be admitted to the ICU. Within three days, he had a visitor informing him he would not be returning home. The house was purchased, condemned, and he would have no legal recourse to get it back. Every opportunity that arose, the Headworks legal team sought to displace residents all along the Green River Gorge. The elderly, in particular, complained about how the Headworks representatives circled like vultures. Some were harassed to the point that their children moved them into their homes and sold off the properties to make the calls and letters stop. For anyone who remained, the pressure to leave grew. The City of Tacoma was hellbent on ensuring the town of Lester disappeared from the public's view.

By 1960, with the Howard A Hanson Dam complete, the Headworks commanded hundreds of acres along the Green River. Gates were erected on all the service roads leading into the watershed, including the one the residents used to access Lester. The only other road into the town was a fourteen-mile logging road from Cle Elum that was hardly maintained and inaccessible for more than six months of the year. Lesterites fought the gates. They wrote to press outlets and showed up to dispute the land action, but the gates remained. This would culminate with the, "Battle of Lester Gate." The story released by the press was about a rogue King County crew that had cut the five-hundred-pound gate loose and dragged it away. The true version was far sadder and suppressed as it would have garnered too much sympathy for the plight of Lester. King County fought valiantly for the town in court, but somehow, the Green River Headworks won every fight.

The battle for ownership over Lester moved from real estate to the courthouse and legislature. The City of Tacoma sued the Corp of Engineers to ensure the recently completed dam could not be accessed by the public, which was a departure from the norm. The city won. King County sued the city in 1965 to fight against the encroachment and outright theft of land perpetrated by the Headworks condemning parcels of land that ran the length of the Green River. The city won, again, under the guise of protecting the watershed. The people of Lester knew better. Logging continued, the mills stayed open, and the railroad ran. Scott Paper was given access to the empty bunkhouses and kitchen hall for their workers to use. The lone condition was that Scott Paper would not hire any of the remaining residents of Lester. The company acquiesced.

The final blow came when the Northern Pacific sold the actual townsite of Lester to the Headworks for $35,000 and consumed the last remnants of the town. It was a backdoor deal, without notice or ability for legal dispute. Only 150 residents remained.

Not long after, the Stampede Pass was downgraded as a rail line, and with fewer workers needed to maintain the station, the town population fell into decline. Trains hardly stopped in Lester, which forced the remaining stores and shops to close.

By 1983, BNSF, formerly the Northern Pacific, made the decision to mothball the Stampede Pass line completely in favor of better grade through Snoqualmie Pass. By this time, the town's residents numbered twenty-four. Rumors persisted about strangers in the woods, and the disappearances continued.

The last handhold the town clung to was destroyed with the culmination of long pursued legislation, effectively closing several Washington school districts, and seeing them absorbed by neighboring districts. The original bill did not pass its first run through legislation, but the criteria were narrowed and voted in. The result: two school districts would be forced to close and one of those was Lester. The school was the last employer in town, and after it was shuttered only two residents remained.

What was left of the town was left to rot. Curiosity persisted, hikers and wanderers who entered to visit the watershed were threatened, removed, and fined. With the passing of the last resident of Lester, the cold war over the last hundred years to gain control over the Green River Watershed had been won.

Talia woke the next morning before the sun rose. As quiet as she could, she rolled out of her bag and slipped on her socks and boots. Summer was dead to the world behind her eye mask and ear plugs. Tiny soft snores emitted from her slack mouth. Talia exited the dew-covered tent. Cool predawn light filled the valley. The air was rich with the scent of pine forest and damp earth. There was an underlying crispness that signaled summer's end and autumn's soon arrival.

Talia would be the only one awake for an hour or more if the prior night's revelry was any indication. Alone, Talia walked along the river's edge away from the town. Walking among the old buildings made her feel like a million eyes were watching her. The forest was safer.

She hugged the tree line along the river, picking her way between the sandy spots and river rock. Her experience the night before returned to her. It was hard to define how it had felt to be removed from her body: the loss of control, the disconnection from time and space, and the sensation of being locked within herself. She had been locked in with the shadow entity. The thought of it made her blood run cold. How could she continue with *Dark Dimensions* if she was unable to confront her fear? How would she overcome the monster that lived there? The pantry door came to mind, and she willed it to remain shut.

Talia considered the encounter with Chase. In the moment, after the terror of being possessed, her desire for connection had been so potent it was overwhelming. And, in the afterglow of that kiss, the part of her that long sought to be worthy had celebrated being chosen by someone like Chase. In her mind, he was still the popular guy, the cool kid. As much as she tried to deny it, there was something appealing about *that* guy choosing her. Somehow, Chase's interest redeemed her, and his urgent need to kiss her was atonement. His want proved she had always been deserving of acceptance, that there was no truth in what the bullies had said and done. She was visible and could be seen. She was no ghost. It was an entirely new experience for her, one she wanted to grasp with both hands and embrace. To her dismay, no matter how she tried to focus on the butterflies, something about it unsettled her. Deep down, she knew it had been a mistake.

The other half, the part filled with a seemingly endless supply of rage, was coming apart at the seams. It was like trying to swallow a bone lodged in her throat. She could not be involved with someone who constantly reminded her of the past she wished to forget.

She remembered the pain of her childhood torment and had allowed her bully to kiss her, and not only that, but had begged him to do it again. The girl that had been harassed and tormented daily all those years was crying out: *Why him? How could you let HIM?* When she considered the kiss, her stomach flipped but in the wrong direction.

That internal voice screamed at her. *You are going to ruin this!* There was truth to that. She had been accepted by the *Dark Dimensions* team and cautiously envisioned a future with them. A family of sorts, something that had been torn away from her decades before. Her throat constricted with the memory of her brothers, missing them, and wondering if they ever thought of her. The thought of them brought into stark relief how much of her life she had longed to belong somewhere. Talia could not enter this group as an attachment to Chase because when it ended, as it no doubt would, she would lose her newfound friendships as well. She had to forge these relationships as a person in her own right. There was a single chosen path, and she did not want to face it. She realized she was going to have to put a stop to the entanglement.

Talia imagined what the conversation with Chase would sound like, and the longer she considered it, the more unwell she felt. The thought of the money gave her pause. She needed what had been promised. If she rejected Chase, would he hold to their agreement on payment? Would he honor his original offer? There was no option, she had to pay off the firm. Talia could not jeopardize the sorely needed funds or the prospect of the job offer with *Dark Dimensions* so she would have to extricate herself carefully.

To make matters worse, they were trapped together until Friday. If she hoped to stay on with the *Dark Dimensions* team, it would look very bad for her to disrupt the dynamic of this trip at the midpoint. Already her reluctance to channel had crushed the team's enthusiasm, and there was still so much filming to be done. If she was careful, she could remove herself with as little disruption as possible. But not until they got home.

With that, her decision was made. She would continue to engage with this until after they left Lester, and she had received the promised payment from the *Dark Dimensions* team. Once that was done, she would put a stop to the romantic involvement. While a small part of her was relieved to enjoy this interlude a little longer, she was disgusted with herself and her fear.

"You know it's the right choice because no one is happy," she reminded herself. Despite the mixed emotions she was experiencing, she could tolerate the conflict for a few more days. It gave her resolve, and she chose to embrace the experience for what it was: a brief lapse in judgment. Talia sighed deeply, wishing in hindsight she had not allowed the situation to develop and become overcomplicated.

With the matter resolved, Talia took in her surroundings and realized she had no idea where she was. She climbed up to the top of the ridge in order to look down at the valley from above and orient herself. As she moved further up the incline, Talia emerged above the trees on steep treacherous earth. She found herself on a talus field below a sharp vertical rock face. The hotel ruins were below and further out, the group's camp next to the river with the townsite of Lester beyond. The sun emerged, peering over the ridge, and filling the valley with warm golden light. It heartened her, the beauty of the day and the love of the forest.

Talia followed the talus field until it ended and found herself looking down at something that stopped her in her tracks. A well-worn groove in the earth lay before her, a trail that only the feet of many humans could have made. No game trail could be this weathered. She checked her surroundings, the discovery giving her pause, then, against her better judgment, followed the cut as it hugged the ridge below the stone wall. She had walked the path for several minutes when the air changed, and she caught a hint of sulfur on the wind. It was unmistakable: the smell of a hot spring.

In all of the reports she'd read about adventurous hikers making their way to Lester, not a single one had mentioned locating the infamous hot springs, even though they were the basis of the hotel's renowned success. Talia had not given it much thought before. They had explored the hotel's ruins and not seen or smelled a single one of the many mineral springs purported to be in the area. She had found one mention, unsupported by anything other than the report of an anonymous internet denizen, that the hot springs had been destroyed by the Green River Headworks long ago to deter visitors. It explained the trail she was on.

Excited by her discovery, Talia hurried along the trail as it wrapped around several outcroppings. The sharp grey rock had compressed into pillars of stone over the millennia. The formations were remarkable; over time lichens, black and soft green, grew in the cracks, and tiny fir saplings clung to the bed of moss at the top of each column. Minute plants grew from the barest nooks of sandy dirt. She noticed succulents and microscopic white flowers blooming at the end of stalks as thin as a needle. Talia found her mind settling, and the exertion had triggered a rush of endorphins. To be this present was better than any drug on the market.

The smell of sulfur became more potent with each step. Coming around another outcropping, she came upon a grove of twisted whitebark pine tucked into the stone side of the mountain. They surrounded three steaming pools of water that were deep and strange. Talia knew in an instant there was something wrong with the water.

Glenn stood gazing languidly down at the edge of one of the pools, and he was not himself. There was an eerie quality to his focus. He hadn't heard her footfalls or noticed her, so she chose to hang back and observe. The water smoked and tangled around him, as if it were caressing him. He was motionless, arms slack, as he stared into the water. Glenn was speaking in hushed tones, murmuring a response to a question that was not asked aloud. She looked at the water, the steam rising off of it obscured her view. Glenn had no reflection in the pool. The water reflected nothing at all. She considered it a trick of the light and then realized with growing horror that what Glenn was peering into was a trap.

"Glenn? Come away from the water," she broke the silence. Glenn inhaled sharply and lifted his head, as if waking from a deep sleep. He looked over to her, and Talia came forward in a rush. She was nervous about approaching the springs, fearful something unnatural would reach out for her. Glenn rubbed his eyes, glanced around at his surroundings, then back at Talia.

"I thought I was dreaming this," he explained. "I was walking in my dream." Talia's arms and neck crawled with gooseflesh, and she tried in vain to rub it away.

"Were you sleepwalking?" Talia asked. He shook his head.

"I don't know, it's all muddy. Someone was calling," Glenn replied. His gaze drifted back to the pool and locked there. His face went slack. Talia followed his sightline.

The water changed, it shimmered opalescent on the surface, shifting beautiful translucent rainbows of color, and a crystalline blue-green glowed underneath. The longer she looked, the more colors appeared. She watched them swirl, shift, and change in a hypnotic dance. How would it feel if she went in?

When Talia returned to herself, she found herself standing at the edge of the pool beside Glenn. She was unsure how much time had passed, but she was certain it had been too long. Glenn gazed at the water. Talia reached out and touched his arm. He glanced over at her, then yawned.

"I was having the strangest dream," he said.

"We should go," she whispered, averting her gaze from the water's surface. In her periphery, something moved, and she restrained herself from turning to look. Glenn's eyes fell back on the pool, and she watched as he drifted away. Talia grabbed his hand.

"Glenn, we need to go. It's time for breakfast." He looked up at her.

"Talia?"

"We need to go now," she said, yanking him behind her. When they disappeared around the outcropping on the other side of the grotto and had gone a short distance, warm tendrils retreated from her mind, like fingers losing their grasp. A wave of emptiness came with the withdrawal, an unexplained malaise, and the thought of turning around crossed her mind.

"Is there a reason why we are moving so fast?" he asked, pulling against her. She released him. He was expressionless and flat.

"Do you know how you got out here?" she asked. He shook his head.

"I was dreaming about water…" he trailed off, looking over his shoulder at the way they had come. Talia grabbed his hand again.

"We really should get back to camp, the others will worry." She tugged him forward. He resisted at first, then came along. She located a trail that would drop them near the hotel gardens and followed it. She would not be returning here. There was something wrong with the hot springs, and it was an element of what was wrong with Lester.

Glenn said nothing to Talia when they reached the campsite, he simply disappeared into his tent. Talia stood there alone, unable to rid the colors of the springs from her mind and feeling those fingers reaching for her. A bud opened inside of her; a small flower she knew as fear. She looked down at the cold fire with her heart pounding in her ears. She grabbed her pack and hustled away, then turned around, and grabbed Summer's as well. She crossed the meadow to the depot.

Talia tossed the bags down beside the stone steps, glancing over her shoulder to ensure no one had seen or follower her, then dug into her pack, pulling out all the food for the next few nights. Aside from the freeze-dried meals, she had packed a collection of snacks: trail mix, jerky, dried apples, cheese and peanut butter crackers, and protein bars. Talia grabbed the package of orange crackers, unwrapping the thin cellophane and biting into one. The salt melted against her tongue followed by the creaminess of the peanut butter.

While eating the crackers, she unpacked her camp stove, walked the short distance to the river to scoop water into the pot, then set it on top of the stove and lit the flame. She selected one of the freeze-dried meals and ripped it open. Barely able to wait for the water to boil, Talia grabbed the baggie of dried apples and popped one in her mouth. The sweetness of the sugar and the spice of the cinnamon warmed her, the fruit tender between her teeth.

Frenzied, she grabbed more from the bag and stuffed them one after another into her mouth. The water boiled. She poured it into the bag, stirring the mixture, and sealing the bag. There was more water, so she went ahead and prepared another, knowing it would be ready when she was done with the first. Talia considered what she was doing before she opened the second meal.

They will know when you have nothing left to eat. They will find out. You need to stop, she thought. The other voice spoke to her, the shadow, and in the darkest corner she felt it there watching her with its many wet eyes.

Moooooooooreee, it hissed. She froze. The creature's slobbering madness bored into her skull, it's desire palpable. Without thinking, the second package ripped open, and she poured the water in.

She tore open one of the bars and took down half in one bite, its grainy texture thick in her dry mouth. She washed it down with a gulp of water. Each snack went into her mouth, and when she could not hold back any longer, she opened the first meal. Steam poured from inside, she stirred the contents and took a searing first bite of noodle and gravy. The noodles were dense, on the hard side of al dente, but edible and delicious. She sucked them off her spoon and went in for another heaping bite. Talia finished the meal in minutes, her mouth and tongue burning. She reached for the second bag, a meat lasagna, and was tucking into it when a shadow fell across her.

"Talia?" Chase stood beside her, looking half-awake with his hair in disarray. He carried a stove pot in his hands. "What are you doing here?"

She nearly spat the food back into the bag. Dropping her spoon, she swept the empty packages behind her. He took a step closer.

"Are you alright?" he asked.

She said nothing in response.

"What are you doing?"

"I was hungry," she offered weakly. There was a slight shift in his expression when he noted Summer's backpack on the steps next to hers. Shame washed over her. Her body demanded she purge, not out of necessity, but out of humiliation.

Chase was silent. Talia remained still. He set down the pot and walked over to sit beside her. He reached for her, to place his arm around her, and she flinched. She was caught, exposed.

"Are you alright?" he asked.

"You can't tell the others about this," she whispered, her voice coming out timid and small. He was seeing it all, but if he was surprised, he didn't say it aloud.

"I won't say anything, Talia," he assured her. "This'll stay between you and me."

***

Late in the afternoon, Talia woke from a dream she could not remember except she was grateful to be released from it. Inside the sweltering tent, still half-drunk on sleep, she unzipped the door to hang her head out and breathe fresh air. A gentle breeze rustled the nylon. A small plant with perfect yellow flowers danced and waved on the current beside her head.

She recalled Chase coming upon her at the depot, mid-binge, and felt a wave of sickening anxiety come over her. After he helped her clean up the mess and carried Summer's backpack to the campsite, he fixed them both a cup of coffee. She took three small sips and excused herself to be sick. When she returned, the others were awake and planning how to utilize the daylight hours. Chase didn't say another word about it.

The team discussed filming interior shots of the depot, the schoolhouse, the bunks, and some of the houses. Dean explained how they would measure locations with EMF to determine which potential locations could be hot spots of activity, and if the readings were poor, they would do energy work. Dean and Chase went back and forth about how the scenes should look until Bam warned them: if they didn't give him one direction and stick to it, he was walking home. Still concerned after their morning interaction, Talia kept an eye on Glenn, who was his usual self: making fun of Lane, flirting with Summer, and all of it with a grin on his face. When the others departed for their tasks, short on sleep and growing tired, Talia returned to her tent for a nap.

Awake, she guzzled the remaining water from her bottle. It was warm with a plastic aftertaste. She grabbed her filter and made her way down to the river to refill her bottle. She found Lane, upriver, skipping stones across a placid stretch, the rocks ricocheting off the surface. She crouched next to an eddy lapping at the sandy bank. The water this close to the source was clear and crystalline. It would taste like the place where the mountains meet the sky. She dipped her collection bag into the soft current and dragged the bag against it, scooping the water inside.

Lane threw another flat stone, and it dashed across the water three times. He watched her, and when she looked up, he quickly looked away. With her collection bag full, she screwed the filter on, wiped the water off the outside and squeezed the water through the instrument into her water bottle until the bag was empty, and her bottle was nearly full. The next rock he threw went off its intended trajectory and sunk after one skip.

150

"You seem right at home here," he called to her as he scanned the ground, looking for the flat, smooth stones worth skipping. He leaned down to pick one up, then tossed it aside. She eyed him, curious why he was out here by the river instead of assisting with preparations.

"I like to think so." Talia forced a smile, packed up her filter, and walked away to search out Glenn. She found him with Alabama doing interior shots in one of the houses. They were jovial, hassling each other the way young men do, so Talia restrained herself from asking too pointedly how he was. His demeanor seemed normal, which made her all the more reluctant to bring up his morning adventure.

"Someone's neglectin' the housekeeping," Bam said, swatting at a cobweb over a doorway and peering into the small musty room beyond. Glenn was carrying a black box the size of thick paperback book.

"What is that?" Talia asked, standing in the doorway as Bam checked the angles through his lens. She noticed he had turned the camera on, so she remained in the doorway.

"Field generator," Glenn explained. "Or a pump. We've had some trouble finding energy in these abandoned buildings. The EMF readers didn't move much earlier. Spirits need energy to manifest. This one showed promise, so I'm setting up the generator, and we'll see what happens tonight."

Talia nodded.

"What's special about this house?"

"Massacre started here," Bam said, turning the camera toward Talia. She faced away from the lens to the outside, looking out at the bunkhouses and school beyond.

"How could you guys possibly know this was the house?" she asked over her shoulder. Bam moved the camera to Glenn.

"Tell us friend."

"Public record. Old deeds. And you can still see the faint outline of the numbers on the outside. This property was condemned by King County before the purchase of the townsite. We found the old deed records, and it was owned by George Donovan," Glenn explained.

"Now, imagine if he used his powers for good instead of evil," Bam said, moving into a back room. Talia stepped inside, glanced around the main room, and wondered why they hadn't destroyed it. There were empty spaces where the fridge and oven should've been. The sink had long ago been ripped out, along with the cabinetry, which revealed bare walls and capped off plumbing. Overhead were the remnants of a hanging light fixture. The ghostly outline of pictures that once hung on the walls remained. The only piece of furniture left was a wooden chair that looked like it might clatter apart with a strong gust of wind.

"All of my best powers are the evil ones," Glenn replied. "Speaking of, you probably shouldn't be here when we turn this on. It's hard on sensitive people." He was no longer smiling, his expression flat. She thought of how he looked as she pulled him away from the hot springs.

"Summer can't be around when it's on. Makes her sicker than a dog," Bam chimed in, switching the camera off and removing it from his shoulder as he rejoined them.

"You're probably right," she replied. "I'll go find Summer and let her know to keep her distance."

"Good call," Glenn said. She searched his eyes for anything to indicate concern.

"Are you good?" she asked finally, needing assurance that he was unaffected by the morning's episode. Glenn nodded.

"Yeah, yeah, do I not seem okay?" He gave her a questioning look. He was ready for her to go so they could get back to business. They were both watching her and waiting.

"No, you seem great. I'll go."

Talia stepped back from the doorway, her sense of unease growing, and went to seek out Summer. As she walked away, she heard the door open and turned to see Glenn leaning out.

"Hey, Talia," he said. "Thank you."

The area surrounding the forgotten town of Lester within the Mount Baker Snoqualmie National Forest is known for being a hot spot for disappearances and strange occurrences. The neighboring communities regard it with caution, calling it the Bermuda Triangle of the PNW. Most people lost there were never seen or heard from again. Those who survived were irreparably changed. The following highlights a few of these odd occurrences.

On July 31st, 1980, a twenty-five-year-old woman named Laurel Robinson hiked to an old fire lookout in the early hours of the day. She borrowed her dad's old Jeep to navigate the gravel roads to the trailhead, following a map with the route highlighted in yellow. When she did not return by nightfall, her father grew concerned. He called her apartment a number of times and drove by. When he did not locate her there, he systematically dialed the phone numbers for all of the friends listed in her address book. No one had seen or heard from Laurel in the last twenty-four hours. He fell asleep in his armchair that night, waiting at the front window in case she arrived back very late. He did not sleep well.

When morning arrived, and Laurel had not turned up, her father phoned the police. Searchers headed out by midday. The parking lot at the trailhead was empty with no sign of Laurel or the Jeep. The hike to the lookout had a steep grade and a narrow trail. Rescuers were concerned she had fallen or been injured. The weather cooperated, and the Forest Service sent out a helicopter to check the surrounding area for any sign. The only item recovered was a torn piece of Laurel's road map, found in a bush beside the trailhead. When the news reports went out, two people came forward with information. The first, Ben Hopkins, was a sixty-three-year-old man who stated he had been present at the lookout on the morning of Laurel's hike. At the tower to capture the sunrise with his Nikon, Hopkins told the authorities Laurel arrived as he was packing his camera away to depart. She reveled in the view and seemed to be in good spirits. There was no indication she was in distress. Hopkins stated Laurel was dismayed to find the hike shorter than anticipated, so they briefly discussed other quick hikes in the area, and Mr. Hopkins suggested Snoquera Falls. They said their goodbyes, and he departed, leaving her at the lookout long before midday.

The other individual who contacted the police was Pat Owens, a man in his early thirties, who had been hiking in the area the same day. He claimed he had encountered Laurel eight miles away from the lookout trail at Greenwater Lakes, passing her near one of the bridges while she was chatting with another man.

This coincided with what Hopkins had reported about a possible second hike, so rescuers diverted the search to the area, and a massive operation was undertaken. Nearly a hundred volunteers combed the forest along the second trail. When no evidence was found, divers were called in as a last resort to check the river. They canvassed the waterway, section by section, checking under log jams and in rapids for Laurel's body. Police would later say it was the most expensive, and dangerous, search and rescue mission they had undertaken in the Mount Baker Snoqualmie National Forest. Laurel was never located.

Pat Owens was brought into the police station three additional times for questioning, once to the trail to recreate where he had last seen her. Inconsistencies in his story had emerged, and police questioned Pat's version of events. A belief formed that he was responsible for her disappearance and deliberately misleading detectives. At the final interrogation, Owens admitted he had made the tale up out of whole cloth. He had never seen Laurel at Greenwater Lakes at all, he'd been forty miles away on the day she was hiking, and he had no idea where she was. He had seen the story getting attention from the local news, and one lonely night, after a few beers, he'd picked up the phone and told the police a story. Part of him hoped he might end up being right and wind up a local hero.

The police decided to charge Pat Owens with obstruction and making false statements to a public servant. When they arrived at his address, they found a vacant lot. His phone number had been disconnected, and no one at his reported place of employment had heard of him. Pat Owens vanished. Not only that, but there was no record he even existed. Authorities arrived at the conclusion Laurel's disappearance was due to foul play, and Pat Owens was likely responsible. Her father continued to search, offering a reward for any information that would resolve his daughter's disappearance. He spent the later years of his life hanging missing posters at every trailhead within a 20-mile radius. Laurel was never seen or heard from again.

Justin Brosh had been a ranger with the Mount Baker Snoqualmie National Forest for two years. Prior to his time in Washington State, he had been employed with Yellowstone National Park, Great Smoky Mountains National Park, and other national forests for over a decade. Justin was well-liked by his peers and regarded as highly experienced in his line of work.

In 1984, a conflict arose between the Green River Headworks, ostensibly controlled by the City of Tacoma, and the National Forest about public land use. The two sides were set to the task of hammering out an agreement that both favored the protection of the watershed and allowed the public to continue accessing the National Forest. Most important to this debate was ownership of, and access into, the town of Lester. Tacoma claimed they were the lease holder for the road, while the Forest Service said otherwise. Brosh took serious issue with the Headworks placing gates on public service roads and limiting entry to the watershed on Forest land. On more than one occasion, he had brought his concerns to his superiors about the abuse of power by the Headworks and was quite vocal on the subject.

Dozens of members of the public, several of which were citizens of Lester, had contacted their office about gates being chained and locked on service roads through the Forest. In one instance, a new gate appeared overnight. Brosh decided to follow up on the reports. He wanted to know why access was being limited on roads that traversed publicly owned land.

Ranger Brosh inventoried the thirty-two entry points into the watershed, a veritable labyrinth of inlets and outlets, and found locked gates on twenty. He discovered a few had new gates installed where none had existed previously and were not known to the Forest Service. Once he had confirmed the reports to be true, he started an unsanctioned and informal investigation. As part of his inquiry, he completed a wilderness patrol once a week, which included cutting the chains and locks off of every gate on public land.

As the opposing sides worked toward an agreement, Ranger Brosh's findings were brought to light. The Forest Service, with the support of King County, had backed the City of Tacoma into a corner by proving the Headworks had been violating the public's right to access while allowing a logging operation within the watershed. Tacoma had argued strenuously against public use on the basis of pollution of the water source because it would require cost-prohibitive filtration. With Brosh's evidence, it looked like the city's negotiator would have to concede to the forest's demands. An agreement was reached in favor of the Forest and the citizens of Lester. Presentation and endorsement were forthcoming.

Just days before the agreement's final approval, Ranger Brosh left for his wilderness patrol and never returned. His parks truck was found at the bottom of a washout in the Green River, near the town of Lester. The determination was made Brosh was not in the vehicle when it went down the hillside and had likely been staged. His disappearance barely made local news; the lone article buried in the back of the paper.

Brosh's wife, Patsy, and best friend, Lloyd Heller, both approached police about statements Brosh had made prior to his disappearance. He claimed he had uncovered an operation within the Headworks that was systematically blocking access to Lester. He had only begun to scrape the surface but was finding ties to the City of Tacoma that spoke of a seedy underbelly at work. Brosh had taken to carrying a revolver, and Patsy stated he had grown paranoid, spending some nights watching the darkened street in front of their house. Not a single witness came forward. The body was never recovered, and no evidence turned up. Justin Brosh was gone.

The negotiated agreement between the Headworks and City of Tacoma with the Forest Service was squashed and instead, a dictate was presented that all the land surrounding Lester would be managed by the Green River Headworks.

In the summer of 1996, a couple hiking from Yakima, through Corral Pass, to Noble Knob was reported missing. They were a part of a larger group from Japan who flew in for a planned excursion. At times throughout the eighty-mile hike, groups were separated by a half mile or more with guides in front and bringing up the back. Everyone would meet at the end of each day at the pre-planned backwoods camp. Every member of the group had reached Noble Knob with little difficulty. On the first day of the return hike, Aya Kojima and Toshi Nakata failed to reach the camp for the night.

This was not addressed immediately, and the investigation never clarified why. The following morning, when Aya and Toshi had not rejoined the group, one of the guides circled back to Noble Knob to see if they could locate them, and when they found nothing, they hiked out to the nearest place where they could bring in outside assistance.

Search and rescue teams were called in. Over twenty-four hours had passed without sign of the pair. Groups were sent to cover the trail between Noble Knob and Corral Pass, employing a helicopter for the surrounding forest. The search area to cover was large, and the terrain, at times, difficult. To everyone's surprise, Aya and Toshi were found two weeks after they were reported missing, wandering along a forest service road, miles north of the trail. Aside from being a little malnourished, they were safe and had survived in the wilderness.

What made their story sensational was in the details. Originally, searchers sought a couple in their mid-forties, but when they located the lost hikers, they discovered they were bordering on elderly. It was chalked up to a communication breakdown. Aya said little. Experts determined she was suffering from a stress reaction from their time out in the forest. Toshi shared his experience, mentioning a portal in the mountains, and how they had come through changed. It was concluded he was exhibiting signs of mental disturbance, likely dementia, which seemed to be a contributing factor in the pair becoming lost in the first place.

There were questions after the fact about why an elderly couple was allowed to hike such a considerable distance. The other members of the hike had flown back home by the time the couple was found. No one could corroborate or refute the original details except for the guide company hired to oversee the hike. The business changed hands shortly after the couple was found. The company advised it was an error in the paperwork; ordinarily, they would not require approval from a physician before permitting a couple of that age. The new owners told authorities they weren't surprised by the mistake; the paperwork was a mess, and they had been forced to hire new staff. Aya Kojima and Toshi Nakata returned to Japan. Later, the interpreter who handled their interviews was fired for drinking on the job.

In 2005, PCT hiker Adam Leckie, known as Trail Tom for his popular Myspace blog, had a growing social media following when he departed from Campo, California in late April. On the trail, Leckie had taken to writing his blogs down in letter form, then mailing them to his little sister back home in Arizona. She published his thoughts and revelations to the blog for all the world to see. Occasionally he would forward a grainy image taken from the cell phone he carried. When his followers spotted Adam on the trail, they would comment where they encountered him. His blog's popularity increased as he traveled through northern California and passed into Oregon. Nearly a million people were reading about his adventure by the time the last letter was sent from a quick stop off-trail near Highway 12 in Washington State.

Several people reported he was seen at Ulrich Cabin where he sat down with a number of hikers to enjoy lunch. He had uncovered a wealth of "chicken of the forest," a mushroom aptly named for its taste, and shared it amongst the group there. After, Adam's trail went cold. He was reported missing when he did not make a planned meetup with friends at Snoqualmie Pass. His family in Arizona was contacted, and the word went out on his blog. No hikers traveling in either direction had seen or heard from him. It was assumed he had skipped the meetup and had chosen to continue north. After three days of using social media and word of mouth on the trail, the authorities were contacted, and Adam was reported missing. Searchers worked the trail for miles in each direction from his last known location. Signs were hung at every trailhead. No witnesses came forward, no sightings were made, and no letter came to update Adam's blog. Over time, the search was abandoned.

Six months later, a tent and hiking gear were found two miles off trail by a couple of snowmobilers. For an experienced hiker like Adam, this was an unexpected development. His body was never recovered. In his tent, buried amongst his things, Adam's phone and journal were found. Adam had entries for five days. He documented how he had stepped off trail to use the bathroom and could not find his way back. He ridiculed the absurdity of the scenario, but it also disturbed him.

There were two photos in the phone from this time he was missing. One was of Adam on the fourth day. He was already thin from the hike, which lent itself to his sickly appearance, but the picture captured his dramatic weight loss, evident by the sharpness of his cheekbones and the hollow circles of his eyes. His unkempt hair stood on end. The other photo was of a light, authorities believed it was the moon.

The journal entries reflected a developing paranoia as Adam mentioned seeing people in the forest. He wrote about how they moved inside the trees. There was speculation that he had misidentified a patch of psilocybin mushrooms. Others believed he had a psychotic break. His family would confirm that Adam had suffered from bipolar disorder since he was a teenager, and his entries were documenting a manic episode. Both scenarios explained why he was unable to recover the trail. The conclusion was drawn that Adam survived many days in the forest and likely succumbed to starvation or exposure or both.

There was a single video, only a few seconds long, taken on the fifth day. In the background, the viewer can hear the sound of footfalls on the earth and the whisper of vegetation. The screen is black. This would be discussed and debated in the backrooms of the internet for years to come. A voice spoke: "We, his finite creatures, actualize the mind of God. Ultimate reality is mind, not matter. God will be birthed in this holy place." The video ends. Adam was never seen again.

Before filming began on the second night, the team sat down for a meal together. Everyone was tucking into one of their freeze-dried stores except for Alabama, who was preparing a more elaborate dish.

"Voila! Spicy chicken chili noodle. Dinner is served," he announced, handing a bowl over to Glenn with a bow and flourish. Packets of prepared chicken and dried noodles were scattered around him as he poured more water in to boil. Talia spotted a small bottle of Sriracha beside him.

"Is that more contraband?" she cried, feigning offense. "I can't believe you carried that all the way out here."

Bam froze and pointed a sly finger in Glenn's direction.

"T'was my little Korean friend. Made a complaint to management about the lack of heat in the dishes we packed." Bam shrugged in an exaggerated way.

Glenn hung his head in mock shame.

"Something had to be done," he admitted. "But I seem to recall a certain hillbilly thought so too!" Glenn flung a pinecone that caught Bam in the side of the head.

"Whoa! Whoa! I think you missed HR's training about good touch, bad touch." Bam rubbed at the spot, then said to Talia. "Have you ever been to the South? Ain't nothing bland about the cookin'. It was a ne-cess-a-tay."

"Why did I even bother weighing your bags?" Talia laughed.

"I was good," Bam objected as he dumped a packet of noodles into the pot.

"You brought a bottle of liquor! And your camera!"

Bam grinned, pleased with himself. Their small campfire made his orange hair vibrant with color. "I was mistaken, please accept my humble apology."

Dean and Chase ate their meals further back from the fireside while they argued over filming arrangements. Dean repeatedly cast glances in Talia's direction. It made her nervous, and her cheeks heated, understanding she was the subject they were debating. Talia couldn't get the thought of Chase catching her binging out of her mind.

"Are they always like this?" Talia asked Summer, who was tucking into a bag containing chicken and rice.

"Mmm-hmmm," she murmured through a mouthful. "Always." She cast a meaningful gaze at Talia, signaling she had long been over their tense interactions. There was little conversation outside of Dean and Chase's exchange. Everyone was tired, so when Lane offered to make coffee, every single hand went up.

"Alright, location assignments," Chase announced, standing with his hands in the pockets of his windbreaker. "Glenn and Bam, start at the massacre house. Lane, we are setting you up on the hotel grounds initially for an hour or two, then move to the depot. Dean and Summer, you will be in the schoolhouse. Talia, you're with me in the bunkhouse. Talia and I will be circulating at some point to check in with all of you. If we are having good energy in one area, then we will reconvene in that location."

Talia's stomach flipped at the prospect of being alone with Chase. Summer glanced over at her.

"Are you alright?" she asked. Talia nodded, and Summer eyed her suspiciously.

"Would you tell me if something was wrong?" Summer asked. Talia shrugged.

"Maybe not," she laughed. "But really, I'm good." Summer didn't believe her but dropped the matter.

"So, you're with me," Chase said to Talia once all the cookware had been stored, and the cameras and devices were passed around. The rest of the group departed for their designated locations and left Talia with a sinking feeling.

Only a few more nights, she told herself as she yanked on a sweatshirt against the chill. She fit her headlamp over her hair, and Chase handed her one of the cameras.

"No spirit box tonight?"

"No, not for you," he replied with a wink. "Let's go."

They walked in the darkness together. Chase stayed by her side, close enough for the back of his hand to occasionally brush up against hers. She found herself reassured by his silence and the casualness of his touch. Perhaps, he would leave the subject of this morning alone. They navigated around the rubble of Lester's main street, the town's old structures gone to ruin. The remaining buildings loomed in the darkness, ominous without lights in their windows. Summer and Dean's headlamps bounced along near the schoolhouse a short distance away. It did not take long to reach the first of the bunks. A sign hung in the window next to the door reading: *Transients Eat $1.00.*

"What's special about this place?" Talia asked.

"This was the dining hall. It was built for the Northern Pacific, but Scott Paper used it about thirty to forty years ago when they were running logging operations out of Lester," Chase replied, scanning the building with his camera. His tone had changed, shifting into presentation mode, and, although she could not pinpoint why, Talia already had a distaste for it.

"I corresponded with a gentleman who worked for Scott Paper. He had some interesting stories to tell. He had a lot to say about the food. The company hired a cook and a pastry chef to provide meals for the employees. He told me he'd never eaten so well in his life," Chase said.

The sideboard where the food had been laid out was intact and covered in a film of dust. All of the furniture had been removed, and the floors were splintered and full of holes. Through a double doorway, where only the hinges remained from the swinging doors, there was a vacant kitchen where the appliances had been stripped. The vague odor of cooking oil permeated the walls.

"They wore cork boots, which had spikes on the bottom, to climb trees, that's why the floors look like this. He told me about a man he bunked up with for a season. Everyone called him Sailor Man. No one knew his real name, but he wore a white sailor hat every day. 'Crazier than a shithouse rat,' his words, but said the guy wouldn't hurt a fly. He didn't sleep in the bunkhouse; he slept under it. The guy drank like a half gallon of McNaughton's in a night. Then one day he quit, cold turkey. They never saw him drink another drop."

"Years after they worked together, he came across a news article about a stabbing in Seattle. The witness in the article said the man who committed the crime was wearing a sailor hat. A week later, there was a mug shot and there he was: Sailor Man."

"That's a strange story," Talia replied, shivering.

"I thought so too" Chase said. "There were thirty-three bunkhouses originally built by the railroad, and we are going to visit a few of them. Ready to move onto the next?"

"You bet," she replied. Chase was all business, and the truth was she was relieved. They passed through the back entrance. The storm door squalled open. Before she could catch it, the door swung shut and slammed against the frame. Chase delivered a withering look.

"Careful," he admonished her.

Talia went quiet. His tone was like a slap and stirred something eluding her memory. They crossed through the darkness, following a path lined with stones embedded into the earth. Trees, shadowy and tall, loomed at the edge of the light their lamps threw. A number six engraved on a wooden placard hung beside the door. When they entered, the smell that met them was of mildew and dust, the aroma of a place that had been sealed up too long. It reminded her of the neglected out-buildings on her Grandfather's homestead.

"Earlier the EMF went off a bit in here," Chase said. "The bunkhouses were built around the turn of the century, late 1800's or early 1900's, after they moved the facilities from Weston. Workers lived here, six to a bunk. Several men in this one were killed during the massacre."

Chase was using the voice again, the fake one. It dawned on her suddenly. It was Craig's tone, the façade he wore when they sat at the conference table. The voice was exactly the same. She noticed too late Chase was filming. He indicated for her to turn her camera on with an impatient gesture. His irritation with her sparked something, and Talia grew uncomfortable. She had expected a little more explanation from him about her role, and here he was expecting her to read his mind. She turned the camera on and trained it onto Chase.

"Follow me," Chase ordered, leading her back to a hallway with two bedrooms. She followed, conflicted seeing this side of him. One room had frames for a bunk bed and a single, the other held three singles.

"People think George Donovan was looking for someone. At the time of the massacre, there were six men staying in this bunk, and five of them were present. One survived. The last one they found in the schoolhouse. There was speculation he was the target, but no one knows why or what triggered him."

Talia pointed her camera into a shadowy corner and found nothing there.

"He was looking for his wife's lover," Talia said. Chase watched her.

"That's not reported anywhere," he said.

"No," she replied. Her head was swimming. She could sense the competing energies in the space, but there was little more than confusion. "He was wrong though."

Chase pointed the camera at her.

"What happened?"

A door appeared at the edge of her vision. She shook her head, and it disappeared.

"He lost his mind."

Chase nodded, never lowering his camera.

"Is there anyone here who would like to come forward?" he called to the air around them. Talia returned to the hallway, shining her head lamp into every corner. She had a dark foreboding the shadow entity was near, watching and waiting. Chase followed with the camera trained on her.

"Is anyone speaking to you, Talia? What are you experiencing?" Chase asked. She turned to face him, confused. She saw his camera and understood his true intentions. He wanted her to channel.

"I think I'm ready to move on," she said and tried to exit into the main living area. He grabbed her hip, and she whirled around to face him, angry. He set his camera on a high shelf and removed his head lamp.

"What are you doing?" Talia asked, masking her alarm with a forced smile. She brought the camera up between them. He plucked it out of her hands and set it aside. His hands went back to her hips, and he pulled her close to him.

"I've been thinking about you all day," he said. He was wearing a charming expression, and it repulsed her.

Chase leaned in and kissed her. There was no part of her that wanted it to happen, but she suffered it just the same. Having been warned her whole life against leading men on, as if their sexual desire was her responsibility and not their own, she feared sending the wrong message. After a second, she pulled back.

"Is something wrong?" he asked.

So much is wrong, she thought. *Let's start with you speaking to me like an idiot and end with you trying to trick me into channeling when you knew I didn't want to.* She tried to create space between them, but his hold on her was firm.

"I think this might be a little inappropriate," Talia replied, indicating the space they were in.

"What do you mean? We're alone, the cameras are off." He brought her in again, and when she tried to resist, he became forceful and pressed his mouth against hers. He was the hungry thing here. His tongue thrust past her mouth, and his hips arched into hers. His firmness pushed into her, and a hand crept around to grab her ass. Without thinking, and harder than she intended, Talia shoved him back. Chase released her, caught off guard. She took a step back, gasping and wiping her mouth with the back of her hand. He gave her an easy smile.

"Is this a game?" he chuckled.

"No, I don't think this is a good idea. Us being involved. It's a mistake," Talia said. It came out before she could think twice. She always deferred to being nice rather than standing her ground, but she knew what he wanted. No amount of money or peace was worth going that far.

Chase snorted.

"You're kidding, right?" He stepped forward. She held her arms up to stop him. Chase grabbed her wrists, overpowering her defenses, and forced her arms by her sides. She backed away but was pressed up against a wall with nowhere to go. Before she could react, his mouth was on her. He squeezed her forearms painfully as his hips ground into hers. She tried to protest and squirm away, but he held her in place. His intention was clear. Fury and terror flashed through her, and she pushed with all the strength she could muster. Chase took a couple steps back, appraised the distance between them, then sucked his teeth and cocked his head.

"Well, I certainly wasn't expecting this from you. Last night, I'm pretty sure you would've let me screw you against a tree. Now, you are playing coy? You're crazy." She noted his balled-up fists, and the danger in their isolation registered. Talia backtracked.

"I had some time to think, and as much as I would like to do this, I don't think it's a good idea," she stammered.

"Oh, it's a very good idea," he replied and moved forward once more. Her arms went up. He stopped, eyeing the length of her in the light cast from his head lamp, then clucked ruefully.

"I don't want it to interfere with us working together," Talia offered. She looked into his face for the person she had spent the last week with, the one she had found herself becoming progressively more drawn to. She hoped he would come to his senses and realize what he was doing.

"Working together?" Chase laughed, plucking the headlamp from the shelf, and pulling the band to hang around his neck. The light angled down at his feet, and he grabbed both their cameras. "I mean, what good are you? There's not much room on this team for someone who is scared of shadows." He walked away, and she followed. He wheeled on her.

"Did you really think we were still going to bring you in?" Chase scoffed. "You knew how to get *here*, that was the purpose you served. But when we leave, there's no more use for you. After last night at the hotel, I thought we'd struck a gold mine. Either you were an amazing actress or the real deal. Let's face it, Summer's lukewarm as a medium at best and terrible at faking it. Then you turned around and blatantly said you didn't want to communicate with the spirits. What is the fucking use of you then? You really have a talent for the dramatics, but let's face it, Talia, you just aren't that interesting to watch without them. I was mistaken to think we could have a bit of a thing, cause after what I saw this morning, you are a fucking headcase."

"I can't believe I fell for it," she said. Rage filled her. Chase kept speaking. His face had taken on an ugly mask, one of disgust and amusement melded into one.

"You were batshit crazy then and you still are," he spat. "What is it that you were doing at the depot? Why did you have all of that food? I'm starting to wonder if I do need to mention it to the others. Maybe we aren't safe out here with you?" He let it sink in, the secret he was lording over her.

"You still want to get paid, right? If you think it was worth ten grand though, then you are a fucking lunatic. I will tell everyone." If an object had been within her reach as he uttered those words, she would have struck him. She would have used it to wipe the smirk off his face and shut his foul mouth. Instead, she stared into his laughing eyes and recalled every time he had watched from the sidelines as they called her "ghost" and asked her if she needed to go to the bathroom. She reviled him for tricking her into coming here at all and luring her into the false sense of hope that she would finally belong somewhere.

Talia raised her fist, blind with fury. She hated him. The storm door's rusty hinges interrupted their exchange. Bam entered the room, his head lamp momentarily blinding her. He looked between them and took a quick appraisal of their stances.

"Everything alright?" he asked. Chase collected himself with eerie speed, hiding his true self behind the mask once more.

"Everything's fine," he shrugged. Bam glanced at Talia, who was fighting to catch her breath.

"I can't find Glenn. Is he here?"

"No. Have you checked with the others?" Chase asked.

"Didn't you hear us calling? This was my last stop. He's missing."

India scrawled a message on a hastily procured piece of stationary and signed her name in a final flourish. She folded up the cream-colored paper, stuffed it into a crumpled envelope, and hid it in the band of her skirt. The letter would be safe there. As invasive as the staff could be, they did not search their person. She had to make it to the station today. She could not wait any longer, she had to send the letter. A knock came at the door of the bathroom, and India, Dia to those closest to her, pulled the chain to flush the toilet. Another knock came, and the knob rattled.

"India? Are you alright? You were supposed to be down in the dining room five minutes ago," Kate spoke through the door, concern and suspicion seeping through the cracks in the frame. Dia grabbed the doorknob and swung the door wide, where she found Kate already working through her key ring. They might not touch her, but they did not allow her even a modicum of privacy.

"I needed a moment," Dia whispered, smoothing the front of her skirt, and stepping into Kate's space to force her back. She closed the door behind her. Kate turned red, either from embarrassment or irritation. Dia was never sure how to read the nurse, but she hoped she was embarrassed.

"Oh, yes, I'm so sorry, but it's time for breakfast," Kate said. "Were you successful on your own?" The nurse blocked her retreat, her face expectant.

Dia shook her head in response, and a wave of dizziness washed over her. She had grown used to her stomach whining and the hunger pangs, but she could not accustom herself to the vertigo that would overtake her. Dr. Handel had asserted, in her usual forceful way, that it was a symptom of an underlying illness, and the dizzy spells would ease with treatment. They hadn't, even when Dr. Handel cut her food intake further, so she lied and said the spells had stopped. Despite her meals returning to normal, the vertigo continued to grow worse. Dia's body was weakening. She would not be able to make the trip to town much longer. If she waited, it would be too late to save London, and London was dying.

Kate placed a soft hand on Dia's upper arm, leading her out of her assigned room and down the hall of the Green River Hot Springs Hotel and Sanitarium. They passed through the sitting room, and Kate's grip tightened almost imperceptibly as she angled Dia toward the dining area. This was a smaller dining room than the one on the other side of the hotel. This wing was reserved for Dr. Handel's patients. The regular hotel guests stayed and enjoyed the luxury of the mineral spring's baths and chef prepared meals in the main part of the resort.

Tables were set in a greenhouse lined with smoked glass at the back of the building. A jungle of plants adorned the walls and hung from the ceiling. The room was humid, making Dia sweat. London was sitting at the far end of the space alone at a table, and she raised a weak hand to wave her over, as if they were in a crowded restaurant. There were only three other patients under Dr. Handel's care. A large man and an older woman sat at a table together. They had arrived within a few days of the other and became companionable, bonding over their fervent commitment to the program. A young man, the newest patient, sat alone. He had arrived the week prior. They were all there for the same reason: Lana Handel's fasting cure.

Kate escorted Dia to where London sat, and London gave a warm smile to her twin. It made Dia wince. Her sister's eyes were sunken deep into their sockets, a pallid cast across her face. Every bone of her body stood out in stark relief, the muscle and fat starved off of her. She resembled a walking skeleton more with each passing day. Dia smiled back and sat. She wondered how long before her face would look the same. London slumped in her wheelchair; the orderlies moved her into one when she became too frail to walk on her own. Dia was surprised to see her upright. She remained in bed most days. When Kate turned and walked away, London moved to dump her oatmeal into Dia's bowl. Startled, Dia blocked her sister's maneuver. London sat back, breathing hard. It pained Dia to see how much the simple gesture exhausted her sister of what little reserves she had. Dia glanced around the room. No one had noticed.

"Still on?" London asked, looking up at her sister with hollow eyes. Dia swallowed thickly, nodded, and took a large spoonful of gluey, unsweetened oatmeal into her mouth. She grabbed her water glass to force the paste down.

"The flowers are blooming beautifully in the garden. I insisted I come to breakfast today so I could smell them. So nice to see the sun," London said in an airy tone. She continued on as Dia choked down each bite in a rush, keeping a watchful eye for Kate.

Dia came to the sanitarium at the behest of her sister. London, ever obsessed with the latest fads in health, had learned of Handel's fasting cure after a friend had returned from a retreat. After reading Dr. Handel's pamphlet, London exchanged letters with the good doctor to inquire about her facility, set in the wilds of the Cascade Mountains, and discuss the various issues London was experiencing.

Dr. Handel advertised her program as a one-of-a-kind health treatment, utilizing a fasting cure to cleanse the patient of toxins. There were a variety of health benefits; weight loss being one of them. London and India had shared a lifelong struggle with being overweight. London had been so enamored with Dr. Handel's responses, she packed and planned her trip to the States without hardly bothering to consult with India. It was an abrupt shift, but it made India proud of her sister for striking out on her own. Dia followed later when telegram after telegram arrived, imploring Dia to come. When Dia had arrived at the hotel in the far west of the North American continent, she learned the truth of it too late. London was basically a prisoner and now, so was she.

"You know the squirrels are so busy, I wish I could feed them sometimes. Always ratholing something away for winter," London said, speaking more to herself than to Dia. India nodded, although London's reference to the season seemed out of place. She worried he sister was losing her faculties, forcing down the last bit of oatmeal as Kate circled back around to their table.

"Clean bowls?" Kate asked, the lilt of her voice accusatory. India fixed her lips into a flat line. Dr. Handel suggested they suppress the urge to finish their meals, it was one of many tenets of the fasting program. It demonstrated restraint, an ability to change prior bad habits. Certainly, Dr. Handel would make her pay for it later, but she needed all the calories she could consume if she was going to make it into town under her own steam. London had given up her portion knowing this.

It was hard for London to eat anything these days, it was like her body had forgotten how to process it. Most of her meals consisted of vegetable broth made from boiled asparagus or tomato, with all the substance strained out. Either was delicious when you were starving for a meal. Kate delivered an admonishing look and whisked the bowls away.

"Those squirrels are always hiding something," London whispered, lifting the blanket she kept across her lap and revealing an orange and cookie hidden there. Dia laughed to herself, relieved, and wondered how her sister had managed to rathole her own stash.

"It's because they are always planning for another day," Dia replied, reaching under the table so London could slip her the items. Dia hid them in the pockets of her dress, then sucked the crumbs of the cookie from her fingertips. The dress itself was too large, feeling like a girl playing in her mother's gown. The housekeepers had tried to wrestle it away from her last laundry day, but she refused to give it up. Much of her collection of dresses, hats, and stoles had already disappeared into the hands of Dr. Handel; each of her many trunks vanishing one by one. Everything else had been taken. Everything would be taken if Handel had her way.

"The train departs soon," Dia whispered. London nodded. She understood what that meant. She would provide the necessary distraction so Dia could slip out. Patients weren't allowed to visit the town unaccompanied, and Dia had to mail this letter. She feared if she didn't, there would be no hope for either of them.

Shortly after receiving London's messages, India departed to the Americas. After a weeklong trip on an ocean liner, she stayed a week in New York visiting friends, shopping, and resting before the next leg of her journey, then booked the train to Lester, Washington for her reservation at the Green River Hot Springs Hotel and Sanitarium. The train ride was another six days. Dia expected to find her sister thin, vibrant, and healthy and hoped to achieve the same outcome herself.

What she found was a wraith who resembled her twin. She was not being treated for weight loss so much as starved to death under the severe oversight of the formidable Doctor Lana Handel. London insisted she felt wonderful despite the gaunt look of her face and the hollow concave of her stomach. She assured Dia everything was proceeding as it should. London had been seriously ill when she arrived at the sanitarium. According to Dr. Handel, London was riddled with toxins and had been most of her life. Her heavy weight was attributed to inflammation, and to remove all the poison from her system, she would need to fast for an extended period. Dia trusted the doctor, suppressing her initial concerns and giving herself over to the process.

It was not long before India learned it was not toxins Dr. Handel was trying to remove from London. She noticed a thin gold watch adorning Dr. Handel's wrist with a striking resemblance to one belonging to her sister. She dismissed it, choosing to believe she was mistaken, until she saw Dr. Handel wearing a dress Dia had purchased for London herself. The garment had been altered to fit Handel's slighter frame. When she confronted the doctor, Lana's expression sharpened, the clench of her jaw noticeable.

"London insisted I take it. A gift," the woman replied coolly. When India asked London about it, her sister seemed confused, then waved it away.

"Oh, perhaps, I did."

A few days later, India entered London's room unannounced to discover Dr. Handel standing over her with a document between them and a mask of barely concealed fury as London fussed and declined as politely as she could. London had always been the sweeter one of the two. Handel swept up the document and admonished Dia for her inability to knock.

"You should show more courtesy in a healthcare facility," Handel said. "London is due for an enema today. You must respect her privacy during the procedure, especially when she is in such a compromising position." She huffed out of the room. London looked ready to collapse into tears. Dia said nothing until later that night when she snuck into her twin's room. After a bit of badgering, London admitted that Handel was demanding she grant her power of attorney and place her estate under the doctor's management.

"She says at least until I am well," London said, fidgeting with a loose thread on her sheet. "She says I am very ill." Dia shook her head.

"No, you don't seem well, but I think it's because you need food. I've been here a week, and I am starving. Where are your dresses? Your jewelry?" Dia demanded. The women travelled with fourteen trunks between them, and London's were noticeably absent from her room.

"They stored them. For safekeeping. Along with all my jewelry," London replied.

"You didn't give the watch to Dr. Handel as a gift?" India asked.

London shook her head.

"After I sent you all those telegrams, a patient, Ivan, died. He was rail thin, shocking to look at, as I imagine I am now. They kept saying he had a weak heart. They told all of us that, although it is rare, there are times patients die before they can remove all the poisons that have built up in their system. They buried him in the garden, underneath the flowerbeds. At night. I watched them from my window. Dia, they don't know I saw them. I managed to convince myself I had dreamt the whole horrible thing until I overheard Kate asking Lana how she wanted to handle the letters from his uncle. I thought it was strange they hadn't notified his family about his passing. Especially since the lawyer had come to discuss his estate. It wasn't until Dr. Handel approached me about updating my will that I understood. When I declined, and told them my will was safe back home, she became relentless. They dialed down the amount of food they were giving me, serving me less and less. The enemas began. Sometimes they would give me nothing but hot water and lemon at meals. But Dr. Handel is so convincing. How she talks about the treatment, what's wrong with my body, I believe her. I believe what she is saying. But when I catch a glance of myself in the mirror or have endured one of her horrid osteopathic treatments, I know something terrible is happening here." London shuddered. "Dia, I want to go home, but they won't let me leave."

After the interaction with Dr. Handel in London's room, Dia's plan for care became more aggressive. Osteopathic treatments were ordered, and the experience was torture. Dr. Handel used her hands and fists to smash her stomach and pound into the muscles of her back, leaving her whimpering and barely able to get off the table. When she declined the next treatment, she was fed nothing. Regular enemas were recommended to release stubborn poisons that held on in the lower intestine. According to Dr. Handel, it was the most efficient way to flush them out, she herself required them. Dia declined and was advised without them, she would be placed into a full fast. She was served nothing for dinner or breakfast the next day. The hungrier she became, the easier it would be to crack her resolve and force compliance. Dia proceeded with the enemas.

India came to understand Dr. Handel's operation. The hotel attracted a wealthy clientele. The lavish amenities, from the expensive paintings on the wall to the one-of-a-kind china, were bait. The staff were tasked with spotting the clients amenable to the doctor's solutions. The clients prone to mysticism or naturalism were her primary targets. If they were a good fit, Dr. Handel would invite them to extend their stay in the sanitarium. Some were released within a month, looking fully refreshed from their stay. It was uncanny. They looked like they had reversed time. Others remained.

Handel's real targets were the clients like London and India. Those clients had little to no close family and more wealth than they could spend in a lifetime. Dia later realized Handel only let London send the telegrams because they were exuberant and regaling the glory of the treatment. Handel lured India to the sanitarium, so she could eliminate London's only other family member and wrap her hands around the entirety of the Williams' fortune. London was nowhere close to being released by the time Dia arrived. They were slowly, slowly grinding her down.

Dia no longer had any hope she would make it out alive if she didn't act. Shortly after London's admission about Ivan, Dia asked to send a telegram. Dr. Handel flatly told her she was not permitted to go to town alone. Instead, she wrote a letter to their governess, who was visiting family in Australia. She asked Kate if she could go into town to mail the letter.

"We mail all letters," Kate replied, holding out her hand.

"They read all the letters," London advised her. "I tried to send you a letter after the telegrams. I noticed it was sitting on Dr. Handel's desk three days later, opened. I suspect she rewrites them in a more positive light."

The only way Dia could get the communication out to Ms. Hemings was to deliver it to the post office herself. Not knowing that Stuart, Dr. Handel's enforcer, had already been assigned to watch her, she snuck off. No sooner had she handed over the letter to the postal worker, but Stuart stepped up behind her, slipped the worker a fold of money, and the worker handed the letter back to him.

India realized how foolish she was to assume they weren't monitoring her every move. She regretted exposing her position. After, Dia only received solid food every other day. The remainder of the time was vegetable broth. She never knew she would come to relish asparagus water like she once enjoyed a chocolate eclair. Dia grew weaker, unable to walk for long without feeling faint from the exertion. Their time for action was dwindling to nothing. Knowing the worker was compromised Dia would bypass the post office altogether. She planned to take it to the train station directly, where she would pass the letter to someone who would ensure it was delivered on her behalf. London begged her to get on the train and never look back. As tempting as it sounded, Dia insisted she would not go without her twin, her other half. And she watched that half slowly die, wasting away to nothing. It was time for Dia to act.

After breakfast, they were sent to the garden to take in the sunshine. It was a bright spring day. London had an air of calm surrounding her as she watched a bumblebee visit the flowers of an effervescent pink rhododendron. Dia felt no such relief, her anxiety at an all-time high. If they caught her, there would be no second chance.

"How are you ladies faring?" a high voice came from behind them. Neither needed to turn to know that Dr. Handel was checking up on them, she often called upon them in these quiet moments. Handel ran a campaign of terror meant to remind them that they were always being watched, and nothing they discussed was secret. Dia believed it was intentionally designed to keep them unsettled at all times. It would ensure they could never talk long enough to form a plan or compare notes.

"Good morning," London whispered, her tone flat and distant.

"How was breakfast?" Dr. Handel asked.

"It was delicious," London replied without missing a beat. "It's been so long since we had something of any substance. Yesterday, it was nothing but watered-down orange juice for every meal. You must have run out of oranges!"

London looked sweetly up at Dr. Handel, both knowing it was a jab. India wished her dear sister hadn't decided to find her spine at that exact moment, but she supposed it was all London had left. It would not be long before she was too weak to do anything but sign her life away in the hopes of a meal. In the late hours after dark, when Dia would come into her room to seek the comfort of her twin, London would plead with her, arguing that they would feed her if she signed off on the conservatorship.

"That's all they want. We will have your half!" London cried. Ever the obedient one, India knew how much it pained her to say no, especially to Dr. Handel. "We could sell the estate in Britain and move to Australia to live out the rest of our days. I always hated that dusty old house."

"Once you sign it, there will be nothing stopping them from killing you," she replied. "Please just hang on." London was growing desperate, knowing her sister, always one of weak resolve, would give in. The only thing keeping them alive was the money, which Dr. Handel was slicing off in bits and pieces. First, it was the jewelry, then the possessions they carried. She had already convinced London to make out several checks, in considerable sums, for the cost of her treatment and stay. India wondered how long before Handel concluded that the entire estate would be left to Dia, and they could dispense of London outright. Why slice up half the pie when you could walk away with the whole thing? The girls were the sole heirs to their family fortune. Their governess had substantiated their claim, verifying that no other living relative existed, which left no one to claim the Williams' fortune.

"You are both doing so well with the treatment," Lana said, stepping in front of them, her hands folded together behind her back. Her auburn hair was swept up and away from her face, the bun held together with an expensive looking fastener. Dia noticed the cameo brooch Handel wore and realized it had belonged to their mother. It was a keepsake passed to London after their mother's passing, and here it was on their doctor. The thought filled Dia with rage, but she bit the inside of her cheeks to stop herself from speaking out loud.

Lana reached out and stroked London's sunken cheek.

"Unfortunately, whatever underlying illness you are suffering from is still ravaging you. I will need to be extending your stay, London, and there are a few matters that need attending to," she said, her lips disappearing into a flat smile. The woman was evil, Dia was certain of it. The essence radiated off of her.

"I will be stopping by your room this afternoon." Lana turned to Dia next. "I believe you are due for a mineral bath today. I can see the toxins building up again. Your cheeks are flush. That high color indicates a poison is at work. We should send you immediately to counteract any damage. I will have Stuart come collect you." Dr. Handel flashed a different face to Dia, one filled with avarice.

"Oh, that won't be necessary," Dia tried feebly to object. Dr. Handel heard none of it.

"As your doctor, India, you are here for my cure. The toxins that live in you are not easily removed from the body. That's why we try to limit food, we must starve the poison and flush it out. But the chemicals are stubborn, very stubborn. Perhaps you need a few days of cleanse? Your reactiveness is another indicator that the toxins have built up. I think we'll get that started today as well. Good day to you both." Lana sauntered back into the hotel. Dia could almost admire Handel's intelligence, how she had manipulated the whole town to work on her behalf and conceal what she was doing behind the scenes. It was any wonder she had managed to pass herself off as human this long.

"You have to go now," London whispered. "Stuart will come and take you for your bath." Dia tried to object, but London gave her a reassuring smile. It hurt India's heart, it used to be such a beautiful smile. London brought something up to her mouth and chewed, then abruptly threw herself into the leather back of the chair and thrashed with great effort.

"Go!" she urged. Dia stood up, shocked, and watched her sister slide down the seat of her wheelchair onto the ground while she spasmed and thrust. Foam poured from her mouth.

"Help!" Dia screamed. "Help! Please help!" She crouched next to her sister to keep her head from hitting the ground, and a wave of dizziness overcame her. Stuart burst into the garden with Kate and Dr. Handel right behind him. They surrounded the frail woman, crowding out India, as they tried to pin down London's seizing body.

"My word!" Kate uttered. Dr. Handel shoved her aside.

"London!" Dr. Handel grabbed both of London's arms as she crashed and banged against the ground. "Stuart grab her head, keep her from biting her tongue." Dia backed away, her presence forgotten, and once she reached the door, she turned and hurried away. The pounding of her heart managed to carry her through the small dining room and into the central hall toward the front entry.

Dia burst through the front door. Temporarily blinded by the sun, she hustled forward into the open courtyard. She set her sights on the hedgerow, praying she would not be spotted. The manicured shrubbery surrounded and separated the property's gardens from the forest, if she passed beyond it, she could disappear into the trees. A horse whinnied, startling Dia. She glanced back. The horse was strapped to an empty carriage, impatiently stamping its feet. Just as she felt relief that no one was there, her toe caught on a stone. For one heart-stopping second, she thought it was going to end with her crashing facedown into the gravel drive, and then she managed to regain her balance.

Once she disappeared behind the hedge, she was able to slow her pace. Her heart pounded in her chest. She took several long breaths, fearing the dizziness would overcome her and was relieved when it didn't.

She followed the road to Lester for several paces, then cut through the forest along a well-worn footpath. If she remembered from her last outing, the trail would place her on the edge of town, in a residential section, away from the main street and shops. After, it would be a straight shot to the train depot. The key was that they would not begin looking for her there or on the outskirts of town. As long as she could reach the station where she would be in public view, none of the hospital staff would cause a scene.

It was a strenuous passage through the trees, but the shade from their branches cooled her. The fern and shrubbery grew dense along the trail. Once her heart slowed, her stomach gurgled, and she remembered London's gifts. Dia crouched down next to a giant Douglas fir and pulled the cookie from her skirt pocket. It had crumbled a bit, but she did not hesitate to cram the entire treat into her mouth. The taste of sugar exploded on her tongue, as the rich butter melted in her mouth. It was without a doubt the best thing she had ever eaten. When it was gone, and each crumb plucked from her pocket and sucked off her fingers, she pulled out the orange. It took some work to get the skin off, which she did in pieces. She was less enthusiastic about the fruit. Dia had been served plenty of orange juice and oranges in her time at the Green River Hot Springs Hotel and Sanitarium. Sometimes, it was all they were given at a meal. But food was food, and she devoured it, taking large bites through its tangy flesh and slurping the juice off her chin. Before she continued, Dia verified the letter remained tucked into her waistband.

The woods in Lester were a dark place, even during midday, and many times, Dia glanced around, feeling eyes upon her. Evil spirits dwelled here, and evil people were drawn to evil places. She was angry she had allowed this wicked woman to infiltrate their lives. She was angry she was trapped in this horrid town in a dump of a country where they allowed hacks to get medical licenses and pretend to be doctors. Her rage helped her continue forward.

The darkness withdrew as she neared the edge of the forest. She emerged in front of a small white house with a dirty, barefoot child standing in front of it. The girl, a towhead with a flat expression and thin, straight strands of hair hanging down to her waist, watched Dia as she passed by. She waved at the girl, who only blinked in response. Dia did not rush but carried herself with an air of confidence she did not feel. If it looked like she belonged here, onlookers would believe she did.

India knew that Dr. Handel had sympathizers and employees amongst the townspeople, and she recalled a warning they would be of no assistance to her if she left the facility. These people had been advised that Dr. Handel's patients should not be aided in any way, especially if they requested food. There would be no refuge here. Lester was full of people who would turn a blind eye to Dr. Handel's abuse. The postal worker proved that.

Dia strode toward the station, the white smoke from the engine stack coming into view. They were preparing to depart soon. Panic flooded her. Had they been wrong about the departure time? She moved faster, remaining on the road that skirted the edge of town in the hopes she would remain unseen by her captors. That is how she thought of them now. She was a hostage, her and London both, and the staff at the hotel were their kidnappers. A wave of dizziness threatened to overtake her, the exertion of the journey was taking its toll. Her muscles had atrophied in so short a time.

The station came into view as she neared a bisecting street. Without thinking, she walked past, exposed, and realized, too late, her lack of caution. She spotted the hotel's carriage coming down the next lane over. Dia panicked, threw herself behind a tree and pressed herself against its trunk. She peered out to find the driver was the garden boy, one of the young locals the hotel employed. She only ever saw him chopping wood and delivering it to various hotel rooms. A wealthy looking couple sat in the back, the woman with a bright red feather in her hat. While the young woman looked at the forested mountains around them, her partner, a man old enough to be her father, ogled her.

Reassured the carriage was on a different course, India made haste for the train station, the engine's white plume evaporating over the river. She slowed her walk again, regulating her breathing to control another dizzy spell. Sweat coated her skin, and her dress weighed on her body. An overwhelming urge to give up welled up inside her, followed by the look of London's face as Dr. Handel stood over her. Dia held her head up and continued.

She was only a short distance away when the thundering of hooves arose behind her. She ducked behind a shrub. Stuart was on the hunt, forcing a black mare into an open run. He turned toward town. How he hadn't spotted her was a wonder, one she had no time to consider. She waited until the bald man on the horse was out of sight, and she fled.

Dia's legs were like cement blocks. The station was so close she could see the people milling around on the platform and the engine's smokestack. Her thighs burned in protest as she forced herself to run. She shoved a hand into the waist of her skirt to get the letter. For a split second, she feared she'd lost it, until her hand closed around the paper. She pulled it from her skirts, running hard with her last hope clutched in her fist. Another wave of dizziness overcame her and darkened her vision.

"Hey!" Stuart yelled. Running faster with the icy finger of fear tracing its way up her spine, she prayed she would not collapse before she could see this task through.

Dia reached the platform, hoisting herself onto the wooden planks rather than using the stairs. Her skirt caught on a splinter, and she yanked the dress until it tore. Stuart rode in on the top of the mare, dismounting in one fluid movement. She turned and ran full out, her boots stomping hollowly on the platform, and the slap of Stuart's footfalls came hard behind her. A new rise of adrenaline overtook her, a primal terror she was about to be snared into a trap she could not escape from. Her legs found renewed vigor as she closed the distance between her and an open passenger coach. She reached it, leaping onto the top stair and collapsed, her overexerted legs unable to launch her fully inside. A woman gasped when India crashed into the car and clutched the young girl beside her. The other passengers stood to look at the commotion. The whistle blasted its final warning as she lay face down on the train car floor, struggling for air and unable to stand.

Dia locked eyes with the girl, no more than the age of ten, and with a practiced flick of her wrist, she threw the letter. The envelope, too light with its short missive, fell short. The girl stared at her, an expression of alarm on her face. The conductor came down the hall toward her. The girl stretched her leg and concealed the letter under her shoe.

"Are you alright?" he asked, helping her to her feet as Stuart climbed into the stairwell behind her.

"Randall, she's with me," Stuart stated, slipping an arm around her waist. She was repulsed by his touch, but unable to fight him. The conductor hesitated to release her from his own hold, his mouth flattened into a firm line and for one second, Dia thought this man might help her. They locked eyes, and Dia believed she could silently transmit her desperation to him. He would keep her, and Stuart would be forced to step off, unwilling to cause a scene. The conductor glanced away, a mask of shame coming over his face, and Dia knew all was lost. Stuart led her off the train. She spared a final glance back at the girl and found her looking down at the letter now in her hand.

"Please," Dia called, and the girl understood, nodding and solemn. Dia fought the urge to scream, wanting nothing more than to call out for help and finding herself incapable. When the vertigo crashed over her, this time she did not fight it and instead, let her world go dark.

***

London gave in to Dr. Handel within a few days of Dia's station run. She signed off on the power of attorney, confident the letter would reach their governess. She assumed once Lana Handel had her fortune, London would be allowed to eat again. She was wrong. Dr. Handel did as Dia had expected and let her waste. Within weeks, she was dead, and it was Dia who occupied the wheelchair.

After her escape from the hotel, Dr. Handel's abusive treatment escalated. Dia was subjected to daily enemas, mineral spring baths so hot the nurses could not put their own hands in the water, and osteopathic treatments like beatings. She endured it, and she prayed. Too weak to swallow solid food, she was served one cup of vegetable broth twice a day. Dia held on, hope waning with each passing day.

When Ms. Hemings arrived at the hotel, Dia wept. The governess took one look at India and contacted the authorities.

Dia weighed a meager fifty-seven pounds on the day she was released from the sanitarium. Doctors in Seattle would spend months nursing her back to health. As it would turn out, India Williams was so ill upon her release, she could not provide a statement to explain the depravity of Dr. Handel's treatment. The investigation was forestalled, so India used her remaining wealth to seek justice for her twin sister. She paid for the prosecution when the county refused and sent an investigator to the hotel. He quit after only a few weeks and returned every last penny of her money, advising she was better off to walk away. He refused to explain further, except to assure her, she would be in grave danger if she continued her inquiries.

Many people had been complicit in her captivity and allowing London to die. India, with the assistance of her governess and the remainder of her substantial wealth, cajoled and bullied the county to act. Eventually, they were left with no other choice, and Lana Handel was arrested.

Talia wasted no time to leave on the pretense of finding Glenn. She blew past Bam and fled into the night. A nearly full moon hung low in the sky.

"Where you goin'?" he called, starting to follow her and stopping when he saw her break into a run.

"There's one more spot I need to check!" she yelled. It felt good to run and put distance between herself and Chase. If Bam hadn't arrived at that exact moment and interrupted them, she would done something she would come to regret. As she weaved between the bunkhouses toward their campsite and the hotel ruins beyond, the weight of the things Chase said began sinking in.

"Damn it," she huffed as she ran, lost except for the beam of her headlamp. Their fire at dinner had been squelched, and she was having trouble orienting herself in the dark. She slowed to a walk. If she found the old road to the hotel, she could locate the footpath to the hot springs above. She had to check there, but the others couldn't know. If it was anything like what she and Glenn had experienced that morning, it would be dangerous for them too. There was something wrong with the water in those hot springs. If Glenn had returned to the pools, she would find him. After, she would talk to Lane, leave him with the map, then pack to leave first thing in the morning before the others were awake. It went against her conscience to leave the team stranded, but she wanted nothing more to do with *Dark Dimensions*.

Through the forest, she spotted the dim outline of the tents in the glomming. Talia moved up to a jog through the campsite. She skirted the tents and their reflective tie downs, then tripped over a backpack, randomly discarded several feet away from the others. She caught herself and frustration welled up inside of her.

It was all falling apart. Another dead end. Had they known the whole time she was just a means to an end? Talia retraced her interactions with Chase, with Summer, framing them through this lens. Had they lured her into believing she would be a part of the team to convince her to sign on to Lester? She continued along the road toward the hotel grounds, contemplating this new reality.

Talia gained speed, and her lungs burned. She emerged from the forest by the hotel grounds and found the well-concealed trail heading up toward the pools. In her periphery, she caught a flash of light gliding across the treetops. Talia stopped and scanned the darkness, holding her breath. She shined her own headlamp over the wild gardens and fragments of foundation. Had she imagined it?

"Glenn?" she called. There was no answer. Talia felt exposed. She turned off her headlamp and removed it from her crown. Her heart raced as she tried to steady her breathing, waiting for the light to appear a second time. Someone was there, concealed in the darkness, she was positive of it.

A sliver of brilliant luminescence crested the ridge above her as the waxing moon rose, looking impossibly large. She relit the headlamp but carried it low, with the beam on her feet. Upon reaching higher ground, she turned to survey the hotel plat once more. The forest below was silent as her eyes adjusted under the moon's aura. The feeling remained. Although she saw nothing in the void, she sensed the energy waiting there. The darkness was full of presence. She was sure now; she was being watched.

Her senses demanded she abandon her errand, but it occurred to her that she might be the only one who knew where Glenn was. Talia took several slow deep breaths to steady herself, then reluctantly turned her back on whoever, or whatever, was below. Finishing her ascent up the mountainside, she found the long flat path hugging the cliffs and followed it to the pools. When she rounded the final outcropping revealing the grotto, she found no one.

"Glenn," she whispered. There was no evidence that anyone had even been there at all. No clothing or shoes, no water splashed on the outside of the pools, no light or equipment. The water reflected no light.

"Shit," Talia said to herself, crouching down with her back against the rock. She tore her gaze away and shielded her mind against their pull. She could feel the thermal energy coming off of them, color shimmering on their surface, and her mind drifted.

"Glenn!" a voice called below her, and it brought her back to herself. It was a mistake to come here alone. Talia turned from the pools and walked away. Her thoughts cleared, the same release of her mind as before, and her concern for Glenn returned. She had been so confident he would be at the hot springs that she had no idea where else he could have gone. Her mood darkened, the malaise after the pools setting in, along with her conclusion that Glenn was really and truly lost. The forest had stolen another soul. She resolved to head back to camp and start a fresh search, unwilling to give up.

As she walked away, she heard the scuff of rocks behind her. Talia wheeled around, bringing her headlamp up to catch the source of the sound. No one was there.

"Glenn?" she asked, her voice shaky. "Is that you?" She waited. "If you think this is funny, it's not. You are genuinely scaring me. Everyone is worried about you." She hoped Glenn would step out from behind the outcropping and surprise her. Instead, she heard a sigh. All of her senses reacted, and she froze. She was experiencing prescience again; she knew someone, human or otherwise, was standing behind the outcropping at the end of her beam of light. For one horrifying moment, she imagined a creature had emerged from the pools, black as ink and humanoid in form, and followed her down the trail.

Calls erupted from below her, her name alongside Glenn's, and she backed away, keeping the light aimed low to watch her footing on the precarious hillside. With enough distance, she turned and moved as quickly as she could to get away. She nearly missed the trail down to the hotel and sliding a time or two in the process of bolting down the mountainside. When she reached the bottom, she didn't stop running until she reached their campsite. A person knelt next to the firepit, nursing a small fire. As Talia drew closer, she saw it was Summer, huddled with her knees tucked into an oversized sweatshirt, feeding sticks to the growing flames.

"Talia! Where were you?" Summer demanded, jumping up and throwing her arms around her. Talia accepted the hug, relieved to see another person.

"I thought I knew where Glenn would be," Talia panted, her breathing slowing.

"This isn't good," Summer said, nervously pacing back and forth.

"Where is everyone?" Talia asked.

"Lane is checking the river. Chase and Bam are walking along the perimeter of the forest. Dean is looking in there." She indicated to the town. "I was so worried about you." She shoved Talia with a gentle hand. Summer looked as if she was about to cry. "What should we do?"

"I don't know," Talia shrugged. "He could be anywhere. But he couldn't have gone far." *Unless he fell in the river,* she kept the thought to herself. She sat down on the weathered log beside the fire. As the adrenaline retreated, fatigue draped across her like a cloak. She threw a few bigger hunks of wood onto the fire, then braced her elbows on her knees and hung her head. What Chase had said to her in the bunkhouse was resurfacing. A voice wormed around in her brain: *They are all in on it. Every one of them in on the joke.* Talia eyed Summer as she threw another branch into the flames and listened to it pop. It was all a lie, an elaborately staged hoax with Talia at the center.

"Were you in on it?" Talia asked. Summer stopped. Her brow furrowed.

"In on what?"

"It's all fake, right? It's been bogus from the start. An elaborately staged fake for the vlog. What's the word you guys keep using: 'exaggerated.' I can't believe I didn't realize it sooner. Were you guys really going to include me on the team, or was it just to get me to bring you out here?"

Summer came closer, her face registering her confusion and shock.

"Talia, what are you talking about?" she asked in a small voice. "We are all stressed out, but what are you saying? Of course…"

Talia couldn't stop. Her rage bubbled over as she awakened to the truth.

"Of course you knew. You and Dean are as thick as thieves, and Chase and Dean are always together. Every single thing you all told me was a lie." It was painful to confront what she had suspected from the start, but the urge to fill that aching hole had been overwhelming. She grabbed one of the backpacks in front of her and unzipped it, rooting around inside, and then dropping it to the ground. She found another and started looking through, unable to find what she was desperately looking for. Frustrated, she cast it to the ground.

"Where's all the food?" Talia asked.

"We just ate. How can you eat right now? Glenn is gone," Summer replied. "Talia, I know you are upset. We are all upset, but you need to calm down." Summer's tone moved from confusion to righteous anger.

"Calm down? Oh, don't worry, I'll be gone at first light," Talia responded, grabbing another backpack, and turning the contents upside down. "Where is it?"

Chase and Bam appeared at the edge of the firelight.

"Did either of you find anything?" Bam asked, then noticed Talia searching through all of the backpacks with increasing frustration. "What's goin' on?" He looked to Summer for explanation, who responded by throwing her hands up in the air.

"You tell me! She's saying she's going to leave in the morning. That everything is a lie. This is all fake. I don't even know what she's talking about!" Summer wailed. Chase folded his arms across his chest, remaining quiet. Bam took a few steps toward Talia.

"Don't come near me," Talia said. Bam stopped and looked around at the others, then shook his head and gave a soft chuckle.

"Is this it? Are we in Lester's Twilight Zone now and everyone's gon' start goin' crazy?" he asked.

Talia snapped.

"Chase offered me a blank check to bring your team out here, and it was bullshit. He offered me a place on the team, and that was a lie. He never had any fucking intention of bringing me in. It was all so I would bring *Dark Dimensions* to Lester. I didn't even want to do it, but I needed the money. I never wanted to come here. He manipulated and lied to me. All your fake setups, your cold reading, your staged bullshit. Try to tell me none of you knew! He even pretended to like me. And I almost fell for it. Was it an act when you apologized for the bullying too? Of course it was! I am so fucking stupid." Talia frantically started tearing open tents to check inside each. The pain of Chase's betrayal and the need to alleviate it was overwhelming. She didn't care anymore. The compulsion to fill this terrific hole inside her, the gaping maw of isolation and sadness that lived and breathed within her, was powerful and all encompassing.

"Where is it?" she screamed.

"He really did all that?" Dean asked. Talia whirled around to find Dean and Lane had returned.

"Are you pretending like you didn't know? This has to be part of the show. Where's the camera?" She gave a dark laugh. "Chase, your best friend, promised me a boatload of money to bring *Dark Dimensions* to Lester. I declined. Twice. So what? Did you guys all agree to send Summer over to persuade me? She's the one who convinced me to join. She said we'd have our own show, just her and I. Where's Glenn? All part of the schtick? The lie that you tell your fans? I want no part in this. He said I'm not getting paid, so I'll leave you a map, and you can find your own way home."

Dean's expression darkened with Talia's words. He looked across the fire at Summer, then back over at Chase.

"You told her we weren't going to pay her?" Dean asked him. Chase shook his head, holding his hands up in mock offense.

"She's making that up. She's lost it," Chase replied. "Look at her. I caught her this morning…" Talia cut him off.

"This is great. Did he tell anyone of you what he really did to me when I was a kid? He had no problem talking about how I got lost out here, but did he tell you how he tormented me after I made it out? How he helped pin me down while the girls at our school made fun of me? How he'd hold his nose whenever I walked by? How he laughed when the other kids joked about me and called me names? Yeah, he's a great guy. One of a kind. Then the minute he got me alone, he tried to get down my pants," Talia stood back, looking at each of them. She knew she looked insane, and she didn't care. She couldn't believe she had let this happen.

"I fucking knew it!" Summer erupted, wheeling on Chase. "You can't keep your cock out of anything. I told you to leave this one alone. We need her. She actually has a gift! It's so much more than what I can do, she could make it happen for us. For all of us! All you had to do was not sleep with her!"

"Oh, please, Summer! Trying to be all self-righteous as if you didn't play your part. I offered her the money, and she still said no. We all know the only reason she bought in was because you 'comforted' her," Chase replied with a smirk. Summer went silent.

"Wait? What does that mean? 'Comforted' me?" Talia asked.

"Summer's medium game is weak when it comes to the supernatural, but she's very good at affecting people's emotions. We call it 'comforting.' Does she touch you? Do you feel better when she does? Then you've one hundred percent been 'comforted' by Summer," Chase laughed, both impatient and irritated.

"Is that true?" Talia asked. Summer took a couple of steps toward Talia, her eyes pleading.

"Yes, I did. I'm sorry. I knew right away you were powerful. I needed you, and I was entirely serious when I told you about my plan. I had no idea how strong you were until we came out here. What you did last night was unreal, Talia. Together, we could be unstoppable. Please don't go. We were going to give these guys a running start, then we can go off on our own," Summer explained, her eyes glassy with shame. Bam scoffed and ran a frustrated hand over his beard.

"And when were you going to tell me?" Dean asked, surprised anger written across his face. "Don't stop now, let's just air out all the dirty laundry. Summer was going to abandon *Dark Dimensions*. Chase tried to stick his dick in the new girl. Again. You told us plenty about her bad home life and how she got lost out here, but conveniently left out the part about you being one of her childhood bullies? What the hell is wrong with you? No wonder she didn't want to do the job!"

"Summer was the one who got her to agree." Chase waved a hand at Summer in an attempt to shift the blame.

"So, you both coerced her into coming out here?" Dean glared at Summer. "How much money did you offer her?" He wheeled on Talia, his eyes filled with fire. "How much did he offer you?"

"He told me to name my price," Talia replied, her tone matter of fact. "He agreed to ten thousand."

"Are you fucking kidding me?" Dean hissed.

"Ya'll need to calm down. You can argue till the cows come home after we find Glenn," Bam interjected.

"Awesome. Fantastic, why not just have Summer 'comfort' everyone," Talia interjected.

"He's right, this drama has to wait. We need to find Glenn. I can address one thing though: Talia, the offer to join us wasn't fake. I can't believe how these two went about it. I had no idea about their machinations. I cannot tell you how sorry I am that you were brought out here under false pretenses. We don't have 'name your price' money. I didn't ask because Chase said he'd taken care of it. Summer convinced me you would be a positive addition to the team. I wasn't sure at first, but after getting to know you, I wanted to formally invite you to join *Dark Dimensions* to stay." He let it sink in. For the first time she understood him. He wasn't standoffish or aloof, he was protective and reluctant. A defense mechanism. They were not so different after all.

"Right now, we need to find Glenn," he finished. Dean was calm and started to walk away.

"We have another problem," Talia announced, her anger evaporated. "All of our food is gone."

In her compulsion to binge, she had discovered a new problem in addition to their missing teammate. Dean strode back over and picked up Glenn's bag. It was empty, save for a few pieces of miscellaneous gear. He checked another. Lane peered into the tent he shared with Glenn and tossed the sleeping bags. Glenn's was still inside, along with a few articles of his clothing. Chase checked the bag on the ground in front of him.

"You have got to be kidding me," Lane muttered, standing back, and watching as the other two men tossed aside the bags.

"What the hell is going on here? What do we do? Where's the food?" Dean asked no one in particular.

"No one has been here for the last hour at least, and before that I was with you," Summer said to him. She was pacing again, absently twirling a strand of her dark hair in a terrified frenzy. Panic filled her voice.

"I thought I saw someone in the forest," Chase announced.

"Why is this the first we are hearing about it?" Dean howled. His vitriol toward Chase returning.

"I thought it was Glenn. I called out to him, but then they disappeared. Just poof, gone. I kind of assumed I imagined it. It was dark. I thought it was a trick of the shadows, my head lamp bouncing off the trees. I was going to say something when we got here, but…" he trailed off. "I could've sworn though, someone was out there."

"Someone was out by the hotel. I saw their light. I called out to Glenn, but no one replied. I don't think he would mess with me," Talia said. "I've been worried about him all day. He was sleepwalking last night. I found him, early, and he didn't seem to have any clue how he got out there."

"Got out where? The hotel?" Dean asked. She hesitated, and when she didn't reply, he asked again. "Out where, Talia?"

"Up in the mountains."

"We should go and look for him." Lane started away from the fireside.

"No!" Talia said, too abrupt to be ignored. "I already checked where I found him this morning. We need to stay together. I think the best course of action at this point is to leave at first light and get search and rescue out here to find Glenn be. We are not trained for this. Our food supply is gone. One of us could wind up hurt, or worse, dead, and it will only exacerbate the problem. We just need to leave."

"No one is expecting us until Friday!" Summer objected.

"Then we find the road and walk until we have cell service. We'll be fine. We can pack up at first light and walk out of here. We don't have any food, our friend is missing, and someone might be out there. This is the Lester we were warned about. Now, it's time to go," Dean said, agreeing with Talia's assessment. He threw another nasty look in Chase's direction, and Chase hung his head, turned away and stalked to the edge of the fire. Dean sat down on the fallen log and fed a few more sticks to the flames.

"We should continue to try to alert Glenn to our position. We can use the whistle. Maybe he'll hear it," Talia said.

"Give me one. I'll do it," Dean offered. Talia removed the emergency whistle from the front of one of the packs, handed it to Dean, and sat down beside him.

"We can take turns," she said and readied herself for a long night.

Not a lot changed after Dr. Handel was arrested. Her lawyer argued that she had patients to care for, and London Williams's death was an unfortunate result of the illness in which she was seeking treatment. Handel was released on bail after a few days. Upon her release, she gave a statement to the press. Lana maintained she was guilty of nothing, that she believed in her medical training, and therefore, would remain committed to the valuable work she was doing.

The Green River Hot Springs Hotel and Sanitarium continued to operate as usual with a few minor adjustments. Dr. Handel advised her faithful servants they would "exhibit caution" given the sanitarium's current legal status. There was a reduction in the more aggressive therapies: enemas were shortened, and manual adjustments were less vigorous. Most notably, there was a marked increase in the amount of food prescribed to each client.

Dr. Handel was staunch in her conviction that the doors remain open while she was under investigation. While it was never abjectly stated, Kate concluded they were going through the motions because closing the practice would insinuate guilt. While Lana's logic was sound, Kate believed that fleeing with the fortune they had amassed was the preferable option.

The inquiry centered around the murder of London Williams and the attempted murder of India Williams. The claims India Williams made had also opened up questions about the other patients who had died at the facility. The few that had gone missing were explained away by Dr. Handel. Lana made a strong case that her cure brought about a central and prominent change in the patients. Who was she to challenge a person who left under their own charge? And if they signed over all their worldly possessions of their own free will, was that truly a police matter? Without access to the bodies, many of those questions were left unanswered.

The police had executed a warrant long ago, taking paperwork and medical records from Dr. Handel's office. Kate half-expected the property to be razed, but it appeared a great deal had gotten past the investigators. There was not much else for them to find. London's room had been turned, Dr. Handel had completed the autopsy and filed a medical report and death certificate. After, her remains were cremated. Despite the accusation that several patients had been murdered, there was hardly evidence to support one charge. The trial was set for January and as it drew close, Dr. Handel opted to remain in Seattle. This left Kate and Stuart to clean up the mess at the hotel.

They had come through Christmas serving the remaining patients a modest dinner of lean turkey breast, green beans, and a tiny dash of mashed potatoes with a thimble-sized serving of gravy. The meal had been received with such a warm response that Kate was surprised at how happy the patients were to be there. As she presided over their meal, she questioned, not for the first time, the work she was doing with Dr. Lana Handel. As quickly as the sentiment arose, she squashed it back down.

In the thick of winter, a week into the trial in late January, a missive was received from Lana via telegram.

Give remaining guests Selene treatment in next cycle. Stop. They will be fit for release. Stop. Accept no new patients. Stop. Keep the hearth warm. Stop.

"How long until the next full moon?" Kate asked Stuart, skimming the telegram again.

"Early in the morning of February 3rd, but we can begin as soon as it rises," he replied. She passed the telegram on to him. He reviewed it and gave a stiff nod. The date was still a couple weeks away.

The following morning, the police arrived to search the premises. They had frequented the hotel enough times, their presence there was unremarkable. Kate had little concern, anything even remotely incriminating had already been removed to reduce the implications against themselves, as well as to protect Dr. Handel. While one group of investigators headed to Lana's office, the other headed out to the back garden with shovels. They immediately ran into a problem: the ground was frozen. There would be no way to proceed with their investigation until after the weather warmed.

When February 2nd arrived, Kate and Stuart set about the difficult task of providing the highly sought after Selene treatment to the five remaining clients of the sanitarium.

"You remember which pool to draw from?" Stuart asked. She nodded but rolled her eyes inwardly. He somehow had developed the idea he was in charge in Lana's absence, but Kate, who had been intimately involved in every aspect of Lana's work in the sanitarium, knew otherwise. There was a hot spring, in fact there were three, located halfway up the mountain behind the hotel. Kate and Stuart would be required to work in collaboration, bringing bucketful after bucketful from the spring, to fill each tub for the treatment. It was a difficult chore for one client, but it would take many hours to perform it for five.

When Lana gave the Selene treatment, it was never to more than one patient at a time. It was undeniably effective, providing immediate and noticeable results. She reserved it for particular guests, seeming with no rhyme or reason to whom she chose, but Kate knew better. Dr. Lana Handel conducted extensive interviews with each and every one of her guests, which amounted to journals packed full of notes. Gleaning over those records, Dr. Handel selected individuals with extensive social circles as the preferred recipients of the Selene treatment. It was better if that person was a "talker" and best if their social groups included individuals with fabulous wealth and limited family. She had termed it "whale hunting," a joke Kate initially took to be a reference to their weight and came to understand it meant the size of their estate.

Once the cold face of the moon peered over the horizon, Kate and Stuart headed up the mountain to begin their work. Kate dunked the first bucket below the surface of the pool, careful not to get the water on her hands. She avoided looking directly into any of the springs and was accustomed to closing her mind to them. They did the task together as a precaution. When she filled her second bucket, Stuart bent over and did the same with his eyes shut tight. He was also well practiced at this.

"We should fill one tub at a time," Kate said, as if they had not already discussed this plan as their course of action. "If we need to, we can stick someone else in the tub to save some time."

"You know it doesn't work as well," Stuart reminded her as they walked along the narrow path overlooking the monstrous hotel below.

"We could try it if we run out of time," she muttered, gritting her teeth as she took her first step downhill. Kate was thrown off balance by the shifting weight of the water, and it sloshed over the side of the bucket.

"It won't help anything if we lose all the water before we get there," Stuart admonished her.

"Well, this is exactly why we only do one of these at a time. It's a lot of work," she snapped back. They were in for a long night. The water piped into the hotel's baths came from a few of the hot springs on the property. The temperature of the pools was a punishing 132 degrees, but mixed with the icy water of the Green River, it was cooled to the perfect temperature for an extended soak with all the benefits of bathing in a mineral spring. It was quite a novelty for its time.

The pools on the mountainside were separate and very different from the spring water piped into the hotel. They had special properties; properties that were still a mystery to Kate, despite her long employment with Dr. Handel. The pools were Lester's best kept secret, and there was a contingent that worked hard to ensure it stayed that way.

Every quarter, close to the equinox or solstice of each season but always during a full moon, a group of wealthy guests would descend upon the town and take up residence in the hotel for a number of days. Dr. Handel catered to them during their stay, accepting no other reservations with the exclusion of her patients in the opposite wing.

Given her background as a nurse, Kate was tasked with managing the sanitarium and keeping the patients separate from the wealthy guests living in the lap of luxury. Stuart managed the hotel, and she preferred to keep her distance when she could.

Over the years, Kate gleaned that their "special" guests included Tacoma city officials, state government, and influential members of Washington's high society. The top priority of their work was the conservation of Lester's surrounding areas. Kate understood this had to do with the hot springs, and it was a sticking point that, for the time being, Lana controlled those springs. This role afforded her certain protections, but it was a delicate arrangement, contingent upon her keeping commitments to her guests. What specifically that entailed, Kate was unclear. Given the powers that backed Dr. Handel, she'd half-expected the whole matter of the Williams twins to be dropped, and she suspected it would have been, if not for India tapping into her own substantial estate to ensure Dr. Handel was prosecuted.

When the elites appeared, the locals whispered, and rumors spread about a cult making virgin sacrifices under the light of the full moon. Kate knew it was more than a rumor and suspected the townspeople would be shocked to know how close to the truth they were. Some guests brought visitors. It was not surprising when they were gone before the end of the stay. The women dressed the part but were confused by the number of forks on the table. Those sacrifices were assuredly not virgins.

The citizens of Lester benefited mightily from the cold, hard cash that flooded the town. The men paid for suites in the hotel and spent their money in the establishments. Several local women, known for their discretion, were employed by the hotel as housekeepers, and they were paid well for their silence. The cultists were welcomed. Their presence, even four times a year, was beneficial enough to the local economy to set aside any potential downsides. It was not uncommon for townspeople to go missing, and anyone with half a mind to speak about it was silenced.

These were matters Dr. Handel never discussed with her directly. Kate was paid to turn a blind eye, to close her ears at the appropriate time, and to keep her mouth shut. She did not ask questions. When Dr. Handel told her to only draw from one particular spring, she listened. Truth was, she was too afraid to ask and wasn't willing to test it for herself, tonight or any other night. She knew something unholy was happening here. She heard the whispers of the God Mind behind closed doors and knew it as blasphemy. No one could know God's Mind, and anyone who thought they did should be struck down by Him. Kate knew it was not her responsibility to ensure God's vengeance, instead she compartmentalized. She was paid very, very well.

By the time Stuart and Kate lugged their buckets back to the hotel, Kate's arms were aching under the strain of the water's weight. They entered the bedroom and private bath of one Charles Widing. Charles had come in an older obese man and, under Dr. Handel's supervision, lost a significant amount of weight. The trial was a setback to Mr. Widing's treatment, which was something he complained about every single day. His weight loss had stagnated, slowing to almost imperceptible, but if they had maintained the fasting cure to the letter, he would have complained about that too. Charles would be discharged today.

"Good evening, Mr. Widing!" Kate called as she burst into the room, arms laden with the buckets. Stuart came in behind her. She heaved the metal cans to the ground. Leaning over the massive tub, she plugged the drain with a rubber stopper and turned the spigot to open the hot water. It spluttered a couple times, then let loose a steady stream. Stuart set one bucket to the ground, lifted the other, and poured them in, one after another. Mr. Widing's eyes opened, glared at them, then rolled over, placing a pillow over his head.

Stuart rolled his eyes. He was not a fan of Mr. Widing.

"I am going to head back up to get water for the next one. Go ahead and get him in, and I will meet you next door in about an hour," Stuart said.

"Is that prudent?" she asked him. He considered.

"I'll be cautious. If I have to wait for you each turn, this will take twice as long," he groused. Kate nodded, accepting his answer. Stuart took all four buckets and disappeared out the door, then turned back.

"If I don't return…"

"Seems unnecessary to take the risk, but I understand what to do." Kate shut the door behind him.

"Alright, Mr. Widing, it's time for a bath," Kate spoke loudly. The bed covers rustled, but the man did not rise.

"Mr. Widing?"

"Bloody hell, it's the middle of the night!" he yelled. "I was having such a lovely dream about Gretchen." Gretchen was one of the housekeepers Dr. Handel employed from town. She was a quiet girl, blessed with more bosom and bottom than she knew what to do with. The poor girl was often bothered by the male patients.

Kate threw off his blankets, harnessing her nursing energy. She found if she acted like she knew what she was doing and spoke with enough authority, most people fell right into line. It was rare when someone stood against her. Whoever she couldn't get under control was dealt with by Dr. Handel, who had an uncanny ability to dominate those who tried to hang onto their own sense of power.

She grabbed Mr. Widing's arm and helped him from his bed, making him lift his arms to undress him. His wrinkled stomach sagged over his nether region, thankfully disguising what remained of his erection. If he was aware of it, he did not let on, nor did he behave with any sense of modesty. His gargantuan weight had made him inactive, which caused his muscles to atrophy over time. With the weight loss, he was able to move again, but not with any speed.

"We are going to fix you up, right as rain," Kate told him, leading him to the tub of water and holding his hand to allow him to step in.

"Don't know why it has to be bloody midnight," he bitched but placidly followed orders and sat down in the tub with a sigh of relief. The water steamed around him, and he shut his eyes. Kate let him settle in as she busied herself around the room, then, without warning, came up behind him and shoved his head below the surface. Kate held him under with one hand, knowing the exposure would compound and making a mental note to track down a couple pairs of waterproof gloves. She released Mr. Widing, and he popped his head above water with a loud gasp.

"How dare you!" he admonished her, his tone incredulous. She tutted at him, gathered up a towel, and set it on the stool next to the bathtub.

"Take as long as you like, we just had to get that part out of the way," Kate responded with a bit of smugness. She dried her hand, but already the magic was at work. The wrinkles in her hand flattened as some unforeseen force ironed them smooth. Mr. Widing continued his blustering, sneezing the water out of his nose. She sat on the edge of the bed and watched. The liver spots on the side of his cheek faded, and the patches of rosacea disappeared. His jowls receded, and the skin firmed, its elasticity repaired. His hair turned from a fragile thin white to a salt and pepper, more salt than pepper, but the color and texture were restored. The bags under his eyes were gone. The hunch in his spine straightened, the moles covering his body vanished.

Kate watched Widing's time reverse. It was a marvel, even if she knew it was something of the devil. This little kiss from the fountain of youth would extend his lifespan, by how many years she could not know, but more importantly, Mr. Widing and his family would be amazed when he returned home. He would be rejuvenated by the healing properties of Dr. Handel's cure. It was only a touch, like Hebe had grazed her hand across his cheek. Nothing like what was possible from entering the actual pool. She had seen the outcome of that too.

Kate had seen what the cultists came for. The young left old, matured by decades. She'd seen their faces in the newspapers: mayors and politicians. The old would leave young, restored to their former glory. Those missing townspeople weren't always lost but transformed, sometimes younger and sometimes older. Sometimes they came back changed, and when they did, Kate steered clear of them. Something had been awakened in them, and she was sure whatever it was, was evil. It was in their eyes, pupils so black it was like the light went there to die.

Mr. Widing's grumbling settled, and he looked at Kate with bright eyes.

"You weren't kidding. I feel amazing," he said, looking down at his body with wonder. "How did you…" He trailed off, flexing his legs and lifting his paunch where he found his penis and seemed to delight in its firm appearance.

"It's one of our most exclusive treatments here at the sanitarium. All of this work you've been doing was to make sure your body was ready to accept the treatment. It doesn't work if your body hasn't been prepared," she told him, using a proud, convincing tone. The spring water would work regardless of the condition of the individual, as long as it was pulled at the right time. It would turn the old and fat into the young and fat, and the result was no less impressive. Mr. Widing was very impressed.

"You can get out whenever you are done," Kate informed him. "We will be discharging you in the morning." She half-expected him to argue, but Charles nodded, staring at the back of his hands again with astonishment.

Wait until he looks in the mirror, Kate thought, exiting the room. She had some time, so she sourced a couple pairs of rubber gloves from a broom closet and moved onto the next patient, entering Mrs. Farmer's suite to start the process anew.

Stuart joined her carrying the four buckets alone, a vein in his forehead bulging with the effort, and they filled the tub together. Stuart stepped out to wait as she dunked the head of Mrs. Farmer into the water and watched the miracle for the second of what would be five times that night.

As they carried the buckets up the hill for another trip, the full moon was high in the winter sky. Her heavy breaths came out in clouds of vapor, and she considered what foul magic was afoot in this place. What horrid thing set these pools here? When she made the mistake of looking too closely upon their surface, she observed how they did not reflect the light. There came the certainty that these pools were not hot springs and instead portals to another place where horrors existed beyond her capacity to understand. Maybe it was the mind of God, but she knew better than to believe that. It was a trap. There was no God in this cursed place.

By mid-morning the following day, each of the remaining patients were packed and ready to depart on the noon train. They were restored, albeit temporarily, as their younger selves, and each was raving as they looked upon the other. The success of the program had been assured. They would go home, and they would tell everyone. Before they left, Kate asked each to complete a testimonial about what they were subjected to at the hands of Dr. Lana Handel. Each reported their incredible healing experience, along with glowing reviews about the illustrious Dr. Handel and her fine staff.

Once the train departed with all five passengers on board, Stuart and Kate returned to the hotel and sent the remaining housekeeping staff home. With the hotel empty, Kate took Stuart to bed. It was not the first time, and while she knew it wasn't very pious of her, she enjoyed it. Given how well-practiced Kate was at compartmentalizing, she didn't spend much time troubling herself about it. Who she was inside the walls of the sanitarium was a powerful woman who was always in control, and at times, that required she do things that flew in the face of her religious beliefs. Outside those walls, she was a devout woman committed to the church of God.

They slept together in one of the suites, enjoying the luxury thread count, and helping themselves to an expensive bottle of liquor. When they woke pre-dawn, they shared a pot of coffee in the companionable silence of two people well known to each other, and then set about their final errand on Lana's behalf. They went to the storeroom and brought out a dozen kerosene lanterns. Kate carried six upstairs, one to each corner and two for the center rooms, lit them, and without ceremony, tossed them into the suites and shut the doors. Kate watched her final lantern ignite the curtains and send flames licking to the ceiling above. When she came down the stairs, Stuart had staged small stacks of firewood and doused them with kerosene. They lit each pyre as they backed out of the building.

By the time they exited the hotel, it was growing hard to see, and although they clasped damp rags over their mouths, it was also hard to breathe. They stood in the circular driveway, watching the flames erupt from the upper story windows and consume the building. Stuart gave Kate a quick kiss on the cheek and walked slowly toward the town to raise the alarm. There would be no saving the structure.

The burning of the hotel, which was a common problem in these remote towns prone to wildfire, was to collect on the fire insurance. Kate and Stuart had not considered that the flames would burn so hot that the surrounding earth would thaw.

The police returned, and several bodies were uncovered on the grounds. Dr. Handel was found guilty of the murder of London Williams and the attempted murder of India Williams, then charged for the additional murders and stripped of her license to practice medicine.

With her indefinite incarceration, Dr. Handel could no longer hold control over the hot springs. The majority of the considerable wealth she had amassed disappeared, alongside her two faithful assistants. The remainder, including the insurance from the fire, was spent fighting the charges against her. Her assistants were never heard from again.

Lana knew nothing about the telegram Kate had received, but the loss of the hotel was worse than any murder charge she faced. The same people who protected her were the same who knew all her secrets. Those people knew Dr. Handel would be forced to give up the springs if the hotel was gone, and she was locked away in prison. Those people had set their eyes on wresting that magic from her grip, and Dia Williams had given them the perfect opening in which to do it.

With the decision made to leave the following day and the argument set aside, everyone fell into a tense silence save for the periodic whistle blasts. Dean and Talia switched off once an hour, sending out the SOS every fifteen minutes in case Glenn could hear it. No one was going to rest well.

Chase grabbed his sleeping bag and walked off into the night without a word. No one stopped him. Bam told them to wake him when they were ready to switch off. He made a big show of putting in a pair of ear plugs, then crawled into his tent, snoring within a matter of minutes. Summer attempted to make conversation, and when she was met with no response, she gave up and disappeared into her tent as well. Lane's restlessness was in evidence as he paced the perimeter of the forest with his headlamp to gather firewood.

"I can't sit any longer. I won't go far," he assured Dean. Dean and Talia were left sitting next to each other leaning against the old log. Talia blew the whistle, three quick blasts. Dean sighed.

"How long before we get tired of this?" she asked. Dean shrugged. "We keep going until dawn." His expression went flat as he gazed into the fire. "Everyone on the team already knows, so it's not something anyone talks about, but Chase is my cousin."

"Is that why you guys are so tight?" Talia asked, venom creeping into her tone. He nodded.

"I guess I feel some responsibility for how things have played out. I'm sorry. I know exactly how he can be, and I still keep him around. He has a gift for motivating people and getting them on board with his ideas. He's a fantastic salesman and marketer, way better than I am, and he's been able to connect the vlog with investors. We make a good team. But he has some less than savory tendencies. Do you know how *Dark Dimensions* started?"

"Just you and a camera. At least that's what the website says," Talia answered, shifting uncomfortably at the topic of Chase.

"Right. Since I know a bit about your past, I'll share mine. I grew up mediocre in a house full of exceptional people. My dad is an architect. He made a fortune running a private firm and is still the vlog's biggest source of funding. He is the reason *Dark Dimensions* even exists. And my mom, she's a powerhouse too. She raised us three boys, and later started her own yoga studio. They are both smart, successful, and rich."

"Then you have my older brother. Straight A student. Class president. Graduated valedictorian of our high school. He was the star pitcher of the baseball team. Everything that guy touches turns to pure gold. Runs in the family. Surprise, surprise, he got into Harvard, and he's working toward becoming a neurosurgeon in a groundbreaking highly specialized field because there's nothing less for Henry than that. And my parents hoped he would be a lawyer." Dean snorted and shook his head.

"My little brother, on the other hand, is a typical youngest child. Quite the troublemaker, but man, he always knows how to get you on his side. He's a lot like Chase, except Evan owns it. Do you know what I mean? He knows that he is always going to talk back to the teacher or crack a joke at the wrong time. People love him for it too. It's part of his charm, so everyone lets him get away with murder."

"And because he makes problems, he's always been the center of attention at home. It's like he gives them something to do all the time, as if they don't have enough. It's always 'you know your brother' followed by a story of how he was caught swimming in a fountain and got arrested. But when Dad picks him up, he's sitting around with the cops, drinking coffee, telling stories, and the whole place is yucking it up. You should see the look on my mom's face when she tells that story. She's *proud*. Evan is smooth. And he's a great guy. I love my little brother. I love my big brother too. He always gives the best advice, and he's even smarter than my dad."

"I'm the middle child, and I grew up feeling like a middle child. Grades were average, I wasn't charming. In fact, I'm loathe to tell people this now, but I was fat."

Talia was taken aback. Looking at the chiseled jawline and slender frame of the man in front of her, she had a hard time imagining him heavier.

"I know it's hard to believe," Dean chuckled.

"I'm sorry. Whatever you did worked so well, I had no idea," Talia replied a little sheepish.

"People usually think I am joking or say, 'you don't look like you could be a fatty.' I was a certified fatass. That's originally why my mom started getting into fitness. The truth is I've been on a diet and exercise program half my life. I've spent a lot of time hungry. What she did helped. It made a difference," Dean paused.

"You were bullied, weren't you?" Talia asked. Dean lifted his head and looked over at her.

"How did you know?" he arched his eyebrows, the sarcasm dripping from his voice. There was no need for her to answer because it was unspoken between them.

"At school, the kids loved to pick on me. It was quite the perk of being fat. They tripped me in the hallway, called me 'piggy' and made snorting noises when I walked by. The usual kind of thing. It was always so uninspired like shoving me into a mud puddle. One time, I came home with a black eye, and no one noticed until bedtime. At home, I felt invisible and spent a lot of time by myself."

"One day I came across my parent's handheld camera. Brand new, still in the box, and gathering dust in a closet. I started filming myself as if I were a celebrity. I wanted to be someone else. I wanted to be cool and smart and likeable. When I was on camera, I could embody all those things. At first it was kid stuff, right? Me filming whatever I thought was interesting. I grew up watching *Unsolved Mysteries* and this British show called *Ghostwatch*. They filmed it like a documentary, but it wasn't real. A lot of people thought it was. So, one day, I'm messing around with the camera, and the wind slammed the door shut. I posted it up on ShareYourWorld, before YouTube, and the reaction was incredible. I got a ton of views. I started staging these elaborate paranormal stunts and grew a following. I avoided being on camera, but eventually I wanted that to change. My mom helped me lose the weight. Laid off the McDonald's and ate salads. After a while, I didn't look like me anymore. That's when I decided to start going by Dean."

"Like James Dean?" Talia asked.

"No," Dean laughed. "Like Dean from *Supernatural*. There's no cooler guy." They both laughed in response to this.

"I met Summer while she was working in a Hot Topic, and we became instant best friends. I had such a massive crush on her at first, but she was clear friendship was all it would ever be. When I showed her some of my videos, it was her idea to go to a cemetery to do an actual ghost hunt. From there, it became *Dark Dimensions*. Chase and Bam both signed on. We still call ourselves the 'core four' because we developed the show together. We have been taking steps to break into the mainstream like *Ghost Adventures* or *Paranormal State*. I want to be famous. I want to be successful. But I have a secret."

Talia tensed a bit.

"I don't actually believe in this stuff. The paranormal," Dean admitted. He glanced over to check her reaction. She stared at him.

"Are you kidding?" She was smiling, waiting for the punchline.

"No, really. The cognitive dissonance is strange, I'll admit. I believe Summer when she tells me what she experiences because she has no reason to lie. And I believe other people when they share their stories too. I just don't buy in. It's why a lot of it is staged, like the saw blade at the Rodriguez's."

Talia shook her head in disbelief.

"You guys faked that?"

Dean nodded.

"Yes. I'm unironically doing this to get rich and famous. And we all have our own motives for being here. Things that are below the surface that we aren't sharing with each other. I assume the fact that you eventually agreed to take us means you have reasons. If I had known you were bullied, and Chase was part of the problem, things would have been handled differently. I had no idea he agreed to that kind of money, and he never should have done that. Hopefully, you and I can work something out because we don't have ten grand in the bank to pay you. I'm so sorry."

"It's not your fault," she said.

"Once we get back home, we will get this sorted out. I have been so preoccupied with the changes everyone wanted to make to the show. It is the next logical step for the team, especially given all the feedback we've received, but that part of me that doesn't believe, wanted to stick with what we knew. Why try to move onto something bigger when I don't even think it's there? I've been so focused on my own goals and problems, I wasn't paying attention to what was happening around me. If I had, I could have seen what Chase was doing. I know what he is. I'm sorry I let this all happen. As for Summer, I'm hurt she went behind my back."

Talia sat and considered the weight of Dean's words, and after thinking for a moment, she replied. "Thank you. I think that is the most sincere apology I've ever received." She gave him a hopeful smile.

"Wow, really?" Dean asked. Talia nodded.

"Really. It isn't your responsibility to apologize on his behalf. But thank you. The truth is I was willing to believe whatever Chase said because I needed the money. When he first approached me, it was so tempting. I worked hard to build my own thing with the guide company. It was amazing how well it was doing, and then the recession happened. After that, it all sort of dried up. The money I made at the firm was better than I could earn anywhere else. Even though it was almost impossible to work there, I thought I could ride it out. Then my boss fired me," Talia said. "I wanted to leave, I just wanted it to be on my own terms. Summer convinced me, but I wanted to be convinced. I didn't want to come here, but I agreed to go because I needed a job. I wanted an easy out of my situation, and it was all served up on a silver platter. I don't even know what I am going to do now. I owe a stupid amount of money, and I have no job."

"So, you are right. I have my own reasons for being here and for signing on. We aren't so different, you know? I watched my mom struggle, and we were so poor. I never wanted to be that desperate again. I was trying to be successful on my own, and I didn't want to rely on anyone else to do it. I learned early on you can't count on people to be there for you."

"That's a shitty lesson to learn," Dean said. "I'm sorry you were bullied. I know what kind of scars it leaves. Kids are cruel."

"Oh, they are so cruel," Talia replied. They fell silent. Talia remembered the whistle and brought it to her lips, releasing three short blasts.

"Do you think Glenn took the food and abandoned us?" Dean asked.

"No," Talia replied. "All the backpacks are here and accounted for. And I don't know how far he would get without a water filter. It doesn't look like he even took one of those, but maybe I missed it."

"Me either. He's young, but he's not stupid. It doesn't make any sense. I can't shake this feeling that something happened to him." Dean tapped the center of his chest. "You guys keep talking about seeing people in the woods."

"I don't know what I saw," Talia said. "I thought there was a light out by the old hotel. Maybe it was Lane. I called out for Glenn, but no one replied. I'm not confident I actually saw anything. I keep getting the feeling like I am being watched, but this place scares me. Nothing has been right since we got here."

A branch snapped behind them. Talia jumped. Lane appeared at the edge of the firelight with a bundle of branches in his arms. He dropped the collection next to the ring where the embers were dying down. Lane knelt beside the fire and carefully added each stick, piece by piece, until sparks rose into the night sky. Entranced, she watched the flames lick over the wood until it glowed.

"What is that?" Dean asked. Talia followed his gaze. In the center of Lester, a warm light was growing. The three of them got to their feet.

"Is that a fire?" Lane asked.

Thundering footfalls approached the fireside, and Chase appeared, out of breath and alarmed. Behind him, flames roared into the night sky above the other houses. The dry cabin exploded, illuminating the dark forest around them with its fiery orange light. Chase checked all over his body for burns. He smelled of smoke and his clothes were singed.

"I went to sleep. When I woke up, the house was on fire. I tried to smother it with my sleeping bag, but it spread too fast. Everything is so dry. I bailed. I almost didn't make it out. The fire was everywhere I turned. Jesus." Chase was panting, afraid. "Did one of you set that fire?"

Dean looked to Lane, who had returned to throwing wood onto their campfire, and before he could say anything, Talia caught movement in the forest.

"Tell me someone else sees that," Talia said, backing away. Dean and Chase followed her gaze.

A group of people walked toward them out of the darkness, backlit by the raging bunkhouse fire. At least a dozen approached, appearing out of nowhere. Their shadows stretched long across the forest floor.

Talia righted herself to run, intent on escaping whatever was coming. Lane grabbed her and slung a thick muscled arm around her throat. He turned her around to face Dean and Chase.

"I think it's time we all sat down and had a little chat," Lane grinned.

Greta Lerner had known since three in the morning that her great nephew needed to see a doctor, but she'd held out hope the fever would break. Things always looked better in the light of day. She had seen it happen many times over the years with the children she cared for: fevers broke at dawn. It had been true with Thomas's mother, Mary Elizabeth, when she was small and prone to illness. Her fever always relented with the rising sun. As the sun rose on July 3rd, she changed her assessment, and accepted Thomas was in actual trouble.

Gret slugged a cup of coffee gone cold, her fourth since the prior evening, as she hovered over the boy. Sweat was plastered to his forehead, but his cheeks were dry from the heat and flared with bright pink color. The fever had held too long with no sign of breaking. She had administered the right medications, and his temperature had not moved a single degree. They were in for a long drive. Lester was an hour away from the city, but at least the emergency room should be quiet on a Tuesday morning. Resigned it had to be done, she carefully wrapped the three-year-old in a blanket, then carried him out to the old Ford. She glanced at the gas tank, put the truck into drive, and backed out of her driveway and onto the long gravel road that wound its way along the Green River.

The day would prove to be a scorcher. The prior day's heat had lingered overnight, and while the air was cool amongst the trees, the sun was already blasting down into the valley.

Thomas rolled over and sneezed into the blanket.

"Auntie Gret, I'm cold," the boy said, his tiny voice almost unheard above the motor. She reached over and tucked the blanket tight over him.

"I know, buddy. I am going to get you warmed up." Gret frowned. If he got any warmer, it was going to cook his brains. She accelerated, pressing down on the gas pedal. They were moving at a good clip when she came around a bend in the road and saw a bright yellow service gate closed across it. She braked hard, and the truck slid in the gravel as it came to a stop. She threw the truck into park, the driver's door protesting as she swung it open, and Gret hopped out.

Strange for the gate to be shut on the only road in and out of Lester. Strange at all they would place a gate across a road where the public lived. There had been rumors. A few people at the schoolhouse had mentioned the new gates being locked. She'd suspected it was another scare tactic to drive out those who remained.

The Green River had been the source of Tacoma's water supply almost as long as Lester had been a town, and the Headworks was established to manage and protect that water. Over the decades, the city had become more aggressive about land ownership within the watershed, tying in with logging and milling operations and buying up acreage around the river from the railroad.

Not only were they purchasing every house placed on the market and letting them sit empty, but the Headworks seemed intent to lock the last hundred residents inside. They knew no one was interested in what a few rednecks who lived up in the willies would have to say. Past the local towns, most people didn't even know that Lester existed.

The gate had appeared a couple of years back without any explanation, and the Green River Headworks waited like the big bad wolf on the outskirts for the next little piggy to fall. On the heels of the massacre, there had been plenty of land to grab. People fled the town like there was something in the water. After all that bloodshed, Gret wondered if there was truth to that.

There was talk that the railroad planned on selling the town site. Some residents made passing mention of the infamous Lester cult as the source of the town's woes. Gret had dismissed those rumors outright. She did not endorse hearsay without evidence, and all evidence supported the city wanting control over their water source. Her stance against the Headworks, like many of the locals, stemmed from their continued allowance of the railway to run and for logging operations to continue, despite their protestations about pollution of the city's water source. They couldn't condemn public access while allowing industry to continue, it was outright hypocritical. But here in front of her was a locked gate, and she was behind it.

Gret pushed on the gate's long arm, hoping it would swing open, but it only clanged in response and did not move. She peered over and found a heavy padlock holding the arm in place. Her throat seized up, and a suffocating heat climbed from the center of her chest into her neck and face. Her body flushed with heat and sweat broke out on her forehead. She suspecting it was less her hormones and more her anxiety. Gret yanked on the lock a couple of times, testing to see if it was actually engaged or just for show, then gave up. She walked back to the pickup, perspiration gathering under her armpits and between her breasts. She looked in the truck bed, hoping to find something she could use to crack open the lock, and her eyes landed on an old, rusted tire iron. She snatched it up.

"Here we go," she muttered to herself. She positioned herself in front of the lock, placed the pronged end of the tire iron against the shackle, and used all the leverage she could muster to pry it open. She was a slight woman, her weight against the lock wasn't going to cut it, but she tried anyway.

"For heaven's sake," she grunted, thrusting all of her strength into the iron. She begged for God to break the lock, but nothing happened. Her hands were slippery with sweat, and it made Gret's anger grow. The Headworks had gone too far.

She slammed the sharp end of the tire iron against the lock, aiming her rage at breaking it. She needed to take Tommy to the hospital where they could treat the fever ravaging his tiny body. When several pointed slashes did nothing to break the lock, Gret went back to the truck. She slammed it into reverse, executing a sloppy three-point turn, then drove like a madwoman back to town.

Gret went straight to the home of the man she could count on to help her. It was early, and although not a single light was on, she did not hesitate to walk up to Bobby Kelly's porch and bang on the door. She didn't stop until she heard his footsteps inside.

"I have a gun!" he yelled from inside. "You better step off if you have any sense!"

"Bobby! I need your help!" Gret called out. The door swung open, and there was Bobby in a t-shirt and shorts, pillow lines still crossing his face. He held a hunting rifle in his hand.

"What's wrong?" he asked, his tone softening when he saw the worry on her face. Greta Lerner had been his schoolteacher, and Bobby had given her hell and a half in the time he'd been in her classroom. He was distractable, a class clown, and relentless when he knew he had the upper hand. She had lost total control of the group many times when he was unmanageable and riling everyone up. Bobby's daddy was a local roughneck, so it came as no surprise for Gret that the boy would follow after the father.

Bobby's mother left, moved on to different pastures. Maybe because she was tired of the isolation, or maybe she was tired of the drinking. No one knew for sure. Bobby was never close to his father, although he admired the man. There was no abuse, but alcohol lands blows just the same. The substance isolates its victims in the long run, and that was how it worked in Bobby's house, creating a wall between the man and his child. There was no connection, and Bobby was convinced his father hated him. His father was too drunk or too selfish to see how desperately the child needed his guidance.

Gret caught onto this. She noticed how no one was washing Bobby's clothes before he wore them to school, or how they hung off his body in some places and had grown too short in others. He rarely brought a lunch when he'd previously always had a paper sack with a sandwich, an apple, and cookies.

One day, she decided it was time to do something, and she held him after school. It made him angry, but she recognized it was one of those circumstances where she would need to press, so she did. The boy crumbled, tears leaking from his eyes. She asked if he would come over to her house the next day, a Saturday, because she needed help in the yard. She said she would pay and feed him. It came as no surprise to Gret when Bobby showed up in the morning ready to work, every bit the earnest child she knew he truly was. Gret fed him lunch and dinner when he took breaks from the work, and she sent him home with a plate wrapped in foil for Sunday.

She brought a lunch to school for him every day. She invited him to come by most evenings to help with a small task or to do laundry, and when he was there, she offered him dinner. Often, he would stay and play cards or dominoes with her. She knew it beat the hell out of going home to an empty house.

The class clown transitioned into her classroom sheriff. And he was good at it. He could corral the other kids and get them to give her attention. He became a wonderful mentor to the younger students. She never had a problem with him after that. Bobby and Gret became as close as two people could be that weren't related by blood or marriage.

She thought of him like a son and did as much as she could to shield him from the emotional wasteland that was his home life. Bobby still had a rough manner. As a teenager, he ran wild and was quick to anger, but he had a heart of gold. Gret saw it, nurtured it, and both their lives were better.

"They locked the gate outside of town. Tommy needs to go to the hospital. I can't get his fever to come down." She pointed back to the truck, its engine running. The teenager was now a man and one who worked for the county. Bobby glanced over her shoulder to where it sat in the door yard.

"Alright, I'll be right behind you," he told her, disappearing back into the house. Gret hurried back to the truck, threw herself into the driver's seat, and checked on Thomas. He was shivering but tiny beads of sweat dotted his brow. She swung the vehicle around, throwing gravel behind her. When she reached the gate, another truck was waiting there on the Lester side, and old Bill Higgins was standing with his hands on his hips next to it.

"Bill, I need you to move your truck," Gret called through her open window.

"The gate's locked," Bill replied, dumbfounded.

"I know. Bobby's coming, Thomas needs to go to the hospital. He's sick." Bill stood at her window to look in at the tiny body laying limp on the bench seat next to her.

"Bloody hell," Bill said, scratching his head. He turned his rig around and parked down the road. As Bill was ambling back to Gret's truck, favoring his right hip, another engine approached. Gret looked to her rear-view mirror in the hopes Bobby had arrived, but the source was a work truck, with Green River Headworks emblazoned on the door, pulling up to the other side of the gate. The vehicle parked, and a fat man slid out. *This'll serve*, she thought.

"I need you to unlock this gate," Gret stated, matter of fact. She exited her truck, the door creaking open.

"No can do, ma'am," the gentleman said. "I'm under orders to keep this gate locked."

"From whom?" Gret asked. "People live here." The man hesitated. Gret sized him up. He wore a tan button-up shirt with the green Headworks logo embroidered above the pocket, the buttons straining over the man's ample belly, and sweat circles peeking out from his armpits. His crisp denim jeans looked like they had never seen a speck of dirt.

"The Headworks owns all this land," he replied, explaining nothing. "I have the authority to arrest trespassers or anyone who tampers with this gate." Greta scoffed.

"Sir, are you new? We live here. This is a public road. I have an emergency, and I need to get through," she replied. The man's face hardened a bit, and she saw the truth. Someone in his life had dominated him, she suspected his mother, and this guard job was going to his head. He wasn't going to listen to anything a middle-aged woman had to say.

"I was told to keep this gate locked," he said, as if that was the end of the matter. Before she had a chance to respond, Bobby arrived in his old diesel. He swung his truck around, backed up to the gate, then leapt out, looking every bit the roughneck in an armless t-shirt and oil-stained jeans. He grabbed a bolt cutter from the bed of his truck, never bothering to look up at the fat man on the other side.

"Excuse me, what do you think you are doing?" the Headworks guard erupted, coming toward Bobby. Bill Higgins approached the gate, nodding to Bobby and the guard.

"Ya'll want to lock the gate, I'm here to open it," Bobby said, giving him a hard stare.

"I will arrest you for tampering with this lock," the man argued, flashing a badge at him. Bobby laughed. He walked around to the other side of the gate, and the fat guard blocked him.

"You ain't no police. Either you open it easy, or I open it hard. One way or another, it's opening so the lady can get through." He stood chest to chest with the man, never averting his gaze, and waited for the guard to move.

"Now, hang on. Hang on. Let me see if I can talk some reason into him," Bill interrupted. "Hiya, name's Bill, and you are?" Bill stuck his hand out to shake over the yellow bar. The Headworks man remained in place, blocking the lock, and refusing to turn to acknowledge Bill.

"I have orders to keep this gate locked, and I have the authority to arrest anyone who tampers with it. You'd do better to get him to stop whatever he thinks he's doing, or I'll have to arrest him," he replied. Greta peered into the truck, noting the growing heat of the day. Tommy was panting. She needed the gate opened, and Bill wasn't proving to be of any help. The guard refused to move.

"Then we will make sure your gate stays locked." Bobby smiled at the man and returned to his truck. He tossed the bolt cutters into the bed and jumped in behind them. After a moment, he lowered a grey tank from the back of his pick-up, along with a pair of darkened goggles and work gloves. He dragged the tank to the gate's big hinge, staying on the Lester side.

"What do you think you are doing?" the fat man yelled over Bill's shoulder.

"I work for King County, and I'm on the county's property. Might want to cover your eyes!" Bobby replied, sliding the gloves over his hands and the goggles onto his face. He lit the torch fixed to the end of the tank and set it to the gate's hinge. Greta turned away as the sparks flew, and the guard raged. The gate made a low creaking sound, then dropped to the ground as Bobby cut through the metal with his acetylene torch.

The Headworks man came around the gate to grab Bobby, but Bill got between them. Bobby, unconcerned with the guard, moved to the opposite end of the gate to finish making his cuts.

"He's got a torch. You'll get burnt," Bill scolded as the fat man tried to move around him. Bill's interference had allowed him to take the necessary actions. Returning the tank to his truck, Bobby grabbed a thick heavy chain from the bed, his arm straining under its weight, as he wrapped it around his tow hitch. Once he was confident the chain would hold, he wrapped the other end around the gate arm and slammed a padlock on it before the guard could stop him.

He'd been watching Greta, and he'd seen the panic in her eyes. Since the Headworks guard was unwilling to listen to reason, there was no time for half-measures. He hopped into the driver's seat without another word and turned the engine over. The guard ran back to his rig, his belly flopping and shirt coming untucked. He reached inside and came out with a handgun.

"Stop!" he screamed, pointing the gun at the back of Bobby's truck. Bill ducked and ran to hide. Bobby revved the gas. The back tires spun flinging gravel as the chain went taut against the gate.

From the corner of her eye, she saw the movement of Tommy's blankets as they began to thrash. The boy was seizing. She leaned into the truck, grabbing the shaking lump of blankets with one frail child wrapped inside. Heat radiated through the comforter. She wrenched it off.

"Bill!" Gret called to him, but her voice was drowned out by the sound of Bobby's engine thundering louder and louder as he revved the gas. The gate groaned in response.

The guard waved the firearm in the air, his yells drowned out by the roar of the engine, as he approached the back of Bobby's truck. Gret could not wait any longer. She pulled Tommy out of the truck and ran with him in her arms toward the river. For a fraction of a second, as she tore across the road, Bobby stopped gunning the engine, and the guard lowered his gun. She careened down the embankment carrying the bundle, Tommy's skinny arms and legs flailing. Gret thanked her lucky stars for the gentle grade until her knee nearly buckled in a loose pile of dirt. The weight of the boy forced her forward, but she managed to keep her feet under her. Tommy thrusted and seized in her arms; his eyes rolled into the back of his head with only the whites exposed.

"Baby boy, hang on, hang on," she muttered between breaths as she ran for the river.

Bobby kicked the truck higher. The tires smoked, the engine roared, and the gun fired. Gret flinched, hesitating long enough to glance back. The fat guard, standing at Bobby's bumper, had fired his gun into the air. She continued on, picking her way across the river rock as fast as her fifty-nine-year-old legs would carry her. The metal arm released with a piercing squeal and was rent open, snapping away from its frame. The gate smashed into Bobby's bumper, the Headworks guard caught between them.

Bobby's truck lurched forward. Tangled in the gate and dragged across the gravel, the man released another shot. The gate slid off the side of the road, thrashing over stumps and shrubbery.

"Bill, get out of the way!" Bobby screamed.

Old Bill had been watching Greta's run for the river and gone a distance down the road. He was directly in Bobby's path. Bobby wrenched the wheel to the side and narrowly missed him, but the length of chain he towed caught the old man at his knees. Bobby slammed on the brakes, the truck guttered, and died.

Gret reached the riverside, witnessing nothing that transpired on the road, and plunged Tommy into the water to cool the fever raging in his body. She washed the water over his head, and the child sputtered and coughed. After a moment, he stopped seizing. Gret, kneeling in the river, erupted with tears of relief.

The Headworks guard made no effort to stand. Bobby stepped from the truck and found him on the ground, making terrible choking sounds as he struggled for oxygen. Bobby pulled open the man's shirt, searching for a wound, and found none. The man turned red and then blue, fighting to get air. He gripped Bobby's shirt, his eyes burning into him, and uttered the word "hospital." He called for Bill to help, but the old man was on the ground with his arm bent at a strange angle. Bobby could not lift him alone. The man outweighed him by at least a hundred pounds. He called for Gret, but it was too late. The Headworks guard died in his arms.

When the dust settled, Old Bill's arm was broken, but his knees survived. He was beaten up and bruised, but able to walk away with a little help. Word around town was that the guard suffered a double pneumothorax due to the impact of the gate smashing into his chest. It popped both his lungs like a pair of birthday balloons.

Bobby didn't stick around after that morning. When the officer turned up at his doorstep to arrest him for manslaughter, he was long in the wind.

No one walked away unscathed. Greta carried the guilt with her. It was on her too. If she had never pulled him into the situation with the gate, Bobby would be living a normal life, maybe starting to settle down and think about a family. But then Tommy might be dead, and when she considered that, there was no other choice. Old Bill never really got back use of his arm, and his health steadily declined after the accident. Tommy lived a life plagued by heart problems. Doctors attributed them to the severe fever that almost took his life. He would die young, they reported. Greta would outlive him.

She never saw Bobby again. But one July day, many years later, Gret decided to spend some time sitting in the garden, listening to the trees whisper, and enjoying a book her niece had dropped off. As she opened her front door, there, set to rest on the porch railing, was a twisted metal padlock.

Without thinking, Talia thrust a hard elbow into Lane's ribs, hip checked him in the groin, and when he instinctively shoved her away, she thrust the pad of her hand toward his nose. It almost connected, but Lane moved with maddening speed. He snagged her wrist and wheeled her around, twisting her arm up high behind her back.

She yelped in pain, the force on her shoulder so violent, she expected it to snap. The group from the forest arrived. Strangers. People she had never seen before. They forced both Dean and Chase to the ground and rousted Summer and Bam from their tents. Summer let loose several shrieks when she realized it wasn't Talia waking her. Chase threw his hands into the air and fell to his knees with no objection. Alabama fought. Two men tackled and pinned him down after delivering a nasty hook. Before Talia could struggle out of Lane's grasp, the arm was back around her throat. She wrestled against it, trying to fight Lane off, but he tightened his grip until her vision grew fuzzy, and then went black.

***

Talia found herself standing alone in the center of a dark place and knew she was at the bottom of the well again. The bottom of her own consciousness. There was no light, no view like before with London, and for a fleeting moment, she believed she was trapped and no longer in control of her own body.

"You're unconscious," a voice spoke. It was the voice of a man. When he stepped out of the shadows, she didn't recognize him. He was an average height and wiry, his chest was bare, and his eyes were empty. He turned to glance at the way he came, and Talia saw the back of his head was gone. In its place was a gaping hole, tattered and bleeding. Talia averted her gaze. He looked back at her.

"Oh," he said, self-consciously touching the back of his skull. "There really was no other way to make it stop."

"Make what stop?" she asked.

"The possession," he said. "You've seen what it can do. It changed me."

"From the water?"

"Yes, the water."

She hesitated, her senses on alert.

"The springs are only the medium for the transmutation. What it reveals is far darker," the man said. Talia perceived the entity was near, lurking in her subconscious.

"Who are you?" Talia asked, glancing around.

"George."

"Why are you here?"

202

"That's not the question you should be asking. You need to get out of here. This is a cursed place," George replied.

"Lester?"

"You need to escape. The pools must be destroyed. What lives there is evil."

"What lives there?"

"You don't want to find out."

"Okay, how do we escape?"

"Find the death door."

George froze, and Talia knew it had appeared. Her body tensed with fear as heat caressed her. George's eyes grew wide with horror.

"You carry a darkness. You must go!"

"But."

"GO!"

A pinhole opened above them, and Talia was yanked out.

She woke on her side with her shoulder bent at a strange angle and her arm numb. Her first thought was one of confusion. She'd been in the darkness, and now she had no idea where she was. She tried to move her arms and realized they were tied behind her back. Rolling over, her sleeping arm tingled as blood flowed back into it. She lay helpless, accepting the pain as it prickled and stung her skin.

"Thank God. Talia, we are all right here," Summer's voice reassured her. Talia arched her back and craned her neck. Summer sat on the ground; her arms tied behind her back. Her mascara and eyeliner had smeared from her tears. They were in a wide, cavernous room with a slanted ceiling, whitewashed walls, and hardwood floors. Light came in through the high windows, and several large roof supports were positioned throughout the room. Evenly spaced along the walls were built-in bookcases with empty shelves. The room was devoid of furniture, wall hangings, or any decorative feature.

"Where are we?" she asked, her voice echoing in the space.

"The schoolhouse," Dean replied. "This is the auditorium."

Talia recalled the fire. Recalled Lane strangling her. Then the darkness. And George.

"Is it morning? What happened?" Talia asked, rolling back onto her side, and hoisting herself up to her knees with a bit of difficulty. Looking around the empty room, Dean and Bam were each tied to separate support posts. Chase had managed to prop himself up against a wall, his arms were tied behind him like Summer and Talia. Glenn was still missing. Summer sat in the middle of the room near Talia.

"Do you remember the fire? People coming out of the woods? All that?" Dean asked.

"Yes," Talia replied.

"They attacked us, tied us up, and here we are. Lane's a fucking traitor. He arranged the whole thing. It was Lane's suggestion originally to come here for the vlog, but now it's clear there was an ulterior motive," Dean replied. His cheek bone was swollen and bruising.

"He's a snake in the grass," Bam muttered.

"What's the ulterior motive?" Talia glanced around at each of them and was met with no response.

"Seems to be a woman in charge, but we aren't sure," Bam mumbled through a split lip. His eye was swollen and turning an ugly shade of purple.

"I don't want to find out," Chase muttered, morose and dejected. Chase was the only one that looked unmolested.

"And no Glenn." Talia said, more as a statement than a question. Her head throbbed. The others fell silent again.

"Alright, now that she's up, how the hell are we getting out of here?" Bam asked, saying out loud what Talia was thinking.

"Ssssh. There's a guard right on the other side of that door. He'll hear you," Chase hissed. "We are outnumbered and outgunned. What are we going to do? Fight our way out?" His tone was cynical.

"Shut the fuck up, you fucking coward," Dean swore over his shoulder. "You held your arms out so they could tie them." Chase fell silent. Dean gave an angry little chuckle. "If we get out of here, you'll be lucky if we don't leave you behind."

"So, we are being watched?" Talia asked.

"They've checked on us a few times," Summer said, exhaustion apparent in her voice.

"That's how we earned ourselves a big pole hug," Bam explained. "Walked in after we got loose. But some of us put up a good fight." He shot a glare in Chase's direction.

"Any idea how many people there are?" Talia asked.

"No way to know for sure. It was dark when they brought us in," Dean replied. "But at least ten attacked us by the fire, and I suspect there's a lot more. They don't seem too concerned about us getting away."

"So, we are being held hostage by random strangers for unknown reasons in a remote location," Talia observed. "Glad we got that cleared up."

The door swung open. A thin woman with dark hair down to her mid-back entered the hall. Her skin was bone white like porcelain. She wore a long flattering dress of navy blue and golden necklaces lay across her collar bone. Her age was indecipherable, but her beauty was unrivaled and terrifying. The woman was timeless. Lane entered behind her, and another man came after. Talia recognized him at once.

"It was you," Talia said, the words out before she could stop herself.

"It was me," said the man, his blue eyes shining like flints of steel. Talia would know him anywhere. Those eyes were the ones from her nightmares.

"Let's try this again now that everyone is awake," the woman interrupted, smiling. "So sorry, Talia, that Lane had to be a little… heavy handed."

"Screw you, bitch," Bam hissed through gritted teeth. Lane walked over beside him, his boots echoing hollowly on the scuffed floorboards. He swung a machete casually in one of his hands. The expression on his face was one of casual indifference, almost businesslike.

"How can you act like this? You were one of us," Summer said to him, hurt leaching into her voice. Lane ignored her.

"It will all make sense soon enough," said the woman stepping forward. "My name is Minerva." She touched her chest with a light hand. "You already know Lane." She pointed to the man Talia recognized. "This is our founder, Jack." The man stepped to Minerva's side, jutting his chin proudly. And it was him. She was certain. It was the man she had met in Lester twenty years ago. The very same, but younger, much younger.

"Lane's objective was to bring you here, and he far surpassed even our expectations," Jack said. His voice carried a hint of an Irish lilt.

"He serves us," Minerva added, her tone firm. Talia caught the way Lane pursed his lips when she spoke. "None of you will be leaving. You belong to this place now. You belong to us."

Chase hung his head.

"Why did Lane bring us here?" Talia asked. Minerva glanced back at Jack, who gave a nod of approval.

"We were looking for something specific. Someone specific," Minerva replied, then took a few steps over to where Summer sat. "And it was you."

"Me? Why me?" Summer asked. She looked up at Minerva, her face broken and fearful.

"Because you have power." Minerva held Summer's chin with a soft hand and tilted her face up. Summer pulled away, a tear pouring down her cheek.

"The rest of you were collateral," Lane said. Talia caught the hostile stare Minerva cast at him. He looked down at the ground, but not before a flash of anger crossed his face.

"We have been looking for a woman. One with psychic abilities. And we got very, very lucky," Jack spoke. "Because he brought us two." Minerva walked over to Talia and stood over her.

"I'm not psychic," Talia said.

"Oh, I beg to differ," Minerva laughed. "You were attracted to the power here even if you don't know why, Talia. Did you dream of this place? Many of us did before we came here. You have a gift. Lane tells us that Summer has a power, an empathic power. But you have power you can't even imagine. We suspect you are connected directly to the Source."

"Source?" Talia asked.

"The engine of the universe. The place where everything began. The source of not just life, but of all intelligence. We call it God."

"This is a joke," Dean laughed. "Where are the cameras? Did someone stage this? Chase? You got me, okay. Very funny, but I think we've jumped the shark with religious crazies, and it's time to call it. Give us the big reveal and get it over with."

"This is no joke," Jack cut Dean off. Talia watched him. He hardly had taken his eyes off of her since he arrived. "I had so hoped you would return. You were powerful then, and you are even more powerful now."

"Talia, after you and Summer met, did you notice she sought to spend a great deal of time with you? Does she touch you? Does she stay close to you whenever possible?" Minerva asked. Talia remained silent.

"I'm going to assume the answer is yes," she concluded. "I can *feel* it coming off of you, even if you aren't aware of it. You draw from the Source, amplifying it. The Source is unlimited but unreachable for most. Your connection to it makes people insatiable; they want to tap your energy. They covet it and want to steal it from you. It invigorates and emboldens them. What they cannot control sparks jealousy and rage, and you have suffered for it. The average person wouldn't understand, but Summer did. She siphons off your power. You are a drug to her: the psychic equivalent of cocaine."

Talia glanced over at Summer, who was resting her head on her knees, averting her gaze, and weeping.

"Who are you?" Talia asked.

"We are the nameless. This has been our place for over a hundred years, and we have been working to prevent it from being exposed to the world. A great deal of sacrifice has been required to protect Lester. Jack has worked tirelessly over the decades to limit access. Everything we have done has been to defend it from outsiders and people who would exploit it. People don't understand what this place is, but of course, it draws them in. It calls to their primal essence, even if they are not aware of it. We've taken every measure to make Lester inaccessible and prevent innocent bystanders from stumbling upon it. Unfortunately, the attraction is inescapable, which is why you are here," Minerva explained.

"We didn't come here by mistake!" Dean interrupted. "You actually sent one of your henchmen to plant the idea and encouraged all of us to come. You act as if we accidentally happened upon this place. There was no mistake, as you so finely detailed in your little scheme. You led us out here. What kind of plan is this? What about the rest of us?"

"We will gift you the option to join our cause, our collective, but you cannot leave. If this place is discovered, it will be harnessed and abused by people who do not understand its purpose. No one can know the power that resides here."

"People know where we are," Bam said. "Our entire fan base knew we were coming."

"We are well aware, and it changes nothing," Minerva replied. "As I said, you cannot leave, and therefore you will not be returning to your former lives. Officially, you will all be listed as missing. Search and rescue will be sent, and they will find nothing. Your website and social media will go defunct. The Internet will move on. And although your families will remember you, most will not. People will speculate, but they will forget. This is not the first time we've dealt with strangers wandering in. Some are with us now. We have all been long forgotten by our pasts."

Talia's stomach clinched at the thought, no one was left to forget her. A silence fell over them. Minerva looked around at each.

"Why?" Talia asked.

"We seek the mind of God. We seek His Will."

Talia stared, not comprehending.

"There is a channel here, one that existed centuries before anything else. Long before there was a railroad or a town, the Natives knew there was both danger and power in this forest. The pools were uncovered when this place was developed. They were here, waiting to be discovered," Jack said.

The hot springs, Talia thought. She recalled their strange quality. She recalled George's words: *transmutation.* An overwhelming sense of unease washed over her.

"That's what they've been hiding here," she said aloud.

"None of this has anything to do with me," Chase cut in. "I can help you. If you let me leave, I will take down all the social media. I will take down our website. There won't be a single mention of Lester connected to *Dark Dimensions*. Lester will simply disappear. I can conceal this if you let me go."

"You are such a fucking coward," Summer muttered.

"Shut up, Summer. You're the reason we are in this mess," Chase replied.

"Are you kidding me? Who wanted to go to Lester so bad!"

"Stop!" Dean commanded them.

"What did you do with Glenn?" Talia asked. "Where are you holding him?" Minerva's bemused expression turned to ice, and she looked up at Lane, who shifted uncomfortably. Talia sensed a tension between them. Another woman entered the room, approached Minerva, and whispered in her ear. Minerva nodded, then turned her attention back to the group.

"We are needed elsewhere. You all have some time to consider your position. Your decision must be made before nightfall. But make no mistake," Minerva said, allowing the pause to hang in the air. "The women are who we are after." Her expression was flat, and her meaning clear. Lane, Jack, and Minerva left the auditorium.

"What do we do?" Dean asked.

"We get the hell out of here," Talia replied. "Summer, I can see your rope. Lane left yours a little slack. Can you get your arms in front of you?"

Summer wiggled her shoulders. "I can try." She was still tearful but laid down on the wooden floor and struggled to wriggle her bound wrists under her rear end. Summer strained and stretched, then threw herself back. "I can't."

"You can," Talia replied. "Get on your knees, it will be easier." Summer did as Talia suggested. Once she got the knot past her backside, she slid each leg through with careful maneuvering, then sighed with relief.

"Untie me," Talia ordered. Summer crawled over and worked at unfurling Talia's bindings.

"I'm hurrying. I'm sorry. These are serious knots. How did Lane find us?" Summer whispered. Her tearfulness was gone.

"Chase vetted him," Dean replied, watching as Summer worked the cord free from Talia's wrists.

"Oh, come on," Chase said. "He probably saw the vlog." Talia turned and untied Summer. When her hands came loose, Summer's face was triumphant. She moved to throw her arms around Talia, then stopped short.

"I came for you," Summer said low for only Talia to hear. "I didn't beg you to join us because he asked me to. I came for *you*. I was serious about everything I told you. It was all real, and I wanted to take you with me. I did 'comfort' you, and I am sorry. Sometimes, it's just an impulse; I don't even realize I am doing it. I know it's manipulative, and I shouldn't have done that to you. Please forgive me." Talia reached out and hugged Summer.

"It's okay. When we get out of this, we'll talk," Talia replied. They moved to untie Dean and Bam. As she worked the rope, she spoke in a hushed tone.

"In case we get separated, follow the river downstream. Downstream leads to civilization. Upstream leads to wilderness and mountains. Some places along the river are like a canyon, and you won't be able to stay close to it, which will force you into the woods. If you get lost, keep moving forward. Eventually you will find a stream, and you can follow it back to the river. There are places like the lookout or old hunting cabins out here, but those aren't things to look for. Hide in one if you need to, but keep in mind, that is the first place anyone will look."

"The forest service roads out here are a tangled mess. It's easy to get lost without a map. There's another train trestle west of here about a mile or so. If you can get across it, and follow the river, you will wind up in what is left of Palmer. If they see one of us crossing, they will follow. We might try to cross at night. Whatever you do, stay off the road leading out of here. It leads directly to the dam."

"And the dam isn't safe? Aren't there people there?" Dean said.

"Chase figured it out. This is why everyone was run out of Lester, and they've been gating it off for decades. These people are the ones behind all of it. The watershed was never to protect the river, it was a cover. The watershed was set up to protect the hot springs," Talia replied, freeing Dean from his ropes.

"What hot springs? What are you talking about?" Dean asked.

"Look who's keeping secrets now," Chase muttered.

"Oh! I am so sick of you!" Summer yelled.

"We need to focus," Dean said. "Is that what she meant by the pools?"

"Yes. I found them in the mountains. I think they are why Lester is Lester. Everything that has happened here goes back to them. And there is something seriously wrong with the water in those springs. We need to go. Just stay out of sight and keep the river near." Talia turned to look at Chase, still bound, and hesitated. He looked hopeful for a split second, then his face broke.

"What in the actual fuck, guys? Are you seriously going to leave me here?" he demanded.

Dean and Talia glanced at each other, considering.

"I'm sorry! I'm sorry about everything. Don't leave me here!" Chase began. Bam stood up.

"I'll untie you, calm down, Princess," he said.

"How are we going to get out of this building? They could come back any minute," Summer said. Talia looked around at the room they were in. Dean noticed her taking in the space.

"This is where the massacre ended," he said.

"Not helpful," Talia replied. Her thoughts returned to George. "Wait. That is helpful. Death door. Does that mean anything to you?"

"Like we are on death's door?" Dean replied, his brows knitted together.

"You say a death door?" Bam asked. "Like the door the dead pass through?" Talia shrugged. Bam went on. "Some of the older houses back home had them, especially on the plantations. It was a door from the parlor to the outside. A separate door for the dead."

There was a door at the back of the room. Talia crossed the space and tried it. She pushed, and it barely budged.

"It's blocked," Talia replied.

"It doesn't lead outside," Dean pointed out.

Summer stood in front of one of the shelves built into the wall and cocked her head. Reaching to the back of one, she pressed on the boards behind it. The wall gave a little.

"Guys, there's something here," she whispered. Bam crossed the room and pushed against the spot where Summer had a second before.

"She's right, I think this is a false wall," he said. Carefully, he lifted one of the shelves from its brackets and with a little effort, it came free. He set it gently aside and proceeded to remove another.

"They were called death doors because on the plantations back in 'Bama, they held their own funerals at home. They had a separate, bigger door to pass the casket through. I think the builders here put this in for that possibility. Not necessarily coffins, but large furniture," Bam explained, dismantling the bookcase. With all the shelves removed, he set himself against the wall. It gave an inch and daylight appeared around the edges.

"No, it was certainly for coffins," Dean said. "The cemetery is on the other side of this wall. Summer and I filmed there last night."

"I see it!" Summer said. Dean stepped in alongside Bam and pressed himself against the door. It started to creak and protest, echoing loudly through the open hall.

"Hurry! They are going to hear us," Talia urged.

"One, two, three," Dean counted. The pair slammed into the wall, which burst open on hidden hinges. The door stuck in the long grass, opening onto an overgrown side yard surrounded by a short fence. They were outside, the Lester Cemetery lay before them. Talia inhaled the fresh air.

"Get on going," Bam said.

Talia started to lead them away and tripped over a flat headstone. The words on the grave marker were too worn to read, but George's words echoed in her mind: *death door*. Her heart fluttered, adrenaline coursing through her veins. She stepped over the fence and led them into the forest.

They weaved through the understory, staying close together. It was like running in a dream, moving in slow motion as the monster approached. No matter how fast they went, it wouldn't be fast enough.

When she saw the man standing on the edge of the forest, it was like time layering in on itself. She was eight again. She remembered how she had fled Lester as a girl, how the forest had looked, and how fear had torn at her heart. She had escaped then, and she would escape now. Talia broke into a sprint, turning deeper into the forest. She blew past Chase and the others, low branches grabbing at her hair. In a trance, she rushed through the trees, jumped fallen logs, and dodged rocks and shrubs as they appeared in her path. Locked in and unthinking, she overcame every new obstacle. A shot fired, its report ricocheting off of the trees. Talia dove behind a fallen log.

"What was that?" Dean yelled somewhere behind her.

"Flare!" Bam yelled.

"We need to move!" she yelled back. Her voice tore at her throat as she gasped for air. They were coming. Talia heaved herself up and ran full out, willing her legs to move faster. Talia focused within, pulling from a deeper resource to run harder, and her body responded. The others were behind her, and she no longer cared. They were coming for her. Talia ran for her life.

She miscalculated a leap over a stump, and her toe caught. She careened over it with barely enough time to put her hands out in front of her. Her already aching shoulder took the brunt of the fall. Rapid footsteps approached as she writhed on the ground. Talia panicked, struggling to get to her feet. Summer appeared, grabbed Talia's good arm, and yanked her up. She brushed dirt out of her hair and spat fir needles out of her mouth.

"Where do we go?" Summer asked. Talia grabbed her hand. Summer's fear radiated off of her in all-consuming waves. Talia yanked her hand away as it overwhelmed her.

"Take a few deep breaths," Talia advised her. Summer nodded.

"Over here," she replied. They were too close to the road, and the man who had fired the flare gun was running alongside them, keeping pace. He was trying to cut them off from accessing the bridge.

The pair ran, tripping and stumbling, the growth around them dense and earth soft with a pad of fallen needles and dead leaves. Summer buckled, nearly rolling an ankle, and Talia pulled her upright.

"I can't keep up," Summer gasped.

"Hide. Go into the forest and hide until it gets dark. Don't move until then. I'll get to the bridge. I know the way. I'll get help," Talia assured her. Summer nodded and headed away from her. She flagged the others down while Talia continued forward. She could no longer see the man. She would beat him to the bridge. She careened forward, branches whipping her face, and her ankles wanting to collapse with every misstep. It was a wonder she managed to stay vertical. Behind her, Summer screamed, and Bam yelled. She didn't dare turn back or look. Talia ran like the wind was behind her, like her life depended on it.

A break in the tree line approached; the road was ahead. Beyond that lay the river and her way out: the bridge. Hope gripped her. *I might actually make it,* she thought. Talia headed for the road where she could run in the open. Once she reached the bridge, she could disappear into the forest. They would never find her. She knew the way. She always had.

Careening through the understory, Talia's mind did not register the open space she found at the edge of the forest. The road was gone. The land had given way, pulled into the Green River, and created a chasm to the roaring waters below. She ground her heels into the earth to stop, sliding feet first into the washout, and grasping for anything as she went. Her hand caught on a root and held. Hanging on the edge of a cliff with the Green River churning below her, she tried to gain a foothold, her shoes slipping under the loose dirt.

A shadow appeared above her. She contemplated letting go. The river would carry her downstream. She steeled herself and let go. A hand grabbed her wrist. Talia tried to wrench free, but the grip was too strong. A man pulled her out of the gorge.

"Did you really think we'd let you go that easy?"

When George emerged from the hot spring, a single brilliant thought came through clear and hard like a diamond: Amelia was sneaking around behind his back, and he was going to have to do something about it. As he sat in the sultry water looking out over the valley, nothing else would occupy his mind, and he did not, for even a moment, doubt his thinking as wrong.

George Donovan, Donnie to his friends, was level-headed, placid, and not taken up by intense emotions or radical thinking. A pacifist by nature, he was loathe to be involved when issues became contentious and hated confrontation. The most extreme feeling he had was the love for his wife, but George was not ordinarily a jealous man. In fact, he was known to be quite the opposite if his courtship with Amelia was any proof.

Amelia was a prize, an ideal woman to make a wife. She was a true beauty with a kind heart and a fine sense of humor. He would do whatever it took to show her he was a man worth marrying. When George became aware he was not the only one pursuing her, he was dismayed. A man hopes to have his lady love to himself, but he knew the other guys asking her out. They might be serious about her hand eventually, but they were more interested in getting her into the backseat of their car. He considered confronting the men but knew how it would appear. He thought of sharing this information with Amelia, then concluded he was underestimating her; she would see through their charade. George decided not to let the competition bother him one bit. He was confident he could offer her a good life. If she wanted him, she would choose him. And choose him she did.

Later, in the early weeks of marriage, after a night of making love, she admitted it was the way George looked at her that had convinced her. As they lay next to each other in the cool dark, perspiration drying, and the smell of their sex heavy in the room, she told him how the other men had a way of looking through her. They didn't really see her. It made her feel less like a person and more like a commodity. Amelia chose George because he made her feel seen. So even though he brought wildflowers when they brought roses, and he took her out for cheeseburgers and milkshakes when they took her out to fancy restaurants, she chose him. After this admission, she rolled over on top of him and asked if he was ready to go again. The simple request and the coquettish smile on her face sent the blood rushing south, and he was more than ready to meet her demands. They were young, and they were happy.

Within a few years, the railroad offered him a promotion to mechanic, but there were a couple of caveats. One, they would require he move to Lester, and two, he would be pulling overnights two to three times a week. He was reluctant, but Amelia encouraged him to take the job.

"You'll get another promotion in no time," she reassured him.

And so it went, and the years passed. George spent a couple nights a week away from home in various cities, and he missed his wife. It was a rare occasion when he had more than one day off in a row, and he sometimes worried she was lonely, especially when he was exhausted from working long hours on the trains and spending uncomfortable nights in strange beds. Amelia never complained. She was happy when he was home and not a word was spoken about him changing jobs. The pay was excellent, and their savings grew. One day he planned to leave Lester, and he would buy Amelia the house of her dreams.

He never considered that her isolation would open up the possibility she might seek comfort from another man. After soaking in the hot springs in the mountains on the far edge of town, it was as clear to him as the water of Friday Creek. Amelia, the sweet love of his life, was fucking Hayden Marks.

Once he extracted himself from the steaming pool, his head filled with muddy thoughts. The visions were a cacophony of flashes and sounds. Here was one of Hayden bending Amelia over the kitchen table, thrusting his hips eagerly into her, and another of her sucking his cock with relish. Every which way a man could take a woman, Hayden had her within the confines of George's mind.

George gagged, nausea washing over him. He tried to focus on anything else, but he could not control the images as they raced through his mind. He dried himself in a rush and dressed. Still damp, he struggled to get his pants on, forgetting his shirt, and slid on his shoes to make his way to the town below.

Thoughts rose and burst like bubbles, revealing new ideas. The other morning, when he arrived home, was that cologne he smelled on her neck? Is that why she feigned she was sick that day? The face of a smarmy Hayden laughing with her in bed, laughing at him for being such a fool, for all the nights he had slipped quietly into their home and had her in their marital bed. He felt no rage at this, just a desperate and overwhelming urgency for the swirl of voices and images to stop.

Once he descended down the mountainside, past the ruins of the old hotel, George broke into a run. Moisture clung to his body in a thin film, his slacks rubbing at every friction point, and tugging irritatingly at his skin. The town was beyond the patch of forest, a half mile or so.

Amelia's happy moans started up, noises he'd never heard her utter for him. Her voice so close, he startled as if she stood next to him, whispering in his ear. He threw a paranoid glance over his shoulder, feeling her hot breath on his neck. George cowered and slapped at his head. He needed to silence the voice, quiet the sounds of another man taking his wife, and hold the replay in his head of every position, slap, grunt, and moan. George wanted to vomit. He needed the cries of her begging for more to end because it was driving him insane.

When he burst into his house, Amelia stood at the sink. She shrieked as the door slammed against the wall.

"George!" she admonished him, realizing she dropped the plate she had been holding, and it had chipped against the porcelain. "What's wrong?" She regarded the plate with dismay, but her expression changed to alarm when she appraised her sweaty shirtless husband. She left the sink and reached for him.

"Honey?"

He gulped down the sickness rising in his throat, then pushed past her, down the hallway, and into their bedroom. Beside their bed, visions of Hayden on top of Amelia played there as he reached underneath the box spring. When his fingers touched the cold metal of his hunting rifle, his racing thoughts slowed, and for the first time since he emerged from the pool, he could breathe.

George went to his knees, leaning under the bed to pull out the deceptively heavy box of 7mm ammunition. The bullets rolled inside, giving a metallic clink as he placed it on the comforter of their perfectly made bed. He reached down again to produce his leather satchel, the one he used to carry extra bullets while he hunted. Placing the pouch on the bed, George spared a thought for his last hunting trip and concluded, based on the thick layer of dust coating the items, it had been several years. A finger of sadness plucked at his heart. He hadn't known then it would be the last time. He opened the box, dumped it into the leather pouch, and affixed the bag across the front of his shirtless body, the weight of the bullets pressing against his hairless chest.

"Honey?" Amelia's voice came from behind him. "Is everything alright?" He checked the firearm, and as he suspected, there was a bullet already in the chamber. Without children, there was no worry about keeping a loaded weapon in the house. Besides, what good was a firearm for protection if it wasn't loaded? He wished he had cleaned his gun.

George turned around with the rifle to look at Amelia. She was holding the dishtowel and drying her hands with a worried expression on her face.

"George?" she asked, searching his face for an answer.

Kill her.

The singular thought pierced through everything and drove itself like an icepick through the center of his brain. He winced as it stabbed him, and he obeyed.

"I love you, Mel," he said as he lifted the rifle and shot her through the center of her chest. The bullet nearly took her off her feet. It walloped her, taking her back several steps until she hit the wall. She hitched air as a crimson flower bloomed from her breast. A single tear fell from his eye. He made no effort to brush it away. All was blissful, serene quiet in George's mind. The voices and visions had been silenced. He sighed with relief, hanging his head.

Amelia tried to suck in a lungful of air, but it was watery. She coughed, and blood spilled over her bottom lip. Amelia looked down at the gunshot, and touched it with a soft hand, then back up at George, suddenly alert and fearful of the man she had spent her adult life with. He could see her urge to run, but she was frozen. Instead, she sank down to her knees, eyes wide and staring, tiny coughs and burbles as she choked on her own ichor.

Amelia fell onto all fours and tried again for air, blood splattering across the wooden planks. She gurgled unintelligible words, then collapsed. George watched, stupefied, as she rolled onto her side, fighting to take in a breath, and drowning as blood filled her lungs. His wife grasped at her throat, scratching and clutching, trying in vain to dislodge her airway. She slowed, then stopped. The hitches continued, the seconds growing further and further apart between each, until they ceased altogether. George stepped past her and out of the house.

As he emerged into daylight, a fine high penetrating tone filled his ears. It was painful and pleasant. Deafened by the keening in his own mind, he walked along the muddy path, pulling a bullet from his pouch, and sliding it into the weapon. He discarded the empty shell onto the ground.

It was going to be a beautiful April day. The snow had released its stranglehold on the town of Lester. Despite the chill of winter holding on, the sun peeked out from behind a white puffy cloud, and the patches of light were warm upon the earth. While there were piles of dirty grey slush still huddled in the shadows where the sun never reached, there was a promise of regrowth and renewal in the surrounding forest. Spring had come early. George held the crisp air in his lungs as he approached the bunkhouses.

The doorknob to the bunk gave easily, and he entered. The group bunks were never locked. It housed Scott Paper's employees, as well as the last of the Northern Pacific workers, mainly laborers who worked in the roundhouse as hostlers or handled the coal chute. Since the railroad had started testing diesel locomotives over the pass, they had quietly tightened up the workers, letting several go or moving them to different stations. The railroad went to great pains to squash rumors about layoffs from circulating. The numbers remaining in Lester had dwindled down to a skeleton crew. It was where Hayden Marks laid his head at night, and George intended to find him.

From the entry, the bunk came into a small mud room, with a bench and a row of hooks on the wall. Several pairs of heavy work boots, covered in dried mud, lay before the bench. Beyond was a common area with a kitchenette. It was a modest set up. The boys could make their own food if they chose to, but everyone ate in the mess, including George, because the food was fantastic. If any of the men went hungry in Lester, it was their own fault.

In the common room, George found David Hanover and Leslie Fallon playing a game of cribbage. They turned to look at him, glancing first at his face, then down at the rifle.

"Going hunting?" Leslie wisecracked. George lifted the rifle and shot him through his cheek. The back of his head splattered onto the table. He tipped over in his chair, his cards dropping to the floor. David jumped up and backed away. George slipped his hand into the leather pouch for another bullet, his fingers quick to close around the cold metal, and slid it into the gun.

"Donnie! Donnie!" David sputtered. The steady ringing in his head allowed nothing to penetrate. He saw David's mouth move and heard no sound come out. He lifted the rifle and shot him in the chest. For George, it was like watching a picture show with the sound turned off. He saw the expressions on their faces, the bullets tearing through them, and the blood spray, but none of it registered. He was single-minded, with only the deafening ringing through his skull.

He flipped open the leather pouch again, popped out the expended shell, and fit another bullet into the chamber. He removed two more and carried them in his clenched fist as he walked to the back rooms. He kicked open one of the bunk doors and found a man he didn't know trying to hide behind a dresser. George shot him once at close range, noting only that it was not Hayden.

He exited the bunk and loaded his gun again. Two men were coming down the narrow hallway from the second bedroom. One he knew was Peter Holt; the other was an older man whose face he recognized but whose name he did not know. He wasted no time, shooting Peter in the shoulder, and when the bullet exited, it grazed the man behind him. The older man stepped back, trapped between Peter's falling body and the end of the hallway. His paralysis bought George enough time to reload the weapon and fire a direct hit into the side of his face before he could duck into the last bunk.

George stepped over the bodies. Peter rolled around on the floor, grasping his shoulder, while the other man was dead before he even hit the ground.

"What the fuck, Donnie?" Peter shrieked and crawled away, blood smearing behind him. George heard none of it, nor did he hear the lowing sound emanating from the common area where David was dying. He checked the other rooms and found them empty. He traced his way back to the front door, leaving the shot men behind without a backward glance.

Back into the morning, the sun was shining in full force. It was powerful enough to break through to him, and for a heartbeat, all was silent while it warmed his face and chest. Immense relief washed over him, and George was himself again. He glanced around, mud squelching beneath his booted feet and the cold rifle cradled in his arms. As quickly as it came, it went. George experienced an extreme sense of depersonalization, as if detached from his own body but also buried within it. Like he was a passenger. The high tone washed over him once more. Somewhere inside him, too far removed to come to the surface, a wail of anguish called out. He sensed it in a vague way, and despite the sun, gooseflesh prickled all over his skin. Better to end it, better to end this. Hayden would have to die, like it would punctuate the end of this hateful sentence, and he knew where to find him.

The exterior construction of the new schoolhouse was completed last fall, and with the winter months in retreat, locals were back to work. The structure was much larger than the old schoolhouse, formerly a single room with an old woodstove and scratched chalkboard. The new building would function as a community center, school, and church for the hundred or so residents of Lester. Many folks in their spare time would go by to lend a hand. If George had heard correctly, they would be painting the interior this week. George was certain he would find Hayden there.

He held the rifle across his bare chest as he made his way to the new school building adjacent to Lester's cemetery. Behind him, George did not see the trickle of men exiting the surrounding bunkhouses, having heard the gunshots, and scratching their heads as they stared up at the sun. The men could not see the hunting rifle tucked close to his body. While gunshots in Lester were not altogether uncommon, it was the wrong time of year. They noted the man without a shirt but did not move to act until the gunfire started again.

George was some distance from the onlookers. He was driven forward as if an unseen force was carrying him along in its current. Like he was directed to this point in time, to this moment. He entered the schoolhouse. It was a long, single-story building with a high roof. The front entry had a collection of cubby spaces and hangers for coats, and several jackets were hanging there. The acrid scent of fresh paint filled the air and made his head swim. A young girl, no older than fifteen, stepped into the foyer and stopped. Her hands clasped her chest, her face frightened.

"Sir?" she asked. George stared at her with a blank expression on his face and held his gun. Her eyes darted back into the building, then she put her head down and rushed past him out the door. The building echoed with the sounds of laughter and voices, idle chatter, and footsteps on the hardwood floor, but George only heard the endless, numbing *EEEEEEEEE*.

He had been here once before and knew the classrooms were to the left. To the right was the main hall that would serve as a gymnasium, community center, and banquet room. He entered the airy space, the vaulted ceiling at an angle, and looked around. A pair of girls were painting in one corner, laughing and teasing each other, while a group of young men worked on a wall in the back of the room.

Their backs were to him. No one noticed him enter. George felt a flutter in his chest, a lapse where he realized he had gotten it all wrong. Nothing was happening between Hayden and Amelia; it was all a dream, just a horrible, insane dream. He must have fallen asleep in the hot spring. This was all a twisted nightmare, not reality, and he would wake up relieved to find none of it was real. Amelia would admonish him for being gone so long on his one day off, and they would sit down and enjoy breakfast together. He swore in the half-second he was going to change jobs, they would leave Lester, and everything would get better. Shattering his self-reflection, an alarm blared inside of him.

Kill HIM.

Before he could stop himself, George shouldered the rifle and fired into the back of the head of a young man with a buzz cut. Red spray and brain splattered across the whitewashed wall. His paintbrush dropped from his hand. The report from the rifle was too loud in the echoing space, and the girls in the corner shrieked in terror. Everyone froze and turned. George was already reaching into his leather pouch, his body shaking. He dropped a bullet as he loaded the rifle, realizing that Hayden Marks was standing at a side door with a bucket of paint dangling from his right hand. He stood stock-still when his sightline fell on George. His expression lacked any recognition, and George knew. He knew he had gotten it wrong.

Lifting the firearm automatically, he leveled the sight at Hayden and fired. The thunderclap ricocheted through the empty space, and the bullet punched into the man's shoulder. Hayden dropped the bucket of paint, the white tide spreading across the floor. The girls shrieked and clamored against each other, their crying drowned out by George's deadened eardrums. The only thing he can hear is his own voice screaming:

KILL HIM!

George fought the urge to vomit, tears pouring from his eyes. He placed another bullet in the firing chamber, letting the empty shell fall to the floor. Lifting the gun again, George pulled the trigger, the shot splitting through Hayden's skull. His body collapsed to the ground. Blood mixed with the white paint, and the colors twisted together, creating a strange work of art.

Against his expectation, there was no peace when the shot pierced through Hayden. Instead, something much worse happened. All at once, George became aware of what he was doing in full color and sound and found he was unable to stop. He reloaded, sighting another of the young men frozen against the far wall. As easy as shooting a buck in rut, his bullet pierced the boy's heart, killing him instantly. Another reload, his hands operating on their own accord. The gun lifted, turned to one of the young girls in the corner, and fired upon its target. Blood sprayed the face of the tiny blond standing beside her. She screamed, backing into the wall, wiping futilely at her face until it was a mask of red. He placed another bullet in the chamber, aimed and fired again, killing her.

"Stop me! Stop me!" George begged as he loaded another round, whirling on another man, and firing. This bullet pierced his gut, and he bent at the waist like he was punched. Automatically, his hands clasped for another bullet, and another casing fell to the floor. The memory of his wife slumped against the wall, choking on her own blood. The recognition of what he had done was like being torn in half. He gasped, and more tears fell from his eyes. His sweet Amelia. The memory of his hands on the gun, blasting the hole in her chest and stepping over her body so carelessly as he left. He cried out, letting loose a single sob.

Footsteps thundered in the great empty room. The townspeople poured into the space, and George turned to face them. There was no return from this. No escaping this terrible conclusion. He thought back to where it had begun, stepping into the hot spring below a splendid full moon, the predawn light beginning to warm the sky.

"What have I done?" he whispered. That would be the last clarity that George would have. He flipped the gun around, took the barrel into his mouth, and pulled the trigger a final time.

Minerva's people flooded the forest in response to the flare. The man dragged Talia back, careful not to hurt her despite how she struggled. Each member of the *Dark Dimensions* team was captured and likewise subdued. It took four men to take Bam down, and he earned a severe beating trying to fight them off. They were forced to return to Lester and held in one of the empty bunkhouses. No one bothered to tie them, but men with rifles stood outside.

Talia's body ached from her near fall into the river gorge. Her skin was a collection of scrapes and bruises, each announcing itself every time she moved. Bam lay on the floor, unconscious. Summer sat beside him, monitoring his breathing, and cradling a swollen wrist. Dean and Chase sat with their backs against a wall wearing mutual looks of defeat, neither speaking to the other. There was nothing left to do and nowhere else to go.

Minutes turned into hours. Eventually, Bam regained consciousness. The guards ignored Dean's request for water and Summer's pleas to be allowed outside to relieve herself. They made use of a back room without any other choice. No one spoke. There was nothing left to say, so they waited. The air inside the bunkhouse grew too warm. When Talia's head felt thick and wooly, she lay down on the hardwood floor and shut her eyes.

She was woken by the door opening, and Minerva entered.

"I thought I was clear," she announced. Two men stood behind her, rifles in hand. The group offered no response.

"Here's how things are going to go," she continued, indicating to the three men. "You are of no consequence to us at this stage. If you decline to cooperate, death is the outcome. So, Talia, Summer, if you fight or struggle, you are putting these men at risk." She snapped her fingers, and two men dragged a corpse into the room. "If you continue to fight, you will see what lies on the other side."

Summer gasped. They dropped the body unceremoniously into the middle of the room.

"This man was supposed to be guarding you, and yet you escaped. Consider, if this is the manner in which I will deal with my own followers, then imagine how I will address you." Minerva let her words hang over them.

"As for you two ladies, I think it's time we have a little chat." Minerva delivered a calm smile. "You, Talia? Come with me."

Unmoving, Talia stared at the woman. Minerva snapped her fingers, and the two men stepped forward.

"That wasn't an option. Come by choice, or you come by force. I'm done playing games. We only have so much time before nightfall," Minerva said.

Talia relented, following the woman out into daylight. Temporarily blinded, she found morning had passed, and the day was slipping into afternoon. She shielded her eyes from the sun. The two men walked behind them, acknowledging the guards at the door with a nod. Minerva walked ahead as they made their way through the wreckage of the town. Talia saw with her own eyes what they had uncovered.

There were a few dozen people moving around Lester. Their campsite had been cleared away. Several long tables had been placed in the meadow near the river, with half a dozen chairs at each. Their white tablecloths fluttered gently in the breeze. Food was being prepared, and the smell of it cooking carried along on the open air. Talia's empty stomach reminded her of her last meal. She wondered where they had come from and why they were here. Approaching the depot, people filed in and out, the interior a hub of activity.

Others were trickling in from the other buildings. There were so many different faces. They all appeared to be average people with no strange identifiers. They seemed relaxed, even happy. Their eyes followed as the two women passed, watching their leader with the newcomer. Minerva led her to one of the tables and gestured for her to sit. Talia sat, placing her hands in her lap. There were no place settings, the surface bare except for a single yellow flower in a tiny vase. Minerva took a seat across from her.

Talia looked around her, listening to the way the people spoke to each other in casual conversation, friendly and elated to see each other, like they were family. A teenage boy walked beside an elderly woman, deep in conversation and laughing like equals. The diversity of the group was striking. A few individuals, both men and women, were dedicated to setting and arranging the tables, while others were preparing a meal in the outdoor kitchen. Talia marveled at the appliances and supplies used to accomplish this task and how quickly the space had been taken over. Minerva watched her.

"Not what you expected?" Minerva asked.

"What is this? Why are there so many people here?" she asked.

"We are celebrating the Autumn Equinox. We meet at the turn of each season," she replied. "It's part of a ceremony. Tonight, there will be a full moon, and the pools will open to the God Mind."

"It really is all about the hot springs," Talia mused. She'd known there was power in the pools, something wrong with the water, and believed there was evil in them.

"They are at the centerpiece of our collective and our work here. Tonight, you will be given an opportunity to enter the hot springs," Minerva informed her.

"And if I don't, you will kill me?" Talia asked. Minerva shook her head.

"I am confident you won't refuse the call."

"But what if we do?" Talia asked.

"We expect you will choose it for yourself. And if we must, we will convince you." Minerva placed careful emphasis on her last sentence, suggesting a darker meaning.

It gave Talia pause. "You and the girl, Summer, are not expendable. Unfortunately, those men in there are. If they don't want to join with us, they will be killed. We will take no risks when it comes to information about this place getting out. We are so close to attaining the next level." Minerva's face lit at the prospect of her words, her excitement palpable. "You have arrived at the culmination of a century's worth of dedicated effort. The future of our collective rests in your hands, Talia."

Talia stared at her.

"Jack discovered this place over a hundred years ago, and it changed him. That's no euphemism. It actually changed him. He was almost sixty when he found the pools," Minerva said. "When he left, his youth was restored, and a seed was planted." Minerva allowed Talia to process that information.

"He was young again," Minerva explained. "And his mind had been opened. He had a vision about what this place was meant for. He would later come to understand that the voice speaking to him was God's."

"How could he be young again?" Talia asked. There was no denying Minerva was telling the truth. She had seen it with her own eyes.

"The hot springs offer an unusual gift, Talia. Each with its own unique power. One grants youth and renewal, restoring your health and vitality. A proverbial 'Fountain of Youth.' Imagine if it had fallen into the wrong hands. Imagine the wars that would be waged over such an amazing gift. You've certainly heard of the Handel business. She exploited the pools for her own gain, and it played out exactly as was foretold."

"The second pool offers wisdom and the gift of maturity, which is far less exciting to some. Our society looks at age as a disability and a weakness, but there are times when age is powerful. A tool. The third pool has the ability to strip us down to our essential selves. It can change a person's nature and reveal what exists within. Then, and only then, are we able to open ourselves to the God Mind. When all else is removed, the purity and essence of the soul is left, and that is when His true intention is revealed."

"Our collective subscribes to the idea that God is found through the consciousness of this community, through the minds and wills of His physical creatures. We believe this is the path to achieve enlightenment. This is the way of the one true God."

"You are trying to become God?" Talia asked.

"God is made real within our minds," Minerva replied. Talia said nothing, and the woman forged ahead.

"What would you do if you glimpsed the mind of God? Would you turn a blind eye? Ignore it? Or would you embrace your vision? Jack followed the path laid before him. The goals were simple: protect this place from people who would misuse it and bring in the people who will move the mission forward. Some of us have been fortunate enough to receive revelations over the years. I am blessed enough to be one of them. I was told to locate a woman, touched by the third eye, to channel the mind of God."

"That woman would birth the future of our collective by throwing the door wide open and share God's vision. Once she entered the pools, she would be gifted the God Mind and lead us." Minerva finished.

"And you believe that's me? Or Summer?" Talia asked.

"Precisely," Minerva said.

"And what do you believe will happen after that?"

Minerva sat back, and an expression of apprehension flashed across her face.

"We seek the true power. To release God's Will."

"You don't know what will happen," Talia scoffed.

"It is not for us to know. This is why we are seeking a vessel. It is God's Will."

"How many women came before me?"

Minerva gave no response.

"And what happened to them?"

"They were not the intended recipient of His gifts."

"Are they here among us?"

Minerva hesitated.

"You mean they died."

Minerva remained silent.

"Did you bring me out here to convince me?" Talia continued. "Did you think I would see all these happy smiling faces and suddenly my mind would be changed? You have been fooled into believing that you are being brought closer to God, but whatever is in those waters isn't holy. What kind of God gives gifts?"

"Don't you see, Talia? This is something bigger than anything you can imagine. You are being offered an opportunity to do something so much greater than what your mundane life has to offer. Granted the God Mind, you have the potential to be omnipotent and all-knowing. You could see into the future." Minerva let her last sentence hang, then continued.

"Do you want to keep living a life of struggle? Of pain? Do you want your life to be insignificant and trivial? Or do you want to have purpose? You could become powerful, powerful beyond measure. What you see here is only a third of our numbers. I have lived many lives, Talia. My existence has been a wonderful thing. I worked on the dam in 1960 as the only female civil engineer. Today, I sit on the Tacoma City Council. Everything I could want is at my fingertips. I live in fear of nothing. And I started here in 1911. A housekeeper. I was nothing, no one, until I met Jack."

"Talia, this will better your life. Part of knowing God is having faith. Have faith something better is in your path."

"This is an evil place," Talia replied.

"I have faith you will come to see. When the moon is full, you will be brought before them, and we will see what you decide then," Minerva replied, standing. Talia hesitated, surprised to find the conversation over.

"We will collect you at dusk," she said.

Talia stood, and the men escorted her back to the bunkhouse. Summer was reluctant to go.

"It's okay," Talia assured her. When they were gone, Talia faced Bam, Chase, and Dean.

"Well?" Dean asked.

"The cult's real," Talia said. She paced the floor, frustrated, processing her conversation with Minerva. "The hot springs I told you about? The ones I found up in the mountains. So much of what has happened here ties back to them. And it's crazy. It's insane. They have special powers."

Bam looked at her strangely. "What do you mean special powers?"

"They say its God or their connection to God. It's not what they think it is. It's dangerous. Yesterday morning, I went for a walk. I found Glenn standing beside these three hot springs, and it was like he was locked into a trance. It happened to me too, something got in my head. The pools have real power."

"That sounds crazy. How is that possible?" Dean asked, inspecting her.

"I don't know. Minerva confirmed they have special properties. The hot springs can change our nature. They can make people young again. That man with Minerva: Jack. I met him when I was lost here as a girl. He was old. Very old when I was eight. And he's not old anymore."

"Wait, what? You never told us that," Chase cut in.

"I didn't tell anyone," Talia said.

"Someone was out here, and you never bothered to mention that? Never thought to warn us about what you saw?" Chase shook his head in disgust.

"Would it have mattered? You didn't care what I thought about coming here. Would it have made any difference if I had told you about a man in the woods? You thought I was crazy!" Talia replied coldly.

"She's right, leave her alone," Dean muttered.

"So, what do we do? What do you propose we do?" Bam asked.

"We agree to join, but whatever you do, don't go in the water," Talia said. "They will kill you guys if we don't agree to cooperate. We can play along, convince them we are a part of their 'collective,' then escape the first chance we get. There are people here of their own free will. How long will they hold us hostage if we agree to join?"

"Eventually, we could leave," Dean agreed, still unsure.

"But then what?" Chase asked the question. "I've read everything there is to say on the subject. Over the last hundred years, there has been a systematic effort to control this place. From court battles to state legislation, and every fight they have entered, they've won. How do you plan on getting away? And when you do, do you really think they will stop? Look at what they did to get us here."

They all regarded his words in silence.

"Remember how far they went to run every single person out of this town. Now convince me you are capable of hiding from them. They have limitless resources and nothing but time. What kind of life is that?"

Dean hung his head.

"What other option do you have?" she said. "If it's join or be killed, then there isn't any other choice for you."

"What's left for you? Or Summer?" Dean asked. "Be hostages? Forever? She isn't letting you two go. Not until they get whatever it is they want." They debated the point, making no headway by the time Summer returned. She took a place against the wall next to Bam and leaned up against him. He leaned into her in response.

"What did she tell you?"

Talia rehashed her conversation with Minerva a second time, comparing notes with Summer. The information was the same. Talia explained her plan.

"If we agree to join, you think they will let us go?" Summer asked, her face a mask of displeasure.

"Yes," Talia replied. "I think if we prove we can be trusted, they won't hold us indefinitely." Dean nodded, unsure.

"They won't let us go," Bam muttered. Chase remained silent. They were divided.

"So, what do we do?" Summer asked, her voice pained, wearing a lost expression.

"I don't know," Talia said, giving into the defeat she felt.

Time passed, and then the doors were thrown open.

"Time to make a choice," Lane announced when he came inside.

"Fuck you," Bam said, his face a stony mask.

"If you don't come willingly, you will be brought," he advised. Two men entered carrying rifles; the implication clear. The sky was dimming, transitioning from the golden hour into twilight. The group went reluctantly, led by Lane and followed by the guards. They were brought to a gathering around a bonfire. A small crowd waited there, a few dozen faces looking across the flames at the new arrivals.

"On your knees," Minerva commanded, indicating to the ground. Talia knelt, as did the others. She found Jack amongst the group of onlookers, and there was a flicker of recognition when he caught her returning his gaze. There was little preamble.

"As you are all aware, we have been seeking the next oracle." Minerva projected her voice for everyone to hear. "In this circumstance, we have additional visitors and in practice, we have always offered the choice to anyone who has discovered this place to join. I would suggest if anyone would prefer not to participate, please step aside until we address this matter."

A handful of people moved away from the fireside and drifted into the glomming. Minerva approached Alabama first.

"Will you join?" she asked. Bam looked like he was trying to find his tongue in order to speak. He sucked in air and spat a wad of blood onto her face, then delivered a blood-soaked grin. There were gaps where his teeth were missing. He looked insane in the firelight.

"What are you doing?" Summer demanded.

Minerva said nothing, unbothered, and flicked her wrist. Lane came forward with his long menacing blade.

"Wait, wait, wait!" Dean yelled. He put a leg under himself to stand, and a man shoved him back down on his ass. Lane centered himself in front of Bam. Dean tried again, and a different man cracked a rifle butt across his face. He collapsed into the dirt like a sack of meat. His eyes open and staring into the night sky. Blood poured from his split forehead.

"No, no," he whimpered.

Lane slammed the blade's point into the top of Bam's skull. It stopped at half-length. Talia gasped. Lane plucked his knife out, the release effortless, the blade sharp as a scalpel, and giving no resistance whatsoever.

Bam's eyes crossed. He snorted, choked, and then exhaled a long gasp. His bladder gave, soaking the front of his pants. His eyes rolled into the back of his head, and with a final shudder, Bam collapsed onto the earth. Blood flowed from the wound in the center of his crown in thick black rivulets. Alabama was dead.

Talia could not look away, her mind uncomprehending. Summer screamed, her tears reflecting in the firelight. Talia grabbed her, and Summer fell into her arms, racking with giant wet sobs. Dean curled in upon himself, covering his face. Chase gave a tiny gasp, and his breathing became panicked. Dean gagged; he rolled onto his stomach to vomit and produced nothing but a thin string of bile. Lane bent down and wiped the blade on the back of Bam's shirt. Summer's cries grew hysterical.

There was a whispered exchange between Lane and Minerva. While Lane remained expressionless, Minerva's words were harsh. She was not happy with him. Jack looked on, observing the pair's dispute without intervening.

"Will you join?" Minerva stepped up to Chase, who held his hands up in defense.

"I can help you," he stammered. "If you let me go back, I can do better than erasing our page. I can broadcast to the public that there's nothing out here. I can edit the video so people can see for themselves there is nothing to see in Lester. Nothing to see in this old ghost town, just a bunch of trees. I won't say anything to anyone."

He prattled off his offer as if he had been rehearsing it in his own head. His charm was easily readable as false. It was nothing like his usual bravado and charisma, but he was sliding it into his tone in the hopes it would overshadow the fear that was coming through. Lane laughed out loud.

"Really? You are going to help us out?" he said, mimicking his saccharine sweet tone. "Cover up for us and make sure no one bothers us out here?" He laughed. "Just a bunch of trees." There was scattered laughter from the people around them.

"That's enough," Minerva interrupted. "Join us or join your friend," She indicated Bam's lifeless body. The chatter from the onlookers stopped. Two more men came forward, lifting Chase to stand on his feet. He looked around, assessing.

"Join," Chase said in a clear voice. Minerva's face lit up. She reached out and clasped his face in her outstretched hands.

"Welcome." She stood on tiptoes and kissed his forehead, then turned away and walked the tight circle of her followers. "He will join!"

Jack nodded his approval, and there was a quiet murmuring from the other members. The two men holding him stepped back, and Chase was alone in the center. There was unbridled terror in his eyes, the look of a trapped animal ready to gnaw off its own limb. He was going to run. Talia saw it and felt a tiny keyhole of hope that he would succeed and send help.

"He won't," Summer whispered. "He won't send help." Talia turned and locked eyes with her. Summer was shaking her head bitterly. Talia bit her lip and turned to watch it unfold. Minerva spoke, and all eyes moved their attention to her. Chase threw a casual glance over his shoulder and bolted, tucking himself down and using his shoulder to blast through a gap between two unsuspecting cultists. On the outside of the circle, he stumbled and nearly fell. Startled, as if he hadn't expected his attempt to work, he looked around wildly, then turned and ran.

"Bring him back," Minerva said. She maintained her cool demeanor, even smiling down at Talia. Several men peeled away to pursue him, each carrying a weapon.

"This is falling apart," Lane said. "Why even give them the choice?" He was angry. Minerva gave him a calculating stare.

"Know your place," Minerva said, then turned to face Dean. "You children must think this is a joke. You can be cannon fodder, that is your choice. Collateral. We were not required to offer you gentlemen anything whatsoever, it was a courtesy we extended to you on behalf of these two women."

Dean did not respond and could only offer a look of pure misery. He had been brought to kneel again and clung to a log round like his life depended on it. Blood poured down the side of his face. His eyes were full of tears as he laid his head down on his hands.

"Why are you doing this?" Summer demanded.

"God has instructed us that a medium, one that can channel, will be able to throw the door wide open and share with us His vision," Jack said, his blue eyes glittering. "We will know His mind and His plan."

"But what happens when you enter the water?" she asked. "You haven't answered that yet. No one has. What if your plan fails!"

The people shifted and watched, their expressions blank. Minerva passed by stroking Summer's black hair.

"Then we have added to our ranks, and we will continue to seek the path to bring Him forth." Minerva crouched in front of Summer. "You or Talia could be powerful in identifying the true one."

She was interrupted when the posse returned with Chase in tow, his hand tied behind his back. His shirt was torn, and his nose bloodied. He struggled and fought against them to no avail.

"Place him here," Lane indicated toward another log round beside the fire. Chase was shoved to the ground behind it. He tried to scramble back up and was forced down a second time.

"Hey! Hey! Can we talk about this?" he yelled, desperate and afraid. "I have money! My parents have money. I can give you everything we've saved from the vlog. My parents will pay. They will. Just let me go, please, let me go. I will give you everything I have."

"You fucking coward!" Summer spat, lobbing the accusation. "How dare you offer up what belongs to all of us for only your freedom! You are a fucking monster!" She grabbed a hand full of dirt and rocks around her and threw it at him.

Chase turned to shield his face, and Lane cold-cocked him. Dazed, he grew quiet and rested his head against the log round. One of the men came forward with an ax.

"Please," he whimpered. "I'll do anything. Anything, please."

The man lifted the weapon overhead, its cutting-edge flashing in the firelight, and dropped it without ceremony. Talia kept her eyes on the darkening sky until she heard him gurgle. Her gaze dropped. His neck, half-severed, hung open. Chase stared at the women, blinking and gaping like a fish. The blood flooded over the edge of the log and down the side. Chase continued to ask through choked air, but no sound came out. Summer screamed again and scrambled back. The man withdrew his ax, and Chase's head lolled. Dean threw himself on his cousin, coming up short as the blade came down again, severing Chase's neck and cleaving Dean's hand.

Talia watched with unrestrained horror, frozen and unable to interfere. Dean did not react. He held the limb up into the light to examine it, somehow removed from the fact it was his own. His fingers were gone, severed. They lay discarded in the dirt, next to Chase's head, and he bent to collect them. A wave of pain hit him so powerful Talia's fist throbbed in sympathy.

Talia pushed Summer aside and pulled a kerchief from her back pocket. Dean stared at his hand, failing to process how half of it was simply no longer there. It spurted blood. Talia brought the kerchief down on it, trying to wrap it, but the effort was futile. The cloth was soaked through in seconds. He brought the hand close to his chest, cradling it to his body. Dean delivered her a pleading, disoriented look and then passed out, falling toward the fire.

"It's too late to continue this mess," Minerva said. "It's time to begin." Talia looked up. A few people were grabbing Dean and examining his mutilated hand. The other members of the group brought her and Summer to their feet.

"Wait!" Talia cried. "Wait, what are you doing with him?" She was afraid if they were separated, he would not survive the night.

"He's with us! He planned to join! Don't kill him! Don't kill him!" Talia yelled as they dragged her away. Above their heads, the full moon peered over the horizon.

PART THREE

It was on a night after the weather had begun to warm, and the prospect of summer was not long off. Talia woke to an alarm. Its rapid pulsing blared through the house, cutting off the moment she sat bolt upright. She looked around her shadowy room, illuminated by her rainbow nightlight. Her heart thudded in her chest, listening to the quiet. Finding herself wide awake and a little unnerved, Talia hoped she could curl up on the couch to watch television with her mother until she fell back asleep. She eased out of bed, navigating around the clothing and toys strewn about her bedroom floor to the hallway. All the lights below in the living room and kitchen were on. Unusual at that hour, she crept out onto the landing on silent feet.

Odd sounds echoed up from the living room, metal squeaking and rattling as if under strain. Quieter was a muffled groaning, as if someone were yelling underwater. Something was wrong. She drew close to the banister, crouching low to avoid detection, and peered over the edge into the space below. Talia did not immediately understand what her eyes saw. Her mother was hunched over her grandfather; his leg kicked weakly, and the entire bed shook. Initially, it appeared she was assisting him, but Grandfather had no face. She realized that her mother was holding a pillow over it.

His left arm flailed to strike her, and Talia's mother accepted the feeble blow, keeping the pillow pressed against the old man's face. Even from her position, she could see the whites of her mother's knuckles and the cords standing out on her neck. His strangled wails disappeared into the pillow's fiber fill.

Sarah's lips were moving, speaking words barely above a whisper. All of her senses warned her to stay hidden; she should not be a witness to this. Talia considered returning to her room but found herself fixed in place. Waves of rage poured from her mother like the waves of a storm crashing on a beach, and it washed over Talia, flooding her with pain again and again. She was repulsed and still could not turn away. The emotions inside her body were not her own. This desperate act of frustration had turned into something intentional, and Talia desired the final result with a surprising ferocity. She wanted him to die. The images of his abuse flashed through her mind, but in these scenes, Talia was not the victim. It was her mother.

After withstanding the old man's abuse her entire life, Sarah had reached the end of her rope. She had escaped him when she met Talia's father and thought she would never have to look back. By some cosmic twist of fate, her young husband was killed, leaving her to care for their four children alone. Grief-stricken and penniless, she packed up her family and returned to her father's home. It was the same house where she had grown up and been subjected to all manner of abuse at the hands of the man she called "Dad." She could not escape him as a child and found she could not escape him now. She was the target of his cruelty, his favorite game of all, and after playing by his rules for so long, something in Sarah's mind finally snapped.

"How does it feel? How does it feel, you fuck?" she muttered, pressing the pillow harder and harder. Talia sensed Grandfather's growing fear and something else: an unexpected excitement. It seemed incongruent, and yet, that was the emotion that came through. The giddy anticipation of a plan at its completion: the outcome of his designs. He had planned this. It was her grandfather's last strike against her mother, and he was relishing in her retaliation.

After what seemed like an eternity, the man's efforts to combat the assault grew weaker, and eventually he ceased to move at all. Her mother remained in place long after she thought he was dead, her back heaving as she panted. When she removed the pillow, Grandfather's face was a mask, mouth open and gasping for air that would never come. Talia was startled when an insane giggle escaped her mother's lips, a laugh of relief and exhaustion. She'd been released from this man's grip after a lifetime of being subjected to his twisted nature. The laughter became a sob, one she stifled by covering her mouth with her hand. She left the pillow on his chest and stepped back from where she kneeled on the bed. Unsteady on her feet, Sarah made her way to Grandfather's bedroom and disappeared into the bathroom within, closing the door behind her. Quiet sobs echoed from inside.

Released from the fever of her mother's rage, her impulse was to hide in her room like she hadn't seen what transpired. Curiosity won over her better judgment. Part of her wanted to confirm this new reality; confirm that she, too, was free of the monster.

Tiptoeing down the stairs, skipping the squeaky step, and dancing to the right side on the next, until she reached the bottom and crossed the room to where Grandfather lay. She looked up at his face. Was that relief she felt? With Grandfather gone, there was hope for a better life. She could be a little girl again, a kid, and that understanding released something she did not know she was carrying. They could be a family again.

Without warning, he heaved a giant gasp of air, and his eyes flicked open. He was alive and thrashing his unparalyzed limbs. Talia stepped back, horrified. They locked eyes as he reached for her. The bedrail was down. He stretched for her, impossibly heaving himself over and falling to the floor. His body slammed to the ground, the air wheezing out of him, and he groaned, stunned and senseless. She found herself frozen with the pillow at her feet, unable to scream.

Talia panicked. It was all going wrong; this was not how it was supposed to be. She picked up the pillow, the fabric soft in her hands but the shape dense. Without thinking, she plunged it over her grandfather's face and knelt on top of it. His frail arm hit her, but she didn't stand or stop. She pressed down, letting the full weight of her body rest on the cushion below her. Acting with little sense of what she was doing, his terror mingled with her own.

Talia heard the bathroom door open, and her mother stood in the frame. The girl faltered and was struck hard by her grandfather. She almost stopped, caught in the act, but Sarah closed the space between them, falling to her knees and pinning her father's flailing limb. Talia looked into her mother's eyes; grey pools devoid of light. Devoid of all joy and happiness, devoid of anything connecting her to reality. The gnawing fear she saw in them was how Sarah survived. It took a while for Grandfather to stop moving, and even when he did, they remained that way, face to face, long after.

"It's okay," Talia's mother whispered. "It's okay." Talia stood, realizing her face was wet with tears. Her mother slipped a hand under the pillow and checked Grandfather's carotid for a pulse. Talia waited anxiously, holding her breath, until her mother removed her hand and uttered a small sigh. Sarah turned and placed a hand on Talia's cheek, locking eyes with her again.

"We can never tell anyone," Sarah whispered. "I will go to jail. Forever. I will go to jail. We will lose the house. Social services will take you kids and put you with strangers. We can never tell, Talia. We can never say what happened. I will call for help in the morning, and I will say we found him like this. They will think it was an accident, that he rolled out of bed or had a heart attack. They know he was stubborn. No one will question that. No one will question you. This house will be ours. It will be our home. Do you understand?"

Talia nodded.

"You can never tell. I need you to understand." Her mother looked at her with deadly seriousness, and when she decided to believe Talia's affirmation, she nodded too. "Okay, you need to get back to bed."

Talia was guided up the stairs and into her room. By the faint golden light of her nightlight, her mother tucked her into the bed and whispered, "You are so brave, Talia. I'm proud of you, honey. What you did tonight was brave, and I know it was scary, but you will see, it was the best thing. I love you, Tali." With that, she kissed her on the forehead and departed. Talia knew everything her mother was saying was true, or, at least, her mother believed it. If she told, her mother would go to jail, and if she did, then so would Talia. She did not want to know what kind of jail kids went to. She would never tell a soul.

The next morning, when Talia came downstairs, her grandfather was covered with a stark white sheet. Her mother greeted her with a tired smile. The ambulance arrived moments later, and Sarah hurried her upstairs to her room. Talia watched from the landing, hiding in the shadows to observe the EMT's at work. Once her mother glanced upward and caught her there but said nothing. The coroner arrived soon after with the police. They poked around, asked a lot of generic questions, and nodded in all the right places. When they finished, one of the officers placed a hand on Sarah's arm and told her how sorry he was. Sarah nodded, tears filling her eyes.

"Thank you," she said. Once they left, and all that remained was the empty hospital bed, she leaned against the door and sank to the floor where she allowed herself to have a real cry. Talia turned away from this, affording her mother the private moment.

Over the next few weeks, her mother returned Grandfather's hospital equipment. She sold the old trucks that had been relegated to the tree line, what remained of his coin collection, and donated his personal belongings to the Salvation Army. All of it amounted to a fair bit of money, but better was that their home was purged of the monster. It was like the first spring day after a long, cold winter.

For a brief time, there was joy in the house. With some of the money, Sara took the kids out for McDonald's and ordered them all a Happy Meal. Next, they went to the toy store and were each allowed to pick out an item. Talia had been torn between the Dream Phone board game or a Polly Pocket beauty set and opted for the latter. It was like nothing she'd ever owned before. The twins combined their money and purchased a Teenage Mutant Ninja Turtles playset and a couple action figures. Jamie got a Rockin' Robot Cassette Player with a microphone attached.

After the toy store, they stopped for ice cream. Life was good again. Life was wonderful. School still had its moments, but the bullying had subsided as summer approached. With Grandfather gone, Talia could see the light in her mother's eyes returning. For Talia, that was good. In fact, it was better than good, it was all that mattered.

On a morning during summer vacation, the four children were parked in front of the television watching cartoons while their mother prepared cinnamon rolls in the kitchen. A knock came at the door. Sarah licked icing from her fingertips and went to answer, her mood cheerful and buoyant. The door blocked who stood on the porch from Talia's view. Sarah's mood changed in an instant.

"Mrs. Michaels?" a male voice said. "We received notice that your father, the resident of the house and property, has passed away."

"You mean owner," Talia's mother replied. "What is this about?"

"That's not exactly true, Mrs. Michaels," said another man. Talia went to her mother's side, wrapping herself around her waist to comfort her. Sarah pushed her away. One of the men handed Sarah a white folded piece of paper. She scanned over it, her brow furrowed.

"Is this a notice to vacate? A notice to vacate the home my father owned?" Sarah asked, holding out the letter in her hand to them.

"Were you aware this property was under a home equity conversion mortgage?" the first man asked. He was heavy set with a small tight moustache, but he had kind eyes. There was guilt in them.

"What does that even mean?" Sarah laughed, like it was all a lark. "There must be some kind of mistake."

"'Fraid not, ma'am. It's a reverse mortgage. The home is bank-owned unless you have the funds to purchase it. We have sent several notices without response, and the bank is ready to sell. Your father came in and signed all the papers years ago. Said he needed the loan," the second man said. He was a bit more matter of fact, trying to keep business on track. He could see his partner was failing to be objective and keep his emotions in check.

"He owned the house," Sarah said slowly, as if they did not understand. "He's lived here my entire life."

"Do you know how many times your father refinanced this property?" the second man asked. "When he signed off, he never had another mortgage payment as long as he remained here and received a considerable payout. As his heir, you have the option to pay off the loan. We have been trying to notify you."

"I thought it was a scam," Sarah said. The two men exchanged a glance.

"Look, we are really sorry, but this is your final notice unless you can pay off the balance."

"I don't have any money," Talia's mother said to the men, trying to hand the notice back to them. "There must be some kind of mistake." They refused to accept the letter.

"Typically, the bank gives seventy-two hours, but they've agreed to allow you two weeks to vacate the premises," the second man said.

"We might even be able to arrange for a little financial assistance to get a truck and some movers over here," the first offered, which earned him a side-eyed look from his partner. "If you want to come down to the bank, we can show you all the documentation." Sarah's mother was too busy melting down to register what they were saying. The two men exchanged another glance and politely excused themselves after pressing a business card into Sarah's shaking hand.

It would turn out to be true. Confirmed by several phone calls and a trip to the bank branch in Maple Valley. Grandfather had placed the house and property in a reverse mortgage and never told a single soul what he had done. Just like that, they had nothing except what they could fit into the truck the bank had helped pay for. Talia's mother tried to sell what they would not be able to take at a final estate sale. The scavengers descended, picking apart what remained in the house. Her mother scrambled to find an apartment with the earnings. All of it went to the security deposit, along with first and last. The small light growing inside of her mother vanished right alongside it.

Thinking back to that night, Talia recalled the energy she had sensed from her grandfather in the moments before his death. How he had grinned with something resembling pure glee. It all made a sick sort of sense now. He had known what would come next for them and delighted in it.

Her mother worked two, sometimes three, jobs to keep them afloat. Talia became responsible for her brothers: ensuring their meals were made, that everyone got off to school, and following up with them about their homework. For a little while, it was fun, like she and her mother were a team. It was a few years of roach-infested apartments, sleazy landlords, and barely scraping by. Any surplus of funds went to a needed pair of shoes or an overdue doctor's bill. Once, when her mother was working third shift and there was no food in the house, Cole had stolen a loaf of bread and a package of lunch meat, so she and her brothers would have dinner. Guilt plagued Talia every time she entered the store after. She promised herself that when they had money again, she would put the right amount of change into one of the charity buckets at the front.

Talia would later recall these years as difficult, but some of the best of her life. She and her brothers were like glue, relying on and taking care of each other. The twins kept an eye on Jamie so Talia could manage the household, and they survived. For Talia, they were together as a family and that was all that mattered.

By the time they reached the top of the path, the night sky had grown dark, but the moon had risen. Summer and Talia made no attempt to run as they were marched up the cliffside. Men flanked them, holding their arms as they followed the trail to the hot springs. The cultists walked in front and behind them in single file. Lanterns were hung to light the way, utilizing carefully hidden nooks, but with the brilliant full moon moving higher and higher into the sky, they were almost unnecessary.

Talia scanned the line; only she and Summer remained. A hollow feeling of complete fear and powerlessness nestled deep within her gut. Inside it, wrapped tight, was the pain.

Her sadness at the unfairness of her father's death. Enduring the bullying from the other kids at school. The abuse at her grandfather's hands and her role in his murder. Her insurmountable debt and the collapse of her business. Now, at the mercy of this cult's fanaticism, Talia would be forced to face an unknown horror. The idea of her having control over her own life was almost laughable. Everything had culminated to this point. As if outside forces had driven here. As if it had been preordained, she was fated to arrive at this conclusion.

They reached the hot springs. Only half of the original group had joined them, and they spread themselves to stand around the pools with Minerva, Lane, and Jack at the center. Steam poured from the obsidian holes. There was no reflection in them, and still somehow, they glowed with a strange iridescent light. Summer and Talia were brought before the springs. Talia glanced around at the many anonymous faces and, for one wild second, considered if she could fight her way out and make it home. But what was home anymore? What was even left for her?

Minerva and Lane exchanged furtive whispers, the exact words drowned out by the shuffling of a dozen pairs of feet and the wind sweeping through the grotto. Minerva's eyes narrowed. Whatever was left of her composure was beginning to fail. Lane looked firm, and although Jack stood presiding over them, he said nothing at all. Things were going wrong. It was evident they had expected a different outcome, and it was exacerbating the power struggle between Minerva and Lane.

"It's because she doesn't know the outcome," Summer whispered. "I know it seems like she carries herself as an authority, but her great prophecy has failed them. We are not the first to be brought here. Lane thinks she should step down. He thinks she's wrong. She was only decisive when she knew what needed to happen, and now that her foresight has failed, she's losing control."

Talia glanced over at Summer, who was watching the surface of the water and looking serene. Her tears had dried. She turned to Talia.

"It's inevitable," Summer said. "Think about it. If we don't go into one of those pools, what happens? We are held and dragged out here again and again, until we do. There is no version of this where we go back to our normal lives, Talia. Think about all those missing people, the ones they never found. I wonder how many of them are standing here tonight. And if they are here, then they went through this too. They made a choice. They are living a life; it may not be what they had once planned, but they are alive."

"Summer, I…"

Summer grabbed Talia's hands and stared deeply into her eyes. Summer's calming energy poured off of her. Talia resisted, until the wave of it crashed on top of her. Her terror abated, and Summer smiled when she saw it go.

"I'm sorry I lied to you," Summer said. "I took it too far. I was excited to break out on my own. But I really wanted you to be my friend. It wasn't just about the power I saw in you. I saw *you*." She hesitated. "I'm sorry for what happened to you. What you've gone through is almost too much for one person to bear. You broadcast it so loud, and you don't even realize. I wanted to help you, and I think I finally know how."

Summer wrapped Talia in a hug, chest to chest. In the center of her being, just below her breastbone, a small thread tugged.

"There it is," Summer said. "Stay with me." Talia tried to pull away in fear of what was happening. Her eyes watered, but she could not tear herself away from Summer's grasp. Talia gasped when the tiny string was yanked through her center and her carefully constructed barriers unraveled. The memories flooded in.

***

Talia, always the early riser, woke as the sun rose and the shell of peace had yet to be broken. She was alone. The night before, her mother had arrived home from work late. The closing of the front door woke Talia as her mother slipped into the apartment and locked the deadbolt behind her. She slept better when her mother was home. They were sharing a queen-sized bed at present, so Talia slid over to one side, expecting her mother would come in. The three boys were stacked in the other room, uncomfortable, but they had not killed each other yet. She heard the television come on, the volume low, and knew there was a good chance her mother would sleep on the sofa. She didn't think twice about it and went back to sleep.

She rolled out of bed to dress. Peeking out the window to see it would be a cool day, she dressed in layers: a sweatshirt over a t-shirt, a pair of old faded jeans, and sneakers that were almost too small for her feet. She didn't want to ask her mom for a new pair, so she chose the thinnest pair of socks she had. Dismayed to find the thread securing the front pocket of her sweatshirt was coming loose, and there was a noticeable flap of fabric, she went in search of the matchbook-sized sewing kit she kept from the hotel days. She went into the bathroom, passing by her brother's closed door, and searched in the medicine cabinet for the kit. When she couldn't find it, she stepped into the living room, reluctant to wake her mother.

The couch was empty. All that she found was the old brown and rust-colored afghan pushed aside and the indent on the pillow where her head would have rested. She confirmed her mother's purse was sitting on the kitchen table where it usually lived. Her car keys lay next to it. Talia slid two slices of bread in the toaster, then thought twice and

238

removed one. She took the jar of peanut butter down from the cupboard and thought, not for the first time, how grateful she was she didn't have to eat eggs.

While she waited for the toaster, she wandered back to the boys' bedroom and peered in, easing the door open slowly so she didn't wake them. They were all fast asleep. She half expected to find her mother curled up next to her baby brother in the bottom bunk, but she was not there.

She closed the door as carefully as she had opened it. Confused and growing concerned, she went back into the living room. She checked the kitchen again. Her toast had come up and was filling the air with its warm, nutty aroma. Talia opened the front door, the deadbolt still locked, and peered out onto the walkway, half-hoping to find her smoking a cigarette with her cup of coffee. Talia hated her mother's secret habit. But there was no coffee in the pot, and her mother was not outside. Her car was parked in the lot below. She double-checked the bedrooms, both of them, peering up into the top bunk in the boy's room and verifying, to be certain. As she exited the boys' room, and having already checked her bedroom, she stood across from the bathroom and knew.

Entering the small room, she stood in its center, staring at the closed shower curtain. She hadn't noticed it before. Her two youngest brothers took baths most evenings and never remembered to close it. Talia preferred it open. She was alone with her brothers so many nights; it was reassuring to know no one was standing behind it, waiting. It was never shut. Reluctantly, she stepped forward and peered behind the curtain. Her mother lay in a ruddy brown pool, wearing only a tank top and underwear, with jagged cuts on her forearms. Talia had no urge to cry. It was a cold ending for a woman she loved with her entire being. Talia sat down on the toilet beside her and stared into those empty grey eyes. She had seen it long before it arrived. Her mother had been ravenous for hope, driven by the hunger to survive.

With nothing left to do, she exited the bathroom and went out the front door to the neighbor's apartment. She knocked for what seemed to her an eternity. When the older woman opened it, the skunky smell inside poured out. She had been told to go to her if there was trouble while her mother was at work. Talia asked to use her phone, and the neighbor permitted it, knowing there was no phone in their apartment. Talia placed the call, punched in the correct three digits to bring assistance, and provided her address without being prompted.

"What's your emergency?" the man on the other end of the line asked.

"My mother cut her wrists. She's dead," Talia replied. And that was it. They asked her to stay on the line, but she hung up anyway. She returned to sit in the kitchen and found the cold piece of toast in the toaster. The last bit of her normal life. She pulled down what little food they had in the cupboards and began to eat.

The paramedics came quickly, and the police shortly thereafter. Social services took much longer to collect them. Matthew, the oldest of the boys, and Talia were placed in foster care. Cole and Jamie were taken in by one of her father's distant cousins and adopted. Their last names were changed. Talia never understood what criteria was followed to make this decision, but the look on Matthew and Cole's faces when they were separated shattered Talia's heart. Matthew ran away from his foster home, and last she knew, he was on drugs in another state. Her efforts to keep tabs on them failed. She employed all the resources available to her at the law office to track them down. It was like they had simply disappeared, and Talia was alone in the world.

***

Excruciating pain overwhelmed Talia's body. In her mind's eye, the pantry door appeared. The lock rattled and shook, the door rocking in its frame. Talia was afraid; she ran to it to hold it shut. The wood slammed against the hasp, buckling and starting to bulge. The white door shattered into pieces, and what she concealed behind it was revealed.

A lifetime of suppressed emotions rushed through her. She'd lived every day like there was a gun to her head, having her face shoved down in the dirt every time she dared to hope. The pain and despair coursed through her. Every time she believed her problems were solved and the future she had hoped for was just around the corner, the world slid out beneath her.

If God had a plan for her, she suspected it was only to cause her pain. The prospect of tapping into His mind made her want to laugh with outrage. What could he possibly offer her after everything she had already been through? To be exploited as a resource? Used as a cosmic generator? What purpose could she serve? What was the purpose of all the agony she had suffered?

Just as Talia thought she could bear no more, it dwindled, then retreated, and was gone. Summer accepted it with a small whimper. The frantic pace of Talia's heart slowed, her thoughts calmed, and she looked around at her surroundings with new eyes. The fear was gone, and along with it, the rage. The sensation she had chased was never to be filled or satisfied; it was the experience that followed. When the pain became too much, she tried over and over to purge the darkness. She was empty. And now she was free.

Summer released her, tears pouring freely from her eyes.

"Who is called on this night?" Minerva projected her voice. Her youthful face glowed, and Talia hated her. Hated how she had single-handedly ordered the murder of her friends and stolen her future.

"You have made me so powerful, Talia. I had no idea what I might be capable of until I met you. I think this will help you do what you need to. It's the only thing I can give you. Freedom from what's been eating you alive." Summer released Talia's hands, then turned toward the pool, and shuddered.

"I'm ready," Summer said.

"No, wait!" Talia tried to stop her, but Summer stepped forward. She turned to face her with a bitter smile.

"There's no other choice," Summer assured her. "All is suffering, Talia. Nobody belongs anywhere." Tears continued to run down her cheeks, but she was smiling. "It's inevitable. Everything is inevitable."

"Summer, stop!" Talia cried. Summer looked back, perfectly framed against the moon's luminescence. Her ebony hair shined. With all of her makeup washed away, her soft, pixie-like features sparkled as if kissed by the moon itself. Her eyes glittered with a mixture of excitement and terror, then her expression hardened.

Summer stepped into the pool.

Steam twirled and tangled around her, pulling her in. She took another step, the depth reaching her mid-thigh. Iridescent rainbows swirled and danced on the water's surface. A strange light emanated from deep within the spring. She stepped in to her waist. Summer turned to face the group of people, locked eyes with Talia, then submerged herself.

Talia held her breath. After twenty long seconds, she grew alarmed, and when the number ticked up to thirty, she stepped forward and found her captors holding her back.

"Summer!" she yelled. Black hair broke the surface. Talia gasped with relief. The mist hung heavy, but illuminated by the full moon's light, it distorted the water and the vision of Summer standing in it. Summer released a long, contented sigh and stepped forward, the water retreating to her waist. Another step, and she emerged from the shadows. Her eyes, ordinarily a pale blue, were shining and black. The change was immediate and terrifying.

"This is different," Summer said, looking down at her hands. She regarded them as if they were newly discovered objects, turning them and wiggling her fingers. She placed them on her body, caressing the flesh on her arms up to her shoulders, then down, squeezing her breasts. The hands traced to her stomach and hips, and her eyes licked all over her body.

"This is new. And unexpected." It was a voice like Summer's, but there was something underneath, something familiar, and Talia understood. Summer's eyes locked with Talia's, and a grin split apart her face.

"I know you," Summer growled. It had gone wrong.

"I am so hungry," the Summer thing hissed, her voice changing and growing deeper. "So hungry. And you gave me this to have? This?" Summer touched her body again.

Talia tore her gaze away, glancing at Minerva. The woman looked on, her expression flat.

"Stop this," Talia demanded, recognizing the wrongness in her friend. Summer was admiring her hands again. Minerva had a curious look on her face, one that reflected an edge of worry in it. Talia knew this would play out; they would not interfere.

"Stop this!" Talia begged, attempting to shake off the men holding her. "Someone needs to stop this!"

"Tsk. Tsk. Tsk," Summer giggled. "What a lovely new thing to play with! What should I do first? Oh, I know!" Summer crammed a finger in her mouth and bit down, degloving the skin and sucking it off the bone with a wet slurping sound. She chewed the morsel delightedly, reacting as if it were a piece of perfectly cooked steak, and swallowed. She looked at the finger with deep interest, her black eyes shining.

"I've been so hungry!" the thing hissed and gnawed on the other fingers. They snapped under her gnashing teeth, blood dripping down her chin. Talia knew what was standing before her. When Summer had opened the door and extracted a lifetime of Talia's pain, she had brought along the dark creature living there. The thing within her that demanded feeding. The entity she had found in the Rodriguez's basement. It had always belonged to her. It was a part of her. It gorged on her pain. No matter how Talia had tried to sate it, it was never fulfilled. She had never been able to expel the darkness. Until now.

The power within the pool had brought the creature to the fore, and the parasite that had been feeding on Talia's pain now had full control over Summer's body. It was as Minerva said: the pools stripped away all but someone's underlying nature. Talia's had been hiding, lying in wait, and Summer had taken it into herself.

Summer unhinged her jaw and closed her teeth around her forearm, biting down into the hunk of flesh. The muscle and sinew resisted, then tore off into the mouth of the monster. It chewed happily, exclaiming in sheer ecstasy. She fell to her knees, ravenous, biting at her hands and tearing at her arms, consuming herself piece by piece. Blood covered the lower half of her face above glittering obsidian eyes.

"Do something!" Talia screamed. Lane came forward with a disturbed look on his face, brought a pistol to Summer's head, and pulled the trigger. Summer hissed, lunged for the gun, and Lane jumped back, firing twice more. She collapsed, her hands ruined, bones exposed and skin hanging in tatters. Lane was panting, and Talia saw the mixture of emotions on his face, both terror and sadness. Summer was gone.

"What did you do?" Talia screamed. She turned to Minerva. "This was the fucking plan God offered you? Was this in your vision? Fuck your God." Minerva was rattled and trying in vain to appear unphased by the tableau.

"Remove her," she said, indicating Summer's disfigured body. No one moved. The collective's members remained in place, warily eyeing the thing that had emerged from the pool.

"Remove her now!" Minerva commanded. The hesitation broke. Lane and one of the men behind Talia came forward and dragged the body away. The cracks in Minerva's demeanor were showing, but she drew herself up to speak.

"This is what God showed me! I saw it the last time I was called to the pool. He said there would be two, and while I know we have found others, these were the two He spoke of! God showed me that she would become the conduit through which His mind would be known!" Minerva frantic, wounded by her own confusion and dismay, was lying. Her plan was going awry, and the members knew it.

"You lie," Lane retorted, and a hush fell over the crowd. "You know nothing about what comes next. How many more will we go through? How many more women?"

Summer had shaken him; Talia could see it. There was something in his eyes, normally steely and withholding, but there was a sadness in them. Minerva looked to Jack, expecting a response. The grip on Talia's arm loosened. Things were falling apart. Their trusted leader had been wrong all along. With nothing left to lose, Talia took the chance and ran.

The moon lit the path below her feet as she thundered away; cries echoed behind her. They were coming for her. She trusted her legs to carry her away from the evil place, praying she would not freeze again if confronted. There was no longer any terror in her heart and no anger to hold her back; she was fearless. Unafraid to pursue escape, even if it meant the end of her life. Nothing was as horrible as what she witnessed Summer succumb to.

And for the first time in her memory, Talia understood her own power. Summer had unburdened her from the terrifying reality of her life and freed her of the tethers of her past. Her eyes were open. Talia was transformed. Without the weight of the pain holding her back, the world was brand new. If she could escape being pulled back into the darkness, escape the people who pursued her and wanted her to embrace the evil within the pools, then her path into the future could be something to behold. Talia wanted that future desperately.

She had nearly reached the path down to Lester when she heard footsteps coming toward her. The voices behind grew louder, but someone was approaching from ahead. They would block her escape. Dismay washed over her. With nowhere to go, she stopped at the edge of the path and turned out to the abyss of night that lay before her. Beyond the moon's aura, stars pinpricked the vast quilt of darkness, and she marveled at its beauty. There was nowhere left to go. She could only guess how long the fall would take, and she hoped it would kill her. In her heart, she believed it would feel like flying. Gathering her will, she lifted one foot over the precipice, and before the air could take her, a voice spoke.

"Talia?"

"Glenn?" Off balance, she tilted forward, falling. "Glenn!" He grabbed her, pulled her back from the edge, and into his arms. She hugged him fiercely and said into his ear, "We need to run."

Talia learned two things in the first eleven years of her life.

Between her father's unexpected and sudden death, the bullying in grade school, her evil grandfather, and the suicide of her mother, Talia had received a full education on how unfair life could be. It was a hard lesson for a young girl. It was like every foster parent, social worker, and school counselor had all been handed the same script. When they instructed her on whatever change was about to take place in her life, they always made sure to say:

"Don't worry, everything will be fine." She wanted to believe them. After the first foster home decided to quit fostering and the second said she wasn't a good fit, she stopped. If the first eleven years of her life were any measure, she decided they were probably wrong. Nothing would be fine. It was like it was built into her DNA to suffer. Talia learned it was always going to be hard for her; there was always going to be pain.

The second lesson Talia learned on the heels of the first. It served her to understand that life throws curveballs, and sometimes it sends meteors falling from the sky. Life was never going to take it easy, but regardless of which, she would live through it because Talia was resilient. Instead of buckling under the pressure and falling into the all too easy trap of becoming a victim of circumstances beyond her control, Talia did something else instead. Talia learned how to survive.

They ran.

Yesterday, it was Talia pulling Glenn down this trail, and it was Glenn's chance to return the favor. The collective was behind them, the beams of their flashlights trailing as they fled. Glenn slipped, and she yanked him upright. They careened down the mountain. Talia could barely keep her legs under her. They ran downhill, the ground treacherous, staying upright out of sheer will alone. They reached the hotel grounds and level earth. The lights were still above them.

"Where were you?" she asked, out of breath.

"Hiding," he replied. "I followed Lane into the woods and caught him talking to those people. They had guns. I hid. I didn't want them to catch me. I thought I could escape, but I couldn't get to the bridge. I saw the bonfire." He frowned. "Where's Summer? And Dean?"

"I don't know where Dean is. Summer didn't make it," Talia replied. She thought of Summer's chin soaked in blood and shoved the vision away. She had to focus. A branch whipped her across the face. The lashing stung and her eyes watered. There was no stopping. They ran along the road toward the town.

"We need to head for the train trestle," she said. They emerged into the meadow, running without caution, and too late stumbled upon the cultists remaining by the fire.

"Shit," Glenn said.

"Grab them!" a voice screamed behind them.

"Go!"

Talia tugged Glenn's shirt, veering him left, guiding them toward the confluence with Friday Creek and the train trestle. Their escape route. They could disappear into the forest if they could just make it across the river. She ran full out, everything in her body screaming at her to move. They ran together. The bridge came into view in the moon's cool light. Her heart leapt at the sight.

A body emerged from the forest, tackling Glenn. Talia pivoted to flee and ran straight into Jack's arms. Even in the dark, his eyes were vibrant and bright.

"We aren't done yet," he said, breathing hard. They'd been cut off. She struggled against his hold.

"Let him go!" she shrieked. "You can't do this to us!" More people arrived, surrounding them, and she submitted. Their last attempt to escape had failed.

Glenn fought as Bam had fought. He made Lane work for every inch, until Lane threw him to the ground and put a knee on his back, binding his wrists. Talia and Jack left them behind, and she was forced back up the mountain. Talia tried to wrench free.

"If you don't behave, I will tie you too," Jack said, his voice eerily calm.

Talia considered, then relaxed.

"There you are. Talia, it is better for you to accept this," he said. "You can try to escape, but you will return here. Again and again. This place fills your waking dreams. You came here because it is your destiny. Your purpose. It is inevitable."

She did not respond. His words, Summer's words, echoed in her mind. Inevitable. They continued in silence.

When Talia reentered the grotto, Minerva was pacing, impatient, and holding off on the ceremony until their return. Many of the cultists had chased her and Glenn back to Lester; now only a few remained. They parted to let her through.

Dean leaned against the opposite wall of the cavern. A mask of blood covered half of his features; no one had bothered to wash his face. His hand was bandaged, and he cradled it to his chest, blood oozing through the white cotton. Talia crossed the space between them and wrapped him in a hug. He winced but returned the gesture as best he could.

"I'm glad to see you," she said.

"Where's Summer?" Dean asked, his face hopeful. He was weak, almost unable to stand on his own.

"She went into the pool," Talia replied.

"Is she okay?" he asked, his voice rasping.

"No, Dean, she's not okay," Talia said. Jack had rejoined with Minerva, and a hushed discussion was taking place between them. Minerva was arguing, her face angry, while Jack spoke in soft tones. A couple of other members returned. She was being overridden. Something was happening.

"What happened to her?" he asked.

"Dean." she offered him a grave look and shook her head. "You don't want to know."

He considered this. "You can't do it, Talia. We can't join. You can't go in the water. Something is wrong here. This place is evil. We should have never come."

All eyes were on Minerva and Jack. Cold metal pressed into Talia's hand. She didn't react, knowing without looking, it was a knife.

"We can still get out of this."

She slipped the object into the back of her waistband and weighed Dean's suggestion. Dean, freshly maimed, with a severe head wound, and barely able to stand. She would have to both carry him out and fight off anyone who tried to stop her. There were almost a dozen members of the collective here and many more in the town below. Every attempt to escape had ended with the same outcome, and she was here in front of the hot springs. It was futile. It was impossible. It was inevitable.

"Talia, we can still get out of this."

Glenn emerged into the grotto with Lane behind him, holding his arms behind his back, and driving him toward the furthest pool. Glenn saw Talia and then Dean.

"Glenn!" Dean called, elated to see their lost friend. Glenn grinned, then spun, throwing Lane off balance. Lane stumbled, fell into one of the springs, and went under. Everyone stopped and waited. No one moved to help. He sputtered up, coughing water and grasping the edge of the pool.

Gradually, his hair began to lighten and thin. His face shriveled. Then all at once, Lane's hair turned white and fell out at his crown. A liver spot appeared on the side of his temple, and his hands grew withered and gnarled. He could not hoist himself from the pool; his strength was gone. He was old in a matter of seconds. Dean, seeing the pools twisted magic for the first time, gasped.

Finally, one of the collective hurried forward and assisted him. Lane emerged an elderly man with a hunched back and wobbly knees. Minerva's face twisted into a sick grin. She was pleased to see her adversary fail, but she was quickly overcome with frustration. This night was to be the validation of her prophecy, the culmination of her vision, and her grand plan had gone wrong.

Glenn, surprised and horrified, tried to back away.

"That's it!" Minerva cried and loosed a handgun from one of the men's belts. She grabbed Glenn by his shirt collar and wrenched him to her, shoving the gun into the back of his head.

"Choose," Minerva's eyes blazed, focused on Talia. Dean shrank back against the cavern wall. "You can save him, but only if you enter the pool." Her voice echoed in the grotto, followed by complete silence. Talia sighed and looked at Dean. Devastation was in his eyes. She gazed over at Glenn. He shook his head.

"Talia, fight back! Don't do it!" he yelled until Minerva cocked back the hammer of the pistol.

There was no escape from this; the only way was through.

"Don't kill him," Talia said. "I'll go."

"Talia, no!" Dean cried out. Without another word, she walked to the edge of the pool. Mesmerized by the colors, moving as if guided by an invisible paintbrush dancing across the water's surface, she entered. The heat rose up through her body as she moved deeper and deeper into the pool until she reached the center. Her aching muscles relaxed, the pain from her scrapes and cuts eased, and her body embraced the warm weight of the water. With one large inhale, she went under.

At first, nothing happened. She was underwater and separated from the surrounding world. Below her, the pool was endless in its depth. A blue light glowed from the bottom, lighting the cavern, so far down she could not see the source. Overwhelming heat rushed in, like a painless fire encasing her. It stole her breath. The thought of drowning had not occurred to her, but she embraced it. This could be the last moment of her life, and she discovered she was unafraid to face it. The thermal energy filled her, and it was blissful, heavenly rapture. The sensation of falling, everything falling away. She would allow death to claim her, and she was without pain.

Talia crested the surface. She stepped forward, up and out of the water, her once green eyes a new shade of vibrant, icy blue. They glowed with unnatural light. As she emerged, she cast her gaze around her surroundings. Errant color shifted and refracted; a rainbow of light danced in her vision, and through it faces, agape and startled. Faces in reverence. Faces in terror. Her ascension had begun.

Talia settled on one aura. It was the color of rich violet with fractures of gold emanating like tiny lightning bolts: Minerva. The woman regarded her with triumph.

"Behold!" She cried. "She is born!"

Talia approached and drew forth the blade. With one swift flourish, she lashed the woman's throat.

Minerva's hands flew to cover the wound, and Talia stepped in close. She flailed, surprised and terrified, covering Talia's face in blood. Talia wrapped an arm around Minerva's body and stabbed the knife into her side.

"Please, don't!" Minerva begged, falling to the ground. A few of the men came forward, and Jack stopped them. Talia fell upon her, jamming the blade into her a second time, opening the hole. The silence held as Talia reached her fingers through the wound, gripping the bone inside.

"Let me count your ribs!" Talia roared.

Minerva tried to scream, but all that she let out was a dying gurgle. Talia tugged on the bone she found there, and with a resounding crack, she broke Minerva's rib, removing it from her body. She stood, heaving, covered in blood, and grinned. Power coursed through her veins. Her mind opened to potential and possibility.

Talia stood and tossed the bone at Jack's feet. He met her gaze, saw the truth there, and bent to kneel to the woman who had emerged: the God Child. Then, the people around her, one by one, fell to their knees.

Author's Note

I started *Lester* in January of 2023. Inspiration struck while I was hiking the Snoquera Falls Trail in November 2021, but as luck would have it, I was two months into drafting my first novel, *Wonderland.* This novel was a long time coming, and what a ride it's been.

The forests of the Pacific Northwest have a certain spooky quality in the right season, and that morning as we hiked the trail, all the elements were there. I am a horror fan, through and through, thanks to Christopher Pike, and the master himself, Stephen King. I envisioned a paranormal research team on a long hike. Each day something terrible would happen, reminiscent of *The Blair Witch Project*, escalating their circumstances until they found themselves trapped and unable to escape. And then the grand finale: a slaughter-fest. For some reason, I kept having this imagery that they would come across an old man. There was something terrifying to me about finding a lost man in the forest, gibbering and mad with terror. But there was always the problem of what they would uncover. My original notes read: portal to hell.

I suspect it was Lester's hot springs that did it. I have a habit of studying maps, and Lester has been a place that has long captured my imagination. When I learned hot springs once existed in Lester, I started doing research to determine whether or not they still existed, and if so, could I hike there. The history and my story idea naturally went hand in hand. I never made it to Lester. Unfortunately, what was left of the town is gone, and to the best of my knowledge, so are the hot springs. The watershed is a protected area and trespassers will be prosecuted.

My research on Lester uncovered an astonishing past. The majority of Lester's political history is real, and I have John Phillip the III's articles in the White River Historical Society's Newsletter to thank for the detailed outline that helped direct my research. Gertrude Murphy was the last living resident of Lester. She was 99 years old when she passed. Greta is very loosely based on Gertrude. I could not write a novel about Lester without honoring her. I tied in other Washington State history to add to the narrative. In particular, the tale about Lana Handel is drawn from the actual story of Linda Hazzard in Olalla, Washington. For an excellent detailing of this, pick up *Starvation Heights* by local author Gregg Olson. Rose Travers' experience in the train was pulled from the train accident in Wellington, Washington, which is now known as Tye. That story can be found in the novel *The White Cascade* by Gary Krist.

The massacre is utter fiction. I took a lot of liberties. There is no cult in Lester or operating through the City of Tacoma or the Green River Watershed. The basis of this novel is completely fiction, and I cannot emphasize that enough. Any factual errors are mine and mine alone.

I want to thank my beta-readers: Carol Scott, Jutta Heller, Allison Baker, Elaina Rardin, Marc Tully, Shannon Schultz, Meilee Anderson, Alison Bowen, and my number one fan, Kelli Buck. And, of course, my mom. Thanks, Mom. Each of you gave me invaluable feedback to bring this story to life. Thank you for making the time, for answering all of my questions, and, most of all, for your honesty. Some of those conversations were absolutely critical to me resolving the bigger questions in this story.

I have a few honorable mentions. Terry Toler for his guidance on marketing. The help you offered me was vital. Joan Tully for showing up on a day when I really needed a friend. Heather Stiles for reading and editing Mads chapter. Josh and Erica Smart, along with the whole Dusty Shelf crew, your early support had brought so much goodness into my life. Stacy Eskridge-Fuller, Gina Nelson, and Bill Gesler, your support is appreciated. Special thanks to Matthew McCollum and his wife for their hospitality. Randall James Marquis had some great stories to share as well. I wish I could have included them all.

To my editor, publisher, and researcher: me. Good job. Your first horror novel and your second full length novel. That's pretty cool, Kim. (If you find any mistakes, be sure to let her know.)

Big thank you to Ash for always being such a cogent voice about what creativity is and how best to care for it. Your cover art is splendid and will be the main reason people pick up my book.

Eternal thanks to my best friend and partner, Chris. Thank you for being my biggest cheerleader as I struggled through this one. Thank you for your patience. Here's to another stepping-stone into our bright future. All my love.

To my readers, thank you for reading my books. I hope you all had as much fun as I did on this journey. It has been an absolute pleasure to make my mark in the horror genre.

-Kimberly Wheelock October 20, 2024

ABOUT THE AUTHOR

Kimberly Wheelock is Stephen King's number one fan. Lester is her second novel.

Sign up for updates at kimberlywheelockwrites.com

Follow my Author Page on Facebook

Instagram: @kimberlywheelock_writes

Tiktok: kimberlywheelock_writes

www.ingramcontent.com/pod-product-compliance
Lightning Source LLC
Chambersburg PA
CBHW020146310726
48970CB00006B/2024